The Janus Room

By

Martha Brygman

To Caro

One day you might read this -

but I doubt it.

The Roman God Janus

Janus had two faces, one looking forwards and one looking back,
since a door can let you in, or let you out.

Prologue
6th January 1969

11.45am

'Gran . . . Granny . . . GRANNY!' each heartfelt word that the young teenage girl screamed, was louder and more frenetic than the last. Lying scrunched between the bottom few steps of the dark cellar stairway and the grimy, lime-washed brick wall that faced it, was a mangled heap of clothing and twisted limbs. Like a nervous toddler, navigating a flight of steps on their own for the first time, she began her uneasy, wobbly descent from the small storage area at the top of the stairs. Steadying herself, by pressing both open palms against the rough, un-rendered sidewalls, she dropped down one tread at a time, using a heavy, uncertain flat-footed stomp. With each descending step that brought her closer to the dimly lit, inanimate figure, her synchronised intake of breath became deeper, until she could feel the cold dank air, squeezing into her lungs, and taste the bitter coal dust, coating the back of her dry throat.

'Granny please wake up!' she said unconvincingly, in a shocked voice that trembled with every syllable. 'Please!' she continued to implore, desperate to detect just the faintest, life-confirming tremor of movement, from the elderly woman's body. Remembering, how in the films, an unconscious person could be dramatically revived by throwing water over them, she twisted around and in the fashion of a monkey climbing the trunk of a sloping tree, she used her hands to pull herself up the crudely cut stairway. At the top she shoved the cellar door wide open, jarring it

1

into the budgerigar's stand and setting-off an outburst of high-pitched indignant chirping.

'Sorry Peter,' she mumbled a reflex apology, and stopped dead for a moment, to stabilise the swinging cage, by grabbing hold of the plastic ruffled skirt that sagged around the bottom quarter of the thinly barred enclosure. Rushing across the room to the next doorway, a harsh, piercing sound of a kettle whistle, needling into her eardrums. A plume of hot, white agitated steam that spun and swirled with a menacing, Cossack-like dance, denied her ingress into the narrow walk-through space of the kitchen. Like a spectral gatekeeper, taunting and teasing with its flicking tendrils, it dared her to enter. Edging inside the galley kitchen, she reached over and swivelled the gas cooker's red control knob, into the "off" position. Instantly this punctured the funnel shaped cloud to the size of a flaccid balloon, which apologetically granted her wish to access the sink. Her right hand snatched a brightly coloured, flower-patterned drinking glass from off of the draining board. At the same time, her left hand struggled to twist open the stiff, steel capstan tap handle. Thrusting the glass into the heavy stream of running water, it filled almost to overflowing in under a second. Concentrating on not spilling too much of the water, she retraced her steps back to the top of the cellar stairs. Peering down, she hoped against hope, that somehow, her grandmother would have magically regained consciousness, and things could go back to how they were. But to her vexed disappointment, her granny's body remained planted at the foot of the stairs, where she had landed. Shuffling down the uninviting stairway again, until she stood directly above her inert grandmother, she poured the entire contents of the glass over the supine woman. When the expected spontaneous recovery failed to materialise, the distraught adolescent called upon the Almighty, to enact a divine intervention and resurrect her grandmother back to the land of the living.

'Please God, make her be all right – *please*, I didn't mean this to happen, honest I didn't. Make her wake up, *I didn't really mean it!*'

Crouching over the body, she decided to shake her grandmother, to see if this would rouse her from her comatose state.

2

The fraught pulling action on the old woman's shoulder, caused her head to flop over, like a chicken that had just had its neck wrung. Emulating the atmospheric luminescence, of a spotlight on a darkened stage, the light-well to the front end of the cellar, allowed a shaft of pearled sunshine, to filter through the cobweb-frosted casement window. The bar of light, cast an ethereal opalescent glow on the drooping, paper-white flesh of the old lady's face, dramatically highlighting it against the surrounding gloom.

The curt realisation that she was looking directly into the accusing, wide-open stare of a dead person, caused a fresh explosion of panic to detonate inside the twelve-year-old girl's brain. Screaming in terror and gripped by a crushing need to get out of the house, she raced up the uneven brick steps. Sprinting diagonally across the living room and straight on through the tiny kitchen, she escaped out of the backdoor, into the sunlit concrete covered yard. With her heart beating to the same wing-fluttering tempo, of an unfortunate house sparrow caught up in the netting of a neighbour's fruit cage, she took a deep breath and fought to clear the sickening image of her granny's white vacant face, indelibly etched in her mind's eye.

'Help Me! Help me somebody, please!' she shouted up and down the length of the back gardens, but nobody answered her call for assistance. Scrambling up the grass banking, she ran through the scratchy twigs of her grandmother's dormant gooseberry bushes, and then, in one bound, she leapt across onto the curved roof of the rusting Anderson air-raid shelter, that for the previous twenty-four years, had seen service as a garden shed. Precariously balanced on the apex of the green-painted corrugated steel construction, she stood up on tiptoe and looked across into the opposite block of houses.

'Help me! Help me please!' she bellowed, as loud as her young lungs would allow, but still there was no sign of life. With a growing sense of despondency and solitude, the girl started to lower herself into the dividing alleyway of the facing back gardens. Sliding down the side of the wall, protruding jagged shards of gritty mortar, from between the burnt-treacle coloured bricks, caught both of her knees and grazed them. Once down onto the black cinder-covered pathway, she ran for all she was worth towards the far end and out into the main road.

'Help me someone!' she frantically yelled out, at the top of her voice.

This time, a young mother, who was pushing a large pram on the other side of the road, called back, 'What's the matter love, have you hurt yourself?'

'No my . . .' the girl started to reply, but just then, out of the corner of her eye, silhouetted against the bright fluorescent window light of the old wool shop, she registered a familiar figure, carrying two heavily loaded shopping bags. Turning her head, she could see a woman walking towards her, wearing a bright coloured lipstick that matched her fuchsia chiffon headscarf, which was knotted tightly under her chin.

'Mum!' she screamed, dashing across the road to meet her.

'Whatever's the matter Linda?' the woman asked, with mounting concern, noticing the bloodied state of her daughter's knees.

'It's Granny. Mum she's . . .' the young girl's head rolled from side to side, indicating her torment at the enormity of what she was about to impart. Instead of completing the sentence, she stood and looked intently at her mother, with horror-struck eyes and a mouth silently flapping in bewilderment, struggling to form coherent speech.

'Linda calm down – and tell me about Granny,' her mother firmly instructed, bracing herself for what she knew would certainly be bad news.

Linda coughed out the excess air that she had inhaled, and forced out the words, 'SHE'S DEAD!'

CHAPTER ONE
11th October 2003

7.45 pm

Linda pressed the button, on her new DAB digital radio.

'That was the Black Eyed Peas, still at number one in the charts, for the sixth week running –surely the Sugarbabes', "Hole in the Head", will knock them off the top spot next week,' the radio presenter calmly asserted, in smooth buttery tones that drifted out into the kitchen like a coiling wisp of cigar smoke.

'Wow! That does sound good, but who the hell are the Black Eyed Peas?' she muttered to herself, turning off the new gadget. From her vantage point, perched up on a kitchen barstool, she scanned her newly installed, "state-of-the-art" kitchen for the hundredth time that week. The contemporary, black marble work surfaces, that conflicted gloriously, against the sleek clean lines of the chestnut units, looked just perfect. It would be a crying shame to disfigure this visual inspiration, by actually using them to prepare food on. Friends were about to arrive for an evening meal, and she wanted the kitchen to remain in pristine condition, at least until they had seen it.

'Steve, have you heard of the Black Eyed Peas?'

'Yep, they've been in the charts for ages,' her husband replied, from the hallway.

'I haven't heard of them, I must be getting really old, or I've been listening to *Radio Four* for too long,' Linda concluded, worried that she was becoming out of touch, with modern pop culture.

'Both probably,' Steve said dryly, as he entered the kitchen and caught the end of her self-assessment.

'Thanks! Don't touch the work surfaces – I've just cleaned them.'

'They're called work surfaces for a reason! You know, we are going to have to do some cooking in here one day,' Steve mocked her unrealistic intention of wanting to extend the new kitchen's flawless presentation indefinitely.

'I know. I just want it to look fantastic for when Rod and Melissa get here, and after that, I'll start to use it. I've ordered a Chinese for tonight, and there are plenty of bottles in the wine cooler.'

'Ooh, get you, *wine cooler* indeed! I suppose the days of just getting a bottle out of the fridge are over, now we have a *luxury* kitchen,' Steve said, continuing to wind Linda up, about her newfound kitchen snobbery.

'What about you and bloody cars, you go on about them for hours,' Linda snapped back, before realising that he was just baiting her. There was a rapping knock at the front door that brought their pointless conversation to a sudden halt, whereupon Steve wandered off to let their guests in. Moments later, the approaching footfall on the wooden flooring in the hallway, heralded the imminent arrival of their friends into the heart of the house.

'Hi, Linda. Whoa! The kitchen looks superb, are you pleased with everything?' Melissa asked, handing over a chilled bottle of champagne to her host.

'Yes, I love it thanks. How wonderful, champagne, thank you,' Linda answered, while gratefully accepting the gift.

'I thought we could toast your lovely new kitchen, with it,' Melissa said, smiling thoughtfully.

6

'Or, I could christen it, like they do a ship and smash the bottle over the work surface,' Steve said, snatching the champagne from his wife and raising it above his head. 'Okay, okay, don't worry Linda, I'm only joking, I'll put it in our wine cooler.'

Steve aimed a little smirk at Linda, stoking the cooling embers of their ongoing private joke. Linda ignored Steve and proceeded to give Melissa a conducted tour of the kitchen's lustrous new appliances, while the two men went through to view the sports channel, that was showing the World Golf Championship, live from the States.

Once the Chinese meal had been delivered, the two splintered gender camps, regrouped around the dining room table, for an evening of wining, dining and lively discourse. With a pervading sense of solace, mixed with a self-congratulatory tinge of smugness, the quartet debated at great length, the topic of house prices and how they were soaring in the SW6 area of London. Various other subjects were discussed during the night, but money and how to make it, was the dominant theme of their discussions.

Bonuses, share dealings, tax avoidance, investments and divorce settlements; Rodney Baxter was an expert on all of them. Ten years previously, Melissa had been his office PA, and in what, on the face of it, looked like a blatant, premeditated ploy on her part, allowed herself to be seduced by him and then *accidentally* became pregnant. Although he had been married for twenty-six years, the enchantment of unexpectedly becoming a father to a child and heir, motivated Rodney to divorce his wife and marry Melissa, some thirty-two years his junior. They lived just four doors up the road, but in a much larger, double fronted house, equipped with all the modern conveniences and luxuries that you would associate with a high-flying millionaire businessman. Over the previous eighteen months, Rodney had taken Steve under his wing and with his network of financial contacts, opened up some lucrative doors for him. So much so, that Steve had resigned from his job at the bank, to become a self-employed financial consultant and was reeling in some big cheques. Finally, as the wine bottles steadily emptied, the chatter became more relaxed and personal.

7

It wasn't too long before Melissa turned the conversation around to her favourite subject; her only daughter, Taylor.

'Rod only wants Taylor to go to boarding school, when she is eleven. I can't stand the idea of her being away from me, for such a long time. You don't approve, do you Linda?'

'Well it's up to you two, to sort that one out, I'm remaining neutral,' Linda answered, deciding that it would be undiplomatic to take sides, in what could become an intense domestic row.

'*Linda*, I was counting on you, to be on my side. You're a successful woman who didn't go to public school – I thought you would champion state schools. I know Steve went to boarding school, so I'm sure he'll side with Rod,' Melissa griped, her speech slightly slurred, by the considerable amount of alcohol coursing through her bloodstream.

'Actually, I did go to boarding school,' Linda announced, taking another swig from her oversized wine glass, before placing it slowly down onto the ceramic coaster.

'Did you?' Steve gasped, astounded by his wife's revelation. 'You've never told me that before – I thought you went to a "secondary modern" school?'

'I only boarded for one year,' Linda answered, amused by her husband's surprised expression.

'Why just a year? Did you get expelled?' Rod asked, with a leery smile, hoping to hear a lurid tale about schoolgirl misbehaviour.

Linda looked into his staring eyes, magnified behind the thick lenses of his glasses, and was immediately reminded of the square jawed, big eyed puppets, from the iconic sixties television series, *Thunderbirds*.

'No, not quite,' she laughed and hesitated for a few seconds, while she invented a fictitious reason. 'My parent's couldn't afford to keep up the fees, so I went back to my local school, Queen's Manor.'

8

'Well, married for nearly twenty-three years and I never knew that!' Steve spluttered.

'Did the experience traumatise you Linda? Is that why you've never mentioned it to Steve?' Melissa probed, hoping this would be the reason, and thereby add some weight, to her side of the argument. 'Only Rod, is always saying, that his boarding school was like the *BBC* – buggery, beatings and cricket.'

Linda's hand shot to her mouth, in a vain attempt to prevent the wine which she was sipping, from escaping and dribbling down her chin, as she vigorously cackled at what Melissa had said. Once sufficiently recovered, she managed to squeal out, 'There certainly wasn't any buggery, I think I would have remembered that! Thank God there wasn't any cricket, I would have preferred the buggery, than having to play, or watch, the world's most boring game. As I recall, there was a bit of beating occasionally.'

'The teachers actually hit you?' Melissa choked in disbelief.

'This was way back in the dark ages Melissa, before you were even born – corporal punishment was the norm then, in schools and in the homes. In those days, kids were seen, but not heard, and we had unconditional respect for our elders,' Linda said, still chuckling.

'Yes, it's hard to believe how easy children have it these days, certainly compared to when I was at school in the fifties.' Rod acknowledged Linda's sentiments, and then continued to put his side of the argument for fee-paying schools. 'Nowadays, boarding schools are very civilized. You get your own room, you can come home for the weekend, the food is good and you get a first class education, which should set you up for life.

'When I went, it was more like a constant fight for survival, where the strong ruled and the weak went to the wall. Prefects were allowed and encouraged to thrash the living daylights out of the younger boys, for the most trivial of offences. When I became Head of House, I caned a boy, just for getting "run-out" during a house cricket match.'

'Rod! That's totally barbaric and not something to crow about!'

Melissa laughed along with the others, at Rod's comment, but felt for the sake of appearances, she should vent her disapproval of her husband's candid disclosure.

'Nonsense, he made an error of judgement, and life is about making the right decisions. That's what it was like back then, our school was a self-governing entity, the masters just let us get on with it. The beatings and cold baths were expected. When I was young, I got canings off the head boy for the terrible crimes, of not having the correct number of buttons done up on my waistcoat, and not cheering loudly enough, when we gave "three cheers" to the opposing house's rugger team,' Rod paused to gauge the reaction of the others looking at him, and then continued, 'Afterwards, I remember vowing to myself that one day, I would be the one to mete out the punishments. So I made damn sure that I fought my way up the school's greasy pole, to become Head of House. When I look back, it was those character building blocks that made me successful in business, and probably helped save my life a number of times, when I was in the army.'

'How did it save your life?' Steve asked.

'The self-preservation instinct that was ingrained into me at school, served me well when I saw active service in the Middle East. In Aden, a couple of times I was in a situation where it was either me, or the other guy – and as you can see, I'm still here. It's amazing how cold-blooded you can be, when your very existence and future depends on taking the life of somebody else.'

'You actually *killed* a person?' Linda asked, her voice saturated with incredulity, as she looked across the table at her wealthy neighbour, who now appeared the epitome of a mature, respectable businessman. She wondered if drinking copious amounts of red wine, had embellished his memory, and he had conjured up this fabrication for shock value.

10

Rod could see in Linda's eyes, her reluctance to believe his story, so he went on, 'Yes, more than one person actually, but after all, that is what I had been trained to do. I was part of an intelligence-gathering unit that operated covertly behind enemy lines. Well, that's what they called it, but in reality, we were a "hit squad" trying to take-out the terrorist ring leaders, in the Arabic quarter of Crater – quite literally, knocking them off in their own backyards.

'Once you have lived with that kind of pressure, closing a dodgy multi-million pound deal, is a walk in the park on a sunny day.'

Rod laughed, trying to make light of the deadly seriousness of his admission, while the others sat around the table, open-mouthed in astonishment. Realising that the alcohol might have loosened his tongue too much, he tried to justify his actions.

'Hey, don't looked so shocked, we were at war, sometimes you have to forget about the *Rules of Engagement*, nasty things happen and people get killed. My experiences taught me a valuable lesson – you don't get anything worthwhile in this life, unless you are prepared to take risks – and that is exactly why I've been successful in the business world.'

'You don't have your business opponents bumped off do you?' Linda broke the stony mood in the room with a lumpish joke.

Rod smiled, and appreciated her intent.

'No, things haven't come to that just yet.'

Linda took another swig of wine from her glass, and then announced, 'Back in the late sixties, my parents thought they were doing their best for me, by paying for my private school education, but they wouldn't have sent me away, if I hadn't wanted to go. Have you discussed this with Taylor?'

'No, not yet, we have nearly another two years before she will have to go, but Rod says, that we have to start to make the arrangements now, if we want to get her into a good school,'

11

Melissa answered, and then she asked, with an unambiguous stress of doubt in her voice. 'You, actually wanted to go then?'

'Yes, I couldn't wait, I was getting picked on by girls in my class, at my local school, so it was an escape really. I'd read a lot of exciting stories about life at boarding schools, which had fired up my imagination, so I wanted to enter that world and be the heroine of my own adventures. When my grandmother fell down the cellar steps and was killed,' Linda paused, and nervously touched her lips with her fingertips before continuing, 'my parents suddenly had enough money, to send me to a fee-paying school.'

'So, was it all midnight feasts, pillow fights and girls' own adventures, then?' Rod asked, mentally recalling some episodes from his own schooldays.

'Well, yes, I did have some adventures and a few scrapes, I made a really good friend and I have to say, it was the most amazing year of my school life. In many respects though, it was much the same as my state school – I still got bullied.'

'But presumably it was a better class of bullying?' Rod quipped, and then raucously laughed at his own joke.

'Why were you bullied at boarding school?' Melissa asked, in a concerned tone.

'As soon as one particular girl found out that my family were actually working-class, she made it her aim, to get me thrown out of the school.'

'Why on earth, would she want to do that?' Steve enquired.

'Perhaps she thought you were on a mission to subvert the middle classes, by integrating with them,' Rod surmised.

'Yes!' Linda let out a drunken laugh. 'I single-handedly tried to bring down the British class system!'

'Do you still see your best friend?' Melissa asked. 'Rod still sees all of his old mates from school.'

12

'And that includes the boy I caned for getting run-out, who is actually in the Shadow Cabinet now!' Rod chipped in, smiling with pride, at the thought.

Linda took a deep breath.

'No, I haven't seen her since the day I left, thirty-three years ago. I tried writing to her, but things were a bit complicated, so I'm not sure what happened to her after that. It was such a shame, she was the only friend that I really felt close to during my school days, and I don't even know what became of her, or whether she is still alive or not.'

Steve suddenly jerked forward and spilt some of his drink.

'Sorry, must have gone down the wrong way!' he quickly reasoned to the others, who all burst into fits of laughter at his *faux pas*. Melissa looked into Steve's flustered darting eyes, and a taunting grin curled on her lips, she knew that the real explanation for his involuntary twitch, was all to do with her uncovered right foot, pressed firmly against his genitalia.

'I'd better get a cloth,' Steve mumbled. 'And while I'm out in the kitchen, would anyone like a coffee or a cup of tea?'

'I'll help you Steve, and make sure you don't mess up Linda's lovely new kitchen,' Melissa said laughing, as she followed Steve out of the room, leaving Rod to regale Linda with one of his many sadistic school anecdotes.

'What did you do that for?' Steve hissed, once they were out of earshot.

'You don't usually complain,' Melissa giggled, as her hand made for his groin. 'Besides, I haven't touched it for ages, I was just seeing if it was still in working order. Now that Linda's company has hit the rocks, she's around all the time, especially at the weekends. We're going to have to find her something to do. Something, to get her out of the way for a couple of days – so that you, my love, can give me what I'm in desperate need of.'

'Okay, I'll think of a way around it,' Steve answered in hushed tones, his eyes rapidly flitting back and forth from the kitchen door to Melissa's half-exposed breasts. 'Anyway her business isn't on the rocks, it just going through a quiet spell – she'll soon be working all hours again.'

'Well, it's been seven weeks since we last did it, and I can't wait much longer.'

Melissa slowly unzipped Steve's trouser fly and plunged her hand in, grasping hold of his penis through the material of his underpants. Steve was stunned for a second by the sudden, unexpected rush pleasure that he was experiencing, but regained his senses enough to firmly push her arm away.

'Are you *mad*? Not here, not under their noses,' he rasped through his clenched teeth.

'Why not? Don't you find it exciting?' Melissa playfully jousted with him.

'You're drunk, now help me find the bloody coffee cups.'

Steve turned away and opened a unit door, just as Linda mooched into the kitchen, carrying an armful of empty wine bottles.

'Not in there Steve, get the posh ones, they're in the end cupboard,' she called over to him, while attentively placing the bottles, one by one, on top of the island countertop. He paused for a heartbeat, and cast a guilty glance at his wife, wondering if she had seen anything. Her demeanour suggested that she had not, so he quickly gathered up the cups and saucers and laid them out on the marble work surface.

'I'll do the coffee, you go in and keep Rod company,' Linda suggested, waving a banishing hand at Steve.

'So, you do think it would be a good idea, for Taylor to go to boarding school?' Melissa, who had remained in the kitchen, continued to solicit Linda's opinion.

'I didn't say that – it might not suit her. What I did say, was that overall, I did enjoy my time away at school – that's not to say, it was all marvellous, there were miserable times as well.'

'Didn't you miss your mum and dad?'

14

'Yes at first, of course I did, I know it sounds *clichéd*, but like Rod said, the environment taught me to stand on my own two feet and deal with problems, like being bullied.'

'I'm surprised to hear that you were bullied at school, you seem a very confident, strong personality,' Melissa lauded Linda's attitude to life.

'Well, I wasn't very confident before I went away to school, but I eventually stood up for myself and fought back. It's ironic – at boarding school I was bullied for being common, and at my secondary modern school I was bullied, for being too aloof to join a gang of shoplifting girls. So, you see, if you don't quite fit in with your ruling peer group, it makes you a possible target at any type of school.'

'How long did you go away for at a time?'

'On average, the terms were about twelve weeks, it depended when Easter fell – back then, only the girls who lived fairly close by, went home for half term, and that was just a long weekend.'

'Were you upset when your parents couldn't afford to send you to the school after a year?'

Linda finished pouring out the last drips of the aromatic black liquid, from the French press coffee pot, before responding to Melissa's question.

'Yes, I was devastated, I had suddenly lost my best friend and I suppose for a while, I was sort of in mourning, but eventually I pulled myself together and got on with my life.'

'What was your boarding school called?' Melissa asked, thoughtfully.

'It was called Grenchwood Hall School for Girls, why do you ask?'

'Oh nothing, just wondered that's all,' Melissa answered with an insolent grin twitching on her lips.

#   #   #

15

Standing in their tiny front garden, at just after one o'clock in the morning, Steve and Linda waved to Melissa and Rod as they entered their large house, just fifty yards further up the road.

'Well, at least we know that they got home safely,' Linda said, double locking her front door.

'Yes, I don't think there was any doubt about that – after all, Rod is a trained killer.' Steve laughed with an air of contemptuous, self-satisfaction. 'Did you believe any of that old tosh he was coming out with?'

Linda pondered the question for a few seconds before answering, 'I don't know, he does have that look about him.'

'How do you mean?'

'There's something about the way he stares at you, with those dead fish eyes, devoid of emotion and unnaturally enlarged behind those thick bottle-end glasses. He makes me feel that I should be confessing some sort of a dark secret about myself.'

'Well you did!'

'What do you mean?'

'Going away to boarding school – you kept that a secret from me for all these years!'

Linda laughed, 'That's hardly a dark secret, I never thought you would be interested in my girly, adolescent school experiences.'

'Of course I would!' Steve exclaimed, smiling like a child who had prematurely unearthed a hidden Christmas present. 'No seriously, I just found it strange that you had never mentioned it before.'

'Steve . . .' Linda started to speak with a solemn look on her face.

'What?'

'Promise me . . .'

16

'Promise you what?' Steve eagerly jumped into the pause that Linda's deliberation had created.

'Promise me . . . that if you ever play cricket with Rod, you won't get run out!' She giggled and ran up the stairs into the bathroom to ready herself for bed.

Steve busied himself clearing the mess in the dining room for ten minutes, before joining her upstairs.

'Penny for them?' he asked, seeing Linda sitting up in bed, gazing intently into space.

'Sorry?'

'Penny for your thoughts,' Steve clarified his question. 'You looked like you were miles away.'

'Oh, I was actually. I was remembering my first day away at boarding school,' Linda answered, without looking at Steve or changing the intense, fixed expression she had on her face.

'Happy memories were they?'

Before attempting to answer Steve's question, Linda nestled down between the sheets and at the same time tried to swallow a rising yawn.

'Yes,' she eventually whispered, closing her eyes she completed her reply, 'mostly happy.'

CHAPTER TWO
20th September 1969

9.55 pm

'And that was Creedence Clearwater Revival, with "Bad Moon Rising". Tune in tomorrow and find out whether they're still, the nation's number one,' demanded the static-coated voice, crackling out from the tiny blue and grey plastic transistor radio. Linda picked up the radio from the top of her bedside table, and with a nifty flick of her index finger, switched it off for the last time. The sudden and ringing silence made her feel all the more unsettled. Carefully she replaced the radio down onto the dust free oblong, where it had previously stood undisturbed for weeks. Snatching up an old love-worn teddy bear, from off of her wooden toy box, she gave it a comforting hug. Sighing deeply to herself, she realised that tomorrow she wouldn't be tuning in, to find out which group would be at the all-important number one spot in the hit parade. In fact, for the next three months, she probably wouldn't be able to listen to any pop music whatsoever. Leaning forward, Linda scanned the Beatles wall calendar that hung from a hook on the back of her bedroom door. With outstretched fingers she slowly traced the parallel lines that divided the weeks, starting from Saturday September 20th until she got down to December 20th. It was only now, that the fateful day had finally arrived, that she fully grasped the consequence of how going to boarding school, was about to change her life, so completely. Being over two hundred miles away from home, her parents would not be at hand, if she needed their

18

unconditional support, and for the first time in her thirteen-year life, she was going to have to fend entirely for herself. The prospect of this caused a growing nervous melancholy to churn within her stomach, which she tried to pass-off, as natural first day jitters.

Going away to school was something she had really wanted; this was to be her escape; something that she had dearly prayed for. Shame, she thought, that Granny had to die for it to happen, but then, she was very old, and if Mum and Dad hadn't inherited her money, they simply would have never been able to afford the school fees. Sitting down at her dressing table, she picked up an Art Deco jade-enamelled hairbrush, recently bequeathed to her by her late grandmother, and while carefully examining her face in the mirror, she ran the soft-bristled brush through a truss of her shoulder-length blond hair. Suddenly Linda's heart began to race fast, like a radiator fan in an overheated car, and her cornflower blue eyes widened with horror and surprise. Materialising from within the depths of the mirror, she could see the intangible features, of her dead grandmother's face, peering at her from the corner of the room. Spinning around to confront this ghostly apparition, the spooked girl beheld nothing more sinister, than a collage of smiling pop star posters, pinned to the wall. Quickly, she convinced herself that the haunting likeness had been conjured up by her blurred peripheral vision, tricking her into thinking that one of the faces on the posters was Granny's. Turning back towards the mirror to resume her hair brushing, Linda noticed in her reflection, that she was wearing an ugly twist of shame on her lips.

'Linda! We are ready to go love,' she heard her mother's penetrating, twitchy voice call up the stairs. It snapped her out of the morbid twinge, that the remembrance of her dead grandmother had triggered, and back into the reality of the present day. Taking a poignant last look around the room, the faded posters of Lulu, Adam Faith and Cliff Richard, which she hadn't really paid any attention to for ages, took on an unwarranted sentimental importance. Looking up at the curl of wallpaper, creeping down the wall from the join at the picture rail, she smiled to herself, remembering the times her father had said he was going to paste it back up, but after a year, he still hadn't found the time. Stepping

19

slowly backwards out through the doorway, Linda's last image of her bedroom was a row of un-played-with dolls that were sitting on a shelf, their glinting eyes, staring accusingly at her as she closed the door.

'Hurry up love – we don't want to be late!' A further piercing request resounded up from the hallway. Linda took a deep breath and began down the stairs.

'Coming Mum,' she mustered a cheerful reply, aware that her mother had great misgivings about her going away to school. 'I was just taking a last look at my bedroom.'

'Well, we won't change anything, it'll be exactly the same for you, when you come back for the Christmas holidays,' her mother assured her.

'That'll be in thirteen weeks,' Linda rather needlessly informed her mother, who was very mindful, of exactly how long her only child would be separated from her.

'Yes, it will fly by – it always seems to be Christmas nowadays,' replied her mother unconvincingly, her insincere words were calculated to reassure herself, more than her daughter. 'Dad's packed the car with all your school stuff, so we'll get going now, just in case there are any hold-ups on the motorway. We don't want to be late on your first day – after all, you're already a week behind the others, because of the damn chicken pox.'

As her mother mentioned the words "chicken pox" Linda's immediate reaction was to inspect her face again in the hall mirror.

'The spots have just about gone, haven't they?' she asked rhetorically, annoyed by the fading blemishes. 'Hope the other girls don't notice them, blasted things, it's bad enough missing the first week of term, I don't want get called "Spotty" or "Pimple Head", as well as being the new girl.'

'Don't worry Linda, I'm sure that the girls at Grenchwood Hall School won't behave like the little cows at Queen's Manor,' her mother angrily expressed herself, remembering how her

20

daughter's life had been periodically blighted by a bullying group of girls at her local state school.

They exited the house together and were immediately confronted by Linda's father.

'Well, what do you think of her?' he enthusiastically beamed. 'Isn't she a brilliant car! It's a Daimler V8, almost brand new, still "running in", so we'll have to take it easy on the motorway. Mr Bryant has lent her to me, so we can arrive at your posh new school in style.'

'Oh Jack! How lovely, now we'll really look the part when we roll up at the school!' Linda's mother exclaimed in surprise, agreeing wholeheartedly with her husband's sentiments. 'Mr and Mrs Bryant have been so good to us – you are so lucky to have such a nice boss. First of all, Mrs Bryant arranged for Linda to go to her old school, and now, they have lent us their brand new car.'

Although Linda knew nothing about cars, she was impressed by the gleaming white machine parked outside their house, which appeared to her, as being twice as big as her father's slightly rusting, Morris 1100. Jack Middlewick opened the rear door and pretended to doff his imaginary chauffeurs cap to his daughter. Giggling at her father's clowning, Linda got into the rear of the car and sank down into the sumptuous, deep red leather upholstered back seat.

#   #   #

The root of the journey, which she was about to commence, was set in motion almost two and a half years previous, back on the day when a mean looking, official manila envelope, from the local educational authority, dropped through the letterbox of the Middlewicks' front door. It contained the disappointing news that Linda had failed the Eleven-plus examination and would have to attend the local secondary modern school, Queen's Manor. This information came as something of a shock to the Middlewick household, as the teachers at her junior school, had assured them that Linda would sail through the Eleven-plus exam. The school even queried the result with the local authority, but to no avail, and the following September, she started at her allotted school.

Queen's Manor School was a Brutalist-inspired, vast slab of glazed panels and salmon-pink brick walls, built in the fifties. It catered for nearly two thousand pupils, many of whom were ferried in coaches, from the town's surrounding satellite villages. Linda was placed in the top form of her year, but with over forty pupils in her class, it was far from being a stable academic environment. After a few weeks, a classroom hierarchy had been established; at the pinnacle of this, were a band of girls, who had appointed themselves into the group of "cool girls". Acceptance into this exalted gang was dependent on good looks and bravado. Linda qualified on the first count, but she lacked the audacity to go out on lunchtime shoplifting sprees in Woolworth's, or to allow herself to be groped by older boys, behind the handicraft block after school. The other prerequisite requirement for admission was to brazenly smoke on the way to school. All these activities were instinctively shameful to Linda, whose strict upbringing had impacted on her personality – she was polite, well mannered and respectful, but she was also shy and low on self-confidence. At first, to emphasise that they were the queen bees of the classroom domain, the gang distanced themselves from the rest of the boys and girls. Linda made friends with a girl called Janet, who was similarly unassuming and her school life began without incident.

After a few months, an uneasy classroom tension started to build; the gang had become bored with their detached superiority, so sought out new ways of demonstrating their supremacy and control over their peers. At first, it was psychological, with whispering campaigns – lies, aimed at smearing the reputations of certain class members. Linda's aptitude and appetite for schoolwork didn't make her very popular with the gang, who regarded her as a swot. Within the twisted ethos of the bullies, being a swot was a punishable offence, and they viewed her as a legitimate and easy target.

When the subtle intimidation didn't have the desired effect upon Linda, the gang members upped the ante, issuing blatant threats of physical violence against her. Things culminated, when

22

some girls set upon Linda and her friend Janet, while they were coming home from school. Despite the fact that no serious bodily damage had been inflicted, just some hair pulling and pushing, Linda's worried parents insisted on reporting the incident to the school, even though Linda begged them not to. Their interference served no purpose, other than to inflame a situation, which may have eventually run its course. Recognising that life at school and the outside world in general, could be combative and dangerous places, Linda became ever more introverted. In her spare time, rather than venture out with her friends, in search of normal carefree teenage activities, she retreated into the fictional school worlds, created by Angela Brazil and Enid Blyton. From within the safety of her own bedroom, she avidly read about schoolgirl adventures, taking place in the secure, self-contained communities of cosy boarding schools. Linda constantly wished that she could go to a boarding school, instead of her secondary modern school, which she now loathed so much. Just a few months later, the sudden death of her paternal grandmother, meant that her mother and father, were unexpectedly in a position to grant her that wish.

Jack Middlewick was a garage manager, and his wife Liz, a part-time nurse, both were working-class people and never in their wildest dreams, had they imagined that one day, their only child would be able to attend a private boarding school. Now due to their inheritance, they had more than enough funds to finance the school fees, uniforms, equipment and extra-curricular activities, for the five years that she would be a pupil there. Although worried by the prospect of Linda going away, they convinced themselves that it would be an investment in her future, and give her the start in life that they never had.

Not knowing anything about the world of private education, Jack asked his boss Michael Bryant for advice. Michael was a very successful businessman with a stack of properties and businesses dotted around the town, but this achievement had nothing to do with being born with a silver spoon in his mouth, or going to the right school, it was entirely down to hard work. However, Michael's wife Caroline did come from a privileged background and in her youth, had attended a minor public school in

23

the north of England. She was only too pleased to advise the family and Linda in particular, on what to expect, when going away to school. Caroline then wrote to Miss Amelia Rutherford, the headmistress of her former school, Grenchwood Hall, and personally recommended Linda to them. Amelia was the granddaughter of the headmistress who had reigned over the school when Caroline had boarded there, before the Second World War. Strangely, Caroline could vividly remember that exciting morning, when her usually dour headmistress, proudly announced in the morning assembly that Mrs Rutherford, her daughter and a teacher at the school, had given birth to a baby girl, called Amelia.

It was arranged for Linda to take the Common Entrance Exam at Queen's Manor and the test papers were then forwarded to Miss Rutherford. After an agonising five-day wait, a letter arrived, which confirmed that the school had accepted Linda and her dream had launched into reality.

#   #   #

'How long now Dad?' it was the fourth time in the preceding twenty minutes, that Linda had asked the same irritating question.

'Not long now,' answered her father, aware of his daughter's mounting excitement. 'It's about five minutes before we get to the village of Upper Grench and that's about a mile from the school. As we are far too early, we'll stop off there and get something to eat, then we can time our arrival to meet your new headmistress at exactly three o'clock.'

On reaching the village, Jack Middlewick found a large parking space in a road just off of the ancient market square and carefully manoeuvred the precious borrowed car into it. When he was finally satisfied that the car was as close to the kerb as he could get it, he turned the engine off and uttered his habitual quirky phrase, 'All ashore that's going ashore!'

It was something he always did, when indicating to his passengers that it was now safe to disembark from the car. Linda couldn't wait to get out of the vehicle and explore the picturesque village, so she quickly opened the door and jumped out onto the grassy verge. Not waiting for her parents, she gambolled up to the end of the road to inspect the busy market square. In the centre, surrounded by the parked cars of the Saturday shoppers, was a weatherworn stone cross, and around the perimeter of the square, a characterful assortment of butchers, bakers, antique shops, pubs and tearooms. After Jack and Liz Middlewick had painstakingly checked and re-checked that the Daimler was securely locked, they caught up with their daughter.

'Right then, shall we go across to that tearoom on the other side,' Jack said, pointing to the rustic Copper Kettle tearooms, on the far side of the square. The family weaved their way around the edge of the square, avoiding the other meandering sightseers and shoppers, until they were standing outside the shop. Silently they scrutinized the menu board in the front window, trying to make up their minds on what to have. Linda, like her parents, had never heard of most of the items on the list. What was "Yorkshire curd tart" or "ginger parkin"? But she thought that "sticky brandy fruitcake" sounded nice. Feeling every bit like anxious incomers, from an alien culture in the south, they entered the shop. A young waitress warmly greeted them and showed them to a vacant table close to the window. Again they all silently studied the menus, which the girl had given to them. Eventually Liz broke the hush by pronouncing a decision, 'I think it would be best if we get the "traditional cake stand afternoon tea" for three.'

Jack slightly nodded his head in agreement, but Linda hankered for something more adventurous.

'Mum, can I also have a slice of the sticky brandy fruitcake?' she asked.

'Well . . .' Liz hesitated, looking at her husband, who again just nodded his agreement. 'Yes alright, we'll ask for a piece of that as well.'

'Thanks Mum. Why do they call the tea, "Breakfast Tea"?'

'I don't know. I expect it's what the posh people drink at breakfast time.'

25

'Do you think that's what I'll get every morning at the school?'

'I'm not sure that the school would be able to afford to give a 120 girls, expensive tea every morning, you'll probably get Typhoo-Tips like we have at home.'

Interrupting the conversation, the young waitress attended their table, notebook in hand, ready to take their order. Having written it down, she then disappeared into the back room, only to re-emerge a few minutes later, carrying a large cake stand, full of assorted sandwiches, warm scones, strawberry jam, and meringues full of cream. She placed the stand down on the table and then withdrew again into the back room. Returning for a second time, she settled down a tray with the teapot, milk, sugar and cups, plus an additional plate with Linda's sticky brandy fruitcake on it.

'Dear me, I wasn't expecting so much,' Liz lamented. 'Will we have time to eat all this and get up to the school by three o'clock?'

'Yes, we still have over an hour, just relax, it won't matter if we are a bit late, you won't get detention!' Jack laughed at his wife, who coloured up in embarrassment.

'Well, we don't want to get off on the wrong foot – standards are going to be a lot higher than at Queen's Manor. I doubt whether Miss Rutherford would stand for any of the nonsense that goes on there. So you be on your best behaviour young lady, we don't want you getting expelled!'

'Linda's a good girl!' Jack reproached his wife. 'I don't think we have anything to worry about there, she's never been in trouble at school before – have you Linda?'

'No Dad,' Linda answered her father, just before taking a large bite of the meringue, causing cream to squirt out from both of its sides.

'Careful Linda, use your serviette,' her mother fussed. 'You must remember your table manners when you are at the school. The other girls will probably come from "well-to-do" families and will know which knife and fork to use.'

'Liz! Leave the girl alone. She's not going to the Ritz. She'll be fine,' Jack interjected, worried that his wife's preconceived ideas about the school, would un-nerve his daughter. At that particular moment Linda's only concern, was whether or not, she would have room for the extra slice of cake that she had ordered.

With their plates cleared, Liz timorously looked at her wristwatch before softly saying under her breath, 'I think I'll powder my nose, before we go up to the school.'

After waiting for his wife to head off in search of the toilet, Jack whispered, 'Right, now that your mother's not here, take this.' He then slid a folded five-pound note across the table to his disbelieving daughter.

'Wow Dad! What's that's for? You know we aren't allowed any money, other than the sixpence a week pocket money that they keep for us.'

'I know, that's why I'm giving it to you, while your mother isn't here, I don't want her worrying about it. Hide it somewhere safe – it's in case you don't like the school and want to come home. That'll pay for a train ticket to London – I've written Mr Hedges telephone number on the fiver, when you get to London, phone him and I'll come and get you.'

'But Dad, I'll have spent the fiver on the ticket, so I won't have the number.' Linda chuckled, exposing the basic flaw in her father's great escape plan.

'Oh yes, I didn't think about that – well copy it somewhere when you get the time and hide that as well.'

'Why don't we get the telephone put in?' Linda asked, while surreptitiously tucking the neatly folded note, into the top of her white, knee length sock.

'We will now. We're on the GPO's waiting list – hopefully they'll be able to connect us before Christmas. Probably get a party-

27

line with Mr Hedges. Anyway, until now, we haven't had anyone to phone, and we don't really know anyone who would want to call us. Here comes your mum, keep that money safe and not a word about it to her,' Jack ordered, as he rose from his seat, to go and pay the bill. When Liz returned from the toilets with her makeup re-applied, Linda noticed that her mother had an unusually nervous look on her face. They both waited in an uncomfortable silence for Jack to join them outside the shop, and then the three of them set off to complete the last small leg of their journey.

#   #   #

The Daimler swept through the school gates and up the drive, bringing Grenchwood Hall into view for the first time. They had all seen Mrs Bryant's blurred black and white snaps of various parts of the building, taken some thirty-odd years before with a Box Brownie, but seeing this magnificent country house in its entirety, with its honey coloured stone *façade*, bathed in majestic sunshine, was just breathtaking. Linda averted her gaze from the building to look at the groups of girls sitting on the lawns, talking and laughing, and observed that they seemed happy and untroubled. This backdrop of a relaxed atmosphere, made the nervous anxiety that had been bubbling away in her stomach all day, subside somewhat. Jack steered the car into the crescent shaped expanse, which fronted the building, the popping, crunching noise that the limestone gravel made under the tyres, announced to those inside the building that a vehicle had arrived. Gradually stopping the car directly outside the main entrance of the house, he jerked up the handbrake and whispered, 'All ashore that's going ashore.' But nobody moved; they all just sat there, not knowing what to do next. A few seconds later, a young woman materialized from the darkness of the doorway and strode confidently down the steps towards them. This descending gait caused her thick golden hair, to bounce and shimmer, as it became exposed to the glare of the sun. Having reached the car, the tall girl leaned forward and smiled at the gaping occupants. Then cupping her left hand over her eyes, to shade them from the blinding sunlight, she said, 'Good afternoon, I presume you are the Middlewicks? I'm Charlotte Drummond, and for my sin's, I'm the school's Head Girl.'

When a sudden breeze caught her hair, she moved her hand from her forehead to smooth the fine floating silk-like threads back into place, revealing her dazzling bright green eyes for the first time.

'If you would like to come with me, I'll show you all to the Headmistress's study.'

Upon this polite request, three car doors simultaneously opened.

'Is it okay, I mean, is it all right to park the car here?' Jack asked, as he bounded around the bonnet to shake Charlotte's proffered hand.

'Yes, it's fine. But I can't guarantee that one of the girls might not steal it! ' Charlotte joked, but then seeing the sudden look of concern on Jack's face, added. 'I'm only joking, Mr Middlewick. We're not as bad as St. Trinians yet!'

'Oh yes, of course,' Jack stammered, embarrassed that he had missed her joke.

Trying to put him at his ease, she moved to the front of the vehicle and openly admired it, saying, 'What a fab car, virtually brand new isn't it? I haven't seen many H registrations yet.'

'Yes, it was new on the 1st of last month, when the letter H came out.' Jack affirmed, going into a bit too much unnecessary detail.

'No wonder you are worried about it – it must have cost you a small fortune.'

'Um . . . yes it did cost a fair bit,' Jack acknowledged, deliberating with himself, whether or not, he should tell her that it wasn't his car, but before he could make a decision, Charlotte had changed the direction of the conversation.

'If you could all follow me, we will pop into the Headmistress's room and I'll introduce you to her, after that, I'll give you all the grand tour of the school.' With this, she spun around on the ball of her foot, like a ballroom dancer executing a

29

pivot turn and marched purposefully up the main entrance stairway, with the Middlewicks trailing in her wake.

Entering the school, their eyes struggled to adjust from brightness outside, to the abrupt darkness of the interior. It was as if, they were walking down a long tunnel, towards a multi-coloured square of light the other end, which was in fact, a stained glass panel, inset into the door of Miss Rutherford's study. Pacing down the wide, oak panelled passageway, Linda couldn't help but be aware that some groups of girls had gathered in the doorways and on the stairway, to catch a first glimpse of the "new girl" and her parents. Charlotte rapped her knuckles on the leaded light Victorian glass panel, then tilted her head up and waited for the green ENTER sign above the door to illuminate. When the filament behind the tiny letters sparked into life, the door was immediately pushed open; Charlotte stretched out her arm and invited the nervous trio to precede her into the room. Sitting behind a large antique desk, which was set against a bookcase-lined wall, a dark haired woman in her mid-thirties, wearing black-framed glasses glanced up at them. The rest of the room, which smelled like a mixture of stale cigarette smoke and rich wood polish, was furnished with an assortment of traditional looking tables and chairs. Two impressive portraits, set in thick carved walnut frames, adorned the opposite wall.

'Good afternoon,' Miss Rutherford greeted her guests with formal cordiality. 'I do hope you had a pleasant journey up . . . from,' she paused for a moment, unable to remember exactly where they had hailed from.

'Hertfordshire,' Jack respectfully volunteered the answer, using his best telephone pronunciation that over-emphasised the initial letter of his home county.

'Yes, of course, sorry I get confused with the counties in the south.'

Miss Rutherford rose and leaned across the desk and shook hands with both parents, but didn't acknowledge Linda in any way. Charlotte dragged a comfy looking drawing room chair over from the sun-bathed bay window area of the room, and then pulled two sturdy looking, ladder-backed chairs across the wooden flooring, placing them next to it. Liz sat down on the well-worn golden and cream upholstered seat while Linda and her father rested on the less relaxing brown uprights.

'I have had a glowing report from Mrs Bryant about Linda,' Miss Rutherford began, making eye contact with Linda for the first time. 'We are always pleased to get recommendations from our "old girls", as they know exactly what we expect here at Grenchwood. Of course, when Mrs Bryant was a pupil here, it was my grandmother, Victoria Fullman who was the headmistress.'

Miss Rutherford nodded towards the portrait hanging on the left hand side of the wall behind them. In deferential unison, the Middlewicks all turned around to pay their respects, to the oil painted image of the long dead former headmistress. Linda examined the picture of the rather fearsome looking woman, dressed in a foreboding black gown and mortarboard. She instantly thanked her lucky stars that she wasn't attending the school back in the old days.

'In 1950 my mother, Emily Rutherford took over the reins,' Miss Rutherford continued with her timeline of former headmistresses, and then waited as her guests switched their attention towards the portrait on the right. This time, Linda judged the woman in the painting, to have a much more compassionate personality, and following that logic; she hoped the present headmistress would surely be, an even more sympathetic character.

'Upon the death of my mother in 1965, I took over the headship and have striven to continue the ideology that my grandmother began, back in the early 1920s, which is, to achieve academic excellence, with a balance between the arts and the sciences. Above all, we are very committed to traditional values and will not tolerate wilful disobedience or laziness.'

Pausing to take a breath, the young headmistress once again made eye contact with Linda, who suddenly became acutely aware, that the last sentence was being aimed specifically at her. Miss Rutherford then gave a quick glance over the top of her glasses, at the girl's parents to see if they were in accord with the standards she had just outlined. Mr and Mrs Middlewick, simply nodded back appreciatively, with expressions of admiration.

'I'm positive that with our help and nurturing, Linda will attain a multi-faceted education that will stand her in good stead, in whichever career path that she chooses to take into adulthood.

'Charlotte will now show you around the school and then you can say your "goodbyes", and let Linda spend the rest of the weekend getting to know her new school friends. Don't worry Mr and Mrs Middlewick, I'm sure that your daughter will be a credit to you, during her time here,' Miss Rutherford concluded the brief, well rehearsed interview and Charlotte opened the study door for them to file out.

'Right, if you will follow me around the corner, I'll show you the Orangery,' Charlotte said, leading off down the corridor. 'When the Hall was first built, it used to be the plant house. I bet back then, they would never have thought that one day, this would be a girls' gymnasium!' she laughed, opening the double doors into the spacious, sun-filled room. On the far side, there were ten south-facing, floor to ceiling, arched windows that afforded them all a splendid panoramic view of the school grounds and the surrounding countryside beyond.

'During the week, this place is hardly ever empty. It's where we have our morning assemblies, dance and gymnastics classes. We also use it for the daily meals, which is why there are trestle tables stacked up over there.' The tour continued, taking in the kitchen, tennis courts, science lab and finally Charlotte showed them the classrooms.

'Well Linda, this is the classroom where you will be taking your lessons.'

'Every lesson?' Linda queried.

'Yes, all of your academic lessons, unless it's science, which takes place up in the lab,' Charlotte answered.

'So the same teacher takes nearly all the lessons?'

'No, at the end of the period the teachers change classrooms.'

'At my old school it was the pupils who went to different classrooms for each lesson, every time the bell sounded, it was mayhem in the corridors!'

'How many pupils were there, at your old school?'

'Nearly two thousand.'

'*Two thousand!* I don't think there are even two thousand people living in Upper Grench. Here, there are about forty girls in each year up to 'O' level and then there are about twenty girls staying on to take A levels. I'll show you the top floor where the prefects and teachers have their bedrooms.'

The little group made its way from the ground floor up the wide ornate stairway, with its beautifully carved balustrade and handrail, their footsteps resonating on the bare, dulled wooden treads, that over the previous fifty years had suffered greatly, from the pounding feet of countless uncaring schoolgirls. Up on the amply proportioned first floor landing, they continued to follow Charlotte along to the foot of another, less aesthetic, set of stairs.

'You are only normally allowed up here, if you are invited by a prefect,' Charlotte warned Linda with a smile. 'But, I thought you would like to see what you can expect when you become a revered prefect.'

Turning left at the top of the constricted second stairway, they passed along the narrow passageway until they got to Charlotte's room.

'This is it – a bit poky, but the main thing is, it's private – after three or four years sleeping in the dorms, you'll think a room like this, is heaven.'

As they stepped back out of Charlotte's small room, a door at the end of the corridor, with a hand-written notice pinned to it, snagged Liz Middlewick's attention.

'What's behind that door?' she asked, while moving closer to read the directive. 'It says – "Strictly out-of-bounds, any girl found beyond this door will be severely punished",' without realising, Liz had read the warning out aloud.

'Oh, the door was installed there years ago, when Grenchwood Hall was a large family estate. This floor was where the servants used to sleep, and the door was the physical barrier between the two sexes. The scullery maids, kitchen maids, chambermaids, and cooks were on this side, while the butler and the footmen were on the other side.'

'So why is it out of bounds now?' Liz enquired.

'I think they discovered some structural problems in the far end of the building and decided to keep it closed off. There are only four more rooms on that side of the door, and the costs of doing the work didn't make it worthwhile to do. Judging from how old that notice looks, it must have been quite a few years ago. It's always been shut off, ever since I've been here anyway. Right, I'll take you back down to the main entrance and see if your car is still there Mr. Middlewick,' Charlotte said, giggling. Her final comment indicated to Linda's parents that it was now time for them to start thinking about departing.

On returning to the ground floor, Charlotte diplomatically left the Middlewicks to unpack the car and say their farewells.

'Right Linda, be a good girl and study hard. I'll write every week with all the news from home and . . .' Liz started her well-prepared goodbye speech, but she could not stop her emotions from welling up and she started to weep.

'Don't worry Mum, I'll be fine,' Linda bravely responded to her mother, although she was inwardly fighting the urge to burst into tears herself.

'Get into the car Liz, before you show your daughter up in front of her new school chums!' Jack jokingly admonished his distressed wife. 'Right Linda, keep your nose clean and remember to write to your mother every week, otherwise she'll be up here, to find out why you haven't!' Jack said, and then waited for Liz to get into the car before continuing. 'Don't forget what I said in the teashop.' He nodded at Linda's right sock and winked at her. Linda couldn't help but smile at her father's furtive attempt to remind her about the escape money. The Daimler's engine suddenly burst into life, shortly after, Jack arced the car slowly around the school forecourt and then followed the driveway towards the main gates.

#   #   #

'Oh Jack, what have we done!' Liz wailed, breaking into a full torrent of tears, which her tiny, lace trimmed handkerchief had no chance of successfully soaking up off her wet cheeks.

'Stop it Liz, or you'll set me off and I'll crash Mr. Bryant's bloody car. She'll be all right – this'll be the making of her, you'll see.'

'Miss Rutherford seemed quite nice, didn't she?' Liz managed to emit her next sentence between sobs and nose blowing.

'Yes, but not as nice as young Charlotte,' Jack chuckled lasciviously.

'Oh you! I saw you looking at her – your eyes were popping out of your head,' Liz chided her husband, but his remark made her crunch through the emotional gearbox in her brain, halting the flow of tears and sending her into a fit of reconciled laughter. 'She was fairly young to be the headmistress of that posh school, don't you think?'

'Well, she inherited the post from her mother, who got it from her mother. Handed down in the family, like a title I suppose. If they had to pay death duties on a place like that, it would have been a considerable amount, no wonder they haven't bothered fixing the problem in those spare bedrooms.' Jack said, turning out onto the main road.

'Yes, that was strange wasn't it? The warning on the door was a bit chilling though, "severely punished", it said. I don't think Miss Rutherford would have written that, it was probably done in her mother's time.'

35

'Yeah, the sign looked really old. Might have been the old battle-axe in the first portrait that put it up? Don't think anyone would have risked opening the door if she was in charge!' Jack laughed, pleased that his wife had overcome her anguish. 'Anyway, it won't be long until Christmas and she'll be home again, playing that bloody pop music noise up in her bedroom.'

#   #   #

Linda stood and watched the white car getting smaller and smaller, as it rapidly took her parents away from her. A few more seconds ticked past and it was out of sight, they were gone from her life for the next three months. The light touch of a hand on her shoulder, immediately snapped Linda out of the morose trance, which she had fleetingly fallen into.

'Come on. I'll show you up to your dorm and see if you can make a few friends. Grab a couple of bags and I'll take your case,' enthused Charlotte, who had returned to complete the final part of her mission, of introducing the new girl, to her roommates. 'Well done on not blubbing, I cried my eyes out on my first day here,' she confided, as they climbed the dark oak stairway. 'Which was surprising really, as my mother is a right bitch.'

Linda's mouth dropped open with surprise at Charlotte's lack of respect for her mother. The tall head girl smiled back at her, pleased that her comment had caused a shocked reaction. Over burdened with Linda's baggage, they clumped along the corridor, until they reached a door marked "Dormitory Five", using her leg and the case, Charlotte pushed the door open.

'Everyone! This is Linda Middlewick, she will be joining this dorm, please make her feel at home,' Charlotte announced, and then in the short time between dropping the case to the floor and departing from the room, she added, 'If you have any problems Linda, you can always come and see me.'

'Thank you Charlotte,' Linda called after her, and then apprehensively turned to face some of her new roommates for the first time. Immediately in front of her, a tawny haired girl with a freckly face lay on her bed reading a magazine. Linda smiled at her,

36

hoping to break the ice. All she got back was a scrutinizing stare. Then, after a few noiseless moments, the girl spoke, 'Middlewick, is a funny name. My brother calls his willy, his middle wicket.'

A synchronised giggle reverberated around the dormitory.

'I'm Louise Bennington, Form Captain. Why are you a week late getting here?'

'I had chicken pox, so I had wait until I wasn't contagious,' Linda answered.

'I can still see some spots on your face, are you sure we can't catch it?'

'No, you can't catch it once the spots stop appearing, but to be on the safe side, we waited an extra week as well.'

'You're over there, next to Mata,' Louise pointed across the room to the bed, next but one from the end of the row. 'Mata's the headmistress's niece –or is it her cousin? Something closely related to her anyway. Did you have a pleasant meeting with Miss Rutherford?' Louise asked, smiling sweetly.

'Yes thank you, she was very nice,' Linda responded.

'The next time you go into her study, she won't be so *nice*, as you so colloquially put it. Will she Mata?'

The bespectacled girl on the end bed, next to where Linda would be sleeping, hardly looked from up from the book that was obviously engrossing her, but answered Louise, 'She can be strict, but only if you have done something really bad.'

'It's all right for you Mata, you can get away with anything!'

Linda sensed some movement behind her; she turned around to see two girls framed in the doorway. They seemed agitated about something and not interested in her at all.

'This is Middlewicket, she's the new girl, but be careful, she has just had the pox,' Louise said. The girls acknowledged

Linda with a brief, cautious glance, but they clearly had other, more important things to discuss with the Form Captain.

'We've got some!' gushed the smaller dark haired girl.

'Really! How many?' Louise replied excitedly.

'Just two,' the girl instantly answered, hopping from foot to foot. 'Shall we then?'

'Yes great!' Louise jumped up off the bed and twirled around to focus a glare at Mata. 'You keep your mouth shout about this Mata Hari.' She then joined the two other girls and they rushed away down the corridor.

Linda shoved her case and bags over to the vacant bed.

'Hello Mata, I'm Linda, what was that all about?' she asked, hoping to start a conversation before Mata retreated back to reading her book. From behind silver wired framed glasses, the girl with short mahogany coloured hair, looked back at her with nervous brown eyes.

'Oh, they have probably got some cigarettes and are going off to find somewhere secret to smoke them. Trouble is – if they get caught, they will blame me for snitching on them. By the way, my name isn't Mata – it's Elaine. Louise calls me Mata after the spy Mata Hari. She thinks because I'm related to the headmistress, I'll sneak on everyone.'

'She likes giving people nicknames then? I see I'm already called Middlewicket,' Linda laughed, melting Elaine's serious expression into a wide beaming smile.

'Yes, she can be quite provocative I'm afraid. She has already been "gated" for talking to some boys, when she was down in the village last week – something she seems to blame me for. So needless to say, nobody wants to talk to me now, for fear of annoying Louise,' Elaine explained, her smile quickly inverting. 'If you don't want to be picked on by Louise and her cronies, you better not let them see you talking to me.'

'Cronies?' Linda inquired.

'Her gang of friends. They all came here from the same prep school, so they all know each other and of course they have stuck together.'

The word "gang" rang alarm bells in Linda's head, causing an unpleasant flashback to her troublesome time at Queen's Manor. A burning bile-like feeling of panic rushed up into her chest, making her confused about what to do next. Should she run with the crowd, or go her own way and be friends with whom she wanted? Linda looked into Elaine's eyes, searching out from behind her slightly damaged national health spectacles, which had fallen down her nose a bit. It was clear from her expression that she was expecting to be rejected again.

'I'm not worried about what Louise and her cronies think, I'd be pleased to be your friend Elaine,' Linda announced positively, although on the inside she had nervous misgivings about her bold declaration.

'Would you! Are you sure? I mean, I don't mind if you want to change your mind,' Elaine exclaimed joyfully, excited by the fact that her enforced loneliness could be at an end.

'I won't change my mind Elaine, I don't think Louise would want me in her gang anyway.'

'Why not? She has half the dorm in it all ready, one more wouldn't matter.'

'Well, I don't like smoking, I don't like boys and I don't like silly nick-names,' Linda said, rather triumphantly.

'Gosh, well said, I agree completely! It will be lovely to have someone to talk to, rather than burying my head in a book all the time. Would you like me to show you around the school and explain how things are done here?'

'Yes please – Charlotte whizzed us around, but I couldn't take it all in.'

Elaine jumped up from her reclined position and Linda noticed that she was quite tall for thirteen, a good three inches taller than herself.

39

'We could have gone down to the village, but it's a bit late to go now. There is always tomorrow afternoon if you would like to?' Elaine suggested.

'Yes, I would like that,' Linda agreed. 'Before we came up to the school, we stopped off there and had a cream tea.'

'Crikey! Lucky you. Did you go to the "Copper Kettle"? The cream tea in there is divine.'

'Yes, I think that's what it was called – it was over in the corner of the square.'

'That's the one! My aunts take me there for a special treat on my birthday.'

'Aunts?' Linda queried the plural usage.

'I have two aunts here at Grenchwood – Amelia, who is the headmistress and Iona, who teaches arithmetic and history. Actually, I call them my aunts, but they're really my cousins. I don't know why I call them "aunt", probably because they are so much older than me, I suppose.'

'Where do your mum and dad live?'

'Oh my mother and father were both killed when I was very young, I don't even remember them,' Elaine informed her casually.

'God! I'm so sorry,' Linda's knee-jerk reaction was to console her new friend.

'It's all right. As I said, it happened when I was a baby. My great aunt, Davina brought me up in Scotland, until I was seven, and since then, I've either been away at prep school in Derbyshire, or staying here during the holidays. Of course, now I'm here all year round.'

'It must be very strange, being here in the holidays all on your own?'

'Actually, it is stranger seeing the place full of girls and hearing all the noise,' Elaine laughed.

40

'So what do you call your aunts now you are a pupil here?'

'During term time, I have to refer to Aunt Amelia as either Headmistress, or Miss Rutherford, and we all have to call Aunt Iona – Miss Iona, so there is no confusion between the two of them. The only problem is, I keep forgetting and saying "Aunt Iona" which causes a riot of laughter in class.'

The two girls spent the next hour happily wandering around the school grounds, while Elaine enlightening Linda, on the proper etiquette required in her new environment.

#   #   #

At four fifty-five precisely, a bell rang to signal that it was time for tea. Girls, who had previously been dissipated around the school, languidly began to converge into the main entrance hallway, to wait outside the orangery. Five minutes later, a second bell sounded and the doors opened into the large windowed room. The sun-drenched orangery was much warmer than the cool, tiled floor corridor where the girls had mustered; Linda felt a wave of heat sweep over her face as she entered the room. Elaine pointed to a table and they sat down together. Seemingly from nowhere, Louise and her pack of followers tumbled into the seats opposite. Linda's stomach turned over at the prospect of the inevitable interrogation that would ensue.

'I see Middlewicket has chummed up with Mata, then,' Louise sneered, instigating the chitchat with a menacing inflection in her voice. 'What is wrong with you? Why be friends with a telltale? Are you one as well?'

'No I'm not, and neither is Elaine, why are you being so horrid to her?' Linda retorted with a question of her own.

'Because, she is the Headmistress's niece and gets special treatment.'

'I do not! I get treated exactly the same as everyone else here,' Elaine indignantly denied Louise's charge.

'All right don't get your knickers in a twist!' Louise laughed, and slumped back in her chair, while she pondered for a few moments her next point of attack. 'Linda, my mother was complaining about the cost of employing gardeners this summer, did your family experience a similar problem?'

This sudden and unexpected civil approach from Louise, threw Linda off-balance, making her wonder, if perhaps, the girl wanted to end the meanness and become friends.

'We don't have any gardeners,' she tentatively replied.

'Does your garden go all around your house?' Louise continued.

'No, we only have a back garden.'

'Oh, so you live in a little terraced house then?' This comment caused a suppressed peal of giggles to squeeze out from the other girls at the table. 'So, which prep school did you attend before coming here?' Louise persisted to pry further into Linda's background.

'I didn't go to a prep school before here, I went to a secondary modern, called Queen's Manor,' Linda innocently informed her interrogator.

'*A state school!*' Louise exclaimed, incredulously. 'What does your father do for a living?

'He's the manager of a garage and my mother is a nurse,' again Linda answered truthfully, but was now realising that Louise wasn't making polite conversation, she was in fact, fishing for information, which she would use against her.

'Your mother goes out to work!' Louise screeched.

'Louise Bennington! Please keep your voice down to reasonable level, we do not wish to hear your conversation on this side of the room,' thundered a grumpy, elderly teacher, standing up on the far side of the orangery to deliverer her admonishment.

Louise quickly twisted around to offer her atonement, 'Sorry Miss Ryan.'

'You will be sorry madam, if there is any more noise from that table, you won't be watching television this evening,' Miss Ryan issued a stern warning and then sat down again.

'That old bat should be apologising to me, for making me sit here with riff-raff,' Louise whispered her contempt for Linda, loudly enough for other girls on the table to hear. The humiliation twisted like a knife in Linda's stomach, and she blinked hard, to stop the burning tears that had pooled in her eyes, from spilling down her cheeks. Sitting across the table, the hateful Louise looked smugly delighted, secure in the knowledge that her barbed comment had hit home.

When teatime was over, amid the hubbub of the cutlery clearing, a muted cheer heralded Miss Ryan and Miss Iona's arrival into the room, carefully pushing a trolley table, upon which, sat a television set.

The girls continued to jostle folded-up trestle tables up against the wall, while the two teachers concentrated on trying to plug the aerial into the set. Then, in what appeared to be, a pre-rehearsed choreographed movement, everyone slid their chairs across the parquet flooring to form a multi-rowed, horseshoe shape around the television set. The next few hours passed by without incident, while all enjoyed the Saturday evening entertainment, of *Dixon of Dock Green* and then, *Shirley Bassey in Stockholm*. To the disappointment of the younger girls, Miss Ryan decreed it was their bedtime, just before the start of the evening film, at quarter past eight.

#   #   #

Up in the dormitory, Linda felt ill at ease about undressing in front of the other girls. She was used to doing this at her previous school, during PE lessons, but the unfamiliar setting and company, made her feel far more conspicuous about this ritual disrobing. Remembering the five-pound note still tucked in her sock, she quickly opened her drawer and hid it under some textbooks. Hastily, Linda got changed into her nightdress while standing with her back to the majority of the girls in the room. Upon completing the task she turned around to find Louise and her sidekicks in close

43

immediacy to her bed. Linda recognised the malevolent smirks that had crept across the faces of the girls, it was the same frightening look that the Queen's Manor gang had worn, just before they attacked her in the street.

'What do you want?' Linda asked plaintively.

'We want to know, if you are as good as your name, little Miss *Middlewicket*' Louise answered, inching ever closer to Linda. 'Grab her girls!' she ordered.

The melee began with Linda falling backwards onto the bed, her assailants deliberately collapsed on top of her, attempting to render their prey defenceless. They each grabbed an outstretched, despairing limb and held her firmly in a splayed horizontal position.

'Stop it!' screamed Elaine, springing across the bed, in an effort to wrestle one of the attackers away from her new friend. Unfortunately her momentum caused her to topple straight over the other side and land on the floor with a thud.

'Right then, let's see if you do have a middle wicket!' Louise shouted victoriously, her fist gripping a handful of cotton material; she then pulled up the front of Linda's nightdress and roughly thrust her free hand up between her legs.

The shock caused Linda to let out a piercing scream, as she frantically twisted her body, trying to loosen the tight grip that the other girls had on her.

'What is going on in here?' Charlotte Drummond bellowed angrily, making a timely entry into dormitory.

'Just having some horseplay with the new girl, Charlotte,' Louise said, rapidly taking her hand away from Linda's indecorously displayed pubic area.

'Anyone not in their own bed in five seconds will come with me to see the headmistress!' commanded Charlotte, in full Head Girl mode, which resulted in a sudden dispersal of shrieking girls, each bounding towards their own bed. 'Are you all right Linda?'

44

Linda could not bring herself to speak, but nodded in the affirmative. 'Well, lights are going off now girls, I don't want to hear another peep from anyone, or there will be real trouble.'

Charlotte flicked the light switch, casting the room into a murky darkness, then she closed the door tight shut and the room became an inky black. Lying rigid with fear and wondering if she was going to be assaulted again, Linda's eyes quickly became accustomed to the gloom, as she searched out for any signs of movement around the grey shapes of the beds and furniture. This wasn't how she thought boarding school would be; it was worse than at Queen's Manor. Back at home, at least she could escape her tormentors in the safety of her own bedroom, but here, she was going to be locked up with them, twenty four hours a day, seven days a week. A warm tear of despair ran down the side of her face, it tickled but she didn't dare move. A second and third tear travelled along the same track, she could stand the irritation no longer and turned her head to the side, feeling on her cheek, the unpleasant wetness that the tears had created on her pillow. She tried not to make a sound, knowing that the rest of the dormitory were probably listening, to see if she would crumple into fits of weeping on her first night. Linda was determined not to give them this satisfaction; instead she comforted herself by thinking about the five-pound note that she had stashed in her drawer. She would simply get up earlier than the others in the morning and then make her way home on the train, like her dad had told her to do.

Eventually the moon came out from behind the clouds and shed some extra light into the room. Linda stared up at the ceiling, noticing that directly above her, was an odd, mottle-stained pattern that at first reminded her of the Turin Shroud, which had recently featured in the newspapers. Then, the more she concentrated on the face area of the strange figure, the more it began to bear an uncanny resemblance to her dead grandmother. Frightened, she buried her head under the covers, and lying in a cold clammy sweat that chilled her entire body, she listened with alert trepidation to every little noise. Throughout the night, each creak of a bed, each cough, each grunt or grating snore, revived her from the edge of slumber

45

back to full consciousness, until at about five-thirty, utterly exhausted, she finally slipped into a deep dreamless sleep.

CHAPTER THREE
21st September 1969

7.00 am

Awakened by a tugging on the sleeve of her nightgown, Linda opened her eyes to see Elaine kneeling beside her bed.

'It's time to get up sleepy head,' Elaine said, smiling at her. 'I'm afraid that we don't get a lay-in on Sundays, because of the walk down to church.'

Linda was momentarily confused; then she remembered the five-pound note and her plan to escape. Looking around the room at the other girls getting up, she realised that it was too late to make good her early getaway. Robotically she latched onto Elaine, who was pleased to continue her role as mentor. At breakfast Linda and Elaine managed to avoid sitting near Louise and her band of henchwomen.

'Are you all right about what happened last night?' Elaine whispered from behind her hand, while they tucked into their dried up sausage and beans. 'Only, I could see you were quite distressed. Louise is such a beast.'

'I was shocked that anyone would do that. I mean, grabbing someone's . . . private place, is just *so wrong*, isn't it?' Linda protested, nervously wondering if this type of behaviour was commonplace in the dormitory.

'Yes, it is completely wrong, if you had told Charlotte, Louise would have been in a great deal of trouble.

47

'I wish I had done now,' Linda sighed, 'I really hate her.'

'It's probably better that you didn't tell on her. I think you will have gone up in Louise's esteem now. They were testing you, seeing how you would react. Have you noticed how they haven't bothered with us this morning – perhaps they have become bored with their bullying and have moved on to something else?' Elaine opined, more in hope than in genuine believe.

'Do you think so? Will they leave us alone now?'

'For a while – with a bit of luck.'

'Thanks for trying to help me, when they grabbed me last night,' Linda said, recognising her new friend's bravery during the fracas.

'Oh, I wasn't much help, I just fell off the bed and clonked my nose,' Elaine laughed, pleased with the commendation. 'We have to march down to the church now and then all the way back up again, for Sunday lunch, but if you feel like it, we can get our pocket money out and visit Grench village this afternoon?'

'Yes that would be great!' Linda exclaimed, feeling a lot happier about the prospects for the day ahead.

#   #   #

Normally Linda only ever attended church for weddings or christenings, so she was thankful when the vicar eventually brought the long and boring Sunday morning service to an end. The Grenchwood girls filed out of the church, each courteously thanking the waiting Reverend, who, save for the odd exception, failed to acknowledge any of their respects. He was more interested in conversing with the more mature members of his congregation. After the ninety minutes of enforced silence, it was a relief for the girls to be outside in the warm sunshine again, chatting away with each other, while they gathered in the lane next to the churchyard. Appearing through the old wooden church lych gates, Miss Ryan came striding briskly towards them. From the angry expression on her face, Linda could tell that the teacher was very unhappy about something.

48

'Helen Richardson and Amanda Penrose!' she shouted, the buzz of chatter instantly ceased and heads turned towards the two girls. 'When we get back to school, perhaps you would like to explain to the Headmistress, why you felt the need to talk to each other during the Vicar's sermon. What was so important that it couldn't wait until the service was over?'

The two crimson-faced girls bowed their heads in disgrace, at their public rebuking.

'Very well, in two's and start back up to the school. Keep talking to minimum while we are still in the village, remember this is the Sabbath.' Miss Ryan shouted, like a sergeant major barking out instructions on the parade ground.

The departing row of schoolgirls, all in their matching uniforms, marched down the road keeping closely in line with each other. Viewed from a distance, the column resembled a giant, bottle green millipede with innumerable white legs, chittering away while it meandered slowly across the fields towards the school.

#   #   #

After lunch, Linda and Elaine joined the queue, which had formed outside a small office next the headmistress's study. Inside the office Miss Iona Rutherford sat behind her desk and carefully recorded the girls' withdrawal of pocket money. Eventually, it was their turn to approach the tabletop, bedecked with its small neat piles of shiny silver sixpences and brass coloured thrupp'ny pieces, placed in rows down either side.

'Can I have two thrupp'ny bits please Aunt Iona?' Elaine asked, and then realising that she had addressed her aunt incorrectly, added ' Sorry, I mean Miss Iona!'

'That's all right Elaine,' Iona smiled, 'After thirteen years of calling me "aunt" you are bound to forget sometimes. Try not to let it happen though, or I will have the whole school calling me aunty!'

'Could I have two thrupp'ny bits as well please Aunt Iona,' Linda laughed, intuitively feeling relaxed in Iona's company.

49

'You see what has happened now!' Iona wailed, depicting her mock despair by theatrically holding her head in her hands. 'Linda, has Elaine shown you around the school and explained all the boring rules to you?'

'Yes she has, thank you Miss.'

'And, you are settling in well?'

'Yes thank you, I'm a bit nervous about lessons starting tomorrow, but other than that everything is fine,' Linda answered, putting up a front to conceal the previous night's unsavoury incident.

'Good. Well enjoy your afternoon out and don't worry about the lessons tomorrow, I'm sure you will be fine, my dear.'

The girls left the office and made their way towards the front entrance.

'Your Aunt Iona seems very nice,' Linda commented.

'Yes she is. Aunt Amelia is lovely as well – in her own way, but I suppose she has to be fairly strict, being the headmistress. Funny that she is the younger sister, you would have thought Aunt Iona would have been the head, as she is three years older,' Elaine reasoned.

'Perhaps she didn't want to be the headmistress,' Linda speculated, and then changing the subject altogether, she added. 'Can you wait here a minute? I've just got to get something from the dorm.' With that, she rushed up the main stairway, leaving Elaine waiting at the bottom looking up. In a few brief seconds, Linda re-appeared and scurried back down again.

'What did you forget?' Elaine asked.

'Oh . . . my sock bands.' Linda hesitated slightly, while thinking up an excuse to cover up for the fact that she had just retrieved her father's five-pound note, from her drawer. 'I don't want my socks to fall down while we're out. I'd taken the bands off after church this morning and only just remembered that I would need them again with these socks.'

50

#   #   #

The girls spent the next half hour, lazily ambling down to the village, which was busy with tourist and local traffic. They sat for a while on one of the public benches, which were dotted around the square and looked across at the village hall. The carved inscription over the entrance to the hall read, "Built in memory of Frank Sumners 1918".

'Wonder who Frank Sumners was?' Linda pondered, as she studied the weathered stone façade.

'Lord Sumners' son – he was killed in the First World War. Lord Sumners owned Grenchwood Hall before it was turned into a school, by Amelia and Iona's grandfather. After the war, Lord Sumners found it difficult to get enough servants and when he died, his family decided to sell up,' Elaine informed her.

'So was Iona and Amelia's grandfather the first headmaster of the school then?'

'Well no, he purchased the hall for his wife Victoria, so that she could set up the school – she was the first headmistress. There is a portrait of her in my aunt's study.'

'Oh yes, we saw it yesterday – she looked really scary.' The two girls giggled. 'Do you think that one day, you might be the headmistress of the school?

'I don't know, I've never really thought about it before,' Elaine mused. 'I suppose it could happen, neither of my aunts have married, so they won't have anyone to pass it onto. I might be their closest relative, so yes, I could be the headmistress in years to come.'

Again both girls burst out into fits of giggles.

'Would you like to be the headmistress?' Linda eventually asked.

'Yes I would! I could make all the rules and get to do the telling off,' Elaine laughed.

'What would you change then?'

51

'Well, I would make the television available every night and not just at weekends; I would make going to church optional; I would ban cross-country runs and I would have cream teas every Sunday, like they serve at the Copper Kettle.'

'Wow! I wish you were the headmistress now,' Linda said, smiling at her new friend. 'Let's go and look in The Copper Kettle's window and see all those lovely cakes.'

The girls stood up and walked diagonally across the square, carefully dodging the passing cars, until they arrived at the shaded opposite corner, where the Copper Kettle tearoom was located.

'Oh, it just makes your mouth water doesn't it?' Elaine uttered, totally engrossed by the menu on the exterior blackboard.

'It certainly does. When is your birthday Elaine?' Linda enquired.

'May the 10th. Why?'

'Oh, you've got months to wait for your treat then.'

'Sadly yes – wish you got two birthdays a year, like the Queen. I'd have my second birthday on September 21st.'

'We could have a cup of tea, we each have enough money for that.'

'No we can't, there is a minimum service charge of one and sixpence,' Elaine pointed out.

'What does that mean?' Linda asked, confused by the term.

'It means, you have to pay at least one and sixpence, whatever you have. It's to stop you going in and just sitting there with a cup of tea for an hour,' Elaine explained.

'We could have a "traditional cake stand afternoon tea for two" if you liked,' Linda announced, to her bewildered friend.

'How could we? It's nine and sixpence for that. We only have a shilling between us.'

'No we have this as well,' Linda dipped down and fiddled with the top of her sock and then, like a magician performing a trick, she suddenly manifested a five-pound note.

'Gosh, where did you get that from?' Elaine hissed, barely believing her own eyes.

'My dad gave it to me, in case I need to go back home. After what happened last night, I was going to use it this morning, but I didn't wake up in time! I've gone off the idea of running away now, so we might as well have a treat. I'm sure he wouldn't mind.'

'Your father might not mind, but we are only allowed to spend sixpence if we visit the village.'

'Why is that then?' Linda queried.

'It's to make everything equal, so the girls from really rich families, don't flaunt their wealth in front of the other girls.'

'According to Louise, everyone who comes to Grenchwood Hall is really rich, except for me of course. Anyway, as long as we don't tell anyone, who is to know?' Linda argued.

'*Shall we?*' Elaine dithered, but Linda could see from the excitement in her eyes she was agreeable to the suggestion. Instead of answering, she pushed the shop's front door open and they both entered.

'Could we have a table for two please?' Linda asked the waitress, whom she recognised from the previous day's visit.

'Would you like it near to window, Miss?' inquired the young waitress.

'Um . . . perhaps nearer the back if we may,' Linda replied, mindful of what Elaine had told her about the spending limit. The waitress ushered the girls to a table, deeper in the interior of the shop and they sat down. Perusing the supplied menus, they were full of eager anticipation for the feast to come.

'Shall we have the "traditional cake stand afternoon tea for two"?' Linda whispered, worried that they would never reach a decision, if they started to choose individual items.

53

'Yes, it looks marvellous,' Elaine agreed.

The waitress returned to their table. 'Are you two young ladies ready to orda yet, or are you still makin' up thy minds?' She smiled, and then recognising Linda from the previous day, she continued. 'Didn't you cum in 'ere yesterday, Miss?'

'Yes, I was with my parents, it was my first day up at Grenchwood Hall – they were dropping me off.'

'Are we goin' see thee both in 'ere every weekend?'

'Oh no, this is a special occasion, it's my friend's birthday,' Linda answered, feeling the need to justify the fact that she was at the teashop two days running.

'Well menny 'appy returns my dear,' the waitress congratulated Elaine on her non-existent birthday.

'We'll have the "traditional cake stand afternoon tea", please,' Linda politely requested.

When the waitress had departed into the kitchen of the shop, Elaine managed to disguise a splutter of suppressed mirth from the other customers, by raising her open palm to her mouth.

'What did you say it was my birthday for?' she squeaked.

'Well it is your *official birthday*, isn't it?' Linda replied, trying to control her own fit of hilarity.

Over the next forty-five minutes the girls sampled with relish, the various sandwiches, scones and cakes, which made up the delectable spread. Laughing quietly at each other, when the cream from the scones accidentally oozed out and smeared their cheeks or chins. After every morsel had been fervently consumed, all too soon, it was time to leave. The waitress brought the bill for nine shillings and sixpence and accordingly, Linda placed the five-pound note on the saucer for her to take away. After her change had been returned to their table, copying what her father had done the previous day, Linda left the odd sixpence as a tip.

While making their way to the door, the waitress called out to them, 'Just a minute, you have left summin' behind!' Linda

54

immediately reached for the top of her sock to check that the fold of banknotes from her change were still there. The money was safe, so she couldn't think of anything else, that they might have forgotten.

'Here, 'ave these as it's thy birthday,' the waitress smiled and handed them a white paper bag with some Pontefract cakes inside. Elaine looked suitably abashed, but they both thanked her and then carefully stepping around the other seated customers they left the shop.

'That was fab!' Elaine proclaimed loudly, as they slowly paced into the warm sunshine of the far side of the square. 'I must have an official birthday more often, or, it can be your turn next time!'

'I feel a bit bad that they gave us these cakes, when it isn't really your birthday,' Linda brooded, her brows furrowed in remorse about the gift.

'Yes, but what could we do?' Elaine answered.

'We'll have to go there again on September 21st next year, to keep up the pretence that it's your birthday.'

'Gosh, I've just realised, what if the waitress remembers me, when I do go for my real birthday treat – with my aunts in May?' Elaine squawked, the pitch of her voice suddenly resembling the cry of a distressed seagull. 'How will I ever explain that?'

Linda couldn't help but to burst out with laughter at Elaine's imagined predicament, and then, to help put her mind to rest, she said, 'Don't worry, May is months away yet, that poor waitress will have served thousands of people by then, she'll never remember us,' she reasoned.

'You're right, why am I worrying! Shall we go down to the river and eat these cakes?'

'I'm completely stuffed, but I might be able to find a little bit more room.' Linda concurred.

At a quarter to five, the girls finally returned to Grenchwood Hall, just in time for an unnecessary teatime meal of bread and jam. Later that evening, while getting ready for bed, Linda reflected on how enjoyable the day had been, even Louise seemed to be no longer interested in taunting her. She looked up at the Christ-like stain above her bed and this time, convinced herself that it looked nothing like her grandmother, in fact she thought it was smiling down on her. Perhaps things were going to turn out for the best after all.

CHAPTER FOUR
22nd September 1969

8.30 am

It was Monday morning and the start of the school week began with a religious assembly, as it did at almost all of the educational establishments, up and down the country. The girls congregated in the orangery with the youngest at the front and the prefects at the back. The teaching staff sat along the side of the room, silhouetted against the large expanse of glass, looking like a line of defending soldiers, manning the battlements. The two swing doors at the back of the room burst open, immediately initiating the grating sound of chair legs scraping, as everyone got to their feet. Miss Rutherford dramatically swept to the front of the room and climbed the two diminutive steps onto the narrow stage. Linda was slightly shocked to see her wearing a black academic robe, which billowed at the sides when she moved and made her look like a gigantic, spectacle-wearing bat. Predictably she started the assembly with the traditional greeting, 'Good morning school.'

The girls responded in unison, 'Good morning Miss Rutherford.'

'Today's assembly will be taken by Amanda Penrose and Helen Richardson. I'm sure you will all do them the great courtesy of paying attention and not talking while the service is being conducted.'

Miss Rutherford's, comment caused a ripple of amusement to discharge around the hall. Linda recognised the two girls who loped up onto the stage and then stood nervously behind the lectern, as the girls that Miss Ryan had bawled out, after Sunday's church service. She then suddenly appreciated, why Miss Rutherford's remark, about not talking while the service was being taken, was greeted with the good-humoured response. The headmistress had obviously decided to make the punishment fit the crime. Amanda announced a hymn number and the small orchestra piped up in a somewhat dissociated pitch. It reminded Linda of the lamentable efforts of the orchestra at her previous school. Unlike at her old school, she was sitting comfortably in a well-lit and airy room and not squashed together with several hundred other pupils, desperately hoping not to faint through lack of oxygen. Linda surveyed the teachers at the side of the room, as they warbled out "He Who Would Valiant Be", mentally trying to gauge how strict, or easy-going, each would be, by their contorted facial expressions. The only blithe looking teacher was Miss Neame, who, in stark contrast to the others, was still in her early twenties and must have been in her first teaching position.

Eventually, after an arid bible reading and another hymn, the relieved looking Amanda and Helen brought the uninspiring service to an end and they quickly vacated the temporary dais. Miss Rutherford returned and thanked the girls for their efforts; she then invited Miss Neame up onto the stage to give a report on the school's first hockey match of the term. The athletic Miss Neame enthusiastically bounded up onto the raised platform in one leap, not bothering to use the steps at the side. She then regaled the assembled girls and staff, with a humorously vivid account of the team's unsuccessful start to the season; colourfully describing the hapless antics of certain individuals and the bravery of goalkeeper Monica Finch-Reeves, in keeping the score down to a nine-goal defeat.

Miss Rutherford returned centre stage to make one final announcement, 'Would Linda Middlewick and Elaine Rutherford see me in my study directly after assembly please.' The school

58

stood as one, while Miss Rutherford regally exited the room and headed off down the corridor towards her study.

Linda couldn't believe that her name had been called out. Surely, she thought, it must have been some sort of mistake. Now it was her turn to stand red-faced with head bowed, in a conscious attempt to avoid the eyes of any of her revelling classmates.

Within the next two minutes, Linda and Elaine found themselves anxiously waiting outside the headmistress's study, apprehensively watching for the ENTER sign to light up.

'What do you think she wants to see us for?' Linda breathed, hoping that there might be some benign reason for their summons to the headmistress's study.

'It must be for having tea in the Copper Kettle yesterday,' Elaine replied with a sigh.

'How would she know?'

'Someone's dropped us in it, I suppose.'

'What do you think she will do?'

'I don't know. We might get the *chair*,' Elaine answered, with a look of deep concern on her face.

Linda's mind raced, confused by the seriousness of her friend's answer and expression. The only connection she could make to "the chair" was from the gangster films that her father liked to watch on Sunday afternoons.

'What . . . the electric chair?' she ventured incredulously.

'Kind of – it's the chair you have to kneel on, in the bay window, when you get smacked with the hairbrush.'

'What! We might get smacked for this? Oh God, in all my time at my previous schools I've never been in any trouble, and I've only been here two days, not even had a lesson yet and I'm already in line for a whacking!'

59

The green "ENTER" light flashed on and Linda followed Elaine into the study, her stomach turned over with nerves, at what might be about to happen.

Miss Rutherford sat stony faced behind her desk, her hands folded before her. She stared ominously at the two girls for what seemed an age, before saying, 'It has come to my attention that you both visited The Copper Kettle tearooms in the village yesterday. Is this true?

'Yes Miss,' came the united demure response.

'Forgive me, I'm trying to understand, how with your joint revenue of just one shilling, you were able to consume the confectionery wares, that they have on offer . . . well, can either of you enlighten me?'

'I had some extra money on me, Miss,' Linda confessed, her voice quaking with trepidation.

'Did you indeed? Then, pray tell me, where these funds materialised from young lady.'

'My father gave me some money in case of emergencies, Miss.'

'So visiting the Copper Kettle is an emergency then is it?'

'Um . . . no.' Linda conceded.

'So then Linda, how much money, did you have upon your person?'

'Five-pounds Miss,'

'Really!' Miss Rutherford's eyebrows appeared above the frames of her glasses in genuine surprise. 'And how much did you spend at the Copper Kettle?'

'Nine shillings and sixpence, Miss – no sorry, I forgot the tip, ten shillings.'

'Well, I must say, you are a generous tipper Linda, I'm sure that the Copper Kettle value your custom very highly. However, we have a rule at this school – pupils in your year, can only spend sixpence on a visit down to the village. It means that every girl is on an equal footing and we don't have petty jealousy or overt extravagance, causing problems. I know Elaine is familiar with this edict – are you?

'Yes Miss.' Linda mumbled.

'So you both saw fit to ignore this rule?' Miss Rutherford paused, as the remorseful girls studied the carpet, rather than look at her in the eye. 'Well Elaine, I told you that I would treat you, exactly the same as any other pupil at the school. In fact, I will have to be seen, to be stricter with you, or the other girls will think I'm unfairly favouring you. I hold you more to blame for this incident, you should have been mentoring Linda, not encouraging her to break the rules.'

'No! It wasn't Elaine's fault – she tried to talk me out of it. Only, I really wanted to thank her for being so kind to me since I've arrived here,' Linda interrupted, her vocal chords activating on impulse, before she had time to think of what she was saying. There was a nervous pause, while Miss Rutherford evaluated Linda's frantic disclosure.

'Very well, I will deem you both as guilty as each other. Your punishment will be "gating" for the next three weeks, and thereafter, I will expect the two of you, to abide by the school rules, or a more astringent fate could befall you,' Miss Rutherford delivered a Solomon-like judgement upon the contrite duo, with an admonitory nod to the chair in the bay window. 'Linda, you will bring me your father's remaining four-pound ten-shillings, for safekeeping. At the end of term you can collect it, and I will let you explain to him, why the ten-shillings are missing. Right run along now.' On concluding the interview, an unseen suppressed smile, twitched at both ends of the amused headmistress's mouth.

The two girls hastened out of the room without looking back, grateful for the refuge of the empty dark corridor, where their eardrums were assaulted by the sound of the school bell, raucously announcing the commencement of morning lessons.

61

'What did she mean when she said "astringent fate"?' Linda asked, smiling at her friend.

'A whacking with the hairbrush I would imagine,' Elaine grinned and nervously giggled back at her.

'I thought so. Well, I think we just about got away with it then?'

'Yes, thanks to your heroic speech!' Elaine replied, beaming with a mixture of admiration and relief. 'I was starting to feel a bit like a condemned French aristocrat awaiting to mount the scaffold!'

'We didn't get away scot-free, we can't go down to the village for the next three weeks, so no sweets or freedom for ages,' Linda concluded.

As they got to the bottom of the main stairs, a cascade of schoolgirls came tumbling towards them and prevented any possibility of their ascent. While they waited patiently, the excited faces of the girls from Dormitory Five appeared, all eager to know the outcome of Linda and Elaine's visit to the headmistress's study.

'How many whacks of the brush did you get?' Louise squealed, her eyes shining with glee and her lips curled with a vindictive excited smile.

'None, but we did get three week's gating,' answered Elaine, at which Louise's mouth dropped with disappointment.

'I just knew that she would let her niece and the guttersnipe off! If any of us had broken the rules and openly scoffed plate loads of cakes, we would have gone to the chair,' Louise spat out her feelings, as she stormed past the two girls, her face twisted in anger at her perceived injustice of it all.

'How do you know, it was for that, that we had to go and see Miss Rutherford?' Linda shouted after Louise, who had moved away towards the classroom.

'Oh, my spies are everywhere, Middlewicket,' Louise sneered, glancing back over her shoulder with a spiteful grin.

CHAPTER FIVE
27th September 1969

11.00 am

For Linda her first school week flashed by in a blurred sequence of lessons, meals and evening prep work, to such an extent, there was little time for anything else other than sleeping. On Saturday morning, the girls were required to converge on the due-sodden playing field, to support the school hockey team. It was a one-sided affair with Grenchwood Hall suffering another trouncing, six goals to one, however, the support from the sidelines was enthusiastic and sportsmanlike, with rousing bouts of applause whenever the visiting school, St Catherine's, scored. At the end of the match, Miss Neame, who had refereed the game, asked for "three cheers" for the victorious St Catherine's school. Standing a few feet behind the touchlines, Linda and Elaine wholeheartedly complied with the request, their gusto spurred more by the relief that the game was over, than from any genuine reverence to the winning team. After this, the mud splattered players headed off for a shower and the spectators randomly dispersed to all parts of the school.

'What shall we do this afternoon, now that we can't go down to the village?' Linda asked.

'Well . . . we could go to my secret room,' Elaine answered cryptically.

'You have a secret room?'

'Yes, it's up there,' Elaine pointed to the top corner of the building.

'But that's out-of-bounds isn't it? It's kept locked – how would we get in there?'

'I have the key! Or rather, I have the key hidden over there in the old greenhouses. Shall we get it?'

The girls wandered over to the old, wrought-iron framed glasshouses, which were left over from the days prior to the First World War, when Grenchwood Hall had a small army of gardeners, who provided a plentiful array of fresh food and flowers for Lord Sumners' household. Elaine pushed the badly rusted door, which opened slowly and made a clangourous metallic tremor when it bounced into some discarded lead watering cans. Cautiously, she ventured into the stagnant atmosphere of the old glasshouse, skipping sideways down the narrow aisle until she reached the end, where she grabbed hold of a large overturned terracotta flowerpot. With both hands, she elevated it up in the air to height of about six inches.

'It's under here . . . oh, no!' Elaine let out a tiny piercing scream.

'What's the matter?' whispered Linda, as she hesitantly advanced up between the old wooden stagings.

'Oh, it's a spider, I can't pick up the keys with it so close.'

'Here, I'll get them,' Linda grabbed the bunch of keys from off of the top of the dirty potting bench, and the girls turned to make their rapid exit, leaving the spider to scuttle away to the safety of the shadows.

'Thanks for that, I hate spiders!' Elaine exhaled, relieved at being out in the open air again.

'That's okay, I don't mind spiders.'

'Let's just take the key that we need,' Elaine muttered to herself, while twisting the biggest brass key around the large ring, until it sprang free from the bunch. 'I'll hide the rest under this brick.' She guardedly lifted up the house brick, mindful that it might be the home to another frightening arachnid.

'How did you get these keys Elaine?' Linda asked, watching her friend burying the jangling key ring.

'I found them last summer, just over there by the tennis courts. They're Aunt Iona's'

'Shouldn't you have given them back?'

'I was going to, but then I forgot about them for a couple of days, and when I went to return the keys, my aunts were having a blazing row about getting another set cut. So I thought it was best to keep quiet about having them,' Elaine answered, with a wry smile.

'Are you sure we should do this?' Linda queried, her enthusiasm waning. 'You know what Miss Rutherford said would happen, if we ended up in her study again. And besides, what can we do up in that attic room that we can't do in the dorm? It's going to be just as boring.'

'No it won't be boring. I've got a load of goodies stashed up there. When I came back here from my prep school last July, I used the other keys – the smaller silver ones, to open all the prefects' rooms up on the top floor. They had left oodles of stuff.'

'Elaine that's stealing!' Linda scolded.

'No, they had all left the school – it was junk they didn't want, or couldn't take home. I got to the rooms before my aunts did their summer clean up, and I found a half bottle of gin; an almost full bottle of sherry; a couple of bottles of cider; some chocolate bars – but I've eaten all of them; a load of magazines, including *Fab 208*, *Mirabelle* and even *Rave*, but best of all, I found a transistor radio!'

'Wow! Does it work?'

'Yes, I'm not sure how long the battery will last though. So are you willing to risk it?'

'Okay . . . but what about the prefects, won't they catch us going down the top corridor?' Linda initially agreed, but then thought of another hurdle to overcome.

'Well, I can't be absolutely sure, but this afternoon most of them go riding over at Appleton's farm. We just need to keep our heads down, and anyway, if we do get caught, we'll just say that we are doing an errand for Charlotte and I'm sure we'll get away with it.'

'Right, let's do it!' Linda said, emphatically coming to a decision. A decision, largely based on her desire to have adventures, like the characters in the Enid Blyton books that she had read, coupled with the overwhelming temptation of being able to listen to some pop music.

#   #   #

After waiting for the school to almost empty out after lunch, the two girls made a conscious effort to stroll nonchalantly up to the first floor, passing the various small groups of girls scattered about, who were not venturing out that afternoon. Pausing by the balustrade, they waited until the coast was completely clear and then hightailed it up the stairway to the top floor. With their hearts racing and palms moist with nervous sweat, they set off down the forbidden passageway towards the obstructing door, its foreboding warning becoming clearer by the second. Elaine's hand trembled, as she unsuccessfully tried a couple of times to insert the key into the lock, on the third attempt it went in and she turned it hard anticlockwise. There was a dull click, she pulled down the handle and the door slowly swung open, to reveal the continuation of the corridor. Once on the other side, Elaine attentively closed and locked the door behind them.

'Gosh that was a bit exciting!' she exclaimed in a loud whisper, feeling all at once exhilarated by the danger, and stimulated by the challenge that they had overcome.

'There's a funny smell in here,' Linda said, sniffing in the fusty odour.

67

'Yes, it's because the windows haven't been opened in years, but you'll get used to it,' Elaine explained, and then led the way up the corridor, until she got to the second door on the left. 'This is the room I use, it's got windows on both sides, so we can keep an eye out, for when the girls start to return from the village and the riding stable.'

Eagerly, Linda followed Elaine through the doorway, whereupon it took a few seconds for her eyes to adjust from the gloom of the corridor, to the radiant sun-filled room. Across the open space of bare floorboards, stood a metal-framed single bed with an old, pale blue and white striped mattress draped over it. It appeared that the wall behind the bed was midway through being painted in a sickly lime green colour, when somebody simply gave up. An assortment of abandoned paintbrushes, hammers, scissors and other miscellaneous tools had been placed in neat piles on the deep windowsills.

'Someone made a real mess in here,' Linda observed, pointing at the brick red stains, splattered on the wooden floor, which, in a way, resembled the type of modern art that her father was always decrying.

'Yes, it looks like they were half way through re-decorating when they discovered the dry rot under the floor and just didn't bother going on with it,' Elaine offered up her slant on the mystery, as to why the decoration work had remained unfinished.

'Dry rot? It is safe to be up isn't it? We won't go crashing through the floor at any moment, will we?' Linda asked, alarmed by the possibility of sudden death.

'No, I'm sure it will take our weight,' Elaine assured her, and then to underscore the point, she jumped up and down a couple of times.

'Don't do that! Someone will hear you.'

'These floors are really thick – during the summer holidays, when my aunts were both visiting friends down in the village, I tested the soundproofing, by leaving the radio blaring away up here, and then going down to the room below, which is our dorm by the way. I couldn't hear a sausage. The rooms at the top of the house were originally used as the servant quarters, and because the big-wigs downstairs didn't want to hear them pottering around all night, they had the floor space in between soundproofed.'

'How did they do that?'

'Don't know, I just remember hearing my Aunt Amelia saying about it. Anyway, let's get the stuff out.' Elaine opened the door of a small wooden bedside cabinet and pulled out a bottle of sherry and some red tinted glasses, 'Is sherry all right?' she asked, rather formally, waving the bottle in Linda's direction.

'Yes, that would be lovely! I get to have a drink of sherry at home, on Christmas day. It's scrumptious.'

Elaine carefully poured out the ruby red liquid into the small-stemmed cordial glasses, until it filled them.

'I think that's too much, at home we only get a small amount, in a really tiny glass,' Linda advised.

'It's too late now.' Elaine giggled, passing Linda a glass 'Well, bottoms up then!'

Both girls took a hesitant sip of the syrupy, sweet smelling alcohol.

'Umm, it tastes divine,' cooed Elaine, who then lifted her head back and took a generous swig.

'Careful you'll be drunk – you're meant to sip it occasionally, not knock it back in one go!' reproved Linda, laughing at her friend's naive lack of respect, for the intoxicating drink.

'Have you been drunk before Linda?'

'I did feel a bit dizzy last Christmas, after some of my dad's snowballs'

'Snowballs?'

69

'It's a thick, milky yellow drink, mixed with lemonade and lime. Oh and Dad sticks a cherry on a cocktail stick in it as well – tastes delicious. Where's the tranny you were telling me about?'

For a moment Elaine didn't catch what Linda was asking, but then the penny dropped and she immediately pulled the cabinet away from the wall, to reveal a hole in the skirting board. Kneeling down, she reached into the void and plucked out the tiny wireless from within.

'I keep it extra well hidden, just in case somebody comes in here. They can take everything else, but I don't want to lose this.'

'Wow! It's good one, almost brand new, wonder why they left it behind?' Linda questioned, bemused by why someone would abandon such an expensive item. As an afterthought she added, 'Perhaps they were too drunk to care?'

'Or, they were in too much of a hurry, to get out of this place for the last time,' Elaine hooted with amusement at her own joke as she flicked the radio on. At once the three hundred year old room filled to the incongruous sound of Mick Jagger belting out "Honky Tonk Women".

'Great the Stones!' Linda exclaimed.

'Are they good?' Elaine asked, oblivious of the group's iconic status in the world of rock music.

'Yes, but I like the Beatles better – I've got nearly all of their singles, mainly because my mum likes them as well, so she buys them, which is a good job, as I can't often afford eight and six. They say that the Beatles are going to split up, but I can't believe that, I'm sure it's just a rumour. The Monkees are good as well, have you heard of them?'

'Yes! I used to watch the Monkees on TV, at my prep school on Saturday evenings.'

'I liked Peter Tork, he was so funny, but sadly he's left the group now – I think the other three are carrying on though.'

'I'll get the magazines out,' Elaine said, rummaging under the bed, 'I've got quite a few – look.' With that, she pulled out a stack of various teenage periodicals.

'Great! This is much better than wandering around the village all afternoon, isn't it? Wonder what Louise and the others are up to?' Linda pondered, while she happily perused the pages of a slightly faded *Jackie* magazine.

CHAPTER SIX
27th September 1969

3.10 pm

Down in the village, at the hub of the market square, clustered on the steps of the stone cross, sat Louise and her five cohorts. They were watching the world go past and hoping to catch the eyes of some local youths.

'We've got to get rid of her,' Louise announced, suddenly breaking the long silence.

'Who?' asked Susan Mollingham, an auburn-headed, tomboy type of girl, who was second in the group's pecking order, so thereby felt, it was her prerogative to ask the question.

'Middlewicket of course,' Louise answered, visibly annoyed that the question even needed to be asked.

'Why do you hate her so much Louise?' piped up Annabel Francis, who, in the interest of self-preservation, had attached herself to the group, but was now having misgivings about the wisdom of siding with its rather irrational ringleader.

'Because she is not one of us, stupid,' Louise rebuked her, with a snarl of distaste quivering on her thin lips.

'What, not a member of our gang?' Annabel continued to chip away, trying to unearth the real reason for Louise's bitter animosity.

'No! It's a class thing,' Louise snapped back. 'She doesn't come from our class of people. Her father's a garage mechanic for God's sake. The school shouldn't take on girls from the working classes, next she'll be forming a trade union, it completely lowers the whole tone of the place.'

'But surely if her father has the money to send her here, they must be quite well off,' Annabel tried to reason with Louise.

'It's not about whether they have the money or not, it's about breeding, let's face it, she is common and we have to get rid of her.'

'How . . . are you going to get rid of her?' Annabel asked cautiously, wondering if Louise meant to murder the poor girl.

'We're going to get her expelled. She has already been to see old Ruthers for noshing in the Copper Kettle, a couple more incidents like that and she'll be on her way – back to whatever grimy little town she came from.'

'What if, she behaves herself and doesn't get into any trouble?'

'We will arrange it, so she definitely does get into trouble! First, we'll plant some cigarettes on her and then make certain, that a prefect finds them. After that, we'll all complain about her, and then Rutherford will have little choice but to give her the boot.'

'Complain about what?' Annabel asked.

'I don't know, I'll think of something – we'll accuse her of being a lez or something.'

The comment provoked an outburst of laughter to echo across the square.

'You can't accuse her of that! What would you say to Miss Rutherford?' enquired Annabel, grinning at the thought of telling an adult about such lewd goings-on.

'Well, we will start with the cigs and see what happens, who knows, she might just skedaddle off home after that,' Louise concluded, with a smack of self-satisfaction.

73

'It's a mean trick to play on someone,' Annabel reflected, unhappy with the plan.

'Why are you so worried about the little guttersnipe, Annabel? Perhaps you would rather be friends with her and Mata, and not be with us?'

'No, I don't want to be friends with them, but it's not a very sporting thing to do. If Miss Rutherford thinks she has been smoking, she'll get into an awful lot of bother.'

'Good, that's what we want!' Louise howled, frustrated by the lack of insight being shown by her minions. 'And just to prove that you are still loyal to us Annabel, you will plant the cigarettes in her bedside cabinet. Then you can write a note to Charlotte, saying, that you think some girls are hiding smokes in the dormitory. You don't need to sign it, just slip under her door.'

'Oh Louise, do I have to?' Annabel moaned, instantly regretting taking a moral stand against the Form Captain.

'If you want to be our friend you do. Now, we have got to get some cigs. Cressida, where did you get those smokes last week?' Louise asked, jumping to her feet.

'We passed a couple of boys smoking down school lane, by the bus stop, and one of them asked if we had the right time, so we stopped and chatted. Then they offered us one each, so we took them and told the boys that we would smoke them later,' answered the impish girl with a bushy mane of lively dark hair.

'Right then, we will start down there, when we see anyone smoking, we will just ask them if we can have one. If we ask enough people, we are bound to get two or three.'

The small group set off from the centre of the square, through the narrow back streets until they reached School Lane, the main through road leading out of Grench village. After arriving at the bus stop, their hopes started to dampen, when all they encountered in fifteen minutes of standing around, were just a couple of old ladies, patiently waiting for the next bus to arrive.

74

Louise quickly became frustrated by the lack of potential targets for their begging strategy.

'This is no good! We will have to try and buy a packet. How much money do we have between us?' she enquired. The question spurred the girls to obediently produce what was left of their spending money. 'One shilling and eleven, I'm sure that will be more than enough for a packet of ten. Let's try the newsagent at the top of the road.'

The window of the small corner shop was completely covered with cigarette advertising, making it impossible for the girls to see inside.

'Right, Annabel you go in and purchase the packet,' Louise ordered, handing her the change.

'Oh, please don't make me do it, I'll get the wrong brand,' Annabel pleaded.

'Just go in and get any packet of ten.' Louise insisted.

Annabel sighed and shrugged her shoulders dejectedly, but knew she would have to undertake the mission. There was a loud unmelodic clang of a bell, as the door pushed open, Annabel stepped down into the dimly lit interior of the shop, where she found herself surrounded on all sides by untidy racks of magazines and newspapers. Across the room, in the far corner, sat a disinterested elderly man, wearing a flat cap and sucking thoughtfully on a stubby red pencil. He briefly looked up from the racing paper that he was studying, and then ignored her again.

Looking past the old man, Annabel could see, stacked up on a shelf behind him, were the prized packets of cigarettes that she was after. Nervously, she paced towards the serving counter.

'Ayup lass. What can I get for thee flower,' the shopkeeper asked in gruff, husky Yorkshire accent.

'I'd like . . . I mean . . . I want to buy some cigarettes, please,' Annabel's faltering stutter, highlighted her lack of confidence.

75

'Do thy now? And what year were thee born?' the old man asked, peering suspiciously over the top of his paper.

'Um, 1956 . . . no, I mean 1954, no thinking about it, it was actually, 1953,' Annabel stumbled over her answer, realising too late, that the question had been asked, to ascertain if she was old enough to legally purchase cigarettes.

'I think thy might be lying to us there, flower – seein' that you are standing in front of uz, in thy school togs. Now buy some sweeties or a comic and run along.'

'Look I've got the money, I would really like to purchase a packet of ten Benson and Hedges please,' Annabel persisted, using her best insistent tone.

'Aye, and I've told thee, that thee are too young! Thy have five seconds to take thyself out of shop, or I'll take uz belt off and come tother side of the counter and skelp thou backside for thee.'

Annabel rapidly stepped backwards until her outstretched palm was in range of the door handle, twisting it furiously until the door finally opened, she tumbled out of the tiny premises.

'Run!' she shouted to the other girls, gathered across the road waiting. Without questioning why, they all set off down School Lane with one hand clamped onto their school berets and their green skirts billowing in the self-made wind caused by their youthful momentum. Not stopping until the shop was well out of sight, the girls found themselves on the fringes of Lower Grench.

'What happened? Did you get the packet of cigarettes?' Louise gasped, trying to get her breath back from the sprint down the hill.

'No, the awful old man in the shop threatened to hit me with his belt,' Annabel squealed, and then added with concern, 'We shouldn't be down in Lower Grench, should we?'

'Who is going to report us – it would mean that they were down here as well, stupid. Now let's find another shop and try again. We'll go down here,' Louise instructed, leading her little troop down a twisting country lane, towards a small estate of tied cottages and council houses. Turning the corner, they found themselves staring at a circle of village girls, all sitting on the top of a wooden sun-bleached, playground roundabout. Both groups of girls maintained a few seconds of incredulous silence, and then a tall, curly haired girl wearing jeans with holes in the knees, spouted out, 'Wha' er you posh gurls doin' daahn 'eear?'

Louise didn't understand all the words, but from the inflection, she took it, that they were being asked, what were they doing in their playground. She studied the tall girl, who appeared to be wearing a string of her mother's fake pearl beads around her neck and was tugging on a long lace of liquorice, that pulled from the side of her mouth. Seeing herself in the role of Captain Cook, boldly confronting a group of savages, Louise realised that there was the possibility of obtaining the cigarettes that they wanted. Enunciating very slowly and loudly, as though she was speaking to a foreign visitor, she said, 'We are looking for a shop to buy some cigarettes.'

'Tobacconist is up at top of hill, you must have passed it on way down here.' replied the girl. Louise was starting to tune into the thick vernacular accent and understood what the girl was saying.

'We went in there but he wouldn't sell us any.'

'Ney, old George is a stickler for the rules.'

'Do you, or your friends have any that we could buy?'

'Hang on a minute, I'll call over to Billy and see.'

With this, she jumped down from the roundabout and shouted across to where a group of boys, using the frame of a set of swings as goal posts, were playing football.

'Billy! These posh girls want to buy some tabs, does thee have any?'

Nobody acknowledged the girl's request, instead they just played on, until the ball was smashed passed the goalkeeper, causing a very small child in red wellington boots, to chase the bouncing plastic football down the lane, like an over enthusiastic ball boy. Then, a large-set youth with thick wavy black hair left the

77

game and slowly came jogging over to where the girls were standing.

'Have you got any cigarettes?' Louise asked hopefully.

'Ney, but I can lay uz hands on some, for a price,' Billy replied, standing in front of the girls rather self-consciously.

'Well, how much are you thinking?'

'Thruppence a tab.'

'No, that's far too much, I'll give you a penny each for them.'

'Louise, they will have cost him more than a penny each,' Susan chipped in.

'Thee won't cost uz owt, I'm going to nick 'em from our dad's stash. But I'm not risking a leathering for a penny a tab,' Billy announced forcefully.

'All right, I'll give you three ha'pence for each one then. I want eight, so that is a shilling – take it or leave it,' Louise bargained hard. Billy stared at her for a few moments, mentally calculating whether or not to accept her offer.

'Ol right, wait on here, I'll be a few minutes,' he decreed, turning around and running off towards a house situated on the far side of the play area.

'We need some matches as well, Billy,' Louise called after him.

'Any of thou want to buy some Spanish?' the curly haired girl asked.

'What's Spanish?' Cressida enquired.

'This,' the girl said, holding up the black thread of liquorice.

'No thanks we'll stick with the cigarettes,' Susan laughed.

Billy reappeared and darted back across the green towards them.

'Here I've gotten them and the matches,' he panted, handing over the eight cigarettes and the loose matches.

'Thank you Billy, you have been most helpful,' Louise purred, taking the spoils from him. 'Here is an extra ha'penny for the matches.' She dropped the change into his outstretched muddy hand.

'Thanks! If there's owt else thee ever need, just come down the hill and find uz.'

'Oh, I'm sure you could help me in lots of ways, Billy,' Louise flashed him her well-practised flirtatious smile, while the rest of the girls whooped. Embarrassed, Billy turned tail and rejoined the football match.

The girls strolled back up the lane, until they found an empty bus shelter, where Louise decided it would be safe to smoke their cigarettes. She handed out the white tubes of tightly packed tobacco and then struck the red headed match on the pavement. Soon they were all puffing smoke and giggling about the afternoon's experience.

'You see, this is why we have to get rid of Middlewicket. Those children were like another species,' Louise laughed, 'I could hardly understand a word they were saying.'

'But we can understand Middlewicket all right,' interrupted Annabel.

'Yes, but she is the thin end of the wedge. You let one in and they all will want to come. Then where will we be?'

'To afford the school fees, your parents have to be fairly well off, I'm sure that nobody down in Lower Grench would have the means to send their daughter to our school,' Annabel argued the point.

'You don't know that. Some common people have quite a lot of money, they can win the football pools or their premium bond might come up. I expect that's how Middlewicket has ended up here. After all, she only lives in a terrace house, probably just like those tiny cottages near the playground. Anyway, after tomorrow she will be on her way.'

#   #   #

An hour later the band of girls wearily returned to the school and ambled up to the dormitory, where they found Linda and Elaine lying on their respective beds reading.

'We've had a great time down in the village while you two lezzers have been confined to barracks,' Louise announced, hoping to provoke a reaction from the girls. 'What have you two, spent the day doing?'

'Oh, just reading, it's been really boring,' replied Elaine, shooting a quick, knowing look at Linda, who responded likewise.

CHAPTER SEVEN
28th September 1969

3.40 pm

The next day the weather turned and a storm blew in from across the Pennines. Frustratingly for Linda and Elaine it meant that most of the girls remained in the building that afternoon, making an attempt to get up to the secret room far too risky. Instead they spent the afternoon country dancing, which had been hastily arranged by Miss Neame in the orangery.

Up in Dormitory Five, Louise sat on her bed holding the two remaining cigarettes from the previous day's dealings with Billy. 'Right then Annabel, there is nobody about, hide these cigs in Middlewicket's top drawer.'

'Oh Louise, it's not fair. Please don't make me do it,' beseeched Annabel, hoping that she might be able to get Louise to change her mind.

'You don't *have* to do it Annabel.'

'Really!'

'But then also, you don't have to be in our gang. It's your choice,' Louise shrugged, as she outlined the alternative outcome.

Annabel sighed deeply and reluctantly took the cigarettes over to Linda's bedside cabinet. She opened the top drawer and made one last plaintive glance at Louise.

'Go on! Make sure they are right up the back where she won't see them,' Louise called over from the room's doorway, where she was keeping watch. Annabel followed her orders and planted the incriminating evidence right at the back end of the drawer.

'Good, well done, now all you need to do is write the note to Charlotte,' Louise said, with a condescending air, rummaging around in her own drawer, in search of a sheet of stationery paper and a pen. 'Write this – "Dear Charlotte, I think you should know that there is a girl in Dorm Five who is hiding cigarettes in her drawer. Yours, a well wisher", that will be enough,' Louise dictated the letter and Annabel wrote down the message, trying to disguise her handwriting as much as possible.

'Right, fold it in two and slip it under Charlotte's door. Don't worry, she won't be there, I saw her downstairs in the orangery, doing that stupid country dancing.'

'But, what if someone else sees me up there?' Annabel asked, worried about being out-of-bounds without permission.

'Just say that you have a message for Charlotte. Well you have, haven't you?'

Annabel grudgingly made her way out of the dorm and up the stairway, turning into the passageway she was immediately confronted by Monica Finch-Reeves, renowned for being one of the more overzealous prefects.

'Where are you going Annabel?' Monica enquired, curtly.

'I've . . . got . . . a message for Charlotte, Monica,' Annabel falteringly answered.

'Very well, take it along to her and then back downstairs straight away please.'

Annabel didn't need to be asked twice, she brushed past Monica, quickened her pace, and kept going until she got to the far end. Bobbing down, she pushed the folded note through the half-inch gap at the bottom of door and promptly retraced her steps back to Monica, who had remained standing where they had met.

82

'Thank you Monica,' Annabel muttered, while once again hurrying past the suspicious prefect. Back down in the dorm, Annabel collapsed with relief onto her bed.

'Well done Annabel! I knew that you could do it!' Louise declared, excited by the activation of her malicious plan, and believing that all she had to do now, was to wait for the fun to start.

After helping to organise the clearing away of the teatime tables and cutlery, Charlotte returned to her room. On opening the door her eyes were instantly fixed to the small piece of folded violet paper, lying almost directly under her left foot. Intrigued by the missive, she picked it up and read the short anonymous tip off. She read it again and smiled to herself.

#   #   #

On Sunday evening, most of the school were gathered in the orangery watching television, until all too soon, the large wall mounted clock confirmed that it was bedtime for the younger girls. As usual, there was the excited hurly-burly, of frantic toing and froing from the bathroom and general larking about in the dormitory. At the stroke of eight-thirty, Charlotte appeared in the doorway instigating an abrupt cessation to the noise.

'Right Dorm Five, I'm going to do an inspection of your bedside cabinets, just to make sure that you evil little girls, aren't hiding any naughty contraband,' she announced, causing an outbreak of stifled sniggering amongst the girls. Charlotte opened Louise's top drawer and raked around, pulling out her violet writing paper and matching envelopes.

'Nice stationery set Louise, Georges Lalo from Paris, very distinctive, very expensive – did mummy give you it?'

'Yes . . . she did, thank you,' Louise replied, quickly realising, Charlotte was aware, that it was her paper that the note had been written on. 'It's not that expensive, I think a lot of girls here, own a set like that one.'

'Do they? Well take good care of it and don't *waste* it,' Charlotte said, with a smile that thinly disguised the look of

83

scepticism on her face. Slowly she went around the dormitory making humorous comments about the random brick-a-brac, that she was extracting from each cabinet. Arriving at Linda's bedside, Charlotte pulled the drawer open to its full extent, causing a disturbing chafing sound, as the woods pinched together. Her hand dipped into the array of assorted items haphazardly bundled together.

'What do we have here then? If I'm not mistaken, it's a couple of coffin nails!' Charlotte cried, holding two cigarettes aloft for everyone to see. There was an audible gasp from the rest of the room, while Linda looked on, truly dumbfounded by the discovery of the strictly prohibited items. She wanted to protest her innocence, but the words would not formulate, all she could do was to stand and stare in open-mouthed disbelief.

'Right Linda, put your slippers on and follow me,' Charlotte directed, with her usual air of authority and sureness. Linda mechanically responded, forcing herself to follow Charlotte out of the room, passing the mocking, enraptured faces that were openly grinning or sniggering at her plight.

'Oh dear, poor Linda has only got her nightdress on, she will need more padding than that!' Louise roared with laughter while bouncing up and down on her bed with exhilaration, overjoyed at the perfect outcome to her plan. Outside in the corridor, Linda followed Charlotte to the top of the stairs, where she looked down and could see the daunting sight of the headmistress's study door. Instead of descending the stairs, Charlotte continue on, until she got to the stairs that led up to the top floor.

'Come on then,' Charlotte said cheerily, leaping up the stairs, taking them two at a time. Feeling totally confused, Linda dashed up behind her and followed until they got to her room. Charlotte opened her door and ushered Linda inside.

'Charlotte, I've never seen those cigarettes before, you've got to believe me!' stressed Linda, regaining her power of speech.

'I know you haven't silly, I'm fairly certain that it was Louise who planted them in your drawer and then tipped me off, to

84

try to land you in the shit. I ask you, who, in their right mind, would hide fags in their own cabinet. When I was in the dorms, I hid my fags in the bathroom – if you give the side of the baths a bit of a bang, the panel pops out, and it's a perfect place to store all sorts of illicit goodies. We used to smoke in the bathrooms as well and then chuck the butts into the opened panel, always remembering to close it of course, before we left. There must be hundreds of dog-ends under those baths, it's a miracle that we didn't burn the bloody place down!' Charlotte guffawed, collapsing onto her bed.

'You used to smoke in the bathrooms?' Linda reiterated, not being able to envisage the upstanding head girl ever doing such a thing.

'Yes of course I did sweetie and much worse things than that,' Charlotte confirmed, her dazzling green eyes sparkled with levity. She reached across and picked up one of the cigarettes, lit it and placed it carefully to her lips. Looking at Linda, she inhaled deeply and then after a couple of seconds got up and blew the smoke out of the open window.

'Have you heard of the pop group the Kinks?' Charlotte asked, to which Linda vigorously nodded in the affirmative. 'Well, when I was about your age, I managed to get hold of a ticket for one of their concerts, in Sheffield. My only problem being, it was a Saturday night during term time. Obviously there was no point in asking for permission to go, so I thought, "bugger it!" and just went!

'I left here on Saturday afternoon with Monica, like we were just going down to the village, but when we got there, I went into the public toilets in the car park and changed out of my uniform, into some slacks and a jumper. Monica took my uniform back to the school, while I started my journey – two bus rides later, I was in Sheffield's town centre. The concert was fab, one of the best nights of my life, but then I had the problem of getting back to school again.'

'Weren't you worried, about what would happen to you if you were caught?'

'I didn't care. I wanted to see the Kinks and bugger the consequences. Sometimes, life is like that, you just have to follow your heart, or you only live a half-life. Anyway, when I reached my connection stop, the last bus to Upper Grench had gone, so I became stranded, there was only one thing to do – hitchhike.'

'God that must have been so dangerous, weren't you terrified?'

'What I didn't know, was that at bedtime, they'd discovered I was missing, and after putting the screws on Monica, she blabbed about what I had done, so they called the police, to warn them that a thirteen-year-old girl might be trying to thumb a lift back to school, along the Sheffield Road. After a couple of minutes of walking down the side of the road, with my thumb sticking out, a blue and white Ford Anglia with "police" written on the side, drew up and the officer told me in no uncertain terms to get in.'

'Wow! What happened when you got back?'

'As you can imagine, Miss Rutherford blew her top. The next day, she phoned my mother and told her that I was being expelled. So would she kindly arrange to have me picked up? My darling mother managed to persuade her to keep me on and give me a thrashing instead!'

'So . . . is that what happened? You went to the chair?' A saucer-eyed Linda asked, in a tone of voice that alternated between disbelief and admiration.

'Yes!' Charlotte laughed defiantly. 'I got a hell of a spanking. The first of Miss Rutherford's reign, she had only just taken over as head back then.'

'Did it . . . hurt much,' Linda asked, the peculiar feeling of morbid curiosity prevailing over her hesitant embarrassment.

'God yes! Hurt to buggery and back. I couldn't sit down comfortably for a week!' Charlotte screamed, giggling uncontrollably. 'But even then, when I was kneeling on the chair waiting, I didn't regret what I had done, for a single moment. It was well worth a sore arse, to see the world greatest rock band. Nobody can ever take that away from me. Like I said before, sometimes you just have to say, "bugger the consequences, I'm doing it".'

'Does Miss Rutherford use the hairbrush a lot?' Linda asked cautiously, not wanting to hear an answer that would confirm her worst fears.

'Not as much as that old cow Miss Ryan would like her to!' Charlotte sniffed in disapproval. 'Sorry, I didn't mean to frighten you, when I told you about my walloping, it's a pretty rare event these days. So don't worry, you would have to do something pretty outrageous to get it. The "chair" is part of the school's folklore, an ultimate deterrent that helps Miss Rutherford keep everyone in line, by just referring to it occasionally. Did they use corporal punishment at your last school?'

'Yes, they used it a lot – mostly on the boys, thankfully – everyday, there was always a long line of them, waiting outside the headmaster's door.'

'So you went to a mixed sex school, how progressive. I bet a pretty little thing like you, had heaps of male admirers!' Charlotte sat down on the bed next to Linda and offered her a puff on the half smoked cigarette. Nervously, Linda sucked hard on the end of the wet paper tube, immediately her mouth was full of warm rushing smoke, causing her to involuntarily gag and splutter, as she fought to exhale the choking vapour.

'God! Why do you do that! It tastes awful, I thought I was going to faint!' Linda coughed, passing the butt back to Charlotte, who took one last drag and stubbed it out, on the top of an old tin plate tea caddy.

'At least, I now know that these fags are definitely not yours!' Charlotte smiled, and then proceeded to methodically answer Linda's question. 'When you get used to taking the smoke down into your lungs, the nicotine gets into your blood stream and it kind of makes you feel happy, gives you a bit of a buzz. Trouble is, after half an hour or so, the feeling goes, so you want another one and then basically you're hooked.'

'I've heard on the telly that smoking maybe bad for you,' Linda cautioned.

'Oh, you don't want to believe everything you hear on the goggle box, they're always scaremongering. Cigarettes are a great way to stop you feeling hungry, all the top models use them, so they don't put on any weight,' Charlotte said, flatly rebuffing any potentially harmful side effects of smoking. Looking thoughtful for a moment, she dropped the extinguished butt end down a gap between the floorboards and then continued, 'I'm going to become a model, you know.'

'What, like Twiggy or Jean Shrimpton?'

'Yes, exactly like them. My father wants me to go to university, but I can't stand the thought of reading anymore stuffy textbooks or taking more blasted exams. I was going to leave this old dump when I was sixteen, but he persuaded me to stay and take my A levels. He promised me five hundred pounds if I did.'

'Five hundred quid!' Linda hissed, accidently inhaling too much air in her surprise.

'Yes, fab isn't it. With that money I'll be able to go down to London, get a place to stay and have my portfolio photos taken by a top photographer.'

'What's a portfolio?'

'It's like a thin case, that you keep all your best pictures in – you take it along with you, when you go and see the art directors, at all the big advertising agencies. Of course, they will immediately sign me up and whisk me away to glamorous places, like Barbados or California, to make adverts for suncream lotion or something,' Charlotte laughed.

'I think they will, you are very beautiful Charlotte,' Linda assured her, with genuine conviction.

'Oh you are sweet – the problem is, there will be a lot of girls down in London trying to do the same as me – it's getting that all important first job that helps. In the Christmas break, I'm going to go down there with my older sister. Her current boyfriend is a disc jockey and he gets invited to all the best parties. So my plan is, to tag along with them and perhaps I'll meet some famous fashion photographers, like David Bailey or Brian Duffy,' Charlotte gushed, full of enthusiasm for her dream. 'Anyway, that's what I'm going to do – if it doesn't work out, I'll have a go at acting or singing with a band, anything that isn't in a boring old office from nine to five. What about you? What do you want to do when you leave here?'

'I don't know? Work in a bank or something I suppose?'

'Nonsense! Look in this mirror, you are very pretty, in a few years time, you could be a model. Imagine it, up there on the catwalk, wearing all the latest fashions and getting paid oodles for it.'

Charlotte looked at Linda, for a few silent seconds.

'You realise that is why Louise doesn't like you. You are prettier than her, and she feels threatened by you.'

'I thought she didn't like me because I'm common,' Linda conjectured, feeling herself blush at Charlotte's unexpected compliment.

'No, she is just using that as an excuse – she would never let on the real reason. Anyway, you're not common, and your dad has be loaded, to afford a car like the one he dropped you off in.'

'Actually, that wasn't his car,' Linda confessed, feeling slightly embarrassed.

'Did he steal it then?' Charlotte questioned, intrigued by this admission. 'Is he some kind of London gangster, working with the Kray Twins then? That would be fantastic.'

'No!' grinned Linda, smiling at the thought, of her father being some sort of underworld criminal. 'He borrowed it from his boss for the day, so that we would make a good impression, when we arrived here. My parents can only afford for me to come here, because of the money my granny left to them, when she died in an accident.'

89

'Oh well, who cares – you are here now, and I'm sure you are going to make them very proud of you,' Charlotte concluded, putting a comforting arm around Linda's shoulder and then leaning in, she gave her an unexpected peck on the lips. Linda immediately felt an impulsive, blurry thrill of pleasure shoot through her, it was a sensation that she had never before encountered, and the effect momentarily confused her.

'Come on, let's go back to the dorm and I'll have a word with little Miss Bennington,' Charlotte said, leading the way out of the door and down the corridor.

#   #   #

The low rumble of excited chatter stopped, the instant Linda and Charlotte appeared back in the dormitory. Linda slowly walked back down the middle of the two rows of beds. She was acutely aware that all the eyes in the room were upon her, trying to analyse from her deportment, what type of fate had befallen her in the previous twenty-five minutes. She gave Elaine a reassuring smile and climbed into her bed.

'Louise, I would like to see you outside for moment please,' Charlotte politely but firmly requested. Louise followed Charlotte out of the room, while the rest of the girls, alarmed by her departure, shot each other worried glances and wondered what was going to happen next. Charlotte strolled about twenty feet down the passageway with Louise in diffident tow and then turned to confront her. Louise sullenly lent back against the cool, pale yellow, distemper painted wall and stared unblinking back at Charlotte.

'You planted those cigarettes in Linda's drawer, didn't you?' Charlotte made her accusation, and moved closer, bending her head towards the girl's face threateningly.

'No, I didn't,' Louise answered, through stiffened lips.

'Well the note was written on your stationery paper.'

'So what? It could have been stolen from my drawer, It's definitely not my writing, you can check.'

'How do you know what the handwriting looks like?'

90

'Um . . . well, I know that I didn't write it, so it can't be mine, can it?' Louise argued, after briefly losing her equilibrium by the question.

'I think we should see what Miss Rutherford has to say about all this, don't you?' Charlotte threatened to up the stakes.

'No! Don't do that. I'll tell you – it was Annabel who did it, she wrote the note and hid the cigs in Linda's drawer.'

'How do you know?'

'I saw her – I was in the dorm when she did it. Ask her, she'll admit it,' without a trace of compassion and unconcerned about the immediate destiny of her classmate, Louise, pinned the blame onto Annabel.

'Wait here!' Charlotte instructed.

The resolute head girl then returned to the dorm and directed Annabel to join them outside. Ashen faced, Annabel moved towards the sullen looking Louise, and could see from her harrowed expression, that serious trouble was pending.

'Right, Annabel did you put the fags into Linda's top drawer?' Charlotte continued with the cross-examination. Annabel cast her eyes downwards and mutely answered with a negative shake of her head. 'Only, Louise says she saw you doing it.'

Annabel's head shot up in shocked disbelief, at the icy betrayal, her eyes instantly glistening with unshed tears.

'If you did do it Annabel, you know what will happen to you, when we go and see Miss Rutherford,' Charlotte tightened the screw a few more notches.

'She made me do it!' Annabel cried, breaking down and sobbing uncontrollably.

'No I didn't, you lying cow!' Louise responded, determined to save herself, by piling the entire blame onto the now incoherent Annabel.

'I'm sure you are both equally to blame for this and I should take you downstairs for your just desserts, but I'm going to give you one last chance. From now on, keep yourselves to yourselves, no more picking on Linda because she comes from a working class family, or perhaps Louise, you are jealous of her looks? If I hear of anything-untoward happening, I'll come down on you like a ton of bricks. And in the next dorm inspection, I will definitely find cigarettes in both of your bedside drawers. Do you understand me?'

Both Louise and Annabel gratefully acknowledged Charlotte's proposal by shaking their heads in agreement. Charlotte escorted them back into the dorm, where the other over-excited girls waited expectantly. Linda could see from the look on Louise's face, that she was furious with the outcome of the evening's events; her reddened features resembled those of a frustrated toddler, who was about to unleash a ferocious tantrum.

'Right, the lights are going out now, remember no talking. Good night,' Charlotte said, as she brought the day to an abrupt end, for the girls of Dorm Five.

CHAPTER EIGHT
25th October 1969
2.15 pm

Frustratingly for Linda and Elaine, consecutive inclement weekends, prevented the majority of the girls from leaving the confines of the school building, which meant, finding a safe opportunity to visit their secret room was out of the question. Instead, they spent their recreation, indulging in some of the more prosaic activities that were available on the rainy weekends. After Charlotte's timely intervention over the cigarettes, Louise's hostile exchanges with Linda were diluted into trivial, sporadic encounters. Mostly, these consisted of Louise aiming a burst of sarcastic comments at Linda, which would ping across the room like tracer bullets, spicing up the classroom atmosphere, for the others. Ultimately, the childish verbal spats, led to nothing more than a brief upsurge in the psychological tension between the two protagonists and a joust-off of rancorous glares and icy scowls, which neither girl would yield to. Louise's standing within the dorm also suffered from a fragmentation of her clique, with Annabel and another girl called Hilary Weston, choosing to distance themselves from her controlling influence.

It was the last weekend in October that provided the next chance to visit the prohibited Shangri-La of the top floor. They devised a plan, which involved taking out their spending money and leaving for the village, as they would be expected to do. Having passed through the school gates and after walking a few hundred yards down the main road, they turned off, doubling back to the rear of the school grounds, where Elaine knew that there was a hole in the old perimeter fencing. They allowed half an hour for the last of the girls to leave and then re-entered the building from the rearmost aspect. For the two girls, this added plot of subterfuge heightened the vivacity of the already perilous exploit. Everything went smoothly and within a few minutes they had jubilantly returned to their secret sanctuary.

'Well, I think we deserve a drink after that,' Elaine said, breathing heavily, from the frantic charge up two long flights of stairs. She opened the cabinet and picked out the half-full green gin bottle.

'Gin! My mum drinks that at Christmas, she has orange squash with it,' Linda revealed to her drinking companion.

'We haven't got any orange, but what about the cider? It's made from apples so it shouldn't be too different – they're both fruits after all,' Elaine said, and without waiting for any confirmation, starting to pour the drinks out. She handed Linda one of the glasses and they simultaneously took a provisional sip, to assess the flavour of the frosted tan coloured concoction.

'Umm . . . not bad!' Linda declared, her lips smacking with appreciation.

'It's a touch bitter tasting but not too bad,' Elaine judged, less enthusiastically. They sat down on the bed and started to pick through the various magazines that were still scattered around the floor from their last visit.

'What is your bedroom like Linda?' Elaine asked.

'It's not as big as this room, about a quarter of the size I would say. I have a small double bed, a bedside table, a dressing table with a large mirror and a wardrobe for my clothes. Oh, and the walls are covered in posters. Why do you ask?'

'It's just that, I've never had my own bedroom and I'm trying to picture what it would look like, if I had one.'

94

'What never?'

'Well, I did have a very small room when I was with my great aunt Davina, up in Scotland, but it was only big enough to have the bed in it – more like a cupboard actually. At the age of seven I left for boarding school, so I've been in dorms ever since. Apart of course, from when I stayed here during the holidays. Then I did have a room of my own, but it was really someone's cast off and I couldn't do anything to it. I think this is the closest I've had to a room of my own.'

'Well it's a great room! We should personalise it a bit – put some posters up on the walls perhaps?'

'Where would we get them from?'

'From out of these magazines – look, there are loads of full-page photographs, all we need to do, is cut them out and stick them up, and then this room will look like a real bedroom. Here are some scissors.' Linda enthused, reaching over and picking up the long bladed wallpapering scissors, discarded by the previous user many years before. 'Looks like someone used these, to mix up the brown paint with! That gives me a thought – we could finish off painting the wall as well. Let's see if the paint is still okay?' Linda took the scissors and popped the lid off of one of the old tins, stacked up over in the corner of the room.

'Oh it's all dried into a solid slab, that's no good,' Linda sighed, disappointed by her discovery. She tried the next two tins, but it was the same outcome, whatever paint had been left over from the abandoned decoration job, had solidified in the intervening years. 'Never mind, we can still stick up some posters with this.' Linda held aloft an unopened sun-faded packet of Crown wallpapering paste.

'Will it still work?' Elaine queried, doubting if it had retained its adhesive qualities.

'It should do, it says the ingredients are mainly wheat flour, so if we mix a small amount of the cider with it and just put a dob on each corner of the pictures, they should stay up.'

The girls flicked through the magazines and sorted a good selection of colour photographs of some famous pop stars that they both liked. Then, once they had managed to disengage the two brown coated, scissors blades from one another, they set about carefully cutting them out. Soon, almost a dozen portraits of singers or groups adorned the far wall of the room.

'That looks absolutely fab!' Elaine asserted, stepping back to admire the vibrant collage that now graced the half-painted wall. 'It's getting to look like a real bedroom. Let's finish off, what's left of the cider and then we better get downstairs before the others start to get back.'

'Elaine, do you have a photo of your parents that we could stick up on the wall?' Linda asked cautiously, mindful that she might be treading on too personal ground.

'No, sadly all their belongings were destroyed in the crash.'

'Crash?'

'The plane crash in Germany. My father was in the army and had just been stationed there. My mother went with him to set up our home. Iona and Amelia's mother, my Aunt Emily, who was the headmistress of this school at the time and married to my father's brother – Donald, was looking after me here, until everything was satisfactory. The plane crashed as it tried to land in a snowstorm, everybody onboard was killed. I was eight months old when it happened'

'How awful! Surely, your aunts must have pictures of your father when he was growing up with his brother Donald, or perhaps when your parents got married?'

'I think they showed me some photos a long time ago, but because I never knew them, I didn't take much notice, it was just like looking at pictures of strangers, and I've never bothered about them since.'

Linda jumped up off the bed and rather unsteadily paced over to look out of the window, checking to see, if any of the girls

96

were returning from the village, or from the riding stables. From her high vantage point, she could make out some small figures approaching the school gates, but found it difficult to focus on them, as they seemed to be continually sliding back and forth. She turned to Elaine and the same thing was happening – the room was spinning uncontrollably. She closed her eyes but this seemed to make the motion inside her head worse.

'Oh Elaine! I feel weird, everything is twirling, I suddenly feel terrible,' Linda cried out, panicked by her loss of control.

'Oh dear! You must have drunk too much cider and gin! We better get downstairs fast.'

Elaine helped Linda to the dividing door in the corridor, then very slowly opened it and peeped through to see if the way was clear. Observing an empty passageway in front of her, Elaine bundled Linda through the doorway and leaned her against the wall, while she re-locked the door. Then it was a rush to the head of the stairs, their arms interlocked, they teetered along resembling uncoordinated contestants in a three-legged race. Ponderously, the two girls faltered their way down the steps from the top floor and eventually reached the relative safety of the first floor landing.

'Elaine, I think I'm going to be sick,' bemoaned a pale-faced Linda, her hand clamped tightly to her mouth.

'Quick, we'll go along to the toilets in the bathroom,' Elaine responded, concerned by friend's distress. Frantically they hurried into the bathroom at the end of the passage, where Linda collapsed against the nearest toilet bowl and heaved the contents of her stomach onto the crackle glazed porcelain with a slapping splash.

'I'm going to get help,' Elaine said, hoping to reassure Linda, who was looking decidedly green around the gills and ready to throw up again. Running as fast as she could, Elaine went directly to the staff room, located on the ground floor, in the rear corner of the building. Bursting through the door she saw Miss Neame sitting by the window reading a magazine.

'Oh Miss Neame, can you help, it's Linda, she is being awfully sick!' Elaine shouted, from the doorway. Miss Neame sprang to her feet, gathered Elaine's hand, and the two of them raced back up the stairs, storming into the bathroom, where Linda was kneeling limply clutching the toilet seat.

'Well Linda what the devil has happened to you?' Miss Neame enquired sympathetically.

'Oh Miss, I feel terrible, the room keeps sliding around and it's making me be sick, I just can't stop it.'

'Oh dear, I'm so sorry, we had better get you up to the sick room, where you will feel more comfortable and we can establish what is wrong with you.'

The trio left the bathroom and gently walked up to the sick room on the top floor. Still feeling light-headed and nauseas, Linda rested wide-eyed and motionless on the bed, too frightened to close her eyes, in case the unpleasant sensation of everything spiralling, including herself, became more intense.

'It's almost as if, you are drunk,' Miss Neame reasoned, analysing the symptoms, but then dismissed the thought as being preposterous. She then asked, 'Down in the bathroom, I thought I could smell a whiff of something appley?'

'We did eat a few apples down in Treadwell's orchard,' Elaine offered up the invention, hoping to steer Miss Neame away from her original correct diagnosis of inebriation.

'Elaine! You didn't scrump the apples did you?' Miss Neame rebuked her accusingly.

'No, the apples have been harvested – we just picked up the ones they left on the grass beneath the trees. Please don't tell my aunt, I mean Miss Rutherford, I'm sure she'll kick up a stink over it,' Elaine begged.

'Don't worry, your secret is safe with me, besides, I think you have learnt your lesson haven't you,' Miss Neame said, grinning at the pair, while she wandered over to the door. 'I'm

98

going to get Miss Iona, I believe she will know the best treatment for something like food poising.'

Elaine turned to Linda, gave her a little smile, blew her cheeks out in relief and then spoke softly with a frayed voice, 'Phew. I thought she was going tumble that we had been drinking for a moment.'

'Well done! How did you come up with that excuse so fast?' Linda whispered in a weak voice. Despite feeling sorry for herself, she wanted to congratulate Elaine, on her quick thinking, which had saved them from getting into very serious trouble.

'I've been scrumping apples from Treadwells orchard every summer for about the last four years, and I know if you eat too many, you do feel sick and giddy. With a bit of luck, Aunt Iona won't be too cross, anyway whatever happens, it's not going to be as bad, as if they found out, we've been out-of-bounds and drinking booze!'

'You're right – God knows what would happen to us, if they knew what we'd been up too. I'll tell you one thing, I'm never going to touch alcohol again, I feel terrible,' Linda lamented.

The sound of approaching footsteps echoing down the empty corridor outside, issued an early warning to the girls and they halted their conversation.

'Been scoffing too many apples have we,' Iona said, with a half smile on her face, as she entered the room carrying a tray with some crusts of bread and jug of water on it. 'Bread and water diet for you two, and then tomorrow, I'm sure you be as right as rain.'

After briefly examining Linda, she was confident that the condition would soon clear up and there was no need to call for a doctor.

'I think it's best that you both sleep here overnight, just in case the urge to vomit returns, we don't want you disturbing the rest of the dorm, do we? Now get undressed and into bed, I'll check on you a bit later and bring you some more bread and water.'

The thought of eating anything, made Linda retch, but luckily she managed not to throw up again. After disrobing and slipping between the bed sheets, she eventually managed to close her eyes without too much uneasiness and drift off into a very deep sleep.

#   #   #

Twelve hours later, as dawn broke, a shaft of amber, dust-speckled light, cut its way through the window and caressed Linda's face. The bright light penetrated her eyelids causing her to wake with a sudden jolt. There were a few seconds of disorientation and then she noticed a bad taste in her mouth, swiftly followed by the pounding ache in her head. She looked across to her right and saw Elaine in the next bed, still soundly asleep. Linda got out of her bed very quietly and tiptoed over to where she lay. Elaine looked very peaceful and for some strange reason, reminded her of Snow White, waiting for a kiss from a prince to wake her up. She leaned over and softly pressed her lips against Elaine's, who despite the contact, didn't stir. Linda did it again but more firmly this time and waited for a reaction. She was going to do it for a third time, when suddenly, Elaine's eyes flicked opened. There were a few seconds of stillness, while she became cognisant with the strange surroundings, then pushing herself up into a half-sitting, half-twisted position, she stared blearily at Linda, who was now kneeling down beside the bed.

'How are you feeling?' Elaine asked, before Linda had a chance to speak.

'Not so bad, the dizziness has gone, but I have a terrible headache,' Linda answered, 'What about you?'

'Yes I've got a bit of a head as well.'

'Oh God! It's church today, hope I don't puke up in the pews!' Linda exclaimed, sending them both into a quiet giggling fit, at the thought of such a sacrilegious act.

'You could always use the font!' Elaine laughed, causing the throbbing in her head to amplify. After a few seconds of contemplation, she slumped back down on the bed again and then put forward her idea, 'We could, ask to be excused from church.'

'Do you think they would let us off?'

'I don't see why not, especially if you say, you think you might heave up.'

Ten minutes later, the sick room door opened and both of Elaine's aunts entered.

'How do you both feel?' Iona inquired.

'Not as bad as yesterday, but I still feel a bit queasy,' Linda answered, and then quickly added for good measure, 'plus I have a really bad headache.'

'I've got a bad head as well,' Elaine pitched in with her current state of health.

'So what you are saying is, you don't feel up to any breakfast, or a walk down to church this morning?' Amelia interjected, in her unfamiliar role as a concerned guardian.

'Um . . . yes please Aunt Amelia,' Elaine said, sheepishly.

'Very well, we better not take any chances, just in case you do have something contagious. You can stay in bed this morning, and if you are feeling recovered this afternoon, you can rejoin the school activities then,' Amelia decreed, with a knowing smile on her face.

'I'll have some toast sent up to you, as I think you should try to eat something now,' Iona advised, turning to leave the room with her sister. After waiting a few moments, to make sure that both aunts were out of earshot, Elaine, forgetting about her bad head, bounced up and down on her bed in a jig of celebration, relieved at not having to attend the stuffy church service.

\#   \#   \#

An hour later the girls peered from their top floor window at the long line of schoolgirls below them, marching two by two, down the main drive and out of the school grounds.

101

'It's a bit weird being in the school when virtually everyone else has left isn't it?' Linda said, watching the long green column of reluctant Christian soldiers, disappear down the main road.

'Yes, this is what it's like during the holidays, really creepy at night. I'm always expecting to meet the ghost of old Lord Sumners, dragging himself around the corridors, aghast at what has become of his lovely home,' Elaine laughed.

'Wouldn't it be great, if we could sleep here all the time, instead of down in the dorm with the others,' Linda ventured her idea to Elaine.

'Yes it would, but unfortunately, we will have to wait until we're prefects, before we get to sleep up on this floor, and then it will be in a room of our own.'

'That will be in just under four years time – that feels like a lifetime away,' Linda sighed. Then changing the direction of their conversation, she continued, 'What do you do at Christmas?'

'Oh I just roam around here on my own, it's very boring really. I never look forward to Christmas, the Easter break is better, I can get out exploring the countryside then, because of the improved weather.'

'Why not stay with me over Christmas?' Linda said, excitedly.

'What, at your parent's home? Would they agree to that?' Elaine responded with a crisp double volley of eager questions.

'I'm sure they will. I'll mention it in my letter home this week and see what they say. Would your aunts let you come?' Linda asked, realising that their consent might be something of a high hurdle to overcome.

'I don't know, I've never been invited to anyone's home before. It would be great if we could spend Christmas together though – wouldn't it!'

CHAPTER NINE
1ˢᵗ November 1969

2.35 pm

Almost a whole week went by, until at last, Linda received the letter from home that she had been anxiously waiting for. She decided not to open it straight away, but rather track down Elaine and go somewhere more private, to see if it was good news or not. After rushing up to the dormitory, where she thought Elaine would be waiting, Linda was surprised to find just Louise in there, lying down on her bed.

'What have you got there, Middlewicket?' Louise sneered, as Linda wandered past her.

'It's a letter from home.' Linda begrudgingly informed her.

'Oh dear, they're probably writing to tell you, that they've run out of money, and you'll have to go back to your pauper school – where you belong,' Louise giggled, pleased to have the opportunity to inflict her obnoxious personal agenda upon her rival.

'Oh, just shut up!'

'What did you say to me? Remember, I'm Form Captain.'

'I said, shut up you bitch!' Linda spat the words back at Louise, unconcerned by what she might do next.

'I could report you for that!' Louise issued her tautly voiced warning.

'Well go ahead then and I'll tell Miss Rutherford why I said it.'

With her bluff being called and without the back-up of her sidekicks, Louise looked confused about what to do next. Linda recognised the obvious look of doubt in the eyes that were meeting her stare, and it encouraged her not to back down. The two girls glared at each other, in a seemingly unbreakable stand-off, neither of them were willing to look away first. From outside in the corridor, the sound of footsteps broke the stalemate, with both girls snapping their heads around to see who would be the third person joining them. It was Elaine who came through the doorway, and she immediately assessed, from the aggressive posture of the two girls, venomous words had just been spoken.

'Come on Elaine, let's go somewhere else, more private, to open my mum's letter,' Linda huffed, as she stalked towards the door, deliberately turning her head away from Louise.

'Somewhere private to have a snog with your girlfriend, Middlewicket,' Louise taunted.

The spiked comment struck an open nerve, and before she could suppress her temper, Linda twisted back towards Louise and screamed, 'Why don't you just fuck off!' Seeing that Louise's primary reaction on hearing the taboo swear word, was an expression of shocked disbelief, Linda decided not to wait for her to recover and stormed out of the dormitory with Elaine chasing after her.

'Wow Linda! That was a pretty bad swear word,' Elaine said, in a tone which was hard to decipher, if she was being congratulatory, or disapproving.

'I know, I wish I hadn't said it. It just came out, I was so angry with her.'

'I wonder if she will report you?' Elaine mulled over the possibility, ruefully.

'If she does – she does. I'll probably get my mouth washed out with soapy water, but I'll make sure that Miss Rutherford knows exactly what that evil cow has been saying to us. I'm just fed up and I'm not letting her get away with it any more,' Linda railed, her final few angry and frustrated words snapped out, like a clap of a whip.

The two girls left the building by the rear door and wandered down to the deserted tennis courts.

'Right, I'm going to open the letter and see if Mum has agreed for you to come and stay with us this Christmas,' Linda announced. Having just calmed down from her row with Louise, she was now getting increasingly tense at the thought of opening the envelope. Without any further procrastination, she yanked the gum sealed flap open, sucked in a deep breath and pulled out the letter. Linda's blue eyes twitched from side to side while they rapidly scanned the white sheet, looking for the vital phrase.

'Yes! My parents are okay about you staying over Christmas!' she blurted out.

'What shall we do now?' Elaine said, beaming with joy at the prospect of spending Christmas with her best friend.

'We'll have to approach your aunts and see what they say about it?'

'Let's see Aunt Iona first, and then, if she is all right about it, we'll go and see Aunt Amelia.'

'That sounds like a good plan, I have a feeling that if your Aunt Iona is in favour, then perhaps she might be able to persuade your Aunt Amelia, who might not be so enthusiastic.'

They tramped back through the school until they found Iona sitting in the small pocket money office. Through the gap in the door, the girls could see that she was leaning over the desk, conscientiously totting up columns of figures. Elaine gave a polite knock on the half-opened door and they both slipped into the room. Iona looked up for a second and then quickly scribbled some figures down on a sheet of notepaper.

'Afternoon girls, what can I do for you two – it's a bit late to go down to the village now, isn't it?

'We're not here for our pocket money Aunt Iona, I've got something to ask you,' Elaine said.

'How intriguing! Fire away,' replied her aunt jovially.

'Linda has invited me to spend the Christmas holidays with her,' Elaine rushed out the words, smiling and hoping that her aunt would be thrilled for her.

'Are your parents aware of this invitation, Linda?' Iona interrupted, with a look of disquiet on her face.

'Yes Miss. I wrote to them asking about it last week, and I received their reply today,' Linda thrust the correspondence towards her teacher. Iona took the letter from within the envelope and read the facts for herself.

'Well, I suppose it would be acceptable for you to visit Linda's home, seeing that her parents are amenable to the idea.'

'Oh thank you Aunt Iona!' surged Elaine, disbelieving how easily it had all gone.

'Just a minute! I'm in agreement on principle, but the final decision must rest with Amelia. Let's go up to her room and ask her now,' Iona said, quickly dampening the mood of celebration, which had been aroused prematurely in the two girls.

A few minutes later they were all standing anxiously outside Miss Amelia Rutherford's private room. Iona gave a rather irresolute knock on the door and opened it slightly,

'Amelia, I have something to ask you,' she half whispered.

'Yes of course, do come in,' came the riposte from inside the room.

Iona motioned the girls to follow her and began the consultation with her younger sister.

'Amelia, Elaine has been invited to stay with Linda Middlewick over the Christmas holidays, and I was wondering if you would be in agreement to this?'

106

'What, she wouldn't be here for Christmas?' Amelia frowned, as she addressed the question in her head. 'I'm not sure?' she continued, still confused by the possibility. 'Aunt Divina is coming down from Scotland and would be very upset at not seeing you Elaine.'

'Amelia, Aunt Divina sleeps for most of the two weeks that she is here. I'm sure Elaine would have a far more entertaining time with her friend, rather than moping around here on her own, during the holiday period,' Iona canvassed on the girls' behalf, trying hard to influence Amelia's decision.

Amelia stared blankly at Elaine for a few seconds, contemplating the situation, then, her normally phlegmatic features, slowly thawed into a radiant smile that illuminated her face, 'Very well, I suppose by the time the Christmas holidays are here, we will have seen more than enough of you. It will do you good to get away from the school surroundings for a change. I will write to the Middlewicks and thank them for their kind offer.'

'Really, Aunt Amelia!' Elaine screeched, unable to contain her delight at the outcome. The two girls returned to the dorm feeling very excited about the prospect of spending Christmas with each other, even though it was still almost two months away.

#   #   #

The following weeks were swept along on a rushing tide of the festive season's hustle and bustle. Any spare time at the weekends, was taken up by singing practice down at the church, in readiness for the Christmas recital, or making decorations out of sprigs of holly and pine cones, glued together and sprinkled with glitter. It was a happy time, and for once, Linda even enjoyed being present in church for the carol service, which as usual, attracted most of the residents of Upper Grench. Afterwards, for over an hour, the sound of excited chatter filled the stone built church hall, with everyone gathering for a post-performance drink of hot chocolate. At almost ten o'clock, the whole school marched back up to Grenchwood Hall in the dark, with the prefects carrying oil lamps to light the procession. As they trudged across the open fields, the wisps of breaths expelled into the cold air by the girls, were captured floating

107

away into the darkness by the blurred radiance of the lanterns. The Christmas holidays were now just a few days away.

CHAPTER TEN
20th December 1969

10.45 am

Eventually it was December 20th, the end of term and the day when parents arrived to ferry their daughters back home for the holidays. From nine-thirty onward, a steady stream of cars appeared on the gravel crescent to the front of the building, sometimes making it look like a municipal car park.

'What time do you think your father will get here?' Elaine asked, inpatient to start her Christmas holiday adventure, away from Grenchwood Hall for once.

'Not until lunch time, he's got a three hour journey,' Linda sighed, as they sat on Elaine's bed and watched the parental comings and goings at the front of the building.

'Oh look, there's Louise's mum and dad, look down there, she's wearing the fur coat.' Linda pointed out a bright blond, aloof looking woman, standing next to a black jaguar car, talking to Louise. 'That means she won't be wearing any knickers.'

'What!' Elaine laughed, confused by the comment?

'I've heard my dad say it, when somebody comes on the TV – he'll go, "she's all fur coat and no knickers",' Linda giggled.

'What does it mean?

'I don't know, but she'll be really cold today if she isn't wearing any!' Linda hooted, pleased that she had made Elaine laugh out aloud.

'And what are you two reprobates still doing up here?' The girls heard a voice behind them and twisted around, to see Charlotte standing at the entrance of the dormitory.

'My dad won't get here for at least another hour, so there's no point waiting downstairs yet,' Linda informed her.

'Oh well, it's not too long to wait. My ride should be here soon. My sister's boyfriend Jonathan, is going to pick me up and whizz me down to London, to stay at their flat for a couple of days. Then we will all join Mummy and Daddy for a tedious Christmas Day. Actually, it will probably be a scream – Mummy will get totally pissed by midday, the turkey will end up getting burnt and Daddy will drive off in his car somewhere.

'Still, I only have to put up with it for a couple of days, and then I'm going back to the bright lights of the capital, to meet all those sexy photographers, at the round of wild parties that Jonathan gets invited to. This is him now – great, he's in his sports car – I'd better go. Have a lovely Christmas you two.' Charlotte waved goodbye and cantered out of the dorm.

The girls watched, as downstairs the passenger door of the red Sunbeam Tiger was thrown open, and a few seconds later Charlotte came into view, bouncing down the steps. After throwing her small suitcase into the back, she gracefully folded herself into the empty seat, and slammed the door shut, all in one fluid motion. Immediately that she was in, the high-performance car backed up to the far side of the crescent. The V-8 engine revved up loudly for a few seconds, before they shot away up the drive, the two rear wheels spinning wildly and sending hundreds of tiny limestone chippings soaring into the raised rose beds.

The minutes dragged on, by midday it appeared that virtually every girl had been picked up and were on their way home.

Then at the top of the drive, a small dark blue, Morris 1100 car trundled into view.

'It's him!' Linda shouted, pointing up the drive. 'Thank God, that bitch Louise has gone, she would have had a field day, seeing my dad arrive in his old rust bucket car!' The two girls quickly ran through the nearly empty school to the front entrance of Grenchwood Hall.

'Linda's father has arrived Aunt Iona,' Elaine excitedly called over to her aunt, who, all morning, had been overseeing the departing girls, and was now taking a well-earned rest, sitting on one of the pair of occasional chairs, which were kept in the hallway.

'Right, I'll just get Amelia,' she replied.

Linda couldn't wait to throw her arms around her father's neck; it had seemed such a long time since she had last seen him.

'Steady on Linda, you'll have me over!' her father joked, embarrassed by his daughter's overt public display of affection.

'This is Elaine, Dad,' Linda extended her hand towards Elaine, who was hovering on the other side of the car.

'Hello Elaine, very pleased to meet you,' Jack Middlewick, stepped around to where Elaine was standing and offered his hand to her.

'Dad stop being so formal!' Linda chided.

Amelia and Iona came down the steps to greet Jack, and there was more reciprocal handshaking.

'Mr Middlewick would you like a cup of tea after your long journey?' Amelia asked.

'Actually, I think I would like to get straight off, it looks like there could be snow on the way and I don't want to get caught up in it, if possible,' Jack answered, nodding towards the slate grey clouds, gathering over the hills to the north.

'Yes of course, very sensible,' Amelia agreed. 'Can I give you these two envelopes. This one contains funds to cover the expenses for Elaine's stay with you.'

'Oh no, we don't want anything for that,' Jack protested, holding his hands up, indicating his reluctance to take the offered money. 'We're just pleased that Linda has made a friend who she wants to come and stay with us.'

'Nonsense Mr Middlewick, you pay for Linda's board while she is here, so it's only right that we do the same,' Amelia continued, forcefully stepping forward and offering the envelope to Jack. Jack decided it was best just to take it and not to argue with his daughter's headmistress. Amelia then brandished the other envelope. 'This one contains the change from the five-pound note that you gave Linda at the beginning of term. I'll let her explain why ten-shillings are missing.'

Jack thanked Amelia and put both envelopes inside his jacket, he then set about the difficult task of getting the girls' suitcases into the small boot of his car. Amelia and Iona each gave Elaine a little hug, followed by a peck on the cheek and then said their goodbyes. With both the cases and the girls aboard the car, Jack switched on the engine and they slowly rolled forward towards the main drive, with Elaine waving farewell to her aunts through the back seat window.

#   #   #

The dark blue Morris 1100 came to a juddering stop outside 142 Junction Road and the journey home was over. Linda didn't wait for her father to utter his little saying; she opened the rear door the moment the handbrake start to ratchet up. Liz had heard the car pull up outside and was on her way out of the house, with welcoming outstretched arms. Their ebullient embrace almost ended with them both falling over the small dividing wall, into the property next door. Elaine watched, as both mother and daughter shed uncontrolled warm tears of joy, at seeing each other again. She was fascinated by the raw emotion being exchanged, the like of which, she had never experienced.

'Don't worry Elaine,' Jack whispered from the front of the car, 'they'll be behaving normally again in a few minutes, arguing about something or other, I don't doubt.'

Elaine ventured out of the car and stood by the front gate, waiting for the clinch to loosen and the swiping away of stray tears from their blushed cheeks to be completed.

'Mum, this is Elaine, my best friend in the whole world,' Linda said, sniffing as she tried to stifle her joy filled sobs. Elaine was both equally surprised and gratified by this unexpected accolade from Linda.

'Hello Elaine, I feel I almost know you already, from all the letters that Linda has sent home,' Liz snuffled out her greeting.

Again, Elaine was shocked, but pleased, to find out that she was important enough to have been mentioned in Linda's letters home to her parents. Liz Middlewick approached Elaine, who started to offer out her hand, which was totally ignored and instead, a warm welcoming hug encapsulated her.

'Now Elaine, you must call me Liz and call Linda's dad, Jack,' Liz said, putting her arms around the shoulders of the two girls to guide them inside. 'We have a few surprises for you inside Linda.'

As they crossed the threshold, Linda came upon the first of the promised surprises.

'Oh Mum! You've had the phone put in!' Linda yelled in amazement, as they all gathered around the big red plastic telephone, imperially perched upon the glass topped, swirl framed, wall table.

'Can I call somebody?' Linda quite literally begged for a chance to use the new device.

'Who do you want to phone?' Liz asked.

'I don't know? Just someone – to see what it's like.'

Liz placed the receiver to her ear and listening for a few seconds.

'I've got to check that Mr Hedges or his wife, aren't speaking on the phone, because we share the line with them,' she explained, and then passed it on to Linda, who pressed the heavy hand piece to her left ear.

'What's that buzzing sound I can hear?' Linda said, slightly alarmed.

'That's the dialling tone, once you hear that, you can dial the number,' Liz answered, carefully placing her index finger into the hole with the number eight in it, and then she pulled the clear plastic disk around to the metal stop plate on the other side. They watched as she took her finger out and the disk whirred back to the starting position. Liz repeated the action again for the number four and then the number six.

'At the third stroke, it will be, three, twenty-six and forty seconds, precisely,' announced a crystal clarion female voice, to an attentive Linda, who couldn't stop herself from laughing out aloud'

'Oh, can she hear me?' she whispered, worried what the woman at the other end of the line would think.

'No of course not! It's the speaking clock – it's a recording. Surely you didn't think she just sat there all day, giving the time out – you silly girl,' Liz jokingly reproached her daughter. Linda offered the phone to Elaine for her to listen to the next time check.

'How did you know the number?' Linda asked.

'I dialled out TIM – see the tiny letters, above the numbers on the dial face. Now, let's go through to the back room, Grandma's waiting to see you in there.'

'Hello Grandma!' Linda shouted, to the white haired, elderly looking woman, sitting across from her in the far corner of the dining room.

'Hello Linda! I didn't 'ear ya come in, when did ya get back from your posh school?' the old lady said, in a broad cockney accent while lowering her knitting needles and allowing a ball of

114

yellow wool to fall from her lap and roll towards where Linda was standing.

'Just a few minutes ago Grandma, we've been testing the new phone in the hallway,' Linda replied, as she stooped to pick up the ball of wool and return it to her grandmother.

'Bloody fing! It went off this morning and I nearly jumped out of my skin! Terrible noise it makes. Now let me 'ave a butchers at ya. I expected ya to be talking all "la-di-da", after spending all that time with those swanky girls. Who's ya little friend?'

'This is Elaine, Grandma, she's my best friend and she is going to be staying with us over the Christmas holidays.'

'I'm very pleased to meet you . . .' Elaine started to introduce herself, but trailed off, not knowing how to address Linda's grandmother.

'Oh, me name is Rose dear, but call me Grandma, everyone else does,' Rose laughed. 'Well, wot sort of mischief 'ave ya two been up to, at the school then?'

The two girls glanced at each other, smiling at the question and the thought of the escapades that they had shared during the term.

'Mum! Linda and Elaine are good girls, they wouldn't get involved in anything naughty,' Liz interrupted, indignant at her mother's comment.

'I'm not so sure Liz, I can see a twinkle in their mince-pies, that suggests to me that they ain't so sugar and spice,' Rose chortled. Then turning to Linda's father, who had just entered the room, she changed the subject. ''Ere Jack, ya got me any more Green Shield stamps?'

'Yes Rose, loads, look,' Jack pulled out a bundle of the trading stamps from his coat pocket.

'Jesus Jack! How much petrol do ya 'ave to put in that jam-jar of yours?' Rose exclaimed, at the sight of the thick wad of stamps.

115

'There not all mine Rose, we get given them at the garage – when people pay for their petrol and don't want them, we just keep them and divvy them up at the end of the week. There should be enough for a couple of books there. Last week, they were doing an offer – *six times* the usual rate, so bloody yards of the things were spewing out of the machine. We had them all over the kiosk!'

'Less of the language Jack,' Liz called through from the kitchen. 'What on earth will Elaine think of us?'

'Sorry love!' Jack called back, at the same time he winked at the girls. 'I'll get the cases up to Linda's room.'

'I hated school when I was young, couldn't wait to leave. I can't imagine being shut up there for three months at a time, worst than being in Holloway!' Rose hissed, screwing up her tiny wrinkled features, in disgust. 'I got the cane every bleeding Monday morning, regular as clockwork for being late. It weren't my fault, it was me old dad's fault. Every Sunday evening, he would get roaring drunk with his chinas, playing cards in our front parlour, and then he couldn't get up to do his first milk round. I helped him most days, but I could leave the round when I got near to the school, so I wasn't usually late. But on Monday mornings, 'cause me mum was petrified that he would lose his job as a dairyman, she would make me do the whole round for him and then I had to take care of the horse when we got back, at about eight-thirty. Bloody good job that old nag knew the bleeding round, I just sat on the cart and waited for him to stop, whenever he did, I just poured out a measure of milk into the jugs and left it on the doorsteps!'

'Didn't they have bottles in those days,' Elaine enquired, fascinated by Rose's story.

'Nah, not on our round anyway, ya had a couple of big milk churns on the back of the cart and ya doled it out from them. At about eleven o'clock me old man had to do a second round, 'cause there were nah refrigerators back then, so people needed more fresh milk for their teas. Linda, wot do you fink of the new wallpapering that your dad's done?'

116

'Yes it's very modern, all those swirls – sort of psychedelic,' Linda decided, having only just noticed the new décor.

'Makes me mince-pies go funny. To tell ya the truth, I fink it looks like a tart's boudoir!' Rose whispered, screwing up her eyes. 'Everyone's gone colour mad these days. Liz wot colour green did ya say the blooming skirting boards are painted in?'

'Groovy Lime Zest,' Liz shouted from the kitchen, laughing to herself.

'Duck-shit-green more like,' Rose quipped, softly.

'We have another surprise for you Linda – come through to the front room,' Liz announced, reappearing into the dining room and beckoning the girls to follow her. 'What do you think about this?'

'Oh my God! *A colour TV!*' Linda gasped, her jaw dropping open, as she emitted a squeal of delight. 'I don't believe it! When did you get it?'

'Last Saturday, we wanted it to be here for Christmas Day, when the rest of the family are coming over. It's huge, the screen is twenty-five inches!' Liz exclaimed. 'The old black and white set was only seventeen. Look, it's got proper sliding wooden doors and it's so heavy, that it took two men to carry it in. We've had a special aerial put up and now we can get *BBC Two* as well. Nearly everything is in colour on *BBC Two*. Your dad has only gone and told everybody, that they can come around and watch the cup final on it – I really don't know where we will put them all! Most of the street have already been in to see it, we've never had so many visitors.'

'You can get *three* channels!' Elaine piped up, equally astounded by the box in the corner. 'It looks so big.'

Liz went over and pushed one of the four buttons; there was a loud clunk and the channel changed to a black and white film.

'Oh put it back Mum,' Linda cried.

117

'But the other side was a game of rugby,' queried her mother.

'Yes, but it was in colour, we only want to watch things that are in colour,' Linda demanded.

Jack popped his head around the door.

'Well, do you like it?' he needlessly asked.

'It's fab Dad, I can't believe we're watching colour pictures in our own front room. Dad, why do the rugger players on one side, all have different colour socks on?'

'Oh they're the Barbarians. They're an invitational side, you have to be asked to play for them, and it's a tradition that you wear the colour socks of the club that you play for regularly,' Jack explained.

'We wouldn't have known that, if we were watching in black and white would we,' Linda deduced.

'Linda, if this match was being shown in black and white, you certainly wouldn't be watching it!' laughed her dad.

A couple of hours later, the two girls managed to pull themselves away from the mesmerizing effect, of seeing actual colour appearing on a television set for the first time. Linda invited Elaine to see her bedroom, and they disappeared upstairs. On entering the room, Linda switched the transistor radio on, and they were at once, reminded of the special ambience of the secret room back at school.

'This is where we'll be sleeping Elaine,' Linda said, patting the pink candlewick bedspread.

'What, in the same bed?' Elaine asked, checking that she had got the sleeping arrangements correct.

'Yes, sorry, my grandma's in the small bedroom, you don't mind do you?'

'No, not at all, it's just, I've never slept in a bed with anyone else before,' Elaine revealed, blushing slightly.

'Haven't you? Come to think of it, the only time I've shared a bed, is with Mum, when I was ill. There should be enough room though.'

'I love your bedroom Linda – especially the lovely mirror.'

'It was my grandmother's – Dad's mum, who died. The dressing table is a bit big and old fashioned, but I do like the mirror,' Linda said, stroking her hand across the polished dark walnut veneer. 'I'd really like a nice modern shiny white one. Still, it's nice to have something that belonged to my grandmother. Do you have anything that belonged to your mother or father?'

'No nothing – all their possessions perished in the plane crash,' Elaine sighed, and quickly changed the subject. 'Where does, your grandma come from? I didn't quite understand all that she said.'

'She comes from the East End of London, somewhere called, Limehouse. She swears a lot doesn't she,' Linda answered, with a glint in her eye, recalling her own indiscretion with Louise.

'I haven't heard her say "Fuck" yet,' Elaine giggled out a whispered reply. 'But at least I know where you get it from! Are there a lot of Chinese people living in Limehouse?'

'Chinese people? I think there are some, why do you ask?'

'She said that her father, got drunk every Sunday, in the front parlour with some Chinese people,' Elaine explained, puzzled by the strange plot to the story.

'Chinese people?' Linda repeated, her mind whirled in circles, trying to fathom a reason, why Elaine would think, that there were drunken Chinese men in the front parlour. It suddenly came to her.

'Oh, when she said, he got drunk with his china's, she meant "china plates" – *mates*. It cockney rhyming slang,' Linda laughed. 'To be honest, I don't understand half of what she says either!'

Linda and Elaine spent the rest of the evening avidly glued to the new television set, watching *Simon Dee* and being enthralled by the mind-boggling actuality of seeing moving pictures in glorious colour, without having to go to the cinema.

After a long and eventful day, the time came for the girls to say goodnight to the adults and make their way upstairs to Linda's bedroom. Although fatigued from the previous hectic sixteen hours, the curious prospect of getting into the same bed together, enlivened them both from their weariness.

Linda switched on the radio, and then she snuggled down into the bed, pulling the covers up to her nose as a defence against the chill bedroom air. For a few seconds they both lay inert, feeling awkward by the closeness of their bodies, fixed together between the fresh cold sheets.

'It's really freezing tonight, it's as bad as being at school,' Linda giggled. She then started to rub her legs briskly over the marble cold material, trying to warm it up by the power of friction.

'It's great listening to the radio in bed. I think we will quickly warm up, being so . . . close together,' Elaine surmised shyly, at the same time the matchless new sensation, of Linda's body heat stealing into her own, excited her.

'Yes, wish we could do this at school,'

'What, get into bed together?' Elaine's voice shifted up an octave in surprise.

'*No!* I mean listen to pop music in bed!' Linda howled, 'Imagine what bloody Louise Bennington would make of us in bed together!'

After a while, their vigorous chatter wound down to a drowsy babble and then finally they drifted off to sleep.

#   #   #

The next day began for the two girls, with them both being awoken by Linda's mother entering the bedroom.

120

'I've put the electric fire on in the bathroom, so if you want to take your clothes through into there, it will be warmer than the bedroom to get dressed in. Your dad's got both fires blazing downstairs, so we should soon be nice and cosy,' Liz advised the two semi-conscious girls. 'I'm doing a big fry up, so don't be too long!'

As Linda sat up in bed stretching her arms above her head, she shivered as the sharp coldness assaulted her warm body.

'Look Elaine! The window is completely covered with ice – *on the inside*!' Linda got out of bed and quickly pulled on her dressing gown, she then approached the frosted glass for a closer look.

'The patterns are amazing, like hundreds of feathers painted on the window, by Jack Frost,' she laughed, and a plume of white breath formed a small cloud in front of her face. Elaine plucked up her courage and made the painful decision to jump out of the snug bed into the refrigerated conditions. They gathered up their clothes and rushed down the landing to the comparative warmth of the tiny bathroom.

Ten minutes later the warm, alluring smell of bacon and eggs wafted up into the cooler atmosphere of Linda's bedroom, the girls, dressed and refreshed from their morning ablutions, ventured down the stairs. Linda pushed the dining room door open and was taken aback by the sudden heat that she encountered. The fire was roaring and crackling loudly in the grate, spitting little flares of bright orange embers across the fireplace like tiny fireworks. Jack burst into the room from the door under the stairs, he was carrying a fully loaded coalscuttle, which he had just replenished from the supply kept down in the cellar.

'Christ it's bloody cold down there!' he growled, placing the scuttle down onto its stand with a dull clang. 'Still, I've got the fire going in the front room, so it'll be nice and warm for this afternoon, when the telly comes on.'

Elaine could hardly believe the size of the cooked breakfasts, which Liz conveyed into the dining room one at a time.

121

She looked across the table at Linda's grandmother and wondered how the petit elderly woman would ever be able to consume the mountain of food placed in front of her.

'This looks lovely Liz – ya can't beat a big Sunday fry-up. Sets ya up for the rest of the day. Lines your stomach for that lunchtime visit to the pub, eh, Jack?' Rose said, winking at her son-in-law.

'How many pints do you think I'm going to drink Rose? The pub is only open for a couple of hours,' Jack responded defensively.

'I've seen my George sink about ten pints during a Sunday lunchtime session down the Grapes,' Rose insisted.

'He must have had hollow legs Rose!' laughed Jack, vigorously shaking the brown sauce bottle over his bacon.

'Don't know about 'olla legs, but his wallet was always empty at the end of the week,' snorted Rose. 'He would just open his gob and in one swig, half a pint would disappear.'

'What did your husband do for a living Mrs . . . I mean Grandma?' Elaine asked, keen to hear some more of Rose's stories.

'My George? He was a doorman at that posh hotel up west, called the Dorchester – he started there soon after it opened in the early thirties. George saw loads of famous people who stayed there – Danny Kaye, Jessie Mathews, and even Vivien Leigh. Douglas Fairbanks gave him two white fivers, as a tip for summit George did for him. Imagine that, a ten quid tip, when George only made four-pound a week. We blew it all on a night-out, up town. We went to a show and sat in the front seats of the stalls, not up in the gods. Then we went to a fancy restaurant and went through the card, ya should 'ave seen the snooty waiter's boat-race. After that, we got a taxi all the way back to Limehouse. It was the first time either of us had ever been in a taxi. George gave the cabbie his last thruppence as a tip, and then he said to me, life's too short to put your bread-and-honey in the bank. It was for him, he joined up at the outbreak of the war and got killed, right at the end, parachuting into bloody Arnhem. I still fink he's going to come through the front door and shout, "Wot's for tea Luv!"' Rose smiled, wistfully. Elaine could see that her pale blue eyes had misted over and for a second she regretted asking the question.

'Are they still going to make you move Mum?' Liz asked, deliberately changing the subject to something that she knew would snap her mother out of the brief feeling of melancholy that she was experiencing.

'Yes they bloody are!' Rose responded with a clap of fury, affronted by the council's plan. 'I love my prefab, I don't wanna to live up in the bleeding clouds with the birds.'

'It's progress Mum, they need the land where the prefabs are, to build a new council estate, so they can house more people,' Liz explained.

'It not natural living that high up, I don't know why they had to knock all those lovely houses down in the first place, just to build bloody 'orrible tower blocks.'

'It all part of a slum clearance Mum.'

'They weren't slums my girl, they were bloody good houses, we were very happy in ours until it got blown up.'

'Blown up!' Elaine blurted out, shocked by the thought of a house exploding.

'Yes, first bleeding night of the Blitz. Fortunately, me, Liz and Harold had been down in the tube all night, 'cause of the rumours that Jerry was going to hit the docks. We heard the bombs landing, even though we were hundreds of feet down. In the morning, when we got home, the gaff was gone. Direct hit. Just the back door frame was standing upright. All we had in the world, was wot we stood up in, but at least we were alive. Both me neighbours either side were brown-bread – I told them to come down the tube with us, but they didn't want to give up their warm beds,' Rose sadly lamented her old friends untimely deaths.

'Do you remember that Mum?' Linda asked.

'Yes of course I do! It's quite an event to come home and your house has disappeared!' laughed Liz.

'What did you do?' Elaine asked, astounded by the story.

'Well I got Liz and Harold on the first train that I could, down to Wales, to stay with me cousin Amy and her husband Will, on their farm. I stayed to carry on with me job at the uniform factory, but we got bombed every night for nearly two months and eventually the factory copped it. So I thought, I've had enough of this malarkey and got meself down to Amy's farm for the rest of the war.'

'Did you miss Grandma when you first went down to the farm Mum?' Linda asked, suddenly becoming interested in the conversation, because she could see a comparable, with her own situation being away at school.

'Well at first I did, but as your grandma said, it was only a couple of months and then she joined us,' Liz answered.

'Can I ask a question?' Elaine said tentatively.

'Of course you can my luv,' Rose replied, pleased with Elaine's interest in her wartime memories.

'What is a prefab?'

Everyone around the table collectively burst into laughter at Elaine's question.

'It's short for prefabricated building,' Jack explained. 'Have you never heard of prefabs? They built thousands of them after the war, all over London because of the shortage of houses after the bombing. It only took about a day to put one up, because the parts were all made in a factory, and then you just clipped them together on the site. They look like tiny bungalows.'

'I love me prefab, it's a little palace. I thought I'd won the pools when we moved in, having a lovely kitchen and bathroom, instead of a bleeding tin bath in front of the fire. Not to mention having a khazi that was indoors – it was heaven! And a lovely

124

garden, where ya can grow all your own vegetables, wot bliss, after that old gaff with the lav out in the yard.'

'That's why the old houses were cleared Mum,' Liz chipped in.

'Well they didn't have an indoor lav, I grant ya, but I'm sure there must have been a way of putting a lav and a bathroom indoors, instead of knocking the bloody lot down,' Rose argued.

Breakfast was over and Liz began to clear the plates.

'You girls can go into the front room and make some paper chains if you like. They're in the Woolworth's bag, in the top drawer of the sideboard. If your dad's not too drunk when he gets home from the pub, perhaps he'll hang them up for us,' she joked.

'Oi you! I'll be perfectly sober when I get home,' Jack retorted.

'Well, if you are taking the car you better be, remember they've got that breathalyser thing now, it can tell if you are over the limit.'

'Yes, I know, I think I'll be okay to have three or four pints, though. I'm going to get the Sunday paper, do you want anything from the newsagent?' Jack asked, as he grabbed his heavy black overcoat that was hanging on the back of the door to the cellar.

'Well, I suppose you could get some sweets and chocolate for later, and do you want a magazine Mum?' Liz called over to Rose, who was sitting in the armchair near the fire, poised to start knitting.

'Ya could get me a *Titbits*, Jack,' Rose replied.

'And a copy of *Jackie* for us Dad,' Linda shouted, from the other room.

'Okay, is that everything?' Jack asked, and on not hearing anymore requests, he slipped out of the kitchen door and made his way down the frosty garden path, to the back gate and then off to the corner shop, a couple of blocks away.

125

Linda and Elaine spent the next hour or so, diligently licking and sticking the coloured paper strips and interlocking them to form yards of Christmas trimmings.

Rose opened the door to the front room carrying a tray with two glasses of lemonade on it, ''Ere you are girls, thirsty work all that licking!'

'Thanks Grandma, I've got a horrible taste in my mouth now,' Linda said, taking several gulps of the clear fizzy liquid.

'Mmm . . . this is lovely, wish we got this at school, instead of the orange squash we have at tea time, which is so weak, you can see through it,' Elaine commented, swigging down the sparkling pop.

'Yes, lovely isn't it? It's Corona, I've really missed it – a man delivers it from a van every Friday, you can get all sorts of different flavours.'

'Can you girls do me a favour,' Rose asked.

'What Grandma?'

'Can ya stick all me Green Shield stamps in these books.'

'Oh Gran! Not more licking,' Linda cried out laughing.

#   #   #

Later that afternoon, Jack returned home from the pub, struggling into the hall with a real Christmas tree that he had bought from a man, selling them out of the back of a lorry, in the pub car park. It was a job to find the required space for the tree in the front room, chairs were squeezed together and the radiogram was taken upstairs to be temporarily stored on the landing. After using an unsteady bedroom chair to clamber up into the attic, Jack carefully lowered down a cardboard box full of old Christmas decorations, to the waiting girls. Linda and Elaine took the box downstairs and quickly set about decorating the naked tree with fragile baubles and hundreds of strands of tinsel. Every time the prickly boughs of the spruce were disturbed by their activity, a fragrant smell of fresh pinewood filled the room. Jack took almost an hour to untangle the

126

fairy lights, which had somehow, inexplicably managed to knot themselves into a ball. After all his efforts, predictably, when he plugged them in, they didn't light up. Painstakingly, he tested every bulb, by individually changing each one, along the long, green twisted wire, until at last they burst into a twinkling radiance. Finally, Jack got to wrap the lights around the tree and he finished it off, by placing a rather bedraggled fairy on the very top. The front room's transformation into a Christmas arcadia was completed when the paper chains were tacked onto the picture rails and trailed all around the four walls. There was just time to watch *Here's Lucy* and once again, marvel at the luminous colours being radiated from the television set, before going through to the dining room, for a traditional Sunday roast.

CHAPTER ELEVEN
24th December 1969

9.30 am

'You don't mind do you?' Linda asked. 'Only it's a bit of a tradition that I go out with my dad on Christmas Eve, to help him choose Mum's present.'

'No of course not,' perched on the edge of the bed, Elaine replied with a somewhat misty voice. She was absorbedly watching Linda slowly brushing her lustrous, caramel and honey-streaked hair in front of the dressing table mirror.

'He's pretty hopeless when it comes to getting gifts for Mum – he's got no idea at all,' Linda giggled, picking up a cut glass, silver collared perfume atomiser that had once belonged to her dead grandmother. She pinched the tasselled, white fabric pump and from the empty bottle, a faint wisp of stale scented air wafted under her nose. The musty lavender smell, was so instantly redolent of her granny, it was almost as if the dearly departed old lady had just entered the room.

'Are you all right? You suddenly looked anxious about something,' Elaine asked, seeing the look of concern spreading on Linda's usually smiling face.

'Oh! Yes . . . I just . . . I mean, I'm a bit worried about what to get Mum, that's all.'

'I'm sure that you will think of something, that she will adore. Your mum said I could help in the kitchen while you are out.'

'She'll be making loads of stuff for tomorrow. In the afternoon, my Aunty Gwen, Uncle Harold and cousin David will come for tea and stay until late,' Linda chirped back in an over cheerful voice, to accentuate that she had recovered from her moment of consternation.

'Where do they live?'

'Only about a mile away, David goes to the same school as me, or rather my old school, Queens Manor. So I'll be able to find out what's been going on since I left.'

'Linda your dad's ready to go!' Liz shouted up the stairs.

'Okay Mum, just coming,' Linda called back, and the girls came bounding down the stairs, a smidgen too quickly and went sliding along the lino in the hallway, ending up perilously close to the new telephone table.

'Careful you two,' Liz admonished, giving her daughter a token smack on the rear end to calm her eagerness, 'I don't want to have to take you around to the hospital on Christmas Eve, it will be full of drunks.'

'Not yet Mum, the pubs don't open for another couple of hours,' countered Linda, pulling her gabardine mackintosh from the red ball-tipped hook, on the multicoloured wall-mounted coat rack. Liz opened the front door and Linda, still in the process of putting her mac on, raced outside in the rain to the car, where her father was waiting for her.

'Right Elaine, now we've got rid of trouble, we can get on with some baking,' Liz said, smiling and slamming the door shut with hefty shove. 'We need to make sausage rolls, mince pies, cheese and pineapple on sticks, chipolatas on sticks, jam tarts, *vol-au-vents*, a couple of egg and bacon pies – oh, and I need to start the trifle.'

129

The list of items that Liz reeled off, as they marched through to the kitchen seemed endless to Elaine, and she wondered how on earth, it all would get done for the next day. The large flap on the larder unit was down and an oval of pastry had already been rolled out on it. Liz handed Elaine a red plastic circular cutter and showed her how to press out tennis ball size circles, of the putty coloured dough.

'So what's it like being the headmistress's niece then?' Liz asked.

'Oh, all right I suppose. I've always called Amelia, "aunt", but actually she is my late father's niece, so I'm actually her cousin. Because of the age difference, while I've been growing up, I've always referred to her as "Aunt Amelia". It is a bit strange calling her, *Miss Rutherford* though, sometimes I forget, which causes quite a laugh. Aunt Amelia warned me that I would get treated exactly the same, as the rest of the girls during term time. One girl thinks that because I'm related, I tell tales to them, but of course I don't.'

'So you don't get along with her then?'

'No not really.'

'But there's no bullying going on, is there?'

Elaine detected from Liz's concerned tone that she was worried by the possibility.

'No, we just ignore her and get on with our own lives' and stay out of her way, as much as possible.'

'That's good. So you are both quite happy at school then?'

'Yes very – we have a fab time mostly. What do I do now Liz?' Elaine asked, anxious to change the subject and having cut as many disks that she could, from the original elliptical shaped pastry mix. Liz opened the oven door and pulled out a tin tray containing twelve pastry cases, each full of glistening mincemeat.

'These are going to be the lids,' Liz informed Elaine, and then she showed her how to crimp the pastry together to prevent the

130

filling from leaking during the baking. Lastly, she took a knife and cut three slits on the top.

'What are you doing that for?' Elaine enquired, perplexed by the strange ritual.

'It's to let the steam out when they're cooking. We don't want them blowing up like our old house did,' Liz chuckled, and then watched Elaine finish off the next mince pie as perfectly as she had done.

'Very good! Have you done any baking before?' Liz applauded Elaine's efforts and realised, that unlike her own daughter, she had a willing and enthusiastic assistant.

#   #   #

For the next three and half hours, under Liz's tutelage, Elaine keenly learnt about and helped create an assortment of savoury treats for the following day's party.

'Crikey, look at you two!' Linda exclaimed, suddenly appearing in the kitchen doorway. 'You've been busy – everything smells great, so when can we sample some?'

'You can both have a selection for supper tonight, the rest we'll have to keep for tomorrow,' Liz informed her daughter.

'It's been great Linda! We made loads of mince pies, sausage rolls, jam tarts, some French sounding things, and we have just started two lovely big, egg and bacon pies!' Elaine said, looking comical, standing in her oversized apron, with her face and tousled chestnut brown hair, covered in dustings of chalky white flour. 'Your mum is a great cook, I've loved every minute of it!'

'*Really?*' Linda replied in utter disbelief 'I hated domestic science at my last school, it was so messy and I was always afraid of burning myself.'

'Elaine's a natural cook, not like you Linda, you can't boil an egg!' Liz joked. 'Do you want to stop now Elaine and go through with Linda?'

131

'I would rather like to help finish the egg and bacon pies, if you don't mind?' Elaine zealously replied.

Linda's eyebrows raised upwards in wonderment that anyone would volunteer to do cooking.

'It's not a problem, I'll go up and help Dad do some wrapping,' she said, departing for the bedroom.

#   #   #

The Christmas Eve excitement continued to build during the day; after teatime, when the dining table had been cleared, Rose taught the girls some card games called Newmarket and Gin Rummy. They played for matchstick stakes, with Rose winning against her inexperienced opponents and collecting the pot, time after time, much to her amusement. The game was interrupted by the arrival of the Salvation Army band and carol singers, who assembled in the street outside and gave a rousing rendition of "Deck the Halls" and "Away in the Manger". They all watched from the warmth of the front room window, except Jack, who found some change and waited outside in the freezing cold, for the arrival of the man, carrying a bucket, into which, he tossed the collection of coins.

Later in the evening they watched *The Cilla Black Show* and then a film called *Genevieve*, about a vintage car race from London to Brighton and back again. The film had some extra significance for Linda, as during the previous summer holidays, on the Isle of Wight, she and her cousin David, had sat in the actual car used in the film and had their photograph taken, wearing Edwardian costumes. Sitting in pride of place on the sideboard, the framed photo showed Linda wearing a flamboyant black hat with a bright red plume of feathers and David in a tweed cloak and deerstalker.

After watching the folk group the *Spinners*, it was nearly midnight and time for the girls to go to bed. Upstairs, as they got undressed, they could hear the stamping footsteps of people walking home from the pub, their bouts of joyful laughter mingling with festive farewells, as they went on their separate ways. Although they were well past the age of believing in Father Christmas, the excitement about what the following day would bring, made it impossible for them to go straight to sleep. Instead they talked quietly about their day, but eventually, after about half an hour they succumbed to the tiredness snaking into their thoughts and drifted off.

CHAPTER TWELVE
25th December 1969

8.00 am

A hard rapping knock of knuckles on the wooden bedroom door, rudely roused the drowsy girls from their pre-waking, half-conscious stupors. Jack popped his head around the door as it slowly opened and announced, 'Father Christmas has been, and he's left two sacks down in the front room.'

'Dad! We aren't seven years old,' Linda reproached her father, but she couldn't help but giggle with a shiver of realisation that it was finally Christmas morning. The invading piquant smell of roasting turkey, full of herbed stuffing, bizarrely circulating in her bedroom at breakfast time, reaffirmed that this indeed was the special day. In no time at all, the girls had donned their dressing gowns and had set forth down to the pre-warmed front room, to see what gifts were awaiting them. Placed at either end of the orange and tan brown sofa, were two pale pink, winceyette pillowcases, full of brightly wrapped Christmas presents. Both pillowcases had a postcard pinned to them, with a name written on it. Linda quickly delved into her sack, pulling out her first present, which she knew from the thin square shape, was going to be an LP. As the holly motif wrapping paper shredded away, she could see it was *Abbey Road* by the Beatles. She gave out a little high-pitched squeak and held it up for everyone to see.

'Wot's that when it's at home – a book?' Rose asked, watching from her seat in the corner of the room.

'No Grandma, it's an LP by the Beatles,' Linda answered.

'Wot's an LP?'

'A long playing record Gran,' Linda laughed, amused by her grandmother's complete ignorance of the commonly used abbreviation.

'Oh, you mean a seventy-eight,' Rose concluded, satisfied in her own mind, that she fully understood.

Elaine looked at her pillowcase and was confused; her aunts had given her three small presents to bring with her, but her sack was bulging with gifts. Lifting the dangling tag attached to the top one, she recognised her Aunt Iona's handwriting. After carefully un-wrapping the adorning paper, a glossy piano-black box, containing an expensive Parker 65 fountain pen, fell out onto her lap. Next she opened the present from Aunt Amelia and was agreeably shocked, to find a bottle of the new Chamade perfume. It was unusual for Aunt Amelia to give such an extravagant present that didn't have a practical use.

'God Elaine! French perfume, how fantastic!' uttered Linda, who was busy opening her own presents. Elaine pulled out the next present, which felt soft and cushiony through the paper; on the gift tag it said it was from Grandma.

'Is this present for me?' Elaine questioned, worried that one of Linda's gifts had been placed in the wrong pillowcase.

'Yes love, it's from Linda's grandma,' Liz informed her.

Elaine pulled at the paper and out sprung a shocking-pink knitted scarf.

'Oh how lovely, thank you Grandma,' she said with genuine feeling, and went over and gave the old lady a hug.

'I've got one as well!' Linda shouted, brandishing identical knitwear. Both of the girls put on their scarves and posed either side of Rose, for Jack to take their picture, with his own Christmas present, a new Kodak Instamatic. The flash bulb cube flared and the burst of white light momentarily blinded the trio.

'Gawd Jack, does that camera do that every time it takes a picture?' Rose bleated, trying to focus her eyes, without getting floating coloured shapes in front of them.

'Indoors it does Rose, otherwise the photos come out too dark when you're using colour film,' Jack explained.

The girls quickly returned to the gratifying task of opening their presents. Linda displayed her delight, by bouncing up and down on the sofa, at receiving a gold wristwatch from her parents and the game Ker-Plunk, from Aunty Gwen and Uncle Harold. Elaine remained astonished by the extra-unexpected gifts that she was opening, from Liz and Jack. A box of three Walnut Whips, a *Judy* annual, a small teddy bear and a *Shirley Flight Air hostess* book were all gently unwrapped and examined with glee.

'Spirograph!' Linda screamed, and then, when she had recovered from the shock of opening the present, that she wanted to receive more than anything else, she added, 'Thanks Mum, thanks Dad.'

'Spirowot, wot on earth is that?' Rose asked, bewildered by the name.

'It's a drawing game Mum, you make fantastic patterns with little plastic disks,' Liz filled her mother in with the premise of the toy.

'Wot will they fink of next,' Rose sighed, shaking her head in disbelief.

Elaine looked into her pillowcase and saw two more unopened presents, she took the long thin one out, knowing that it was from her Aunt Divina and when she opened it, she was not surprised to find a one pound premium bond. Aunt Divina always sent a pound bond to her, for every birthday and Christmas present, as far back as she could remember. She took out the last gift, it was very small and the attached tag, made from an old Christmas card, completely dwarfed it. Elaine read the message, 'To Dear Elaine,

136

thanks for being such a lovely friend, have a merry Christmas, lots of love Linda.' A surge of panic flooded her mind, she turned around to see Linda watching and smiling at her.

'I haven't got you anything Linda, I didn't know you were going to do this!' Elaine remonstrated, feeling guilty about not reciprocating.

'Don't worry, I wasn't expecting anything – well open it then,' Linda said, impatiently waiting to see her friend's reaction. Elaine pulled at the sticky tape and the wrapping fell away, inside there was an expensive-looking pearl-white box, with a gold trim running around the top edge. Gingerly she lifted the lid and her eyes caught a glimpse of something shiny and silver in colour. Using her forefinger and thumb, she very gradually drew it out of the presentation box and held the focal point in front of her face, where she could see that it was an italic, lower case letter e on a chain.

'Well, do you like it?' Linda said, examining Elaine's features for any telltale signs as to what she might be thinking or feeling.

'It's ... it's absolutely fab! I can't believe that you got me this!' Elaine cried out, and then for the first time in her life, a spontaneous wave of emotion swept through her, as she threw her arms around Linda and squeezed her in a tight embrace. 'I shall treasure it always,' she continued in a shaky voice, while Linda helped her to fasten the clasp of the chain around her neck.

'It looks really good, we got it yesterday, that's why you had to stay with Mum and help with the cooking – I wanted it to be a surprise.'

'It is a surprise! And I didn't mind helping with the baking, I loved it actually.'

Liz and Jack cleared up the discarded Christmas wrapping paper, while the girls knelt down at the coffee table and endeavoured to produce intricate colourful patterns, using the new Spirograph toy.

At eleven o'clock, the television was turned on for Rose, who wanted to watch Leslie Crowther, enjoying a Christmas party with some unfortunate children, who had to spend the day in hospital.

'Liz, when's the Queen's speech on today?' Rose asked, screwing her eyes up in an attempt to focus on the Christmas Day listings page, in the *TV Times* bumper festive issue.

'There's not one this year Mum, they're showing a documentary about the Royal Family instead – it's on at twelve-thirty, so we'll watch that and then have Christmas dinner,' Liz answered, while hovering in the doorway. 'Elaine, would you like to speak to your aunts on the telephone and thank them for their gifts?'

Elaine was at once intrigued and fearful about using the unfamiliar technology.

'Um . . . all right then, if you don't mind?' she replied warily.

'Of course not, come on, let's call them now.'

Elaine nervously joined Liz in the hallway and watched as Linda's mother carefully dialled out the number.

'It's ringing,' Liz said, thrusting the receiver into Elaine's hand, 'I'll go back into the front room and leave you to talk to them.'

Elaine, waited for a few more fidgety seconds, and then she heard, 'Good morning, this is Grenchwood Hall school for girls,' it was the disembodied voice of her Aunt Iona, echoing down the telephone wires, all the way from Yorkshire.

'Hello . . . hello . . . this is Elaine, Aunt Iona . . . I'm calling you from Mr. and Mrs Middlewick's home.'

'Elaine! How wonderful to hear your voice. Amelia! It's Elaine on the telephone.'

'Thank you for the lovely pen Aunt Iona.'

138

'You are very welcome Elaine, I look forward to seeing how it improves your handwriting in the New Year – I'm going to pass you over to Aunt Amelia.'

'Elaine, what lovely a surprise! Are you having an enjoyable time?' a new voice filled her eardrum, but it was one that she was very familiar with.

'Yes, a marvellous time, thank you Aunt Amelia, and thank you for the lovely perfume.'

'Well you are not a little girl anymore, so we thought it was time for you to have a grown-up present. I hope you are behaving yourself and remember to thank the Middlewicks for their very generous hospitality. I had better say goodbye now, this is a long distance call and must be costing a lot of money.'

'Goodbye Aunt Amelia, have a lovely day . . . and a happy New Year!' Elaine called out, as the line clicked dead. Elaine's first ever telephone conversation was over in under sixty seconds; she replaced the receiver and returned to the front room.

'That was quick love, you could have talked for longer,' Liz said.

'Oh no it was fine, I thanked them and wished them a happy New Year as well. It was strange hearing my aunts on the phone, it was like they were tiny and were trapped under the floor, like characters from that book called *The Borrowers*,' Elaine laughed.

After the documentary about the Royal Family, everyone went through to the dining room to await the first course. Linda was disappointed that she was missing *Top of the Pops*, but decided it was not a good idea to ask her mother to delay the meal for another forty-five minutes. Her disgruntlement soon evaporated when she heard the pistol-shot sound of the Christmas crackers being pulled and saw her father, wearing his purple paper crown at a jaunty angle.

'What has a head, a tail, but no body?' Jack demanded, reading out a joke from the curled paper slip that he found in his discarded half of the pulled cracker.

'I don't know – what does have a head, a tail and no body?' responded Linda, knowing how her father loved bad jokes.

'A coin of course!' he roared with laughter, as the others around the table smiled, not at the joke, but at his exaggerated jocularity.

'It's prawn cocktail for starters,' Liz announced, placing on the table a tray with five glass fruit bowls, filled to the top with a lumpy pink sauce that sat on a bed of bright green chopped lettuce. 'Do you like prawns Elaine?'

'I've never had them, what are they?' Elaine enquired, as she tried to analyse the contents of the dish set before her.

'It's seafood luv,' Rose fielded the question. 'Seafood's lovely, cockles, whelks, mussels, winkles, all that sort of fing.'

Elaine was even more suspicious of the curious concoction, but decided it would be bad manners not to try it. She took a spoonful, but only allowed a small amount to pass her lips, in case the taste made her feel sick. Conversely and to her surprise, the flavour was very palatable, so she finished the rest on her spoon and took another.

'This is really lovely!' she proclaimed, with the zealous fervour of a culinary convert.

'My George loved his seafood, give him a bowl of winkles and a pin and he was as 'appy as a sandboy for half an hour, listening to *Henry Hall's Dance Orchestra* on his home made cat's whisker. When I was a girl and we couldn't afford meat, 'cause me old man had spent the housekeeping down the boozer, me mum used to boil up whelks and we'd 'ave em in a stew.'

'What are whelks Grandma?' Linda asked.

'Well, they're snails I suppose.'

'What, you used to eat snails!'

140

'It was better than going hungry my girl. Anyway the French eat snails and if yer go to a posh restaurant, they'll charge you a pretty penny for 'em.'

'Mum, you'll put everyone off their Christmas dinner!' Liz quickly pitched in, looking at the horrified expressions on the girls' faces.

#   #   #

After the meal, everyone, except Jack, who had volunteered to do the washing up, returned to the front room and watched Julie Andrews introduce scenes from Disney films. An hour later, they were jolted out of their languid state by the sound of the front doorbell chiming.

'Oh it's not five o'clock already,' Liz muttered under her breath, while shuffling through into the hallway, to let her guests in. Harold, Gwen and their son David, shuffled into the front room still wearing their coats, there was a brief nod of greeting to the girls, but their attention was completely captured by the colour television set.

'Merry Christmas Mum,' Harold said, managing to drag his concentration away from the screen for a second.

'Merry Christmas Son,' Rose replied. 'Wot'd ya fink about the TV then?'

'It's amazing isn't it?'

'Don't seem natural to me, I prefer me black and white set, wot I got in 1957, with me insurance money. I've only ever had to replace one valve, in over ten years,' Rose announced proudly.

'I bet the football looks fantastic in colour, doesn't it Uncle Jack?' David said, interrupting his grandmother.

'Only when Chelsea are winning, David,' Jack joked.

'Can we get one Dad? It would be great.'

'We can't afford to buy one, but perhaps we'll rent a set from Granada,' Harold said, giving his wife a hopeful look.

141

'We'll see,' Gwen answered diplomatically, leaving the subject open for discussion at a later date.

'I wouldn't bovver Harold, I can't see 'em catching on,' Rose interjected.

Once the colour television had loosened its grip on the attention of the newly arrived guests, the customary exchanges of appreciation for yuletide gifts, were undertaken between the family members. To make more space, Liz suggested that the children go into the dining room and play cards or Ker-Plunk, while the adults remained in the front room. Jack vanished down into the cellar, only to emerge again a few minutes later, carrying a cardboard box full of bottles and cans, which he placed down on the kitchen table.

'Dad, are you going to make us a snowball?' Linda asked, excitedly.

'Yeah sure, but let me get the others their drinks first,' Jack called back, amid the noise he was making, banging a screwdriver into the lid of a Watneys Red Party Seven can. There was hissing sound and then a dirty cream coloured fountain of bubbles erupted, soaking Jack and the tabletop, much to the amusement of the three onlookers. Quickly, he opened up another aperture, on the other side of the lid and then picked up the large, red tin receptacle in both hands and poured mainly froth, into the two dimpled glass pint jugs, that were placed on the draining board.

'Right, I'll let them settle a bit and get your Aunty Gwen's Cherry B ready.' Jack hunted around under the sink for the correct glass and eventually pulled out a gold rimmed, thin-stemmed goblet with three cherries on the side. 'Excellent! I knew we had one of these somewhere.' After another couple of minutes pouring and mixing, he had all the required drinks stacked onto a tray, ready to transport into the front room.

'David, could you take these drinks through?' Jack asked his nephew. 'Oh, by the way, what do you want to drink?'

'Can I have a lager and lime Uncle Jack?' David made his request, with an optimistic twang to his recently acquired, raspy broken voice, as he carefully carried the tray out of the kitchen.

142

'I suppose so . . . but don't tell your mother,' Jack called after him, smiling to himself. He looked into the box and located a white and blue can of Ind Coope, Long Life beer. The lip on the can was not too deep; so this time he could puncture it with the claw end of the butterfly tin opener. Tilting back the half-pint glass, he slowly poured in the fizzy amber liquid, until the white frothy head of carbon dioxide bubbles, almost reached the rim, leaving just enough room to add a measure of lime.

'Right then, two snowballs coming up,' Jack announced, taking some tall glasses down from the kitchen cabinet. First he tipped a good slug of the pale yellow, viscous Advocaat into each glass, and then he filled the remaining space almost to the top with sparkling lemonade, finally adding the requisite splash of Rose's lime juice.

'Dad, you've forgotten the cherry!' Linda reminded him.

Jack went to the cupboard and got out the specially purchased jar of Maraschino cherries, along with a box of cocktail sticks.

'Here, you can stab your own cherry.' He said, offering the open jar to the girls. They each pulled out a bright red ball with their cocktail sticks and dropped them into their drinks.

'Just a minute you've haven't got your straws,' Jack said, handing over a couple of candy striped, waxed paper straws. 'Right that's everyone done, I'll go back in the other room and save your Uncle Harold from being bored to death, by all those women, nattering on about the price of eggs.'

The girls joined David at the dining room table where he had set up the Ker-Plunk game. Elaine pursed her lips around the straw and took a hard suck, then she exclaimed, 'Wow that's divine! I can't remember ever drinking something so wonderful.'

'Divine! I suppose soon, you'll be speaking like that as well Linda,' David, teased his cousin.

'Like what?' Linda snapped back.

'All posh!'

143

'Shut up David!' Linda came back at him and kicked his shin under the table.

'Ow! I'll have to go and put my new shin pads on if you're going to keep that up all evening,' David yelled, which made the girls laugh. 'So what's it been like, being away from home for such a long time?'

'It's been good, I've had a great time,' Linda answered firmly.

'Better than Queen's Manor?' David persisted.

'Yes, loads better.'

'In what way?'

'It's just not so big and chaotic, plus the teachers are very good. I've learned loads of stuff, since I've been there.'

'I'm not surprised, you're at school all the time, seven days a week.'

'Yes, but we don't have lessons the entire time silly. We have plenty of free time as well.'

'What do you do in your free time then?'

'Well, we can go out, down to the local village.'

'When we are not gated,' piped up Elaine, and the two girls burst into fits of closed-mouthed giggles.

'What the hell is "gated"?' David asked, bemused by the jargon and the mystery of boarding school life.

'It's like detention. Only it lasts all weekend, not just half an hour. You have to stay within the grounds of the school.

'So what did you do to get gated then,' David pried.

The two girls looked at each other and smiled, 'We had a cream tea down at the village. You are only allowed to spend sixpence at the weekend, but I spent *ten bob*!' Linda declared with a loud bravado laced laugh. 'We got gated for three weeks,' she

144

added proudly, hoping that the confession would impress her cousin.

'Is that all you did! Ten bob for some tea and cakes, I could have bought a brand new Subbuteo team for that,' David dismissed her bad girl act out of hand.

'Oh, you and blooming football,' Linda retaliated, disappointed by his reaction. 'I bet, everything you got for Christmas, was connected to blasted football.'

David considered the question for a few seconds and then concurred, 'Yes, I think everything was football related, except a boring old French dictionary from my Aunt Celia, which I'll never use, because I'm giving up French next year. Oh, a couple of weeks ago, I saw your friend standing outside Mrs Platt's office, looking very sorry for herself.'

'Who . . . Janet? What on earth would she have done, to have to go and see Mrs. Platt?' Linda pondered about Janet's improbable circumstances. 'Are you sure it was Janet?'

'Yeah, dark hair in bunches and tortoise-shell framed glasses. She must have done something pretty bad, 'cause it looked like she was going to burst into tears at any second. Those other girls from your class were there too. The ones that you had the dust-up with.'

'Why would Janet be there with them?'

'She goes around with them now. I bet they all bunked off to go down the market on Friday morning,' David hypothesised.

Linda was stunned by the thought of Janet befriending the gang of girls, who had given them so much trouble the previous year. While David continued to speculate, a feeling of betrayal gripped her.

'Well you can't blame her, you had cleared off to your posh school, and she was left on her own – so it was probably her best bet.' David said forcefully.

145

Linda paused and considered what David had said; he was correct, what right did she have, to feel let down by someone, she had not even given a second thought to, when the chance arose for her to escape the torments of the bullies. A dark mood of personal remorse quickly replaced the spike of anger that she had felt about her friend's perceived disloyalty.

'Do you ever get bullied David?' Elaine asked, breaking the momentary silence.

'Nah, I'm in the school football team, so the tough guys tend to leave me alone,' David answered.

'Why docs being in the school team give you protection?' Elaine pressed.

'I dunno really, it just does. Colin Hooper and me got hassled by an older kid on the way to school once. He wanted our dinner money.'

'What happened?' Elaine implored, anxious for the details.

'Colin punched him really hard on the jaw. You should have seen the look of shock on the guy's face as he toppled back over a garden wall,' David laughed gleefully at the memory.

'What happened then?' Linda said, sucking in another mouthful of her delicious snowball.

'We legged it down the road as fast as we could, just in case he got up!'

'Did you see him again?' Linda grilled her cousin for more information.

'Nah, I think he was either bunking off from another school, or he had left school completely and was trying to steal money from easy targets. Either way, we never saw him again. Are you two getting some bullying at your school then?'

'We get a bit of trouble from a few girls. Please don't tell your mum David, 'cause she'll tell mine, and then she'll just worry all the time that I'm away,' Linda pleaded.

146

'Nah, don't worry, I won't. Must be nasty if you're getting aggro off of these girls and can't get away from them. You'll have to stand up to them, like Colin did and see what happens,' David advised.

'What, punch her in the face? I don't think I could do that,' Linda smiled, while imagining herself doing it.

'Well you did tell Louise to "fuck off" the last time that she annoyed you, Linda,' Elaine whispered, trying to suppress a giggle.

'*Did you!* I didn't think you knew words like that, I'll have to tell Aunty Liz that the posh school isn't working!' David goaded, guffawing with laughter. 'What did she do when you said it?'

'Nothing really, she just looked a bit amazed that I had said it,' Linda replied, feeling her face blush, agitated by the pang of guilt that her confession had provoked. But she was pleased that David finally looked impressed by something that she had done.

The door opened and Jack came in carrying a tray of empty glasses, 'Who's winning the Ker-Plunk thing then?'

'We haven't really started yet Dad,' Linda said, as her father rushed past into the kitchen.

'Are you lot ready for another drink as well?' he shouted, as he put the tin tray down on the yellow Formica kitchen table, causing the glasses to jingle against each other.

'Yes please!' the three underage drinkers shouted back an enthusiastic chorus of approval to his suggestion. 'And can we have two more straws Dad? These have gone soggy and flat at the ends,' Linda added.

#   #   #

At seven o'clock Liz came through from the front room, to tell them that she needed the table to put the evening savouries and snack food on. After the game had been carefully replaced into its box, another round of over-eating began. Soon it was time for *The Morecambe and Wise Christmas show*, which everyone wanted to

147

see, so with the addition of a couple of straight back chairs from the dining room, they all squeezed into the front room, to watch the television highlight of the holiday. A John Wayne comic western film called, *McLintock!* rounded off the day, but this failed to hold the attention of the female component of the room, and general chit-chat sporadically broke out, much to annoyance of the male watchers. At half past eleven, Christmas Day was almost over and the girls stood shivering at the open front door, waving goodbye to Gwen, Harold and David, as they started their fifteen-minute journey home on foot. By the time the trio had got back to their house, Linda and Elaine were already tucked up in bed and were indulging in drowsy pillow talk about the various high points of the day.

'Thank you again for my lovely silver necklace, it's quite simply the best present I've ever been given,' Elaine sighed, with contentment. 'I'm not going to let my aunts know I've got it, because, jewellery isn't allowed during term time and I'll only get to wear it in the holidays. I thought, I could hide it up in the secret room and then put it on whenever we go up there.'

'That's a good idea. Dad told me, when we were out yesterday, that he needs to take us back a day early – will that be okay with Miss Rutherford . . . I mean your aunt?'

'Yes, I'm sure that will be fine, there are always some girls who have to come back a day or two earlier, especially if they live overseas and can only get flights back on certain dates.'

'Great! With hardly anyone about, we should be able to smuggle a few things up to the room, on that Friday.' Linda speculated and then changed the subject. 'Did you like David?'

'Yes, he was funny and very good looking,' Elaine quietly approved and then batted the question back to Linda. 'Would you like him to be your boyfriend?'

'Oh no, he can't ever be my boyfriend, because we are cousins, and if we did get married and had children, they might be deformed or not all there in the head, or something. Mum told me that ages ago.'

148

'*Really?* I never knew that?' Elaine gasped at the revelation.

'You can marry him though,' giggled Linda. 'I saw him giving you a look over when you weren't watching.'

'Did he! I never saw that,' Elaine suppressed a squeal, the best she could.

'He was probably wondering what it would be like to kiss you on the lips.'

'Is that what boys are thinking when they give you a look over?'

'Yes, I think so? Who would you like to kiss?' Linda asked.

'I don't know – Cliff Richard?'

'He is very nice looking isn't he, but I think if I could kiss anyone it would be Charlotte, she is just so beautiful.'

'Have you got a "pash" for her then?'

'Yes I think so, I get this funny feeling whenever I see her, and she is so perfect I just wish I was her.'

CHAPTER THIRTEEN
16ᵗʰ January 1970

12.15 pm

Friday the sixteenth of January came around all too quickly and it was time for Linda and Elaine to return to school. After making good time on the motorway, Jack pulled into the drive of Grenchwood Hall School for Girls just after mid-day.

Aunt Iona was there to greet them and was soon joined on the front steps by Amelia, who was uncharacteristically affable. While the girls' bags and cases were taken from the car boot, the adults had a brief exchange of niceties, regarding the holiday break, and not long after, Jack was back in the car and heading out of the grounds of the school, on his return journey.

Once in the building, Aunt Iona invited the girls into her little office for a cup of tea, where Elaine regaled her with a few anecdotes from her cookery adventures, whilst staying with Linda's parents. After finishing their tea, the two girls lugged their suitcases through the strangely silent corridors and up the echoing stairway into the empty Dormitory Five.

After the considerable effort of conveying the luggage, Linda threw herself onto her bed, and looking up at the ceiling, she suddenly called out, 'Oh! The Turin Shroud has gone!'

'What?' Elaine queried.

'The strange stain on the ceiling that reminded me of the Turin Shroud, has been painted over.'

Elaine looked up.

'Oh my aunts will have had some local decorators in over the holidays to patch things up a bit – it does look a bit better now.'

'I got used to looking up and seeing those blotches. I pretended the shape was my guardian angel, looking over me!' Linda chuckled at the inane comment that she had made and then jumped down off the bed to open her case. 'Look what I've got!' she said triumphantly, holding up a full bottle of Advocaat.

'Where did you get that?' Elaine screeched, open mouthed with surprise.

'I found it down in the cellar, and I've got half a bottle of lime juice and a full bottle of lemonade. The only thing we haven't got are the cherries!'

'Won't your dad miss it?'

'No, he doesn't drink it, neither does Mum – if I hadn't taken it, the bottle would still be down the cellar next Christmas. Anyway if he does notice that it's gone, I'm two hundred miles away!' replied the self-assured Linda, smiling smugly. 'I've also got some batteries for the tranny, a set of cards, a pack of drawing pins – so we can put up some more posters, and a large box of Maltesers, which Mum did give me to bring back here. When shall we move it all up to the room?'

'Let's do it now, while we are the only ones here. It will make a change not having my heart in my mouth when we go up to the top floor,' Elaine decided.

'Right, I'll put all the stuff in my duffel bag, so it'll be easier to carry. Where's the key?'

'Before we came away for the Christmas hols, I hid it under the brick, down by the greenhouses, where the other keys are, just in case anyone looked under my bedside cabinet.'

151

Elaine set off to retrieve the key while Linda carefully transferred the plundered goods into her duffel bag. Ten minutes later they were ready to advance up the stairs to the "out-of-bounds" area of the school. Even though they were confident that they were alone in the school, there was still a small doubt at the back of their minds, that they might be seen. Cautiously they tiptoed all the way along the unlit top corridor, with Linda cradling the duffel bag like a baby in her arms. In the shadowy half-light, it was difficult to focus on the keyhole, Elaine slowly offered up the key to the brass lock, when from behind her, the unmistakable cracking sound, of a door opening, froze her like a pillar of salt.

'And what do you two, think you are doing up here?' came an ethereal voice, from the darkness. Slowly the girls turned around, their eyes ever widening, probing through the murk to see who had caught them.

'It's all right, it's only me,' they immediately recognised Charlotte's voice. 'Your faces! You look like you have just seen a ghost!' Charlotte laughed. 'Were you going to try and open that door?'

'No . . . we were just exploring,' Linda offered up the most plausible excuse she could muster in her shocked state.

'You *were* trying to open it, *weren't* you! What have you got in the bag, come on hand it over,' Charlotte firmly instructed. Linda passed the heavy bag over to her and the glass bottles clinked together, making it obvious to Charlotte that she was about to uncover something worthwhile.

'I see . . . this looks like a bottle of Advocaat, and a bottle of lemonade, and here are some sweets,' she groped her hand around the bag. 'So, do you usually go exploring laden down with booze, and how were you going to get into the closed off part of the school?'

'I've got a key,' Elaine said faintly, swallowing her dry throat. 'Are you going to report us?'

152

'No of course not! I've always wanted to know what's behind this door, come on, open it up, let's explore,' Charlotte beamed.

Elaine unlocked the large oak door and its own weight caused it to gently swing open, allowing them all to step inside.

'Um . . . strange smell,' Charlotte said, sniffing at the stale chilled air.

'You do get used to it,' Linda informed her.

Charlotte pushed open the first door that she came to and ventured inside.

'Christ, it's got the feeling of the *Marie Celeste*!' Charlotte judged, as she viewed the time-capsule bedroom. 'Everything is just the same, as on the day that it was vacated, except there's about a quarter of inch of grime over everything now.'

She picked up an abandoned magazine lying on the top of a set of drawers and knocked off the grey veneer of dust from it, causing a cloud of tiny particles to rise around the room. Covering her mouth against the floating lint Charlotte examined the cover of the *Picturegoer* magazine, with its typical fifties duo-tone style printing. The young film star Jill Ireland stared back at her through the remaining film of dust.

'May 1955, these rooms can't have been used for nearly fifteen years, except of course, by you two,' she smiled.

'Our room is next door, it's bigger and has windows on two sides,' Elaine said, leading the way down the darkened corridor.

'Oh look, there's another door,' Charlotte shouted, pointing to what looked like the continuation of the wood panelling. 'Behind here, there must be a staircase that leads all the way down to the kitchen, in the basement. The male servants would have used these stairs to get up to their quarters in the evenings. Just think of all the generations of housemaids and footmen, who were kept apart by the dividing door in the corridor – what would they have given

153

for your spare key!' Charlotte giggled. She pulled at the door but it was locked. 'Do you have the key for this door Elaine?'

'I might have, I found a bunch of them, but I haven't got them on me, they're buried down by the old greenhouses. I never ever realised before that this was a door,' Elaine answered, while turning around and entering the next bedroom. 'Well, what do you think?'

'Wow! This room is really groovy – I love the posters on the wall, not sure about all these tools scattered about though. Did you start to paint the wall?'

'No, this is how it was left, when they decided to block this section off,' Elaine responded.

'Seems strange, why would they leave all their tools? Anyway, who cares, let's get the booze out!' Charlotte commanded, plonking down on the mattress.

Linda opened up the transistor radio and replaced the 9-volt battery, instantly the room reverberated to the beat of Edison Lighthouse's "Love Grows". Charlotte jumped to her feet and started dancing. 'This is the kind of dance they're all doing in the discothèque's and nightclubs in London. One night we went to the Marquee club, it was just fantastic!' Charlotte breathed, her blond hair swinging out of control, as she gyrated around the room.

'Did you go to many nightclubs?' Linda asked, admiring Charlotte's suggestive dance moves.

'Yeah, every night while I was in London, it was great. I met all sorts of interesting people.'

'Did you meet any famous photographers?'

'Well, I met some that wanted to be famous!'

'Are any of them going to take the pictures for your portfolio?'

'No, all they wanted to do, was take shots of me in the nude,' Charlotte laughed, collapsing back onto the bed, when the

154

song finished. 'What about you two, did you have a good Christmas?'

'We had a great time down at Linda's parents home, and look at the lovely present Linda gave me,' Elaine said, proudly showed off her silver e, to Charlotte.

'That looks fab, what a nice gift. Let's all dance to this one, it's my fav,' Charlotte enthusiastically pulled the girls to the middle of the floor and they vigorously cavorted about on the bare wooden floorboards. 'I love the Tremeloes, don't you?'

After several more energetic dances that helped them all keep warm, Linda prepared three snowball drinks, which were eagerly consumed, with murmurs of appreciation.

'One night, I got really pissed after I drank a load of cocktails, called Whiskey Sours,' Charlotte announced to her captivated audience. 'I puked up in a dustbin somewhere in Soho, at about three in the morning. I had a terrible head the next day. I don't know why I had so many, I didn't even like the taste very much.'

'Why have you come back a day early?' Linda asked.

'Oh, my bloody sister's boyfriend, Jonathan, made a pass at me, while she was out shopping. So I decided not to risk a lift with him and got the train up here yesterday.'

'What . . . did he do?' Linda tentatively pressed for further details, hoping that it wouldn't be obvious that she was excited, by what Charlotte was saying.

'I knew he was going to try something – he had been looking at me a bit funny for a couple of days. As soon as we were on our own, he pounced on me, trying to snog me and his hands were everywhere. I told him NO, but of course he didn't stop, pushed me onto the sofa and tried to get my knickers down.' Charlotte didn't spare the wide-eyed girls any of the sordid facts. 'Anyway, I managed to grab hold of his stupid lava lamp and banged him over the bonce with it.'

'Did you knock him out?' Linda enquired, enthusiastically.

155

'No, but he had quite a lump on his forehead though!' Charlotte laughed. 'I think he only stopped because he thought I would damage his silly lamp. If he had asked nicely, I might have let him do it, he is very dishy and it would have pissed off my sister,' Charlotte guffawed with a burst of laughter, at the thought of annoying her sister. Linda and Elaine joined in the merriment, but both were inwardly shocked that Charlotte was so unrestrained when talking about sexual matters.

Encouraged by Charlotte's accessible demeanour, Linda pushed for more tantalising enlightenment, about what was for her, the taboo subject of sex.

'Have you . . . ever done it?' she asked, the tension in her voice rising noticeably, in the second half of her short sentence.

'What, had sex?' Charlotte clarified, nonchalantly.

'Yes, actually done it with somebody?'

'Yes! I've "done it" four times.'

'Have you!' the girls exclaimed in unison, looking at each other with eyes and mouths open in astounded wonderment.

'Yes, the first time was last summer, with a boy who lives a few houses up from ours. He's a couple of years older than me and was home from university. His parents have a tennis court in their garden, so I used that as an excuse to pop around and have a game with him. After a few times, he started to get more confident and it wasn't long before he hit on me. We went up to his bedroom on the pretext to listen to his *Between the Buttons* LP by the Stones, after a few minutes we were snogging like mad on the bed, and then . . . well, things got a bit more intense and before I knew it, I'd been shagged for the first time.'

Charlotte's candid confession released a torrent of agitated questions from the two rapt girls.

'Did it hurt?' Elaine asked.

'Only a bit, it's nothing to worry about,' Charlotte answered succinctly.

156

'Were you frightened?' Linda continued the cross-examination.

'No, it just felt right.'

'Did you tell your mother?' Elaine inquired, naively.

'God no! If I had, she would have been around there, wanting her go!' Charlotte made a nasal sniggering noise at the idea.

'Were you in love with him?' Linda continued to quiz.

'No, I liked him, but I didn't love him.'

'My mum says you have to be in love with someone to have a baby with them.'

'Well, your mum is right, but we were just having sex, not making a baby.'

'What's the difference? How did you know you wouldn't have a baby?'

'Because, he used a rubber johnny.'

'What's that?'

'It stops the man's sperm from reaching the woman's egg. Soon, when I go to London – now that you don't have to be married to get it – I'll go on the contraceptive pill. Then the guy doesn't need to wear a rubber. How much about the "birds and the bees", do you both know?'

'Not that much,' Linda replied for the both of them.

'Have you started your periods yet?'

Linda and Elaine turned to each other with awkward smiles, but nodded a definite "yes" to the question.

'Linda, hasn't your mother had a talk to you, about the "facts of life"?'

'Not really, but at my last school, just before I went to the Christmas disco, she warned me, that if they played a slow song and

157

I let a boy dance close up to me, and I felt something hard pressing onto my tummy – I was to slap his face and walk away.'

Charlotte let out a screaming laugh.

'Well, did that happen?' she asked, hopefully.

'No, none of the boys would dance – they all just stood over to one side of the hall and watched us girls jigging about. It wasn't until we had a sex education film shown to us at school and I saw a cartoon of a boy's willy swelling up, that I realised what she had meant!' laughing uncontrollably, Linda threw her hands up to her face and felt the flush of heat, that her words had caused.

'So, what else did the film explain?' Charlotte asked, with wry smile.

'Well, it was mostly cartoons about rabbits and then some cartoons about how boys' and girls' bodies would change shape. Oh, and then a man said, that when they are "in love" the man and the woman would lie together in a special way to make a baby. So, I sort of know what happens, I think?' Linda concluded hazily.

Seeing the vague expressions on the two girls' faces, Charlotte decided it was high time to enlighten them, on the real intricacies of love-making.

'Right, I'm going to tell you everything you need to know, and it won't involve rabbits or cartoons of boys cocks.' She then spent the next twenty-five minutes extolling, the intimate carnal delights that they could expect to experience in the future. The girls viewed Charlotte's disclosures, as being variously; fascinating, unbelievable or disgusting, but by the end, there was absolutely no lingering uncertainty in their minds, about the act of sexual intercourse.

After the impromptu sex education lesson, there followed the imbibing of more snowballs and the fervent decimation of the box of Maltesers. The trio, then set to work, to completely cover the half painted wall, by pinning up more photos of pop stars, cut from the magazines that littered the bare floorboards. The watery winter sunshine, which had softly illuminated the room during the

158

afternoon, began to fade, resulting in a sharp fall in temperature and grudgingly, they agreed to go back to Charlotte's room for a warming cup of tea. Before leaving, Elaine put her precious silver necklace and the transistor radio, into the skirting board cavity for safekeeping, and then she pushed the cabinet over to conceal the tiny hidden chamber.

CHAPTER FOURTEEN
17th January 1970

1.55 pm

By lunchtime on Saturday, the majority of the pupils and teachers, had returned to the school, it seemed, that all anyone wanted to do, was to talk about their Christmas break. Throughout the building, little huddles of excited girls clustered together; screaming with laughter and waving their arms in manic animation, as they described something amusing that had happened to them, during the holiday. Linda's happy mood quickly transposed to vexation, when she caught sight of the dreaded Louise. She had secretly hoped and silently prayed, that the loathsome girl would have met with a fatal accident while on holiday. It wasn't long before Louise was holding court in the dormitory, determined to quickly re-establish herself as the undisputed leader of the group, after losing some dominion toward the end of the previous term.

'Hands up, who saw the *Morecambe and Wise* show on Christmas Day,' she ordered, virtually every girl raised their hand up in the air. 'Keep your hand up, if you saw it in colour!' she continued, her trademark puffed-up grin, smirked across her face, as she watched nearly all the hands begin to lower. Panning the room, she was noticeably shocked, to see Linda and Elaine, still with their hands up. 'I said, in *colour!*' she reiterated loudly, thinking that they must have not been paying attention.

160

'Yes I heard you,' Linda said, smiling sweetly back at her. 'We watched it in colour.'

'Not at your own home?' Louise postulated, unable to comprehend, how on earth Linda's parents would be able to afford something so extravagant as a colour set.

'Yes, in my mum and dad's front room, to be absolutely exact,' Linda informed her, in a mocking tone, which caused the rest of the room to giggle nervously. Louise's face was like thunder; her frustrated rage revealed itself by the way her fists tightly clenched the top blanket on her bed. Picking up on this, Linda prepared herself for an onslaught.

'I expect your father, got his colour television, off of the back of a lorry,' Louise taunted.

'Well, it was delivered by a lorry and it took two men to carry it in,' Linda quipped back at her, which again, made the onlookers snigger. 'But, I'm sure he bought it from the Coop.'

'My father says, all trade unionist should be put up against a wall and shot, before they completely ruin the country,' Louise announced, deciding to attack Linda's family antecedents.

'Then, he wouldn't have anyone to fix his car, when it went wrong, would he?'

'We would just buy another one,' Louise laughed, ending the squabble by contemptuously strutting out of the room with Susan in tow. The significance that only Susan left the room with Louise was not lost on Linda.

\#   \#   \#

On Monday morning, before the first lesson began, Miss Iona handed out a small square of paper to each girl, and while walking around the classroom she explained, that the paper was a voting slip, for the new term's Form Captain.

'Right then girls, can I have your nominations for Form Captain?' she asked.

161

Susan's hand shot up and without waiting for permission, she called out, 'I would like to nominate Louise Bennington, Miss.'

'Louise, are you prepared to continue as Form Captain for another term?' Miss Iona asked.

'Yes, I would regard it as an honour, Miss,' Louise declared, with a supercilious grin of victory already shivering on her lips.

'Do I have a seconder for Louise?' continued Miss Iona. Immediately Cressida raised her arm.

'Remember, if you nominate or second someone, you are honour-bound to vote for them. Now, are there any more nominees or will Louise run for office unopposed?' Iona said, looking around the room hopefully. 'Anyone else?'

Annabel slowly put her hand up and stunned the room, by proclaiming, 'I would like to nominate Linda.'

Without bothering to ask if Linda was prepared to stand as Form Captain, Miss Iona requested a seconder. Elaine spiritedly volunteered her arm to this proposal and the contest was ratified.

'Very well girls, we will have, what is called a secret ballot, you will write on your piece of paper, the name, of whom you want as your Form Captain, either, Louise or Linda, then fold the paper in half and put it into the cardboard box on my desk.'

Each girl in turn, left her seat and went up to the front of the classroom to post her vote. Miss Iona gave a brief lecture about the voting system of the United Kingdom, which was largely ignored, as the girls' attentions were entirely focused on the possible outcome of the mini-election.

'At least I'll get three votes,' Linda whispered, to Elaine.

Miss Iona tipped the contents of the box out onto her desk and then unwrapped each folded slip of paper, placing the open sheet either to the left, or right of her.

'The result of Dorm Five's Form Captain election is – Louise Bennington six votes,' there was a pause for dramatic effect,

162

before Miss Iona delivered the final result. 'Linda Middlewick six votes.' A high-pitched audible gasp of surprise that sounded like escaping gas, filled the room.

'It falls to me, to cast the deciding vote,' Miss Iona announced. 'The new Form Captain will be Linda.'

There was a spontaneous burst of applause, which with some reluctance, the vanquished supporters of Louise, joined in with. Louise shot Linda a look, her face set in brooding anger, which transmitted a definite hostile intent to the new Form Captain.

#   #   #

Throughout the rest of the week, the still seething Louise, provoked Linda into a series of verbal altercations, in an attempt to undermine and criticise everything that she tried to do.

The following Saturday, Linda and Elaine intended to visit the secret room and finish off the remaining sweets and lemonade. After breakfast, whilst it was still quiet, Elaine went to collect the key from where it was hidden, down by the old greenhouses. During the morning, the girls noticed an ominous leaden sky and could hear rumblings of thunder echoing around the hills, which sounded like they were coming ever closer. The prospect of bad weather, meant that most of the other girls would be forced to remain within the confines of the school building for the rest of the day, so at lunchtime, Linda and Elaine agreed on the cancellation of their illicit expedition to the top floor.

During the afternoon, up in the dormitory, a continuing series of terse exchanges between Linda and Louise, served to slowly tighten the mounting tension between them, stretching it close to breaking point.

Elaine decided that she had better return the key back to its usual hiding place, in case somebody discovered it in her top drawer. Clutching the key in her right hand, she skipped around the end of her bed, but caught her foot on the leg, causing her to stumble. Instinctively, she threw her arms out to steady herself, but this sudden jerking movement, resulted in the key slipping from her fingers. She made a desperate grab for it, while it tumbled in midair,

163

only to knock it further away from her. The key clinked on the wooden floor, bounced twice, end over end and came to rest under Linda's bed.

'What's that?' demanded Louise, alerted by the metallic pinging sound that broke the silence of the dorm.

'Nothing!' Elaine shouted, the panic apparent in her voice.

'Yes it is, show me,' Louise badgered, leaping from her bed for a closer look.

'It's nothing to do with you,' Elaine said, and then slid full length under Linda's bed to retrieve the precious key.

'Let me see what you have in your hand.'

'No get off me!'

Louise pushed Elaine down onto the bed and grabbed at her hand in an effort to make her release her grip.

'Get off her,' Linda yelled, giving Louise a forceful shove from behind.

Louise twisted around and threw out a hand, which caught Linda on the side of her head. Linda reacted impulsively, sending an instant retaliatory blow that smacked loudly across Louise's face, the shock from this, made her stagger back a couple of steps, before she gathered herself and mounted a counter attack, by lunging at Linda with both hands. The two girls fell to the floor in a heap, grappling with one another, pulling at clothes and trying to scratch at any exposed skin. The rest of the room massed around and screamed encouragement at the two combatants, the hubbub that this caused, intensified the general pandemonium of the fracas. Linda's shirtsleeve ripped down from the shoulder and her head snapped back against the iron bedstead with a sickening thud. The blinding pain caused her to swing her free right arm wildly; there was jolting impact to her clenched fist as it hit something hard. Louise's grip slackened and then went limp, as she convulsed with the anguish from the blow to her mouth. Unsure of what to do next, Linda glanced up to see Annabel's contorted face, radiating ruthless pleasure. Above the commotion being made by the other girls, she

164

heard her screech, 'Hit her again!' It was an instruction that Linda was more than happy to comply with. Pulling herself up onto her hands and knees, she made her small hand into a tight fist, drawing it back, so that it was ready to launch another punch. The release of the pent-up anger Linda felt for Louise, powered her fist into the dazed girl's cheek. Descending like a stupefied boxer on the ropes, Louise slumped from a sitting position, to lying prone on her side. Linda experienced an incomparable sizzle of pleasure, from her complete dominance over her hated rival. Just as she was going to inflict another exhilarating blow, she felt her arms being seized and her body being pulled up to the standing position.

'What in the name of God, is going on in here?' Miss Ryan screamed, expelling tiny flecks of spit, which landed on Linda's face, causing her to flinch. The dormitory was now in complete silence and full of teachers, prefects and other pupils keen to see what all the excitement was about. Miss Neame and Monica Finch-Reeves had pulled Louise to her feet and were both holding her tightly by her arms.

'She hit me! Look at my lip,' Louise spat out her accusation.

'Louise started it Miss, she attacked Elaine and then slapped Linda across the face,' Annabel piped up from the gaggle, motivated by the irresistible urge to exact revenge on Louise.

'No I never! It was her, she lives on a council estate, what do you expect,' Louise pleaded, in a whining drone.

'I don't care who started it, you are both going down to the headmistress, she can deal with you,' bellowed Miss Ryan, who then turned to lead the way through the crowd, which in urgent deference, parted to allow the procession to pass. Linda meekly followed, her arms being held by two prefects, who both towered over her and resembled two police officers arresting an unresisting anti-Vietnam war demonstrator. In stark contrast, Louise was not going to submit with dignity, she tried to thwart the inescapable march down to the headmistress's study, by attempting to break free from her escorts. Her efforts were futile, Miss Neame and Monica were far stronger than her and she was simply dragged along, until

165

they were all almost running. The throng made its way past the girls waiting on the landing and down the stairway, where Louise attracted the attention of the few remaining members of the school, who were not aware of what was happening, by wailing her innocence in a soprano pitch. As the troupe passed along the oak panelled passageway, leading to the headmistress's study, Charlotte came striding towards them. Witnessing the dishevelled state of the two smaller girls, within the advancing group, she pensively asked, 'What the hell has been going on?'

'These two have been fighting like common fishwives,' Miss Ryan informed her, without breaking stride. 'I'm taking them to the headmistress for punishment.'

'Wait, don't you think they have administered enough punishment on each other?' Charlotte proposed, trying to get Miss Ryan to stop and inspect the two contused miscreants. Miss Ryan declined to answer Charlotte's question and instead continued to walk briskly down the corridor. On reaching Miss Rutherford's room she grabbed the door handle and without knocking, threw the door open, affecting a dramatic entrance. Miss Rutherford was clearly startled at the sight of over a dozen, animated individuals, spilling into her study, without invitation.

'These two girls have been fighting each other,' Miss Ryan, curtly informed the headmistress, her face twisted with anger. Yanking Linda and Louise by their wrists, she roughly propelled them, so they both stood directly in front of the large desk. Miss Rutherford took a moment to study the girls standing apologetically in front of her. Louise's face, was bright red and tear-stained, her top lip was seeping a slight graze of blood, which she nervously licked away, and just under her left eye, there was a discolouration of a small bruise. Linda was breathing heavily from the adrenalin rush that the fight had produced. She had red wine coloured scratch marks on her cheek and hands, with her torn shirt revealing more vertical rake-like marks on her upper arm. The injured condition of both girls bore testimony to the ferocity of their brawl. Miss Rutherford seemed to lack her usual self-assurance and the room remained totally silent, waiting for a reaction from her.

166

'They need to be severely punished for such a display of hooligan behaviour, this is a girls' school not a wild-west saloon,' Miss Ryan broke the silence by opening the case for the prosecution. Glaring at the girls, she continued to press for the maximum sentence. 'I know it's an old adage, but "Spare the rod and spoil the child" is as valid now, as it ever was. You have to eradicate this type of behaviour quickly, or it will become the accepted standard.'

Miss Ryan, had made her thoughts about what she saw, as the breakdown of discipline, known to the younger headmistress several times before. Observing the various members of staff present, Amelia Rutherford correctly deduced that they had used this serious affray, as an excuse to gatecrash her study and see for themselves, whether she was up to the task, of curtailing any future schoolgirl anarchy.

'It's not fair, it wasn't my fault,' Louise cried, deciding to conduct her own defence and feeling deeply uneasy by the fact, that a visit to the legendary chair, was an imminent possibility. 'She just attacked me!'

'You hit me first,' flared Linda, her lacerated cheeks reddening still deeper with indignation.

'That was an accident!'

'You were hurting Elaine.'

'That was just horseplay.'

'Stop!' Miss Rutherford finally spoke. 'You are, of course right Miss Ryan, this kind of thuggish behaviour simply cannot be tolerated. However distasteful I find it, as the headmistress, it falls upon me, to administer any corporal punishment that is necessary. You will both receive six of the hairbrush.' Like a high court judge, she passed the mandatory sentence on the two sorry-looking girls. Dipping down to her right, Miss Rutherford opened the bottom drawer of her desk and produced a large, shiny hardwood backed, Mason Pearson hairbrush, which had been solemnly used on such occasions, since the school had opened in 1922. For both condemned girls, the arresting sight of the instrument of castigation,

167

caused time to stand still, as they envisaged their very immediate futures. 'Louise, please go over and kneel on the chair by the window,'

'No!' Louise screamed in a blind panic, 'I won't, it isn't fair, she attacked me!'

Miss Ryan grabbed Louise by the arm and tried to drag her across the room, but the frantic girl physically resisted, by tensing her body and flailing her free arm around wildly. Miss Neame and Monica came to the assistance of the struggling elderly teacher, each managed to clutch a part of the Louise's body and scramble her over to the place of execution. The unseemly performance of delivering and positioning the hysterical girl onto the chair, played out in a single act, before the astounded assembly of onlookers. Louise continued to writhe against the holds that enshrouded her, but she was no match for the combined strength of three adult women. Miss Rutherford quickly located herself to the left of the writhing, pinned-down girl, then without pausing, raised the hairbrush, which she held tightly in her right hand and brought it down viciously, across the squirming posterior, presented in front of her. The distinct smack of the blow was paralleled by an asphyxiated scream of pain. Even before the trailing resonance of the cry had been fully absorbed into the study walls, Miss Rutherford had unleashed a second strike onto the intended target. Like Anne Jones, the previous year's Wimbledon champion, discharging a barrage of ferocious cross-court forehands, the headmistress meted out the full six strokes of the punishment. The instant that Louise was released, allowing her the unrestricted use of her hands again, she shot them both to her burning backside, and then falling to her knees on the floor, she wailed like a wounded animal.

Miss Rutherford took a deep breath, titled her head around and for a few seconds stared directly into Linda's eyes. Using the hairbrush, she pointed at the chair. Although visibly shaking, Linda answered the gesture, by advancing unaided towards the seat, stepping over the sobbing, recumbent Louise on route. She vowed to herself, not to lose her pride and dignity in front of the crowded room of enraptured viewers, certainly not in the same, piteous way,

168

as her reviled adversary had done. She slowly knelt up onto the springy cushioned seat of the upholstered chair, placed her arms on the side wings and braced her torso against the gently sloping inside back. Looking out of the bay window, she could make out the blurred colours of the distant traffic, speeding on the hillside road, which skirted the village. A vivacious squirrel darted up the thick trunk of the single yew tree, lonely situated in the corner of the lawn, and there right in front of her, a shiny blackbird, obliviously pecked away, looking for worms in the rain-sodden grass. Linda felt like she was cocooned in some kind of bubble, nothing seemed real, this should not have been happening to her, how could the rest of the world be going on as usual, while her world, was in such turmoil.

A movement behind her that she detected in a reflection on the windowpane, signalled that her arduous ordeal was about to commence. Having just witnessed Louise's punishment and the resulting histrionics, Linda should have been all too well aware, of just how potentially painful, the application of an oval piece of heavy solid wood to the buttocks, was likely to be. The resulting raw pain, which exploded on her rear, was like no other burning sting she had ever experienced in her life. The intense shock caused an involuntary arch in her back and her hands to lift from the top of the chair. Miss Rutherford interrupted her rhythm and allowed a second, to see if Linda would recover her position. When she did, the headmistress instantly delivered the next blow. Linda's back arched again, as she desperately fought the temptation to cry out a plea for mercy. On the impact of the third strike, she tried unsuccessfully to stifle a cry of anguish, by pressing her open mouth against the padded upholstery. The rapid flurry of spanks continued to relentlessly find their mark, causing her distress to intensify, as the hurt had no time to dissipate itself. Linda clamped her teeth furiously on her bottom lip and tensed all her muscles against the torturous attack on her rump. The metronomic smacks of the hairbrush stopped, and through glassy, tear-filled eyes, Linda could make out the shape of the blackbird still on the lawn, below her. She blinked the wetness away and the outside world refocused into perfect clarity. The blackbird pulled a worm from the ground, flipped it around a couple of times and then swallowed it in one

169

gulp. Looking up, it seemed to notice Linda staring back; after nodding its head in acknowledgement, the bird sang a short refrain to her and then flew away to the safety of the yew tree. Although in pain, Linda couldn't help but smile to herself, at the surreal absurdity of the previous sixty seconds, even though, the sharp throbbing in her buttocks was uppermost in her mind. She unhurriedly reversed herself from the chair and turned to confront the breathless audience, who, from the looks on their faces, had been variously affected by what they had just witnessed. A gamut of different expressions peered silently back at her, ranging from the pity, shock, and concern, end of the spectrum, through to the antonym, of scorn, amusement, and inappropriate, *schadenfreude*. As an act of passive defiance, Linda resisted the almost overwhelming desire, to rub away some of the smarting in her hindquarters.

She tried to catch the eye of Miss Rutherford, but it was obvious that the headmistress did not want to return the glance.

'Now! Would everyone please, kindly leave my study, *immediately!*' Miss Rutherford vociferated, clearly unsettled by the unpleasant episode. Heeding her command, the room was quickly vacated. Outside in the corridor, Charlotte prised herself between Linda and Louise and took hold of their hands, like a boxing referee, about to announce the winner of a bout, by raising the victor's arm.

'Right, I'll take you both up to the dorm,' she declared, waiting for the crowd in front of her to disperse. She looked at Linda and mouthed, 'Well done!'

Linda didn't know what she was being congratulated about, but assumed it must have been for bearing the punishment, better than Louise, who was still sobbing and clearly broken by the humiliating experience. On the way up to the dorm, they had to run the gauntlet of almost the entire school, most of whom had gathered along the route, out of curiosity to gawk at the two recently castigated girls. Linda refused to be shamed by their superior, exultant demeanours and countered them by setting her head high, while fixing anyone, who had the temerity to stare directly at her, with a stolid look of contempt.

Entering Dormitory Five, they were greeted by an embarrassed silence from the rest of the girls. Still weeping, the humbled Louise collapsed theatrically onto her bed, burying her face deep into the pillow. Linda, on the other hand, knowing that all eyes were upon her, rebelliously swaggered down the middle of the two rows of beds, then she derisively bounced, bottom first, onto her iron framed squeaking bed. This performance was contrived to demonstrate to the rest of the room, just how insignificant she considered, the punitive effect of the headmistress's hairbrush. In reality, it was an unwise thing to do, and something she instantly regretted. Managing to mask the agonising spike of pain that the act of bravado caused her, she smiled casually back at the astonished faces looking across at her. Like iron filings being attracted to a magnet, every girl immediately rushed over to her, leaving Louise isolated and alone down at the other end of the room. Questions and praise were met with uncharacteristic exaggeration and self-satisfaction, as Linda milked being in the spotlight. After so many years of being a "bit-part player" in the theatre of life, the feeling of starring centre stage was intoxicating. Glancing over, to where Louise was lying forlornly alone on her bed, she felt no sympathy for the girl whatsoever. Savouring her moment of triumph, she knew that the days of being apprehensive of her were over – Linda Middlewick was top dog now.

CHAPTER FIFTEEN
12th July 1970

1.00 pm

It was the penultimate weekend of the school year, a beautiful sunny July day that served to amplify the shimmering anticipation, rising amongst the girls, about what the summer months would bring. Numerous chairs had been conveyed from the orangery and were being carefully lined up at the bottom of the main entrance steps. The whole school had gathered outside in the hot gravelled crescent, where a turmoil of frenzied preparation was in full swing, in readiness, for the taking of the annual school photograph. Busily setting up his tripod-mounted camera on the raised flowerbed, some thirty-five yards away from the hurly-burly, a young male photographer cut a lone, uneasy figure.

After everyone had heeded their instructions, as to where to sit or stand, the chaos gave way to a semblance of order and the final light meter readings could be taken. The nervous photographer asked those sitting, to fold their arms in a unified fashion. This simple instruction caused a ripple of confusion as all the girls checked with each other, to see if their correct forearm was to the front or not. At last, the photographer was satisfied that the composition of the picture, was as symmetrical as it was going to get, he then comically ducked under the black hood, attached to the back of the big mahogany framed camera.

172

'Please keep very, very still, until I lower my left arm,' the shrouded man shouted, holding his arm aloft. He made a couple of adjustments to the extension of the pleated leather bellows, there was a faint audible click, followed by two seconds of tense, concentrated stillness, which ended immediately his left arm came down.

'Thank you! I'll just take another one, to be on the safe side.' Dropping the plate negative, into a black, draw-pull velvet bag, he quickly loaded another one and then repeated the process for a second time.

'Thank you ladies! That's it, you can relax now,' the photographer called out, bringing about a rumble of giggling and small talk, as everyone took their ease.

'I can hear the music from down at the village fete,' Elaine said, cupping a hand to her ear.

'Oh yes, I can hear it as well, sounds like a brass band,' Linda remarked. 'I can't wait to get down there – when are we allowed to go?'

'As soon as the photographer has finished here, Aunt Iona will start to hand out the pocket money – because of the village fete, we can withdraw two shillings today. Once we have our money, we can go,' Elaine answered, with an excited ring to her voice.

#   #   #

Just over an hour later they were promenading around Grench Village Green, their nostrils being teased by the stimulating mixtures of sweet and savoury essences that wafted around them, on the warm breeze. The first port of call for the girls was the candyfloss seller, where they watched in amazement, as he expertly spun a fluffy pink cloud onto a thin white birchwood stick. While walking around and dodging in and out of the crowd, it was difficult to eat the sweet, sticky wisps, without getting a frosting of coral coloured dried sugar, fused all over their faces. They waited for a while by the coconut-shy and watched, as a procession of middle-aged men, tried their best, to knock off a coconut. Encouraged, or ridiculed, by jocular family members, they hurled the wooden balls

173

down the track, as though they were opening the bowling in a Test match, but each of them, ultimately failed to win the prize. The exertion and embarrassment of failure meant that most participants, then disappeared into beer tent, strategically situated close by.

Next on the list of treats to sample, were toffee apples, followed by a glass of cloudy homemade ginger beer, which Elaine thought tasted like spicy soap and so Linda finished off her glass. In the roped-off middle area of the fete, a series of sheepdog trials were taking place, and the sound of different shrill whistles pierced the buzz of ebullient chatter. They wandered into the various marquees; where trestle tables strained under the weight of the prize vegetables, flower displays and homemade cakes, all vying to catch the judge's eye. There was a sudden change in the general ambience of the crowd, as the "tug-of-war" competition, between Upper and Lower Grench began. When it came to contests of any kind, between the two bordering communities, the villagers had fervid loyalties. The support for both teams was raucous, as they tried to encourage their eight men, to pull the other side over the line. It was all over fairly quickly, with Lower Grench winning, two pulls to none and the atmosphere then reverted back to the more subdued rattle of chitchat and laughter.

The girls sat down on the perimeter of the green, away from the happy commotion, to enjoy a little quiet.

'I think we've seen it all now,' Linda sighed, looking a bit bored while she concentrated on making a daisy chain.

'Yes, I think all they do now, is announce the prize winners. We could go and queue up at the ice cream van and get a Fab ice lolly or maybe a Ninety-Nine ice cream, with a chocolate flake in it?' Elaine suggested.

'Or . . . we could go back to the school and visit the secret room,' Linda paused, to see what Elaine's reaction would be. 'There would be hardly anyone about – virtually the whole school is down here. We haven't been up there since the beginning of last term.'

174

'Well, after your fight with Louise, we couldn't really risk it, if we had been caught, you would have probably got expelled. It would be nice to go up there, I haven't seen my lovely silver chain for ages.'

'Yes, and we could listen to some pop music, instead of this brass band oompah sound,' Linda laughed.

'All right then, we should be able to spend an hour up there – if we keep watch, we'll be able see when everyone starts to come back.'

Returning to the school, they collected the hidden key and made the familiar jittery intrusion up into the prefects' corridor, keeping their heads well down just in case somebody was still in their room. Quickly Elaine unlocked and gently eased the door open and they both slipped into the one time, male servants domicile.

'All the pictures have stayed up,' Elaine said, pleased that everything was just how they had left it.

'I've just thought. What if, your aunts check these rooms, they would know that somebody had been up here, wouldn't they?' Linda reasoned.

'When I first came into this room, nearly a year ago, there were no footprints in the dust, so I don't think that anyone has been up here for years. The only time that they are ever likely to come in here again, is if they decide to reopen up these rooms. And with at least five unused rooms, still on the top floor, it is unlikely that they will go to that expense.'

'Yes, you're right – there's no reason for them to come up here. What a shock they would get though,' Linda smiled, gaping at the collection of mess scattered across the floor. 'Various empty booze bottles, sweet wrappers and magazines everywhere – not to mention the fantastic display of posters that we've put up.'

'If and when they do come up here, they will think it's been done by prefects, who have long since left the school. There is nothing to connect us two to this – only Charlotte knows and I don't think she would squeal on us.'

175

'What if they found your silver chain, with the initial e on it? They would know that somebody with a name beginning with e, has been up here,' Linda extrapolated, on the theory.

'Well, there is that quiet prefect, Evelyn Stanford, who wouldn't say "boo to a goose", she would get the blame,' Elaine sniggered, her face reddening with guilt, at the thought of such a thing happening.

'Would you let her take the blame,' Linda giggled.

'If it saved you from being expelled, I would,' Elaine retorted, with a half serious look on her face, which diffused into a grin, when Linda held her eye for a couple of seconds.

'Would you?' Linda asked softly.

'Yes, I can't imagine what my life would be like without you. You're my best friend in the whole world, and I'd do anything for you,' Elaine answered, shocking them both with her unforeseen emotionally charged, candid admission.

Linda was thrown off-balance, by Elaine's proclamation. She gathered that what Elaine was really saying, was a coded, declaration of some kind of love.

'I'd do anything for you as well,' Linda replied, in a deliberate tone, befitting the importance of their conversation.

'I know you would – you did – you fought Louise for me and took the awful punishment, when it should have been me.'

'That was ages ago, and I had a fight with Louise because . . . I really wanted to hurt her . . . it sounds terrible I know, but I really enjoyed hitting her, it made me feel, sort of strangely nice inside. It was something that just had to happen. If she had seen the key and reported it, your aunts would have guessed that we had been coming up here, and then, all hell would have been let loose. So it wasn't your fault, it was just an accident, that sparked everything off.' Linda looked into Elaine moist eyes and wanted to hug her, but was unsure, if it was the appropriate thing to do; instead, after a moment of awkward silence, she decided to change the subject.

176

'Let's have a drink, I'm sure there's some Advocaat left,' Linda said, feeling her face blush hot, as she averted her eyes from Elaine's fixed, hopeful stare. Stepping over to the old wooden cabinet, she bent down and opened the rickety plyboard door.

'Here it is, there's enough for one snowball each,' she announced, holding up the bottle. 'Oh, it seems to have gone solid!'

Elaine laughed, at the humorous sight of Linda, trying to pour out the conglomeration, which resembled cold, set custard in looks and density.

'I think, it will have to be flat lemonade instead, I'm afraid,' Linda said, joining in with the joke, by turning the Advocaat bottle upside down and holding it above her head.

'I'll put the transistor radio on,' Elaine murmured under her breath, pushing the cabinet along the side of the wall, until she could get her hand into the cavity and pull out the radio and her silver chain.

'Can you fasten the clasp of my necklace for me?' Elaine asked, and Linda was happy to oblige. She stood behind her, swaying and shaking her head to the beat of the song, "In the Summertime", being sung by Mungo Jerry on the diminutive radio.

'This is my most precious possession – I'm going to keep it forever. Once I leave school, I'll wear it every single day,' Elaine affirmed to her friend. 'Next Christmas, I'm going to get you something special, I can't think what yet, but it will be something really special.

'Hopefully, you will be able to come and stay again, would you like that?' Linda asked, already knowing the answer that was about to rush from Elaine's lips.

'Yes! That would be fab. I would love to see your parents again – they were so generous to me. And your grandma, with all of her funny stories, about the war.'

'What about David?' Linda asked, engineering the framework of their conversation to pore over Elaine's true feelings.

'Yes, he was very nice, it would lovely to see him as well, but I doubt whether he would remember me.'

'I bet he will, I'm sure he fancied you!'

'No, I think he is more interested in you. You're so pretty, why wouldn't he?'

'He can't fancy me, I'm his cousin – I told you, you can't go out with your cousin,' Linda tried to impress on Elaine, the social stigma of dating your cousin. 'Anyway, all he cares about is bloody football, why do all boys love talking about bloody football? It's not as though we go on forever, about hockey or netball, is it?'

'That's because we don't like hockey or netball either,' Elaine pointed out, suppressing a giggle with her hand.

'That's true! But they wouldn't listen anyway.'

#   #   #

The two girls whiled away the next hour or so playing cards and listening to the latest hits, flowing out of the pocket sized radio. Linda decided to check the window, to see if any girls were returning up to the school. She could see a couple of groups frolicking around on the road, leading to the main entrance.

'We had better get going, they're starting to drift back in dribs and drabs.'

Elaine carefully prised the tiny catch on her necklace with her thumbnail, allowing the slender string of fine silver links to collapse down onto itself, tickling the palm of her hand. Fascinated by how it resembled a liquidised stream of mercury, dribbling down into her hand, and liking the aesthetic feeling that it created, she did it a few more times.

'Come on Elaine, hide it away we've got go,' Linda admonished Elaine, snapping her out of the abstraction she had been lulled into.

'Oh sorry!' As Elaine got up from where she was sitting on the floor, there was a soft clinking noise, which caused both girls to search for the source of the faint disturbance. To their horror they

178

realised that Elaine had dropped the necklace and the silver letter e had slipped between the floorboards. The weight of vowel pulled the chain down as well; it disappeared like a thin silver worm slithering down a hole.

'Oh my God! What have I done!' Elaine cried, slapping both her hands to her rapidly reddening face.

'Don't panic, we can get it, I've seen my dad lift the floorboards at home,' Linda quickly reassured Elaine, who looked on the point of bursting into tears. Taking another look out of the window, she added, 'We've still got five minutes – they're larking about down the road. This is what we need to lever it up.'

Taking an iron crowbar, which was laying on the windowsill, she jammed the tapered end between the stained floorboards and pulled back with all her strength. There was some cracking as the holding nails started to lift away, allowing the wooden plank to rise slightly. Changing her position, Linda moved six feet down the room and repeated the action, again there were some rattling sounds as the floorboard elevated even more.

'All we have to do now, is get the crooked end, under the board and we should be able to lever it up,' Linda declared, looking pleased with herself. Elaine helped pull at the bar and gradually the wooden board lifted up and then flipped over with a crash, sending a billow of dust particles swirling across the room.

'Done it! Oh look, there are thousands and thousands of little white shells, they must be the soundproofing,' Linda exclaimed. Grabbing a handful, she let them slip back through her open fingers, so that they rained back down into the gap, where they made a rattle of tiny clinking noises. 'The chain should be somewhere down here,' she plunged her arm down into the mass of tiny bleached crustaceans. 'It goes a long way down. Ah! I think I've got it? Oh, it's caught on something. Hang on, I don't want to snap the links.'

Linda carefully pushed the crowbar down next to where she could feel the delicate necklace was trapped, and then twisting the crooked end under the obstruction, she gave a hard tug. All at

179

once, there was an eruption of seashells onto the wooden floor, as the chain and whatever it was caught on, emerged up to the surface and out into the room.

'What the hell is that?' Elaine enquired, studying the strange shape of the impediment. 'It looks like a tree branch.'

Linda gently unhooked the silver chain and then took a closer look.

'Shit! It's a bloody arm! Look it's got a wristwatch on it!' she bellowed and sprang to her feet, propelled into the air by a jolt of electric panic. Elaine released a piercing scream of revulsion and also recoiled, jarred upwards into a rigid standing position. She then continued to scream, walking aimlessly backwards, until she collided with the wall. Shrieking hysterically, she slid down the side of the wall, tearing down several posters, which drifted down beside her, as she sat choking for breath.

'Come on, we've got to get out of here!' Linda yelled, grabbing Elaine tightly by the hand and pulling her up upright. Keeping their backs against the painted, crumbling plaster, they slithered around the surrounding walls, to keep as far away from the decomposed limb, as they could. Out in the corridor they both rushed to the door, Elaine was shuddering uncontrollably and so Linda snatched the key from her, rammed it into the lock and twisted as hard as she could. There was a "clunk" sound of the catch releasing, followed by her frantically pushing and banging against the heavy oak panelled door. In her frenzy, she had forgotten that the door pulled towards her; remembering, she grasped the handle with both hands and yanked it open. The very moment there was enough of a gap, they both squeezed through and blindly ran out, straight into Charlotte, who had been waiting on the other side.

'Whatever's the matter?' Charlotte asked, concerned by the highly agitated state of the two girls.

'There . . . there . . . there's a dead body in the room!' Linda stammered, watching Elaine collapse into Charlotte's arms.

180

'What's all the noise about?' Monica called out, advancing up the corridor.

Charlotte glanced around for a split second but didn't reply to Monica; instead she refocused on what Linda had just said.

'A dead body? There can't be, there just can't be! You must be mistaken, let's go and take a look.' Charlotte and Monica led the way back up the corridor, with Linda and Elaine reluctantly following them several paces behind.

The two older girls entered the room and stared at what looked like a pallid stump, sticking out from the middle of the floor. Charlotte slowly moved closer for a better look, her reticent minuscule steps, suggested to the others, watching from the doorway, that somehow, she thought it might come to life and grab her. She knelt down and examined, what looked like a ball of gnarled stick-like fingers, tightly welded together, clenching as if in a final tormented rage. Moving even closer, she could make out that the two-tone watch face, which had slid halfway down the wedge shaped stump, had a distinctive Omega logo on it. Brushing more of the shells away, revealed a roll of light blue and maroon plaid material.

'Jesus Christ! It is a fucking body,' Charlotte screamed, abruptly shattering the tense silence. 'Monica, run down and get Miss Rutherford; and don't, for God's sake, speak to anyone else about this.'

Without uttering a word, Monica athletically sprinted away down the passageway. Charlotte took the key from Linda, marched back to the door and locked them all inside. Leaning back against the panelling, she sighed thoughtfully, 'I don't want anyone else wandering in – the fewer people who know about this the better.'

'Who on earth could it be?' Elaine pondered.

'Probably, someone from a long time ago, before this was a school, perhaps one of the footmen, or maybe a butler,' Linda speculated.

181

'I don't think butlers, or footmen had expensive wristwatches back then. Anyway, the watch doesn't look that old, it must be a man, who has taught at the school in the last twenty odd years,' Charlotte logically analysed the facts.

'I don't think any men have ever taught here,' Elaine mused. 'Except for my Uncle . . .' the vociferous sound of distressed banging on the door interrupted her line of thought. Charlotte unlocked the door and allowed the leaden-faced headmistress and her sister Iona access. Without being instructed, they both rushed past the girls and went straight to where the gruesome find was located.

On seeing the lifeless appendage, protruding out from beneath the floorboards, Iona slumped to her knees and was violently sick, all down the front of her blouse. Amelia Rutherford just stood, fixed like a statue, totally bewildered at what was in front of her.

'I told you, this would happen one day,' Iona bawled, using her hand to wipe away the residue of the spew and tears, which disfigured her normally cheerful face.

'*You know, who this is?*' Charlotte enquired, with an undisguised modulation of disbelief and shock in her voice.

'Yes, we know who it is. It's the body of our father,' Amelia answered quite calmly. There was a moment of silence, as her words penetrated into the minds of those present.

'How? . . . Why? . . . What . . . is he doing up here?' Charlotte finally managed to cough out the next question.

'I killed him!' Iona screamed, bursting into another flood of tears.

'He was . . . raping me,' Amelia informed the room, in a cold, deadpan voice. 'Iona came into the room and saw him on top of me, so tried to get him off, by stabbing him in the back, with a pair of decorating scissors – those ones down there, on the floor.'

Linda gulped at the disgusting thought, that she had been using the same scissors, to cut out pictures from the magazines.

182

Through her sobs, Iona expanded on what had happened, unburdening herself of the dire secret, which she had carried with her, for more than 14 years, 'I didn't mean to kill him, just hurt him – stop him from hurting Amelia. The scissors just went straight in, I couldn't believe what I had done, so I quickly pulled them out again, but in just a few awful seconds, he was dead!'

'Elaine, I have something very important to tell you, about who you really are,' Amelia paused for a few seconds while she considered how to continue, 'it's going to change your life forever.'

Elaine stood blank-faced, still stunned by her Aunt's Iona's revelation.

'No! Don't tell her now. Not like this, it's too much,' cried Charlotte, who had worked out what Amelia was going to say.

'I've always wanted to tell her, it's been hell all these years,' Amelia whispered, with silvery tears trickling down her cheeks that dropped off her chin and spotted the dusty floor.

'Well, one more day won't make any difference,' Charlotte responded in a calm, authoritative voice. Knowing that she had to take charge of the situation, she then turned her attention to the girls. 'Monica, can you take Elaine and Linda to the sick room and lock yourselves in?'

Charlotte took the bunch of keys from Amelia's limp grasp and handed them over to Monica.

'What did you want to tell me, Aunt Amelia?' Elaine asked, in a quiet, plaintive tone. Amelia said nothing, tears were still falling from her face, as she wrung her fingers and stared with eyes full of sorrow, at the floor. Monica gently pushed Elaine and Linda out of the room and escorted them, in silence, up the corridor to the sick bay room. Charlotte ushered the two distraught sisters into her bedroom and then went down to the headmistress's study to dial 999.

CHAPTER SIXTEEN
12th July 1970

6.15 pm

Locked inside the sick room, Elaine sat quietly on the bed; her shoulders were slumped forward, as she dejectedly hugged a pillow to her chest for some small comfort. Staring ahead at the wall, with a vacant expression etched onto her features, she suddenly turned to the others and asked a stream of questions.

'What do think that Aunt Amelia was going on about? What did she mean, when she said that she was going to tell me – who I really was? I know who I really am – I'm Elaine Rutherford. And what could be so important, that it will change the rest of my life?'

'I don't know? How could, just saying something, change the rest of your life?' Linda petitioned, from across the other side of the room, where she was standing at the window, keeping lookout.

'Don't worry about that, she was in shock, she didn't know what she was saying,' suggested Monica, who was nervously pacing around the room, causing an irritating squeaking sound, each time she changed direction and her rubber soled plimsolls purchased against the lino covered floor.

'I can see three police cars coming down the drive, no four . . . no there's another one and a motorcyclist. Why are so many coming?' Linda demanded.

Elaine and Monica joined her at the window, to see the plethora of pale blue and white constabulary vehicles, draw up and park to the front of the building.

'What's going to happen to Aunt Iona?' Elaine asked, suddenly realising that the situation was far more serious, than she had first considered.

'She will probably, have to go to the police station and answer some questions,' Monica informed her.

'Why have they sent so many cars? Look there are more coming down the drive. They won't keep her there will they?

'They might . . . she may have to stay overnight . . . while they make their enquiries. Like they do on *Dixon of Dock Green*,' Monica proffered, unconvincingly.

'Why was Aunt Amelia's father, doing that terrible thing to her?' Elaine enquired, her mind being stampeded by countless unanswerable questions.

'I don't know, but he shouldn't have been doing it. Iona was right to try and get him to stop. It's just . . . maybe, they should have gone to the police straight away,' Monica's offered words, only added to Elaine's feeling of spiralling despondency.

'Look! The police have blocked off the main entrance to the school grounds, and some people are standing up there by the gate. Why are they doing that, what do they expect to see?' Linda pointed with a dramatically extended index finger to the new development.

Elaine went over and sat on the bed again, placing her elbows on her thighs and lowering her face into her awaiting cupped hands, she sighed deeply and began to sob. Linda hurried across to Elaine's side, wrapped a comforting arm around her heaving shoulders and whispered, 'Don't cry Elaine, everything will be fine, it will all get sorted out and we can go back to normal.'

'I don't think it will. It's too messed up – I'm frightened,' Elaine whined like an abandoned puppy.

185

#   #   #

Finally, after two hours of moping around, there was a knock at the door. It was Charlotte with Miss Neame, who was carrying a tray crammed with cups of tea and plates of sandwiches.

'What's happening Charlotte?' Elaine cried, ignoring the offered refreshments.

'Elaine, you are going to have to be brave. Your aunts are going to make a statement at the main police station in Sheffield, and I don't know what will happen after that. Linda, your parents are on the way to pick you up, they will be here in about an hour,' Charlotte explained, her young face carried the weight of the day's events, as she imparted information that she sensed would not be well received.

'I don't want to leave Elaine, I'd rather stay here, until everything is sorted out,' Linda protested.

'Elaine is going to come and stay at my parents' house for a few days, my father will pick us up early tomorrow morning. So don't worry Linda, I'll take good care of her. Let's all just think of it as an extra week's holiday,' Charlotte's assertive rhetoric doused the flames of any discontent.

Within the hour, there was a knock on the sick room door, to alert them that Linda's parents had arrived and it was time for her to leave. Elaine looked impossibly sad and lonely sitting on the bed. Linda searched for some comforting words to say to her.

'Goodbye Elaine, I'll write soon and you can come down and stay with us for some of the summer holidays. I'm sure that everything will be all right.'

Elaine looked at Linda and managed a faint smile in return, but said nothing. Linda reluctantly started to leave the room, but then remembered that she still had Elaine's silver chain. Fishing about in her gymslip pocket she clutched the thin metallic strand between two fingers and hooked it out.

186

'I forgot to return this to you after, I . . . well you know,' Linda said, pressing the shiny chain into Elaine's palm, who again smiled and nodded a silent acknowledgement to her best friend.

Down at the front of the building, Linda embraced her worried mother and father, while answering an initial barrage of agitated questions from them. Before getting into the car, she took a glance up at the sick room window, where she could just make out Elaine's silhouette against the fulvous backlit interior of the room. She waved, and watched with an oppressive sense of sadness as Elaine motioned back to her. In her heart, Linda knew she was not going to see her friend again.

CHAPTER SEVENTEEN
12ᵗʰ October 2003

9.30 am

Linda awoke with a start, for a few seconds she couldn't remember what day it was. Her eyes strained to focus on the radio alarm; the blurred luminous blue digits shone out 9.32, and filled her with momentary panic. A wave of relief washed over her, when she suddenly realised that it was Sunday morning. Her head fell back onto her pillow, causing a billowy thud, then without looking, she flopped her right arm across to the other side of the bed, to discover that it was empty. Steve had obviously gone off for his game of golf without waking her. Linda couldn't decide whether she was pleased, or annoyed, by his absence, but the pounding in her head, quickly shunted this train of thought into a siding and launched her out of the bed in search of some much-needed aspirin.

Down in the kitchen, while waiting for the electric kettle to boil, she started to stack the dishwasher. Seeing a black plastic container, half full with cold, greasy egg fried rice, left over from the previous evening's get-together, she was overcome by the craving to try a spoonful. It tasted surprisingly good, so she avidly consumed the rest, together with a few mushrooms and some beef chow mein, which she found in the other abandoned containers.

For a change, Linda was being self-indulgent, lounging about in just her dressing gown and foraging around in discarded plastic cartons, for uneaten morsels, of room temperature Chinese cuisine. Her relaxed state was suddenly interrupted by the harsh sound of the front doorbell ringing, which exploded the comfortable silence of the kitchen, like a fire alarm going off in a library. She jumped off of the stool and half skipped her way to the front door, where she could see through the dimpled glass panels that waiting outside was Melissa.

Linda opened the door and was confronted by her excited looking neighbour, who was clutching a bundle of A4 sheets of paper.

'Hiya, Linda, I didn't get you up did I?' she chirped in a gleeful, rising trill.

'No, I was just clearing away some to the debris from last night, do you want to join me for a coffee?

'Yes please, and I have something to show you,' Melissa shook the clump of paper that she was holding. The two women sauntered down the hallway and into the kitchen, where Linda made two cups of instant coffee and then joined Melissa on the white leather sofa in the extension partition.

'Right then, what's all this about?' Linda asked, intrigued by the mysterious printouts.

'Well, we had to get up early this morning because Taylor is playing in a seven-a-side football competition, in Streatham,' Melissa started.

'Football! Do girls play football nowadays?' Linda interrupted, astounded by the possibility.

'Yes lots do. Taylor is really good, and she might even play for a boys' team next season.'

'Why didn't you go and watch her?'

'I didn't feel too good this morning, so I didn't really fancy a car journey, and Rod definitely didn't fancy me throwing up in his new Lexus, so we agreed, that I would stay at home this week. Instead, I spent a couple of hours surfing the net and look!'

189

again, Melissa brandished the sheets of paper. 'Let's start with this one, Victoria Ellington? Does that name ring a bell?'

'No – should it?' Linda shrugged, still unable to comprehend what Melissa was going on about.

'Okay, what about Rebecca Harrington?' Melissa asked, again Linda shook her head in a negative response. 'What about Annabel Francis?'

Linda felt that the name rang a distant bell, she concentrated for a few seconds and then responded, 'I think there was a girl in my dorm at Grenchwood, called Annabel Francis.'

'Yes! Well, she is – "a happily married mother of three lovely girls, and is about to become a grandmother in December. Her husband of twenty-three years is called Simon and he works for the Town Planning Department of Leeds Council. She works as a part-time receptionist in a doctor's surgery",' Melissa exultantly declared, to a bewildered Linda.

'How do you know that she is the same Annabel Francis that I went to school with?'

'Because I got these, from a website, that has all the schools in Great Britain on it, I simply looked up Grenchwood Hall School, Yorkshire, and up came eighty-one names. I reduced the list, to those girls who would have attended, at about the same time as you, which brought the total down to twenty.'

'Annabel is going to be a *grandmother*! It doesn't seem possible. Oh God, that means I could be a grandparent now, I feel so old, all of sudden!' Linda grouched at the thought.

'The next on the list is Amanda Penrose.'

'No can't remember her.'

'Louise Bennington?'

After thirty-three years, the name still sent a shudder down Linda's spine and caused a colour to rise in her cheeks. After recuperating from the unexpected shock, she affirmed her recognition of the name, by barely nodding her head.

'She is – "married, with one son and one daughter and lives happily in Cheadle with hubby Daniel, who is the CEO of a refrigerated shipping company".'

'What a shame, I was rather hoping she would be dead!' Linda articulated in a cold and scornful voice.

'I take it, you didn't get on with her,' Melissa smiled, moderately shocked by Linda's reaction to Louise's name.

'No, I hated her,' Linda snapped, and then, feeling embarrassed by her overt, hostile over-reaction, laughed a false laugh and assumed a fake smile, in an effort to soften her comportment. Melissa rattled off a series of names, 'Caroline McKenzie, Suzanne Narroway, Jackie Wales, Polly Reader, Theresa Puttock, Jacqueline Holmes-Browne, Rosalind Lindford, Amanda Pascal, Jayne Richards?' none of which, triggered any recognition in Linda's memory bank. 'Penny Davenport, Evelyn Standford, Jenetta Foss, Monica Finch-Reeves.'

'Yes! I remember Monica, she was a prefect, what is she doing now?'

'Um . . . she's the head of the physical education department at Braymall Grammar High School for Girls'.'

'That figures, she was very sporty at school,' Linda said, reflecting back to her schooldays.

'Do you think she's a lesbian?' Melissa asked.

'Why?'

'I'm sure all the women PE staff at my school were rug-munchers. They would stand by the entrance to the communal showers and watch us. Weird or what?'

'Rug-munchers?' Linda queried the term.

'You know. It's a euphemism, for a woman, who performs oral sex on another woman,' Melissa explained, slightly discomfited by having to describe the actual physical act.

'Why rug?' Linda gave her an odd look.

191

'Rug, means her pubic hair,' Melissa whispered quietly, as if she was afraid that somehow, unseen ears might overhear their conversation.

'Oh, I get it!' Linda inhaled with sudden awareness.

'I see that Charlotte Drummond the actress, went to your school,' Melissa continued, taking another sheet of paper from the pile.

'Yes, she was Head Girl when I went there – what message has she left?'

'Oh, she hasn't listed herself, somebody has put her into the famous ex-pupils section, along with Mary B. Grantham, a novelist who went to the school back in the forties. Someone as famous as Charlotte Drummond is unlikely to want people emailing her.'

'Is that what happens with this website then?'

'Yes, you could send Louise whatshername a message, saying that you still hate her guts, after all these years!' giggling like a mischievous child at the idea, Melissa continued, 'So how well did you know Charlotte Drummond at school?'

'Quite well.'

'Do you think she would remember you?'

'Yes . . . I . . . think she would,' Linda warily replied, recalling stark images from that fateful last day at school.

'Do you think she would recognise you now?'

'I doubt it! The last time that she saw me, I had only just turned fourteen. It's been strange seeing her on television over the years, slowly growing older. I remember the first time that I saw her on TV, way back in the seventies, in some dire sitcom, I was just so excited to recognise somebody who I actually knew, on the telly. Is she still on the box these days, I haven't really watched much TV over the last ten years?'

192

'Yes, she crops up fairly regularly. She is still very attractive, for a woman about fifty. Usually plays sexy mother-in-law types or a recently divorced neighbour, who has an affair with the married man who lives next door,' Melissa felt herself colour up, as she realised what she had inadvertently said.

'Is that everyone?' Linda asked, not noticing Melissa's momentary unease.

'Um . . . yes, oh no, there is one more, Elaine Rutherford.'

'*Elaine!* Elaine has posted on this website!'

'Yes Elaine Rutherford, what's up, you look like you have had an electric shock!'

'I can't believe it – she was my best friend at school – the one I told you about last night. I just didn't think that Elaine would ever want to hear from anybody, who went to Grenchwood!' exclaimed Linda, who was both dumbfounded and thrilled at the same time.

'Why wouldn't she?'

Remembering the lie that she had told the previous evening, regarding why she had left after a year, Linda had to tread carefully – the last thing she wanted, was to divulge to Melissa, the real reason.

'Oh . . . the headmistress was her aunt – well . . . you can imagine what that was like for her,' Linda improvised an ambiguous answer, and to throw Melissa off of the scent, she hurriedly added, 'Does, she say anything about herself?'

'Yes she does – "Hi, hope that some of you remember me. I now run a B&B in the heart of the peak district – cheap rates for all Grenchwood Hall old-girls".'

'I can't believe it, after all of these years!' Linda murmured, taking the printout from Melissa to read it for herself.

'Well, are you going to join the website and send her a message then?'

Linda contemplated the question and slowly she shook her head.

'No, it's been far too long, we were just children then, what happened back at school, is a lifetime away now. Best let things lie. I'm glad to see that she is still alive and kicking though.'

'Don't you think that she would like to know, that you are still alive and doing well?' Melissa asked.

'No, it's very complicated, I'll leave it,' Linda decided, sliding the sheet of paper back over to Melissa. 'Now, I must get on, I have to look at some quotes and things for my business.'

Melissa correctly interpreted this as a benign request for her to leave, so she gathered up the paperwork and the two women walked silently through to the front door.

'Are you sure you don't want to contact her, just to say hi?' as she left the house, Melissa made one last attempt to change Linda's mind.

'No, it's been too long, but thanks for taking the time to download all those names, it was nice to remember them . . . well some of them,' Linda's voice trailed off towards the end of the sentence and she gave a nervous laugh.

After Melissa left, Linda showered, got dressed and then cleared up the mess left over from the previous evening's Chinese meal. Throughout these mundane activities, she was subconsciously annoyed with herself, for not having the courage, to do what Melissa had suggested and contact her old friend. She went up to her small office, which had once been the box room, of their Victorian terraced house. Taking out a letter, from an already opened envelope, she read the contents of it again. It was probably the tenth time that she had scrutinised the wording, each time the text remained exactly the same, but her resistance to what it offered changed a little. For the past twenty years, Linda had built up her function and events company, by spending most of her weekends, travelling the length and breadth of the country, to oversee exhibitions, product launches, boring conferences, promotions and even private social events. Work was getting harder to find, as

194

bigger companies, with more resources continued to undercut her. One such company, called All Rite On The Nite, had offered £200,000 to buy her out, and it was the contract from their solicitors that she was studying. Written into the deal, was the requirement, that if she accepted the offer, thereafter she would either work as a consultant for them, on a moderate salary for a set period of time, or alternatively, she could sign another legal document, agreeing that she would not start up another events based enterprise, for at least three years. These stipulations were there, to safeguard the buyers, against the core of Linda's clients, gravitating back to her, if she started up a business again straight away. Linda conceded that it was a reasonable assumption on their part, that some of her clients, would want to remain personally loyal to her. When the offer was first received, she dismissed it out of hand, but the more she thought about it, the more tempting it became. Linda knew that her rivals could eventually squeeze her out of business, however, that would take time and cost them many thousands of pounds in reduced fees. The time was rapidly approaching, to bite the bullet and make a decision, before the offer was withdrawn. She knew if she procrastinated, the next time that they went to the negotiating table, it would result in a reduced cash offer. The end of the month was the deadline for an answer, which gave her, just over two weeks, to make the hardest decision of her life. The morning meeting with Melissa and the very real possibility that she would have to sell her hard-earned business, left Linda's mind in a whirlpool of flustered thoughts and emotions. In an attempt to free herself of these cogitations, she chilled out on the sofa reading the Sunday supplements and awaited Steve's return from the golf course.

CHAPTER EIGHTEEN
12th October 2003

11.30 am

The bright white golf ball, rolled smoothly across the closely cropped grass. Gradually, as it lost speed and reached a subtle slope, it faded to the left, clipped the rim of the hole, teetered for an agonising instance and then, almost in slow motion, dropped with a satisfying plop, into the sunken plastic cup.

'Great putt!' shouted Robin Weatherby, Steve's playing partner, who was standing just behind the four and a quarter-inch circular cavity, holding the black and white striped flagstick, safely out of the way. Attempting to emulate the legendary Jack Nicklaus's victory salute, Steve walked over towards him with his putter raised above his head, waving to an invisible crowd of spectators.

Robin reached down and picked up the ball, then diligently replaced the eighteenth pin back into the hole.

'You realise, now I'm not going to sign those agreements next week – you should have let me win!' he joked, tossing the ball over to Steve. 'That putt just cost you about twenty grand, in lost commission.'

'Isn't it always the way, I was trying to miss, but the ball just kept on going, probably the longest putt I've sunk in a year!'

Steve responded, modestly proud about his long distance effort. 'I hope you are joking about that lost commission!'

'Yeah, we know we are in safe hands – you came with a glowing endorsement from Rodney Baxter, and what he doesn't know about the world of finance, isn't worth knowing. Haven't seen "Ruthless Rod" here for a while, has he given up golf on Sundays?'

'No, but his daughter is in a junior football team, so he has to transport her and her team mates around south London virtually every weekend,' Steve explained.

'What some fathers will sacrifice for their daughters, eh?'

'Yes! He's certainly besotted by her. Rod didn't become a father until he was in his fifties, so I guess it's really important to him, not to miss any part of her childhood.'

'It's hard to believe that he has a soft side to his character, having seen him at work, asset striping companies. That's where he gets his nick-name "Ruthless" from – I suppose to become successful in that game, you have to be merciless when it comes to making a profit.' Robin reasoned.

'I guess it does help not to have any scruples, if you want to make shed loads of dosh,' Steve concluded.

'His lovely wife looks quite a bit younger than him?'

'Melissa. Yes she is in her early thirties – she's his second wife.'

'Lucky old sod!'

'Yes!' Steve smiled smugly to himself, picturing in his mind, the erotic memory of Melissa's naked body, stretched out on a bed. As soon as the two men got back to the clubhouse, Steve automatically checked his mobile, for any missed calls. There was just a text message from Melissa, which simply read, "ring me B4 12o/c!".

'I've got to make a quick call Robin, I'll catch you up in the bar where you can buy me a swift half,' Steve called across the changing room, as he slipped out into the car park.

Quickly he pressed out Melissa's number and put the phone to his ear, waiting impatiently for her to answer.

'Hello Melissa, what did you want?' he asked hastily.

'I thought I made that clear last night,' Melissa giggled, alluding to their kitchen rendezvous the previous evening. 'I have an idea on how we can get Linda out of the way for a whole weekend.'

'Listen, I'm not going to do anything, at either of our homes,' Steve vigorously interrupted.

'No, I know. But with Linda occupied for at least two days, I'll tell Rod that I've got to visit my sister and her new baby in Spain, then *we* can go somewhere for a romantic weekend. A place where nobody will know us, and we can behave like a proper couple, without having to skulk about and rush things in a few stolen hours, here and there.'

'Sorry you have lost me, why has Linda got to go away?'

'Because I want you all to myself, for the *whole* weekend, two days and two nights – not just part of Saturday or Sunday, I want the entire forty-eight hours.'

'What about Rod, won't he want to come to Spain with you?'

'No, he can't stand my sister – I'll suggest that he takes Taylor, to see his aged parents down in Somerset, before they both kick the bucket. Rod feels guilty about not going down to see them, so I'm sure he'll agree that it's about time that they saw their only granddaughter again.'

'Where will Linda be, when all this is going on?' Steve asked, still confused by the various machinations.

'I'm working on that at the moment. Hopefully she'll be in the Peak District, visiting an old school friend. When you get in this

198

afternoon, tell her, that you have to play golf next weekend with a new client. I'll come over a bit later and all you will have to do, is generally support whatever I say.'

'But . . . what if . . .'

'Steve! Just leave things to me. Remember to tell her, that you have golf next Saturday. I can hear Rod's car, I've got to go.' Melissa abruptly ended their conversation.

#   #   #

Two hours later, from her reclined position on the sofa, in the kitchen extension, Linda heard the familiar metallic rattling sound, of a full golf bag being dumped down on the hallway's wooden flooring.

'Steve! Don't leave it there, it takes up too much room – put it away in the spare room wardrobe,' she shouted through to him, but it was too late, a couple of seconds later he strolled into view with a sardonic grin of victory on his face. 'I take it, from the look on your face that you won your golf round thing then?'

'Golf match,' Steve corrected her phraseology. 'I did, as it happens. I wasn't trying that hard – perhaps I should always play that way? The main thing though, was that for at least the next twelve months, Robin Weatherby, has agreed to let me optimise his company's capital investments. With his turnover, it should be worth between twenty and twenty-five thousand pound per annum to us. If things keep going well, my portfolio of clients could bring in about 400k next year.'

'What? You will earn four hundred thousand pounds! Are you sure? That sounds an awful lot of money to me!' Linda questioned, with an astonished rise in her voice, as she poured out two cups of the coffee that had been percolating for the previous thirty minutes.

'Well, this year, since January, the FT Index has gone up about fourteen per cent – I concentrate most of my investments in the twelve highest yielding shares in the One Hundred Index, and presently, they are returning an average of around nineteen per cent.

199

'I don't understand all the jargon, but that does sound a lot more than the interest that you would get, putting it in the bank,' Linda observed, but although she was pleased by the prospect of her husband raking in a large amount of cash, a small part of her was a bit resentful, of how easy it all seemed. Ruefully she worked out, that at its present rate of profitability, her events company would take over ten years, to earn her a similar sum.

'That kind of money is still southern league, compared to what Rod pulls in each year. Last year, his bonus alone, was over half a million. I mustn't grumble though, at least our bank balance has been in the black for a few months now. Oh, before I forget, I said I'd have a round of golf next Saturday with a business associate of Robin's, unless of course, you have anything planned for that day?

'No, sadly my diary is mostly empty for the foreseeable future.'

'Great, only Robin thinks that this chap will be able to put . . .'

A loud rat-a-tat-tat knock on their front door stopped Steve in mid-flow.

'I wonder who that can be?' he muttered to himself, as he wandered out of the kitchen to investigate.

Linda heard Melissa's distinct phonetic estuary accent, reverberating along the front hallway and was instantly annoyed. There was something she didn't like about her, but couldn't quite put her finger on it. Perhaps it was the fact that the woman was more than a decade younger than herself and head-turning attractive, or perhaps, it was more to do, with the way she had seemingly purloined another woman's husband, for her own personal gain. Either way, for Steve's sake, Linda steeled herself to act amiably towards her.

'Linda, I've done something rather naughty,' Melissa confessed, as she breezed into the kitchen area, with a flicker of a nervy smile on her delicate-featured face.

200

'Have you?' Linda responded dispassionately, and then pointedly took a slow sip of coffee from the cup that she was holding, which was irritatingly too hot and burned her lips.

'Promise you won't be angry with me,' Melissa pressed. 'Only, I've sent a message to your friend Elaine.'

'Why did you do that?' Linda asked, confused by Melissa's admission.

'I joined the website in your name and sent it from you.'

'What . . . Melissa!' Linda shouted, but managed to check her temper, before it tore open at the seams and she said something that she might later find regretful. 'What did you write to her?'

'Just this,' Melissa raised a sheet of paper and began to read out aloud. ' "Dear Elaine, hope you are keeping well. Glad to see that you are living in a beautiful part of the country. I'm married to Steve and we live in west London. Best wishes Linda." And this is her reply . . .'

'*She's already replied?*' Linda interrupted, surprised by the speed of the response.

'Yes, do you want me to read it to you?' Melissa asked and Linda nodded her head in approval. 'Okay this is what she wrote – "Dear Linda, I can't put down in words just how excited I felt when I received your message. It's been so long since we last saw each other. Should you ever have a free weekend, it would be absolutely wonderful if you could come up for a visit, so that we could reminisce about our times at school together, and that fantastic Christmas I spent at your parents' home. Now that summer is over, it's my quiet period, so I should be free most weekends up to the New Year. All my love, Elaine . . . kiss . . . kiss." ' Melissa guardedly peered up from the sheet of paper, to monitor how Linda had reacted to Elaine's message. Linda was staring back at her with a strange contemplative expression on her face.

'What a nice message,' Steve broke the taut silence. 'You must have been really good friends back in your schooldays. She was truly pleased to hear from you.'

201

Linda held out her hand and took the sheet of paper from Melissa, silently she began to read it again, but this time, in her head, she heard the words being voiced by Elaine.

'I hope I haven't upset you Linda,' Melissa murmured softly, gambling that Linda would respond positively.

'No . . . of course not.' Linda's face transformed effortlessly, from a serious pout, into a warm grin. 'It was a very nice message, and it would be good to see her again, but so much time has elapsed, I'm not sure whether it would be the right thing to do?'

'Well, I've got to go, we are taking Taylor and a couple of her footballing friends to the cinema, to see *Finding Nemo*. If you do want to contact Elaine, her email address is at the top of the page,' Melissa announced, giving Steve a sideways glance as she started to make a move towards the kitchen door.

'I'll see you out, I've got to move my golf bag,' Steve said, accompanying Melissa out of the kitchen, into the darkened passageway between the staircase and the dining room. When they got to the front door, Melissa turned to Steve and whispered, 'She's warming to the idea of going up to see Elaine – it's up to you to spur her on.'

'Well, I don't know if I should . . .'

'Do it Steve,' Melissa hissed, nestling her right palm gently into his crotch and then smoothing it gently, until she felt Steve physically respond. 'Or this is what you'll be missing.' Melissa gave a little gurgled laugh and with her other hand turned the latch on the door and opened it.

Flustered, Steve closed the door behind her and forgetting about his golf bag, went straight back through to the kitchen, where he saw that Linda was still intently studying Elaine's email.

'Why don't you drop her a line and see if she is free this coming weekend?'

Linda looked up at Steve and mutely replied to him, by screwing her face up in an expression of negativity.

202

'What have you got to lose, I'm out all day next Saturday and you haven't got anything booked. It would do you good to get away for the weekend – give yourself a bit of space to think about things.'

Linda's resistance was fragmenting, in her heart she wanted to jump into her car and race off up to Derbyshire, but something in her head was struggling to keep this yearning at bay. Repeatedly intruding into her mind's eye, was the still-frame memory she held of Elaine, forlornly waving to her from the sick room window. With each successive time that this sad vision invaded her thoughts, she felt the last remaining strands of resistance breaking away.

'Sod it! I'm going to email her and see if I can go up next weekend,' Linda incisively declared, jumping down off the kitchen bar stool, she almost broke into a run, en route to her office upstairs.

#   #   #

Nearly two hours later, Steve heard the recognisable rhythmic sound of Linda's footsteps, descending the stairs, a couple of seconds afterwards, she appeared holding a sheet of inkjet paper.

'How does this sound? – "Dear Elaine, thank you for your very generous offer, to come up and stay with you for a weekend. It would be great to meet up again – we certainly have some catching-up to do! I know it's very short notice, but I was wondering, if I could visit you this coming weekend, staying overnight on Saturday the 18 th and Sunday the 19th? Best wishes Linda." '

'Blimey, have you been all this time just writing that, I thought you were re-writing *War and Peace* up there,' Steve could not resist the chance to rib her.

'Shut up Steve!' she limply remonstrated with him and gave out a low bubbling laugh, that indicated how nervously excited she was. 'It was difficult, I couldn't think of what to say, so I've done about half a dozen different versions, but I think short and sweet is best, don't you?'

'Just like you,' he laughed.

203

'Is it okay? Not too pushy?'

'Look, she has invited you up there, if she can't make this weekend, then I'm sure there will be other times when you can go.'

'It's strange isn't it, this morning I completely shunned the idea of contacting Elaine – I suppose, the thought of it scared me, but now, I can't wait to go up and see her. I'll have to apologise to Melissa later, I was a bit sniffy with her, it must have taken her ages to download all those names and print everything off. It was a very thoughtful thing to do.'

Steve smiled, and in his head ruminated, on exactly how *thoughtful* Melissa had been to Linda.

Linda returned to her office, sat down at her computer and read her email to Elaine, one more time. As she fought the last few demons that were darting around in her mind, her index finger hovered over the "send" key. She touched the key with her finger and then pressed, a fraction of a second later, a line of green text flashed up on the screen – "Your message has been sent." Linda exhaled a long sigh of relief, as the mental exhaustion from the tension of the day, caused her to slump back in her chair. For the next two hours, she deliberately stayed away from her computer, fearing the disappointment that she would experience, if she found her mailbox empty. Finally, in the late afternoon, feeling restless and frustrated at not being able to concentrate on the simplest of household tasks, she decided to check, if Elaine had replied. Next to the "New Email" in the left hand column, there was the figure one, glowing out at her. Linda clicked the link and the email window opened, the subject read Re: Weekend visit; again she urgently clicked on the subject and the message appeared.

Dear Linda,

It would be fabulous to see you next weekend! I can't believe after all this time, we will actually be together again, very soon. Bring some walking shoes or boots with you and I will give you a guided tour of the surrounding countryside. Check out my website for directions – if you get lost (most people do!) call into

204

the village pub, the Poacher's Pocket and they will direct you.
Can't wait until next Saturday!

> *All my love*
>
> *Elaine xx*

Thrilled by the response Linda immediately wrote back.

> *Hi Elaine,*
>
> *That's great! I will leave early Saturday morning and*
> *hopefully be with you by about 11 in the morning if this is OK?*
>
> *Linda*

Just a few minutes later, the computer made a "bing" sound, announcing that her inbox had new mail. It thrilled Linda to think, that at this very moment, somewhere in Derbyshire, Elaine was sitting in front of her screen, and they were communicating, in real time, for the first time in thirty-three years. The thought briefly crossed her mind, to check Elaine's website for her telephone number, but somehow hearing her voice, before seeing her face would spoil the big reunion on Saturday. She hit the link and opened Elaine's latest message.

> *Dear Linda*
>
> *11am is fine, it will give us nearly two whole days to catch*
> *up on what has happened during the past thirty odd years – not sure*
> *that will be enough time tho!*
>
> *See you Saturday morning, hope you have a good journey*
> *up.*
>
> *Love*

Elaine xx

CHAPTER NINETEEN
18th October 2003

5.45am

At 5.45am the unwelcome sound of the alarm beeping, concluded Linda's seven hours of fitful sleep. Throughout the night her slumber had been regularly punctuated by a series of strange, school related dreams. She hastily stabbed the off button, not wanting to disturb Steve, who rolled over onto his left side, but didn't seem to regain full consciousness. Lying motionless for a couple of minutes, Linda tried hard to remember the imagery of the disturbing dreams, but tantalisingly, just before she could make any sense of them, they seemed to evaporate out of her memory, like melting snowflakes on a windowpane. Carefully, she slid out of the side of the bed and with cushioned steps, padded her way through to the main bathroom. The coldness of the ceramic tiles in the bathroom, caused her to stand on tiptoe, as she tugged down on the light switch cord, which she noted for the first time, made a loud clicking sound on being activated. Without waiting, she peeled off her pyjamas, stepped into the shower cubical and closed the magnetically sealing door behind her. She pressed the "on" button, and the shock of the initial cold water caused her to make an involuntary shudder, as it splashed against her face and breasts. This unpleasant feeling was soon replaced by the agreeable heat of the hot water spray, which surged powerfully, down the length of her entire body. The stimulating effect of the streaming hot water, banished any residual

207

drowsiness and her thoughts fixed on the exciting day ahead. In just a few hours time, she would once again be meeting with her old school friend – the idea filled her with a nervous excitement that she had not experienced for a long time.

#   #   #

At seven-twenty, Linda lightly placed a cup of hot tea down on the frosted glass top of the bedside table, adjacent to her husband's head.

'I'm off now Steve,' she said, sensing that although his eyes were closed, he was half awake.

'Right, have a great time and drive carefully,' Steve mumbled, without opening his eyes.

'Are you sure that you will be okay about your meals, I can come back Sunday afternoon and we can have something to eat in the evening?'

'No! I'll be fine!' Steve asserted, with a sudden snap to his voice. 'I'll have a hot meal at the golf club, where I'm playing today, and for tomorrow, I'll get a take-away and gross-out in front of the telly, watching football. Don't worry about me, you just have a good time with your old friend, and I'll see you Monday evening.'

'Okay, if you are sure?' Linda bent down and pecked him on his unshaven cheek. 'Bye then, see you Monday!'

Outside, in the dimly lit shadowy street, a strange squeaking noise, emanating from further up the pavement, momentarily unnerved Linda. She smiled to herself and felt a bit foolish, realising that it was only the paperboy's bike causing the noise, every time he touched the brake lever. Waiting a few seconds, for the hooded youth, with a large fluorescent reflective bag slung over his shoulder, to cycle past her, she then stepped forward and opened the door of her black Land Rover Discovery. At seven-thirty on a Saturday morning, Linda had the unusual experience of encountering very little traffic congestion, zipping through the back-street labyrinth of south-west London, until she joined the A40 Westway and then on to the M1.

208

Just under three hours later, the very insistent female voice on the sat nav, announced in an omniscient tone, 'You have arrived at your destination.'

Linda looked across to her right, but could see only a dry-stone wall, with a dense plantation of trees and bushes behind it. Looking straight ahead, it appeared to her, that the main village of Basington was about a hundred yards further down the road. Suddenly she remembered Elaine's advice in her email, that if she should get lost, to call in and ask at the local pub. Driving the car slowly down the approach to the village, Linda kept a careful look out, for any obscured turnings or signs, which might indicate to her, as to where Elaine's bed and breakfast establishment was situated. Rolling the Land Rover quietly into the front car park of the Poacher's Pocket public house, she could see a man up a step-ladder, watering the hanging baskets, which were now past their prime.

'Excuse me!' she shouted over to him.

'Hang on,' the man replied, and having jumped athletically down from the ladder, he started to stride towards to her.

'Sorry to interrupt the watering, but could you direct me to Elaine's bed and breakfast, please?' Linda asked, looking up at his smiling face. 'Only, my sat nav told me, that I had reached my destination back down the road, but there was nothing there.'

'Oh, I see that you've got one of those new GPS gadgets have you?' the man looked past Linda and into the car. 'Is it any good?'

'Well usually – it's got me this far, but now it's saying I have to do a U-turn back down the road.'

'Well, the damn thing is right,' laughed the man, the attractive creases next to his deep blue eyes suggested that he laughed a lot. 'You missed the driveway opening about hundred and fifty yards back down the road, don't worry, everyone does! Elaine's house is just up there, behind those massive old trees – in a

209

couple of weeks, when all the leaves have fallen, it'll come back into view. To get there by car though, you have to use the dirt track, which runs almost parallel to this road, but it takes you up the hill to the house. Are you staying long?'

'Just for the weekend – Elaine and I went to school together, so this is a sort of reunion for us.'

'When was the last time you saw her?'

'Thirty-three years ago.'

'*What!*' the man staggered back in mock amazement and let out another throaty chortle, which disturbed the sleepy tranquillity of the village. 'You must have gone to nursery school together.'

'I'll take that as a compliment,' Linda smiled.

'I'm James Guthrie, landlord of the village pub,' he offered out his hand. 'I expect Elaine will drag you in here, sometime over the weekend.'

Linda shook his hand, and politely replied, 'Thank-you, I hope so – your pub looks very inviting.'

She turned the car around and as she drove past James, she waved a thankful good-bye towards him. Keeping at a leisurely speed, this time, Linda spotted the concealed opening, which was now on her left. The soil and stone track-way, was uneven and bumpy, but the Land Rover, which had never been off a tarmac road before, made easy work of it. At the top of the incline, the track veered to the right onto a pebbled parking area, set a few yards further back from this, was a large, double fronted Georgian style building, which reminded Linda of her old dolls' house. She parked up and just sat there, contemplating the house for a few moments. After taking in a nervous deep breath, she got out of the car, and trudged across the beach-like expanse, with her heels sinking into the pebbles with each crunching step. Before Linda had managed to reach the front door, it opened. Ahead stood a woman, with clear, deep brown beaming eyes that shone out brightly from an intense and expressionless suntanned face. Stopping in her

210

tracks, she stared closely at the features looking back at her; she focused hard, but was unable to muster a flicker of recognition. Frantically Linda absorbed the details of the woman's physique, her short, variegated ash blonde hair and her generous lips, covered in a matt coating of rose lipstick. To her dismay, the face did not bear any resemblance to the memory she carried in her mind, of her old school friend.

'Elaine?' she asked, tentatively.

'Yes of course it is!' Elaine squealed with excitement, as she stepped forward and welcomed Linda by warmly hugging her.

'I'm sorry, I didn't recognise you,' Linda apologised.

'Well, who did you expect to answer the door, a thirteen year old girl in school uniform?'

'Ridiculous as it sounds, I sort of did!' Linda laughed. 'I still expected you to be three inches taller than me; and still be wearing those national health specs; and to have the same hair style. You look . . . amazing! When did you get these!' Linda screamed with laughter and pointed to Elaine's voluptuous breasts, straining against the material of her faded pink tee shirt.

'At fourteen, I stopped growing upwards and these popped out instead,' Elaine said, laughing so hard that she had to take a tissue from her jeans pocket and dab her eyes. 'I wear contacts now, which is great, because I hated those bloody glasses, and I dye my hair, because . . . blondes have more fun!'

Linda took a step back to re-appraise Elaine's now relaxed and jovial countenance, this time, much to her relief; she could see the ghost of her friend's adolescent face shimmering through the mascara and make-up.

'I recognised you immediately!' Elaine boasted, with feigned hubris.

'You did not!' Linda countered, indignantly.

'I did! When you got out of your car, you had the exact same expression on your cute little face that you had, when you first

211

walked into the dorm, all those years ago. The same expectant smile and eyes full of hope. I grant you – you are a bit more shapely now, than you were back then.'

'What you're saying is, my bum is much bigger now,' Linda giggled, feeling instantly at ease with Elaine, even though, they had been apart for over thirty years. The two women continued to tease each other, as they walked through the rambling old house to the kitchen at the back.

'Were you hiding behind the door, waiting for me to arrive?' Linda asked, while surveying the big, eclectically cluttered kitchen that was the absolute antithesis of her own.

'I was going to keep a watch out for you, when it got to about eleven o'clock. At the moment, my bloody doorbell doesn't work, so when I'm out here, in the kitchen extension, I can't always hear people knocking on the door, so I've put a note on the window, saying to come around the side of the house, to the back door. Luckily, Jim gave me a call, to tell me that you were about to arrive, so a scurried through and nervously waited.'

'Jim? Oh, James – the rather dishy landlord of your local pub, the guy who gave me the final directions.'

'Yes that's right, lovely man, shame that he and his wife are having to sell up.'

'Doesn't he get much business then? The pub looked so idyllic, I would have thought it would have been a little goldmine.'

'It does get busy every weekend, with all the walkers, but it's a bit dead in the week, especially during the winter months. The trouble is, there aren't many regulars – over two thirds of the houses in the village, are either holiday lets, or weekend getaway homes, for the wealthy citizens of Manchester or Derby. We only have one general store now, which thankfully also acts as a newsagent, but I don't know how much longer that will survive.'

'The aroma in here is fantastic, it reminds me of Sunday mornings at my parents' house, when I was young girl,' Linda said, silently sniffing in the palatable redolence of the room.

212

'The smell of egg and bacon must have infused into the brickwork of the building over the last forty years – speaking of which, I'll make us some bacon rolls,' Elaine said, bending forward to open the door of her ancient fridge, as she did so, Linda noticed a gleam of silver, flashing against the pink of her tee-shirt.

'That's not . . . *it is!* It's the silver e that I got you for Christmas! Did you dig it out especially?'

'No, I've worn it most days for the last thirty years. I've gone through about half a dozen chains in that time mind.'

'I'm . . . surprised that you kept it . . . after what happened,' Linda warily ventured.

'Of course I kept it – this is the only thing from my childhood that means anything to me. When I look at it, I remember all those great times that I had with you at the school. It doesn't remind me of that one awful day.'

'So how long have you been here?' Linda asked, tactfully changing the subject, and then to break eye contact with Elaine, she began to wander about the room, taking in the multifarious array of cookery books, kitchenware, food processors, and strong scented herbs that spilled out from ceramic pots. These various jumbled items were disarranged on shelves, hanging from hooks, laying on the work surfaces, or were bulging out of half open drawers.

'I've been here for four years, before that Amelia and Iona ran it, I came back to look after my . . . mother, before she died. I suppose, you must have guessed that Amelia was my mother, not my aunt or cousin?' Elaine shot Linda a circumspect glance, and then tossed some rashers of thickly cut bacon, into the roasting oven of the blackened Aga.

'Yes I did, but not until some years later. I'm sorry to hear that Amelia is . . . no longer with us. Is Iona still alive?'

'No, she drove the wrong way up a dual carriageway, swerved to miss the oncoming traffic, smashed through a fence and a hit a tree – died instantly. Mother, who was in the passenger seat, survived, but was badly injured, after six months of recuperation

213

she was allowed home, here, and I came to look after her. I finally got her, all to myself, but it was not for very long, she never really recovered and had to go back into hospital, where she died of pneumonia.'

'I'm terribly sorry to hear that.' Linda automatically offered her condolences.

'Anyway, I discovered that Amelia was my mother, the day after we . . . you know . . . found the body, of what turned out to be my grandfather, Donald . . . who of course, was actually my father as well,' Elaine emitted a nervous giggle. 'And, my Aunt Emily, his wife, was in fact my real grandmother, the only member of the family who I was correctly addressing back then, was Aunt Iona – who really was my aunt . . . well actually I suppose she was my half-sister as well. Gosh, it's complicated when you start to analyst it, isn't it?'

Linda could not think of an appropriate response other than to whisper back, 'I'm sorry Elaine – it must have been so confusing for you.'

'Well not at the actual time, it was all too much to take in. The thing that shocked me the most, was the fact that the parents, whom I thought I had lost in a plane crash, when I was just a few month old, never really existed. They were just contrived to explain my existence.'

'So what happened to you, after I had been whisked back home by my parents?'

'The next day, the school was in total chaos, with parents arriving every fifteen minutes or so, to collect their over excited daughters and the police milling about everywhere, like ants in a sugar bowl. Amelia was released from custody, came back to the school and explained things to me, none of which really made any sense. All day, I watched the comings and goings from the sick room window and then, at about six o'clock, Charlotte came up and told me that I was going to spend a few weeks at her parents' home. The next thing I knew, I was in her father's car, heading off to somewhere in Cheshire.'

214

'What was that like – staying with Charlotte?'

'Very strange,' Elaine carefully cut some bread rolls as she spoke. 'After two days, Charlotte had a terrible row with her mother and flounced off down to London, in search of fame and fortune. So, I was stuck with her parents, who didn't talk to each other and who seemed permanently pissed! Charlotte's mother, Vivian, was having an affair with some student, who was young enough to be her son. He lived up the road and would pop in during the day, when they would disappear upstairs together. Sometimes, if she knew he was coming around, Vivian would give me money, to go out to the pictures, or to the local swimming pool. One day, I was on my way to the pool and I suddenly realised that I had forgotten my towel. When I got back to the house, I trotted upstairs, only to find Vivian bent over the banister rail, being royally rogered from behind!' Elaine's eyes sparkled with impish delight, as she related the sleazy story.

Linda remembered seeing the same enchanting grin, when they were both at school together, it triggered a strange warm feeling within her that regressed her back to her teenage years.

'What did they do?' she asked.

'Nothing! I just said sorry, I've forgotten my towel, and walked past them!'

'Did she mention it later?'

'No, she just carried on, as if nothing had happened,' Elaine let out a hearty laugh and took the bacon out of the Aga. 'Do you want sauce on yours?'

'No thank you, it'll be fine as it is.'

Elaine showed Linda over to the far side of the room, where a sofa and a chair, draped with thick multicoloured throw covers, were placed at right angles to each other.

'Mmm . . . these bacon rolls are delicious,' Linda enthused, speaking with her mouth half full.

215

'Well, I've cooked bacon, virtually every day for the last four years, I should be able to get it right by now,' Elaine joked, her eyes held Linda's smiling gaze for a few lost seconds, which caused a shiver to tickle down her back, as she also felt the intervening years melt away. 'I can't believe it, I just can't believe it,' she blurted out, suddenly breaking the stillness.

'Can't believe what?' responded Linda.

'I can't believe that we are actually here, in my kitchen, eating bacon rolls, after not seeing each other for over thirty years. It's like I'm having some kind of surreal dream and I'll wake up in a minute.'

'Yes, I know what you mean – everything does seems so unreal at the moment.'

A pregnant pause followed, terminated by Linda deciding to ask Elaine about something that had bothered her for years.

'Why didn't you write to me, while you were staying at Charlotte's parents or even after that?'

Linda's question provoked Elaine's bright wide eyes to instantly mist over and she averted them away from her.

'I couldn't. At first I didn't, because I wanted to have some time on my own, surrounded by just my thoughts, but then, when I realised how I had come into being, I felt so ashamed. That feeling of shame turned into a terrible guilt and then a burning anger. Each week, I would receive a letter from Amelia, updating me on what was happening, regarding Aunt Iona and the school. It soon became obvious, that I would never ever be going back to Grenchwood and I wouldn't be seeing you again. I dreaded getting those letters, and then in early September, I got one containing a couple of postal orders. The first was for the Drummonds, to cover my "keep" for the nine weeks that I had stayed with them. The second, was for me to cash, and then to buy a train ticket up to Scotland, where, I was informed, I would be starting school in a few days time.'

'What was your new school like?'

'It was a strict, convent boarding school, run by nuns, which made Grenchwood look like a holiday camp. As you can imagine, my head was pretty mixed up when I arrived there, and I turned into the archetypical rebellious teenager. From the very start, I behaved terribly, continually antagonising the nuns with my outspoken views on the non-existence of God, which made me popular with my new classmates, but public enemy number one, with the teachers. I don't know whether the nuns knew about my parentage, but they soon decided that I was sperm of the devil, whom God had sent to them, as some kind of holy ordeal.'

'What did they do?'

'They tried to beat the devil out of me,' Elaine made a throaty chuckle while she kneaded her left palm, with the thumb of her right hand. Subconsciously she was remembering the pain of the punishments, by soothing the skin where the castigations had been cruelly inflicted.

'God Elaine, how terrible for you, it sounds like something from the Spanish inquisition. Did they succeed?'

'Succeed?' Elaine looked at Linda for a moment and then realised what she meant. 'Succeed in beating the devil out of me? No, the more they tried, the more I came to enjoy it, so the joke was on them.'

'How could you have enjoyed it? It sounds absolutely awful?' mooted Linda, her mouth staying open in a look of puzzled incredulity.

'I found the pain a welcome release, from the continuous tension that gripped me on the inside. It's a fixation that has followed me into adulthood – look.' Elaine twisted her left forearm around so it was visible to Linda.

'Elaine! How did that happen,' Linda exclaimed, openly disturbed by the series of thin white scars that criss-crossed her flesh.

'I did it. I cut myself with a razor blade. I didn't do all these in one go, they have amassed over the years. Whenever I found myself overwhelmed by a situation or depressed about it, I would cut myself – it became deliciously addictive and in a strange way, sometimes the pain even made me feel sort of ecstatic.'

'Do you still do it?' Linda gingerly asked, almost fearing her answer.

'No, as you can see these scars have faded, I've not done it for a few years now, but the urge to punish myself, never completely goes away.'

'In heaven's name, why?'

'Because of the pain that I have caused to others, by being born, I suppose. I'm a terrible jinx, anyone that I become close to, has terrible luck after meeting me,' Elaine giggled at what she had said, but Linda sensed that there was a real underlying belief, cloaked in her jocular declaration.

'Well, we were very close at school and I haven't had terrible luck – quite the reverse, actually. We were best friends back then and I'm sure we will be best friends again, now that we have found each other,' Linda rallied, leaning over to give Elaine's hand an affectionate squeeze.

'Good, I'm surprised that you haven't got into your car and headed back off to London, I must seem pretty weird to you,' Elaine smiled.

'Well it's good to get some things out in the open straight away.' Linda reassured her.

'So what are you going to confess about yourself then – that you've just got out of Holloway, after spending twenty-five years behind bars, for committing an axe murder?' Elaine quipped.

Linda hesitated for a second, before saying, 'Sorry, I can't think of anything remotely interesting that I've done in the past, apart from getting married twenty-two years ago.'

'Have you got any children?'

'God no! You must have guessed that, by the fact, I didn't thrust a dozen pictures of them under your nose during the first

218

minute that we met! What about you, do you have a brood of offsprings?'

'Um . . . no, which brings me to my next bit of earth shattering news that I should get out into the open straight away – I'm a lesbian,' Elaine announced calmly, and then added, almost as an afterthought, 'Are you shocked?'

Linda tried hard to swallow the last mouthful of her bacon roll without coughing, as the bread seemed to get stuck to the back of her throat and she involuntarily choked out her unconvincing reply, 'No.'

'You look shocked,' Elaine fixed her with a mocking smile.

'Well, you did sort of spring that on me,' Linda laughed, placing her hand across her mouth, to mute the sound of the continuing coughing fit. 'It's hardly surprising that I'm gay, considering the fact that for the first sixteen years of my life, I was incarcerated in "female only" institutions. When I finally got out into the real world, the male of the species seemed to have come from another planet.'

'In truth, I think they do!' Linda giggled. 'So do you have a . . . partner or girlfriend?'

'I did have a partner for nineteen years.'

'You split up, after nineteen years together?'

'Yes, but only because she died.'

'Oh, I'm sorry Elaine, how ghastly for you.'

'Yes it was very sad. Yvonne was older than me . . . quite a bit older actually, twenty-six years to be exact. I know what you are thinking and you'd be right.'

'What ?'

'That she was a mother substitute for me.'

'I wasn't thinking that. Lots of couples today, are from different age groups. Our friends up the road for example – the guy is about thirty years older than his wife. How did you meet Yvonne?'

'After I got expelled from that wretched school,' Elaine started, but Linda couldn't resist the temptation to butt in.

'Expelled! What on earth did you do?'

Elaine's eyes narrowed with amusement as she recalled the incident.

'I wrote something on their precious lawn, the one, we weren't even allowed to walk on.'

'What did you write?' Linda asked, intrigued by the escapade.

'It wasn't just me, there were four of us, we had stolen a big can of creosote and some brushes from the gardener's shed, then during the night, we all sneaked down to the front lawn and working as a team, in the pitch black of a moonless night, we managed to burn into the sacred grass, "STAN LIVES" in ten foot capital letters.

'Who was Stan?'

'Nobody! We managed to cock it up, it should have read SATAN LIVES, but Mother Superior was still suitably mortified and typically threatened to punish the entire school, if the culprits of the heinous crime didn't own up. So I decided to take the blame, or the glory for it, all on my own.'

'That was a brave thing to do,' Linda muttered, admiring Elaine's act of schoolgirl heroism.

'Not really, by then, I wasn't afraid of them – they had tried unsuccessfully, to break my spirit for nearly two years. They had beaten me, locked me under the stairs, made me kneel on dried peas and once, one particularly vicious nun, tipped a bowl of hot porridge over my head, for talking at breakfast time!' Elaine laughed. 'So, I just didn't care what they did to me, but I was amazed when the MS told me that I was expelled, they had finally

220

given up – it was as if, I had won. She even gave me the money for the train ticket, so I could leave right there and then.'

'What did your aunts say, when you turned up out of the blue? Sorry, I mean, what did your mother and your aunt say?'

'Mother wasn't best pleased, mainly because, I had nowhere to sleep, all the rooms here had been taken by paying guests. Plus, Aunt Iona was just about to be released from prison and was coming to live here as well. Anyway, I soon got a job with Derby County Council in Matlock, working as a filing clerk and general dog's body. I was only fifteen miles away from them, but I found a bedsit, close to the office, which cost me most of my eight pounds a week wage. It was a very depressing and lonely time and that's when I began self-harming, the pain was a form of comfort to me. After a while, to help make ends meet, I managed to get a weekend job, at a local hotel, helping out in the kitchen. I loved doing that and for a few months I stopped cutting myself. I struggled through the ups and downs of the next few years, but gradually my pay improved and with my weekend earnings, I could afford to rent a proper flat. Then I met Yvonne – she worked at the offices in Matlock as well, but our paths hadn't crossed, until the day she became the head of my department. There was something about her and the way she looked at me, that I found increasingly exciting. We would socialise after work – not just the two of us, other girls from work as well, but it always seemed that it was Yvonne and me, who were the last to leave for our empty cold flats. This is going to sound corny, but she gave me a lift home after a work's Christmas party and I invited her up to my place for coffee. I was so naïve back then, I didn't realise that I was effectively inviting her to join me for some slap-and-tickle,' Elaine giggled.

'So you actually got it together that night then?'

'Yes, I could hardly say "no" to my boss, could I! Not that I wanted to, she was everything that I had always fantasised about, confident about her sexuality and extremely affectionate towards me. I was suddenly in heaven!' Elaine's face blushed at the memory of that special night.

'So how was it at work after that?'

221

'We had to play it very cool at work, at first I would only see Yvonne discreetly at the weekends, but after a few months, things developed and she wanted me to move in with her. Outward attitudes to same-sex relationships were very different back in the late seventies. The good people of the Peak district, weren't the *avant-garde*, sexually liberated, modern freethinkers they are today,' Elaine paused and a small ironic smile formed on her lips. 'It was very unusual for women to live an openly gay lifestyle, so we told people that I was just renting a room in Yvonne's flat, while I saved up to buy my own place. Strangely, everyone seemed to believe that this was true, including my mother and aunt – I suppose, like Queen Victoria, most people back then, refused to admit that there were such creatures as lesbians living amongst them. Five years later, the council offered Yvonne redundancy, so I gave up my boring office job and we took over a . . . guess what!'

'I don't know! What did you take over?'

'A tea room in Bakewell!' Elaine squealed. 'It was great, finally I was doing something that I loved, making scrummy homemade cakes, scones, maroons and sandwiches – with their crusts cut off of course!

'Gosh! I've just realised, I haven't asked after your parents, how rude of me, I've been constantly babbling on about myself . . . are they both okay?'

'Yes, they are both alive and well, living just outside Welwyn Garden City, in a lovely bungalow,' Linda quickly updated her.

'Thank goodness for that, after all the deaths I've told you about, it's a relief to hear that they are still with us,' Elaine sighed. 'I suppose Granny is not around anymore?'

'Granny?' Linda quizzed, with a perplexed look on her face. 'Oh you mean Grandma – sorry, I used to call Dad's mum Granny, and Mum's mum, Grandma, so that they knew who I was talking about. Grandma has gone, but only four years ago. She so much wanted to see in the new millennium, but didn't quite make it.'

222

'She seemed quite old back in 1969, how old was she when she died?'

'Ninety-six I think.'

'So whelks are the secret to a long life!'

'Pardon?' Linda questioned, in a tone of total confusion.

'Your grandmother told us, that when she was a girl, if her dad had boozed away the house-keeping money, she had to eat whelks in a stew, instead of meat.'

'Did she? I don't remember that.'

'Ever since, when I see something about whelks, I always think about your grandmother,' Elaine burst out into a giggling fit. 'Did she have to go and live in that tower block – which she detested so much?'

'No, because when I went back to Queen's Manor school, Mum and Dad had a load of spare money, so they bought the bungalow and my grandma came to live with us.'

'That must have been nice for her – and you?'

'Yes, but we only really overlapped for about eighteen months. I went off to Cardiff University, where I met my husband Steve. After we had both finished our respective courses, we got a flat together in Kent, so that we could commute into London for our jobs.'

'What do you do?'

'I run an event management company.'

'Wow! That sounds very glamorous!' Elaine drooled, enthusiastically.

'Well, it's not really, all I do is make hundreds of phone calls, liaising with people over venues, presentations, delegates packs, posters, badges, travel, hotel accommodation – you name it, the list is bloody endless, and I have to get everything out of a tight budget. For the last twenty years, I've spent most of my weekends

223

onsite, in some soulless conference hall, smoothing out the perennial problems that always crop up.'

'Does Steve go with you to these events?'

'No, his weekends are spent on the golf course, brownnosing company directors, in a hope that they will let him manage their company pension funds or something. To be honest, I'm not really sure what he does, now that he works for himself, but he earns a fortune, whereas I just about break even.'

'So you can't see much of each other then?'

'Just a couple of hours in the evening and then he is usually engrossed in some dreary football match. Anyway, I've decided to sell my business, so I'll soon have every weekend off,' Linda gave a bitter laugh and then in a sarcastic voice added, 'Perhaps I'll take up golf as well.'

'You live near central London now?'

'Yes we've moved four times, each time we've got a bit nearer to the centre of London and that pretentious, aspirational city lifestyle that you see on all those property programmes. Each time, the cost of the house doubled our mortgage and reduced our floor area. The last move was four years ago, we bought a derelict terrace house in Fulham, for the then bargain price of £220,000, but we had to spent nearly that much again, making it fit to live in. We put in an attic bedroom, a new bathroom, an en suite bathroom and then to get some more living space, we had the kitchen completely rebuilt and extended, so that we now have a garden the size of a postage stamp,' Linda's mouth formed a wry smile as she looked out the window, at the rambling garden that surrounded Elaine's house. 'We have literally spent every penny we have on the house, we're mortgaged up to the hilt and until very recently, all our credit cards were maxed out.'

'And has it been worth it? Is living in the heart of a vibrant city, all that's cracked up to be?'

'I don't know? You hear people saying, how fantastic it is, to live in a location where everything is on your doorstep, with its

224

marvellous mix of amenities, like the West End shops, theatres, restaurants and bars, but perhaps we're just too old now to make the most of them. We hardly ever go out after dark, because it's too dangerous.'

'Dangerous, in what way?' Elaine frowned back at Linda.

'Muggings. Even though the houses are ludicrously expensive, they are situated cheek by jowl, with some pretty dodgy council estates. Every week, I read in the local paper about people being mugged at knifepoint by gangs, who are after their mobile phones or watches. It just makes you scared, whenever you see a group of kids walking towards you.'

'I'm pleased to say that in Basington village, we only have one dangerous delinquent . . . and old Joe Woodger is in his eighties,' Elaine laughed, her middle and index fingers twiddled with the silver e, balancing it just under her chin, while she stared attentively back into Linda's eyes.

'I suppose you know just about everyone in your village?' Linda asked.

Elaine thought for a moment, 'Um . . . I must know just about everyone who lives here permanently. If you go to the pub as much as I do, sooner or later, virtually everyone in the village will pop by for a drink and a chat.'

'We've lived in Fulham for four years and there is only one other couple who we are friendly with, the rest of our immediate neighbours, we just nod to – we don't even know their names. Everyone keeps themselves to themselves, there is absolutely no community spirit. At one time, not too long ago, our street would have been like this village, with everyone knowing each other and meeting up down the local pub for a gossip. The old pub on the corner, is now a private house and apparently owned by a high court judge.'

'I have to say, if our pub closes, this village will go the same way as your road, people will just stay indoors and never see each other. That's why I'm hoping that Jim finds a buyer for his

225

place, who is going to keep it open and not turn it into a private dwelling.'

'Out of interest, how much do they want for it?' Linda asked.

'Four hundred thousand pounds.'

'That sounds very reasonable. A great big building like that – when you think, that in London last year, a tiny garage in Chelsea, was up for sale for over a hundred thousand pounds! The world has gone completely mad and I'm afraid, that Steve and I, along with hundreds of thousands of others, have contributed to that madness, by buying into the ethos that "greed is good". I've just realised that over the years, I've slowly turned into a clone of that dreadful girl at school called Louise.'

'Louise, the girl you had that fight with?' Elaine bellowed, excitedly lurching forward in her seat, almost upsetting the empty plate off her lap, but still causing a shower of tiny breadcrumbs to scatter onto the woollen throws.

'Yes, the snooty cow who always had to be "ahead of the Joneses". Well, I'm just like her now, I have a cleaner who comes in twice a week, even though there is hardly ever any mess – a gardener, for our garden, which is half the size of this room and consists entirely of patio slabs, with a dozen pot plants dotted about on it. We have a giant plasma television on the wall that cost a fortune and a Land Rover, because that is the "signature" car for the area that we live in. Everything we buy, is carefully chosen, not for us, but so that we are in sync with our other *nouveau riche* neighbours. Go into any house down our road and you'll find the same regimented, uniformed white walls and hardwood flooring,' Linda suddenly spouted forth, with the passion of a religious convert.

'Have you only just come to this conclusion,' Elaine said, slumping back into her armchair.

'No, I realised I wasn't happy about twelve months ago, but by then, Steve's freelance career had really taken off, and he was even more obsessed with the mythical inner-city village

226

lifestyle. So, I thought I would keep quiet and leave it for a while, in the hope that he would eventually come around to my way of thinking. Unfortunately, the more money he makes, the more he wants, it's sort of become an addiction to him.'

'What are you going to do about it?'

'There isn't anything a can do really, my own event's company is grinding to a halt and if I don't sell now, it will be fairly worthless this time next year. Soon, we will be totally reliant on Steve's earnings, so in practical terms, I'll have to like it and lump it.'

'It's amazing isn't it? Elaine said, jumping to her feet.

'What is?'

'The way that we have just been chatting, like we used to, back at school.'

Linda beamed at Elaine, 'Yes . . . it is amazing. It's as though, the last thirty odd years were an overlong double period of maths, and we both can't wait to get out of the classroom and babble on about the more interesting things in life.'

'Well, would you like to go out for a walk? The weather is fantastic for this time of the year and the countryside will look stunning today,' Elaine suggested.

'Yes I would like that – I can't remember the last time I took a ramble in the countryside.

'Get your walking shoes then and let's get going!'

CHAPTER TWENTY
18th October 2003

9.20am

Leaning over his suitcase, Steve simultaneously tugged the leather pull-tabs on the zips, so that travelling along the track in opposite directions, they eventually drew together and sealed the top flap shut. Leaving the case precariously over-hanging the edge of the bed, he straightening up and glanced nervously at the radio alarm clock to check the time. Sauntering over to the bedroom window, he briefly looked downward at the white Volvo V40, a car that he had hired for the weekend, which had been delivered just thirty minutes previously. Seeing it parked outside his house, caused the gnawing feeling in his stomach to become a little more intense, as he knew, it was now time to leave. There could be no more procrastination; grabbing the case from off of the bed, he headed down the stairs and out of the front door. For a few frustrating seconds, Steve fiddled with the strange infrared key fob, without gaining admission to the car. As his panic and frustration grew, he swore at himself under his breath, until he realised, with a burst of embarrassment that he was pressing the wrong button. The loud symmetrised clunking noise, of the car's disengaging locks, trumpeted the welcomed news that access to the vehicle had finally been granted. He opened up the sloping rear hatchback and swung his suitcase into the empty load space. Mindful that he still had to go back to the house for his clubs, he pulled the cargo cover over the case and

closed the door. The golf bag was slumped against the wall in the hallway; Steve hung it over his shoulder, stepped backwards outside and slammed the front door shut. After double locking it, he popped the key into his trouser pocket, while at the same time, to reinforce his conviction that the door was secure, he gave it a robust shove. Satisfied in his mind that it was correctly locked, he made an about turn, back towards the car, when seemingly from nowhere, Rodney Baxter appeared.

'Why didn't you tell me!' he shouted.

Steve was like a rabbit caught in a car's headlights, paralyzed by fear, at the unexpected confrontation with his lover's husband. His thought processes were scrambled by Rod's question and the certain horrendous ramifications of being found out – all that he could do, was groan out the auto-pilot reply of, 'What?'

'That you were getting a new car!' Rod exclaimed.

Steve almost collapsed with relief, and through an uneasy chuckle, he explained the reason for the unfamiliar vehicle, 'No, it's a hire car, Linda's taken the Land Rover up to Derbyshire to visit an old school chum – so I've hired this, to get me out and about over the weekend.'

'Who are you playing a round with?' Rod asked.

'Pardon?' again Steve's mind froze, as he analysed the question. Somewhere from out of the guilty mire of his brain, he managed to elucidate what Rod meant. 'Oh you mean . . . sorry, who am I playing golf with today?'

'Yes, is it anyone that I know?

Put on the spot, Steve searched for a plausible opponent, whom Rod wouldn't know.

'No, I'm just playing my old neighbour, from when we lived down in Kent,' he said, with as much conviction that he could squeeze into his unsteady voice.

'Where are you playing?'

'Um . . . Sandwich.' Steve fudged another answer. Sandwich being the only golf course that he could think of, situated in the county of Kent.

'Royal St. George's?'

'Yes.'

'Where the Open Championship was held, back in July? How fantastic! So you'll be treading in the mighty Tiger's paw prints,' said Rodney, impressed by Steve's disclosure.

'Only if I hit the ball straight,' Steve laughed, feeling more at ease, as his heart rate began to calm down.

'You'll be fine, you bandit! Anyway I'm just going to drop Melissa off at South Ken tube station, she's going to Spain for a couple of days, to see her sister and her new sprog.'

'Aren't you all going then?' Steve inquired, feeling his confidence rising.

'No, after I drop Mel off, I'm continuing on down to Yeovil with Taylor, to see my parents – I've been promising them a visit for months now, so I was feeling a bit guilty. Taylor wasn't very happy about missing out on a weekend in the sun, but I've bribed her with a few of those Game Boy video things, for her to play with on the journey.'

'Hiya Steve!' Melissa's shrill voice rang out down the street.

'Hi there,' Steve called back to her. 'Going to Spain, you lucky devil, hope you get a nice tan.'

'Oh I doubt it, I'm planning to remain indoors most of the time – helping with my new little niece,' Melissa shouted back, her face cocked to one side, was a picture of impudence.

'Well, I hope you all have a good weekend,' Steve waved goodbye and slid his golf bag into the back of the Volvo; climbed into the driver's seat and set off on the first part of his journey.

#   #   #

230

Being a Saturday morning, he managed to find the first parking bay in the quiet "no through road", directly outside Ravenscourt underground station, and patiently kept an eager eye on the two adjacent exits. All the time, in his head, he was promising himself that this would be the very last time that he ever did anything so duplicitous. His unexpected meeting with Rodney Baxter earlier in the morning, had hyperextended his nerves, leaving them like over-tightened harp strings, full of tension and ready to snap. He concluded that he was just not cut out for the cloak-and-dagger stuff, of surreptitious assignations. In the past, all of his extramarital dalliances, were just that, brief encounters in cheap hotel rooms, or worse, in deserted lay-bys, late at night. After such trysts, he always felt a tinge of remorse, which usually melted away just few hours later, helped on its way by the self-deliberated, mitigation that his sex life with Linda had become prosaic and occasional. His deep thoughts were interrupted by the hurried movement of a handful of people, spilling out of the station doorway. They all marched past him up the road, except for one woman who placed her shopping bags down and stood next to a telephone box, on the opposite pavement waiting for a lift. For a further sixty seconds, Steve watched the dark opening opposite his car, hoping that Melissa would materialise from it and then, just as he was about to return to his introspection, there she was. The sun seemed to act as a dramatic spotlight, as it reappeared from behind a cloud, to shine with a sudden intensity, sublimely greeting the moment of her arrival. Within one beat of his heart, all of Steve's misgivings and doubts vaporised, as he watched her sashaying towards the car with a broad, lascivious smile on her face. In his excitement he fumbled about with the car door handle, which for some reason wouldn't open. Then when it did, he almost fell out onto the kerbside. Composing himself, he strode across the road to meet Melissa, kissed her on her cheek, breathed in the intoxicating fragrance of her honeysuckle scent, and in a pointed act of gallantry, took hold of her suitcase.

'See, didn't I say that everything would go like clockwork,' Melissa said, reassuringly hugging his arm.

'What about this morning, when I spoke to Rod in the street? For one ghastly second, I thought he had somehow found out.'

Melissa giggled at the thought, before commending him, 'Well you handled it fine. You even remembered to put your golf clubs in the back of the car – it's the little details that make all the difference.'

'You should have been a spy, the amount of manipulation and covert organising that you've done, to make this weekend happen.' Steve praised her back.

'I like the idea of being a spy, you can interrogate me later, but I won't talk, no matter how much torturing you put me through!' Melissa's dirty chuckle was worthy of Sid James in his prime.

Steve started up the engine and then bided his time, to allow the woman shopper to get into a car that she had been waiting for. Once she was safely settled into the front passenger seat the driver sped on further up the street in search of a turning point. The space he left, was sufficient enough for Steve not to have to do the same, but instead, execute a swift three-point turn, to get them facing in the correct direction to leave Ravenscourt Place.

'Right, where are we off to?' Steve asked, still struggling to adjust his seatbelt.

'It's a secret,' Melissa giggled.

'Look I've got Speedy Gonzales coming back up behind me, should I go to the left or the right!' Steve snorted, with amused frustration.

'Head for the M1.'

'The M1? That's where Linda was going today,' Steve questioned with concern, as he flicked the indicator and turned the car left into the main road.

'I know, but she started off nearly three hours ago and will probably be at her friend's place now.'

232

'What if she has broken down?'

'Steve! Don't be so paranoid, if by some bizarre coincidence that Linda has broken down, she will be looking out for an AA breakdown van, not a . . . what make of car is this?'

'It's a Volvo.'

'Has she seen it?'

'No, it was delivered after she left.'

'Well then! Just make sure you keep to the fast lane,' Melissa laughed.

'Sorry, of course you're right,' he conceded.

#   #   #

Three hours later, despite his many requests and pleas, Steve was still driving north on the M1, without a clue about their final destination, when Melissa suddenly announced, 'Turn off at the next junction, number thirty-four.'

After leaving the motorway, she took a printed sheet of instructions from her handbag and guided Steve, first through the roads of the built-up urban city and then into the rural area that surrounded it.

'Take the next left and we are here,' Melissa declared, while she neatly folded the paper sheet in half and replaced it into her bag.

'Wow! Look at that, what a lovely building,' Steve expressed his genuine surprise, as he turned into the driveway of the Grenchwood Hall Hotel. 'How on earth did you find this?'

'I came across it online, when I looked up Linda's old schoolmates on that website – this used to be her boarding school.'

'Linda came here?' Steve muttered, astounded by the sight of the fine building.

'I just couldn't resist it, when I realised, it's quite possible that we might be going to "have it off" on the exact spot, where just

233

over thirty years ago, Linda would have been bored to tears in a history lesson.'

'God, you really are wicked Melissa.'

'Yes I am,' she snickered. 'And over the next two days, you're going to find out, just how wicked I can be!'

CHAPTER TWENTY-ONE
18th October 2003

12.35pm

Serpentining around an assortment of flowerbeds, overgrown Hydrangeas and other leafy bushes, Elaine led the way up her back garden path, until the stepped, concrete trail ended. Continuing their slog up the gradient, they waded through the knee-high grass and passed a raised bare earth island, where the last of the remaining summer vegetables prevailed. Set back a few feet from the vegetable patch, was a dense chaotic array of shrubs, mostly made up of elder and hawthorn that formed a boundary hedge. Almost hidden within this wall of overgrown lush foliage, was an old sun-bleached wooden gate, which Elaine, fighting against the build up of long grass and unidentifiable plant stems, yanked open. Once through the opening, Linda found herself standing on a shadowy woodland track way, covered by the gangling, overhanging branches of the nearby trees. The grass pathway was flanked by a mass of undergrowth, consisting of bracken, large ferns, exposed tree roots, and clusters of tall stinging nettles.

'If we just walk up here, we'll soon be out in the sun,' Elaine pointed the way towards the oval of bright sunlight, about fifty yards to their right.

The two women walked out of the naturally cooled woodland copse, into the bright open ground and immediately appreciated the comfort afforded to them by the increase in temperature.

'Wow! It's really warm today and what a view!' Linda admired the breathtaking autumnal landscape, stretching across the shallow valley. 'I can't believe how beautiful everything looks and the golden and scarlet colours of the trees, are just to die for!' she shouted out, with a real childlike enthusiasm.

'Yes, if you get a nice day, I think this is the best time of year to walk in the Peaks, and we've certainly got an unusually lovely day today,' Elaine confirmed her friend's observation.

'I just can't get over the sky – how big it is. In London, I never notice the sky – all those bloody buildings I suppose?' Linda looked up at the quiescent ocean of cloudless blue sky that dominated the landscape. Her skin welcomed the warm rays of the sun and her face the temperate breeze, which seemed to caress her. For the first time in an age, she felt relaxed, carefree and almost serene. Elaine stood for a moment, delighted to watch Linda drink in the scene around her.

'I know it's a sort of *cliché*, but the air out here, really does feel fresher and cleaner. I'd forgotten how relaxing the countryside can be,' Linda said, as they continued on their way.

'When was the last time that you did some country rambling?' Elaine asked.

'I can't remember, it's so long ago. I would love to go on a walking holiday, but Steve would never do it. His idea of a walk – is chasing after a silly, little white ball. And his idea of a holiday – is to fly thousands of miles away and sit around a swimming pool for two weeks getting drunk.'

'You don't enjoy it?'

'I did at first – I used to get excited about jetting off to hot places, but over the years, I've just started to find it boring. The hotel, really could be anywhere in the world, but each year we've flown further and further, just to brag to people that we've been to Bali, Barbados, Brazil or Bahrain and a host of other places

236

beginning with bloody B,' Linda paused for a moment, to smile at her own accidental joke. 'It usually takes almost a day to get there and even worse, with the spate of delays recently, two days to get back. Sometimes I'd return feeling more exhausted than before I'd left!'

'To be honest, I've only been abroad twice and both occasions were a disaster – the first time, we went to Crete and I got badly sunburnt, so I had to stay indoors for most of the holiday. The second time, we went to the Algarve. On the third day there, I got food poisoning, so again, I had to stay indoors, close to the toilet!' Elaine laughed.

'Last year, we didn't go away, because of Steve's work and we haven't booked anything for this year either. He's always so busy now, with his various deals that we just can't get away. So this weekend, is going to be my holiday.'

'Well, I hope you are going to enjoy yourself, I can't promise you much excitement, but at least you won't take two days getting home.'

'I'll settle for that and perhaps a visit to your lovely village pub for a drink and something to eat?'

'Certainly, we'll call in on the way back. Now, you didn't tell me what happened to you, directly after leaving Grenchwood?' Elaine asked.

Before attempting an answer, Linda pulled up a long stem of grass from the ground and began to knot it, lost in a moment of reflection.

'After we got the awful letter, saying that Grenchwood would be closing, my parents decided that they didn't want me to go away to school again. It was Mum really, she became very stifling when I returned home and didn't like me out of her sight for too long. As I mentioned earlier, I went back to Queen's Manor, the school that I had gone to, for the two years before Grenchwood.'

'That was the school where you got bullied wasn't it?'

237

'Yes, but when I went back, it wasn't so bad. Everyone had grown up a bit by then, and it was also the year that we had to choose our options, on what subjects we were going to study for our 'O' level and CSE exams. This meant, for each subject, the classes consisted of a different set of pupils.'

'Did you have any more fights?' Elaine hooted with laughter as she stumbled a bit on the uneven surface.

'No! Louise thingymabob is the only person I've ever thumped, but I have to say, over the years, I've felt like punching hundreds of obnoxious people!'

'You said that you went to university? Cardiff wasn't it?' Elaine reprised her question from their earlier conversation in the kitchen.

'Yes that's right – in those days not many pupils stayed on at Queen's Manor to do A levels, it was generally accepted that when you got to sixteen, you found work and contributed to the families' income. I decided to stay on, I knew that my mum and dad could afford it and would want me to do as well as I could at school. I also saw, that by going away to study at university, I could unshackle the emotional grip that my mother had on me. She would have to let go, and I could make my life my own again, for the first time since the freedom of being at Grenchwood.'

Descending to their left, the trail dipped and narrowed as it ran through another dappled woodland area. A group of silhouetted figures trudged slowly, up the incline towards them. As they got closer, Linda could see that the leader of this pack was a fairly elderly gentleman, kitted out in all the latest walking gear, including an encapsulated A4 map, which dangled from around his neck. It appeared to Linda that he had a ski pole in each hand, as did many of the others who followed him up the slope.

'Good afternoon ladies,' the man said, when they were in close proximity to each other.

'Afternoon,' Elaine and Linda replied, standing to one side, to allow enough space for the column of walkers, some weighed down by bulky backpacks, to pass by. Each one offered

238

some form of greeting or thanks, as it was their turn to edge past the two waiting women.

After they were out of earshot, Linda turned to Elaine and asked, 'Does everyone in the countryside say hello to you?'

'Yes, it's part of the countryside code,' Elaine smirked, leaving Linda unsure of whether she was being joshed or not.

'Do you think that lot, were the British over sixties, downhill ski squad, training ahead of the new season?' Linda's remark caused a quizzical look to appear on Elaine's face. 'What were the ski poles all about?'

Elaine laughed, suddenly realising what Linda was referring to.

'They are walking or trekking poles, lots of people use them nowadays, helps with balance and enables you to walk faster apparently.'

'Perhaps we should get some – help us stagger home from the pub,' laughed Linda, who felt gloriously carefree and happy, strolling along in the company of her old school friend again.

'So how did you get on at Cardiff,' Elaine returned to the subject that they were chatting about, before the interruption of the other walkers.

'I had to study hard to get there, and then, I had to work very hard to keep my place there. I wish I could say it was all beer and skittles, but in reality I spent most of my time, in my digs reading and writing extremely long and boring essays.'

'You must have had some time enjoying yourself, didn't you say you met your husband there?'

'Yes, we both had rooms in the same student boarding house, so we gradually got to know each other, over lunchtime cornflakes in the communal kitchen. I liked him, because he was shy and not as mature as some of the other guys at uni. I suppose, he was the male counterpart of myself, so I was drawn to his vulnerability, honesty . . . and availability,' Linda snorted out a suppressed giggle. 'It took a fairly long time . . . before we . . .'

'Had sex?' Elaine finished off the end of Linda's pondering sentence.

'Yes, it was a big step for me, not like the kids of today, who seem to jump into bed with each other, after just a couple of hours.'

'So he was your first?'

'Yes, and the only.'

'How romantic!' Elaine smiled approvingly.

'Well it wasn't quite Romeo and Juliet, but we have been together since we were both twenty – nearly twenty-six years, and married for twenty-two of those.

'Which is a fair bit longer than Romeo and Juliet managed,' Elaine joked.

'Do you think it's strange?' Linda asked, lifting her left eyebrow slightly, to emphasis the seriousness of her question.

'Do I think what is strange?'

'That I've only had one sexual partner in my whole life!'

Elaine's bellowed with laugher, which disturbed a partridge nesting in some nearby ground cover, the resulting turbulent rush of its wings, frantically flapping, startled both women for a split second, until they realised it was just a bird.

'No of course not! Millions of people have sexually monogamous relationships.'

'It's unusual for today though, isn't it?'

'I suppose it is less common, but listen, you have something very special.'

'Were you and Yvonne in an exclusive sexual relationship?' Linda bit her lip, in the realisation that she may have delved too deeply into the privacy of Elaine's past. Quickly, before

240

her friend had the chance to answer, she added in a contrite tone. 'Sorry, how rude of me, to ask such a thing.'

'That all right, we never had secrets between us, when we were at school together, why should we now?' Elaine reassured her. 'The answer is no. We weren't in an exclusive sexual relationship – I did have other sexual partners during our time together.'

'Did Yvonne know about them?' Linda almost whispered.

'Probably, but you have to remember, we weren't a conventional lesbian couple, if there is such a thing. She was a lot older than me and I think she expected me to have the occasional fling,' Elaine stared at Linda and playfully chided her. 'You have that shocked look on your face again!'

'Sorry! It's my repressive parents fault,' Linda laughed an embarrassed little chuckle. 'My life is so tame, compared to most people's. So, how many "flings" did you have?'

'Oh, I'm a terrible slut, it must have been about twenty-five.'

Quite unable to control her astonishment, Linda exclaimed very loudly 'TWENTY-FIVE!' and then cringed slightly, half expecting another unseen partridge to take off from the adjacent scrub land. 'Oh dear, you must think I'm such a prig! Where on earth did you meet these . . . girls . . . I mean women?'

'Hang on a moment, it's not as bad as it sounds, that was about twenty-five different partners over a nineteen year period, I wasn't jumping into bed with a different woman every week. My first *lover*,' Elaine accentuated the word 'lover' and paused, to see how Linda would react to the term. She was amused to see a shrinking expression looking back at her; it was as if, Linda was afraid of what she was going to hear next, 'I met in our teashop. She was an attractive, smartly dressed, brunette in her late thirties. I had noticed that she had come into the shop, alone, at the same time on three consecutive lunchtimes. She ordered the same thing each time, sat at the same table in the corner and she caught my eye, whenever I shamelessly allowed her to. When she came to pay on the third

241

day, she pressed a small card into my hand, said nothing and left the shop without looking back.'

'What did it say?' Linda impatiently tried to hurry her along.

'It had her phone number written on it and a note saying "my name is Veronica, call any weekday up until six".'

'So what did you do?'

'I waited for Yvonne to go across to the bank, just before they closed, at about three o'clock – once she was out of the shop, I asked Margaret, who used to do some washing-up and cleaning for us, to watch the counter for a few minutes. Then I nipped upstairs to our flat, which was over the shop, and gave the woman a ring.'

'God! What did she say to you?' Linda said, agog with excitement.

'She told me . . .' Elaine threw her head forward, to hide her sly smile. 'Exactly what she was going to do to me, if I called around to see her.'

There was a still second of silent cogitation and then both women roared with laughter.

'Bloody hell Elaine . . . so you . . . went . . . to see her?' Linda stuttered, shaking her head in disbelief.

'I wasn't going to, but I just couldn't stop thinking about her, it was like an itch I couldn't scratch – driving me mad. The following Wednesday was half-day closing, our normal routine, was that I went to the wholesalers, while Yvonne cleaned up the flat. After I had stocked up, I found a telephone box that hadn't been vandalised and called her again, to see if I could pay her a visit there and then. She said yes, gave me the directions to her extremely swanky house on the outskirts of Bakewell and that was that.'

'You must have been very nervous?'

'Hell yes! I was shaking like a leaf when I pressed her front door bell, but the feeling of trepidation and my heart pumping, somehow made me feel really alive.'

'So what happened?' Linda hissed, gripping Elaine's arm.

'She was as good as her word!' Elaine gave a wide-eyed smirk and gently elbowed Linda in the ribs.

'How did she know, in the first place that you were . . . um . . . that way inclined?'

'Once people realised that Yvonne wasn't my mother, I'm sure we were the subject of much gossip, at the various local coffee mornings and the evening candle-lit soirees. I suppose, Veronica decided that she would find out for herself,' Elaine giggled like a naughty child.

'Did Veronica have a partner as well?'

'Yes, a husband and two boys away at boarding school.'

'A husband! She was married and still wanted to . . . well you know,' Linda said, her voice caught in a fluctuating mix of surprise and intrigue.

'Half of the women I've slept with have been "happily married" – the kind of women, to look at them, butter wouldn't melt in their mouths – pillars of society, who drop their kids off at school and then spend the rest of the morning swanning around shopping centres.'

'God, really! I had absolutely no idea that anything like this went on. So how many times did you see Veronica?'

'Only three times, she passed me on to someone else then.'

'What! How do you mean she passed you on?'

Elaine smiled at Linda's sudden ire.

'Not in a sex slave sort of way! She just gave me the details of someone, she thought I might like to contact.'

'And you did?'

243

'Yes, it was easier the second time – still exciting though, not knowing what I was letting myself in for, I guess that was why I did it, really.'

'Other peoples' lives are always so interesting! I'm just amazed at all these rural, clandestine shenanigans.'

'I'm sure that it goes on in the cities and towns as well, more so, probably. Someone as good-looking as you, must have been "hit-on" loads of times. All those weekends away at conferences, living out of hotel rooms, it must have happened.'

Linda cheeks coloured up, and she hung her head a little, to avoid Elaine's searching gaze.

'Well . . . yes . . . there have been times when some clients have become a bit frisky, after one too many drinks at the bar.'

'So what happened?'

'Oh nothing!' Linda lifted her left hand and pointed to the gold wedding band on her finger. 'I just reminded them that I was married and not interested in cheating on my husband.'

'And that deterred them?' questioned Elaine, her own experiences with the opposite sex, making her sceptical.

'Yes, along with pouring the contents of the ice bucket down their pants!' Linda screamed out in jest, and then continued in a more serious vein. 'In truth, I try not to upset some guys, as they are putting the work my way, so I do indulge in some light-hearted flirting. After all these years, I'm experienced enough to recognise when the banter is getting a bit too serious, and then I excuse myself from the bar, on the pretence that I still have to sort out some problems, regarding their exhibition. It's really a case of being diplomatic and not letting myself get caught in a vulnerable position.'

'Have you ever been tempted?' Elaine asked.

'Not really, I haven't fancied any of them, and I don't think I could have handled the guilt trip, that I would have been on afterwards. I've always, been too afraid of the consequences of

244

doing anything wicked, since I . . .' Linda's voice disappeared away to a hush and a look of disgust covered her face, as an unpleasant memory from her childhood, spiked into her thoughts.

'Since you did what?' Elaine asked swiftly, seeing her friend's tortured expression.

Linda didn't reply, but stared for a few moments, into the mid-distance, scanning across the landscape of rolling hills and grass fields, all neatly divided by lines of dry-stone walls.

'What was the wicked thing you did, that you regret?' Elaine repeated her question. Linda snapped out of her trance-like state and smiled vacantly back at her.

'Oh . . . punching that stupid girl and getting my backside tanned by the headmistress . . . I mean Miss Rutherford . . . I mean your aunt . . . NO sod it! I mean your bloody mother!'

Both women dissolved into convulsive laughter, which reverberated down the valley towards another group of walkers, making their way up the trail. Elaine sensed that Linda was not telling the truth about her true regret, but decided it was best to divert the conversation onto safer ground for the rest of the walk.

#   #   #

Just as the two women, marched down the hill and back into Basington, the church clock released four brassy chimes, which resounded around the otherwise silent village. Elaine led the way to the main entrance of the Poacher's Pocket pub, where various pairs of walking boots were stacked up to the side of the door, much to Linda's amusement.

'We'll have to leave our footwear here,' Elaine said, dipping down to untie her bootlaces. Linda concurred with Elaine's request and pulled off her trainers.

'Will they be safe out here?' Linda asked, feeling the coldness creep up through her sports socks and into the soles of her feet, as she stood on the bare concrete.

'Yes, who would want to steal somebody else's boots?' Elaine laughed at the absurdity of Linda's question. 'We'll go into the public bar, it's a bit small, but that's where the locals usually hang out, and it should be fairly quiet at this time in the afternoon.' She pushed the black door to her left, which opened with a groaning shudder. Following her in, the pleasing sweet aroma, of fruitwood burning in an open fire, assailed Linda's senses. This smoky bouquet was complimented by clouds of pipe tobacco smoke, drifting towards them from the other end of the bar. A middle-aged couple, sitting at the nearest table to the door, politely nodded their acknowledgement at Elaine, who waved back at them.

'Elaine! Fancy seeing you here,' shouted the pipe-smoking old man huddled over the end of the bar, nursing an almost empty pint glass in front of him. 'Jim told me, that your much younger, prettier sister had come to visit you.'

'Shut up you old goat,' Elaine responded, trying to curb a smile. 'See, what I have to put up with Linda.'

Jim Guthrie appeared through the connecting door between the two bars, and greeted them, 'Hi Elaine. I wondered if we would see you in here this afternoon.'

'Jim, can't you ban this old sod, I've only been in here five seconds and he has already insulted me,' Elaine pleaded, with mock indignation.

'I'd love to ban the old bastard, but without old Joe's weekly pension money falling into the till, my cash flow would incur an insufferable shortfall.'

'The first time I was barred from this establishment, George the Fifth was on the throne,' Old Joe informed the room, with an undertone of misplaced pride.

'Hello again,' Jim smiled at Linda. 'Has Elaine been dragging you around our beautiful countryside and informing you about all the points of interest?'

246

'Well, we certainly did have a very informative chat, while we were trudging up and down those pathways!' Linda answered, slipping a veiled look at Elaine.

'And what can I get you two lovely ladies?'

'Can I have two glasses of white wine please Jim?' Elaine replied, casting a quick glance at Linda for approval, which was returned immediately with an enthusiastic shake of the head.

'Coming right up – take a seat ladies and I'll bring them over to you.'

'Thanks, we'll be over in the back corner.'

Elaine advanced up the narrow corridor of space between the barstools and the single line of tables next to the window seats. As she squeezed past Joe, his left hand shot back and pinched her on the rump.

'OWW! That hurt Joe! If I get a bruise there, it'll cost you two bottles of your homemade wine,' Elaine squawked, lightly smacking him around the shoulder with her open hand.

'Fair enough! Of course, I'll have to check for myself that you really do have a bruise,' Joe growled out a deep rumbling laugh, and slapped his palm down onto the dark brown, wooden bar counter, indicating that he would be very pleased with that possible outcome. Linda approached him, nervously wondering if she was in for the same treatment. Joe's coal black eyes twinkled mischievously as he peered at her from under his thick, Father Christmas white eyebrows. 'Don't worry my love, I only pinch the bottoms of the pub regulars – the ladies that is!'

Linda slipped past him and quickly slid down onto the bench next to Elaine.

Twisting around on his stool, Joe fixed Linda with a toothless smile, 'Of course, if I see you in here again, I'll class you as a regular.' There was another rumble of shoulder shaking laughter and another slap of the bar top, then Joe swigged back the final dregs of his pint. 'I've got to go now. Elaine, I'll be up later to trim your bush.'

Another clap of raucous mirth accompanied his frequently used *double entendre*, and then Joe waved his goodbyes to all those present in the tiny snug bar. Linda watched him unsteadily amble his way out of the room, but instead of leaving the pub, he went through the internal door into the much larger lounge bar.

'This is what we call "Joe's long goodbye",' Elaine said with a little smile of amusement. 'He'll go into the lounge bar, see someone he knows, spend half an hour chewing the fat with them, and then he'll pop his head back in here, spot somebody else, who will have just come in, and he'll start nattering on with them. I bet he's still here in an hour's time.'

'Who is he?' Linda asked.

'That was Joe Woodger – lived here all his life, nobody knows how old he is, but he must be over eighty. Joe does some gardening for me and in return I take cooked meals down to his cottage three or four times a week.'

'A sort of "meals-on-wheels" bartering system?' Linda observed, smiling at her own joke.

'More like "meals-on-heels", as I only have to trot thirty yards down the steps to his place,' Elaine sniffed out a laugh through her nose. 'He makes the most divine homemade wine, so every time he does something naughty, like pinch my bum, I fine him a bottle of his wine.'

'I've not seen anyone get their bum pinched for ages, hasn't Joe heard about political correctness?' Linda giggled.

'No! In Joe's world, it will always be 1955 in this village!'

For man in his eighties, he seems so . . . well . . . alive, I suppose. When I see old people in London, they always seem to cut sad forlorn figures, anxiously shuffling back and forth to the few remaining local food shops. Most people are only interested in them when they are about to kick the bucket – then they are like vultures circling, waiting to pounce on a potential money-spinning refurbishment project. The sad thing is, Steve and I were part of that flock of vultures.'

'Was the house that you bought, previously owned by an elderly person?'

'Yes, an old lady in her nineties, who had lived in the house all her life, her parents bought it in 1908 for the princely sum of £275. Just think – all those, happy and sad times, which she must have experienced there, during her lifetime.'

'Gosh, she must have seen some changes in the street over ninety years,' Elaine reflected.

'Nothing had been done decoratively to the house for years – it was like walking into a fifties time warp.'

'Here you are, ladies,' Jim appeared at their table, carrying two glasses of white wine on a tiny tray.

'Can you put that on my slate please Jim? Oh! Is the kitchen still open and if it is, is there anything left to eat?

'We've only got lamb shanks or cottage pies. We've been swamped by walkers making the most of this fantastic weather, it's hard to believe that the clocks go back next week, isn't it?'

'Yes, I always think, that when the clocks go back, it's the onset of winter,' Elaine agreed, and then turning to Linda asked. 'What do you fancy Linda? Besides Jim.'

'What? Oh you! I'll have the lamb shank please,' Linda answered, slightly ruffled.

'Two of your finest lamb shanks please Jim! And can you put that on my tab as well?' Elaine placed her order and Jim disappeared back into the kitchen to tell his wife.

The middle-aged couple that had been sitting over by the door waved goodbye to Elaine, as they placed their empty glasses on the bar and straggled out of the pub. Elaine called out to them, 'Don't forget the fancy dress party next Saturday.'

'It's very warm in here,' Linda said, carefully pulling her lightweight sweater over her head and placing it down on the bench beside her.

'The fire will die down in a bit, they have to light it in the afternoon because in about forty minutes time, the sun will go down and the temperature will plummet,' Elaine explained.

'It's nice to see a real open fire again, reminds me of our fires at home, when I was a girl.'

'Yes, when I stayed that Christmas, I remember your dad "drawing the fire" by holding a newspaper over the opening, to get it going and then fetching up the coal from the cellar.'

'Shortly after that Christmas, they had gas fires fitted into the fireplaces. My mum loved them – she would say, "There's no messy ash to clear up, you don't have to have the chimneys swept anymore, and you get instant heat at a flick of a switch," I suppose she had a point, but there is something special about gazing into real flames,' Linda surmised wistfully, and then she picked up her glass of wine and took a sip. Placing the glass back down on the table she studied it, with a contemplative expression on her face.

'Is there something wrong with the wine?' Elaine asked.

'No, the wine is very nice – it's just that I haven't seen a normal size glass in a pub for ages. In London pubs, you virtually have to have a large glass, which makes it look like you're drinking a half pint of the stuff! Then you get charged a fiver for it.'

'Five pounds! Jim would sell you the whole bottle for that price.'

'It's little wonder that you see young girls paralytic in the streets nowadays,' Linda theorised. 'It wasn't like that when we were young, was it?'

'Actually, I do seem to remember you getting very drunk one afternoon, when we were at school,' Elaine said, with a sanctimonious smile curling on her lips. Linda's hand snapped to her mouth and her eyes widened in feigned horror, 'Oh God! I had forgotten about that! And you told Miss Whatshername that we had been eating apples.'

250

'Yes, that's right, I did and she believed us, or maybe, she pretended to believe us? Miss ... Miss ... what was her name? Something like Miss Green?

'No Miss Neame!' shouted Linda, pleased that she had remembered the teacher's name first.

'That was it – she was the only young teacher at the school, all the rest must have been over forty.'

'Like us now!' Linda sighed.

'Hello Elaine!' shouted a woman dressed in a blue kitchen apron, suddenly appearing from the side opening at the end of the bar. Her dark hair was scraped back in a tight bun and a glaze of perspiration covered her forehead. In her hands, which were wrapped in tea towels, she carried the two meals that Elaine had ordered earlier. She briskly walked down towards their table and precisely placed the two large white plates in front of each of the women. 'Now, please be watching yerselves, the plates are very hot, I'll get yer cutlery,' she said in a velvety, Irish accent as smooth as Guinness.

'Thanks Finola, this is my old school friend, Linda, who I was telling you about,' Elaine called after her.

'Ah, the one who yer haven't seen for tirty years or more?'

'Yes that's right!'

'Well did you recognise one another, after all that time?' Finola asked with a broad grin on her face.

'I recognised Linda but she thought I was the cleaning lady,' Elaine laughed.

'Elaine! I did not!' Linda protested.

'Well I would be surprise if yer did, the last time yer saw each other, yer must have been tiny girls. Nice to meet yer Linda, I hope yer have a great weekend.'

'Have you had any luck with the sale of the pub?' Elaine asked.

251

'Naw, as a last resort we might have to apply for planning permission ter de-licence the pub and change it to residential, but that could take an age and the last thing we want to do, is leave the village without a boozer.'

'Oh dear, somebody must want to buy this lovely pub, I'll keep my fingers crossed for you – and for the village as well – that they'll show up soon!'

Linda could see from the look on her face, that Elaine was genuinely concerned.

'Tanks, anyway yer ladies enjoy yer meal now and hopefully we'll get a chance to chat later.' Finola returned back to the kitchen, leaving Elaine and Linda to tuck into their lamb shanks.

CHAPTER TWENTY-TWO
18th October 2003

2.40pm

From the elevated position of his double aspect, second floor suite, Steve looked down longingly at the immaculately manicured green of the nearby par four, seventeenth hole.

'What a beautifully laid out golf course they have. From up here, you can really make out the distinct dogleg of that fairway – it must be at least thirty degrees. And it has a couple of sand traps on the right, ready to catch you out if stray down into the light rough,' Steve's enthusiastic description fell on unheeding ears. He glanced hopefully across at Melissa, who was lying on the bed reading some of the hotel literature. Her set expression suggested that she was not the remotest bit interested in his appraisal, of how potentially difficult it would be, to play the hole. Undaunted he continued, 'I think, I would risk trying to draw the ball over the small stand of trees that are placed near the joint of the dogleg, leaving just a seven iron pitch, straight up to the green.'

Grasping his hands together he threw his arms in an arc of a golf swing, as he imagined playing the shot he had just described to his inattentive audience. Casting another quick glance over to see if there was any reaction from the muted Melissa, and not detecting any, he risked muttering, in a low voice, 'I've got my clubs with me – I could do a half round while you . . .'

'Don't even think about it!' Melissa said firmly, still keeping her eyes fixed on the brochure. 'I'll tell you what we'll be doing this afternoon and evening.'

'I suppose you have it all planned out in fine detail, like the way you've engineered everything else today,' Steve chuckled.

'That's right,' Melissa dropped the hotel pamphlet, rolled over onto her back and stretched her arms out above her, like a contented feline in front of a warm fire. 'First, we'll take a leisurely stroll down to the village, where we will window shop at the many antique emporiums situated in the celebrated historic square, then we will have a drink in the quaint sixteenth century, Five Bell Tavern.'

'That sounds like advertising blurb – you've just memorised that from one of those leaflet.'

'I haven't!'

'Okay, what does quaint mean then? Steve asked, watching Melissa trying hard to keep a straight face.

'Um . . . it means quiet and sleepy,' Melissa pictured a country pub and took a guess at the definition.

'No it doesn't,' Steve answered in a playful stern voice. 'You have obviously not been doing your homework young lady – detention for you.'

'What does it mean then – know-all?' Melissa rolled back over and supported her upper body weight on her elbows, while looking up at him with narrow eyes and a challenging smile on her full lips.

'It means . . . charming and old-fashioned,' Steve answered in his most pompous voice.

'You're a bit quaint then, aren't you,' giggled Melissa, elevating herself up from her horizontal position and grinning mischievously, she wrapped her arms around his neck. 'I might not have known what quaint meant, but I don't think you'll have any

254

complaints about my 'O' level. If you're a very good boy I might even let you test me on my 'A' level tomorrow.'

Steve swallowed hard at the mental image pulsating in his brain.

'We could make start on those examinations right now if you want?'

'No! I want everything to be just right,' Melissa barked at him. 'This afternoon we're going to unwind after that journey, with a nice stroll down to the village, followed later, by a relaxing swim in the hotel pool and maybe a go in the hot tub. Tonight, we'll have a lovely romantic evening meal, with lots of champagne. Then tomorrow . . . starting from three o'clock we are going to have a marathon sex session, only finishing, when either, you have a heart attack, or they bang on the door demanding that we vacate the room – I've already ordered room service for Sunday's evening meal and for breakfast on Monday morning.'

'I guess I can wait a bit longer then,' Steve decided that it was in his own best interests, to go along with all of Melissa's intricate plans and smiled a smile of surrender, as he willingly capitulated to a higher power. 'One thing though, I haven't got any swimming trunks.'

'I've brought some for you – see I think of everything!'

'There not . . . Rod's are they?'

'Why?'

'Well, I don't like the thought of my tackle being next to something, that he has had his sweaty balls rubbing all over.'

Melissa head jerked forward, causing her satiny hair to fly about unrestrained, the silent sobs of laughter that she was emitting, quickly grew into a fit of hysteria, momentarily rendering her so incapacitated that she had to plonk back down on the bed.

'What's so bloody funny?' Steve asked, unable to see the joke.

Between pants of laughter and clutching her aching stomach, the breathless Melissa managed an answer, 'You don't seem to have a problem getting your tackle close up and personal to his wife's vagina! His sweaty balls have been all over that.'

Steve thought about it, before admitting, 'Oh yeah, I see what you mean now.' He managed a half-hearted chuckle, shrugged his shoulders and moved towards the door. 'Come on, let's go down to the village and visit that quaint pub.'

'They're new by the way,' Melissa said, peering into the mirror to check her eye make-up and comb her hair. 'The trunks I mean, not his balls.'

'Good, I'm most relieved. Now, if I can get the mental picture of Rod's balls out of my mind, I might have a relaxing afternoon.'

#   #   #

On their promenade down to the village, Melissa turned around and slowly walked backwards to admire the gleaming Grenchwood Hall, set like a cream-pearl jewel against a palette, daubed with rich autumn shades of gold, russet and brown.

'So what do you think of Linda's old school then?' she asked.

Steve stopped and turned around to enjoy the view.

'It's fantastic! I assume it wasn't so luxurious when she attended.'

'No, I bet she wouldn't believe it, if she could see it now.'

'Strange, that in all the time that we have been together, she never mentioned once, about going to boarding school, until last weekend.'

'Perhaps there is some deep dark secret, connected to her time here that she doesn't want to share with you?'

'She only attended for a year, more than likely, nothing exciting happened during her incarceration here. I can think of

256

several different years of my boarding school experience that were mind numbingly boring.'

'Oh poor darling! Never mind, I have a special surprise for you tomorrow.' Melissa teased.

After a languid turn of the village square, perusing the cluttered windows of the numerous antique shops, Steve and Melissa decided it was time for a drink at the Five Bells. Melissa sat down on a wooden bench table, situated at the front of the pub and while waiting for Steve to bring the drinks out, she watched the people mill about the sunny square.

'There you are, half a lager,' Steve said, placing the two glasses down on the sun-warmed table.

'What have you got?' Melissa asked, looking at the golden copper coloured liquid in the pint glass.

'A pint of real ale – want to try some?'

Melissa picked up the full pint glass in her two hands and quaffed a mouthful of the draft. She allowed the beer to slosh around in her mouth and detected a pleasing nutty flavour to it, which she considered for a few seconds before swallowing.

'It's quite nice,' she said, with a clear note of surprise in her voice. 'But not cold enough.'

'You can't serve chilled real ale, you wouldn't be able to taste the subtle balanced flavours between the hops and the malt,' Steve said, fervently championing the age-old art of brewing, with the indignant passion of an affronted connoisseur.

'I'm more of a champagne kind of girl actually, as you are going to find out tonight and tomorrow.'

'I've a feeling that this weekend is going to become a bit expensive!'

'You can afford it, with all the work that Rod has been getting for you, just consider the bill, as a finder's fee – payable to the finder's wife.'

257

'Not sure how Rod will write it off on his tax return?' Steve laughed. 'Claiming for your wife's dirty weekend away with a neighbour, might be a bit difficult to get passed as a legitimate business expense, even for the creative accountants that he employs.'

'Would it be okay for us to sit on this end of the bench?' asked a tall bearded man with a very expensive looking camera hanging from a strap around his neck.

'Yes of course, there's plenty of room,' Steve invited the standing couple to sit down. The man looked every inch the weekend tourist, with his knee-length, baggy olive-green shorts and the bright red backpack that he was busy stashing down by the side of the table. His partner on the other hand, with her large sunglasses and headscarf, had more of the look of a woman who didn't want to be recognised in public. Steve gave a sly look at her face and thought that he did recognise her from somewhere – perhaps she was an actress that he had seen sometime, on one of the many soaps, that littered the television schedules. The man had no sooner sat down, than he was up again, taking photos of the buildings across the other side of the square. He finished his impromptu photo-shoot, by taking a couple of shots of the five bells and one of the his partner as she took a swig from her wine glass, which she castigated him for, by waving her hands angrily towards him.

'I think it's time to christen those new swimming trunks,' Melissa said, after downing in one, the remaining half-inch of her now tepid lager.

Holding hands, Melissa and Steve strolled leisurely out of the village and then along the well-trodden country path that took them back up to the hotel.

'So what's this surprise you have for me tomorrow,' Steve asked, hoping that it would rekindle some spark to their conversation.

'It won't be a surprise if I tell you!' Melissa dismissed his attempt to discover her secret intentions. 'But, I will let you have a go around the golf course tomorrow morning, while I pamper

258

myself with a manicure, pedicure and a full body massage. Just as long, as you're finished in time to take me out for Sunday lunch.'

'Great! Yes I'll start early so that nobody holds me up and on my own, I should complete in about three hours or so,' Steve said with a schoolboy glee, delighted how the weekend was working out so perfectly for him.

CHAPTER TWENTY-THREE
18th October 2003

6.10pm

After their pub meal, which was complemented by several glasses of white wine, Linda and Elaine left the Poacher's Pocket in high spirits, linking arms, they skipped across the road and climbed the dirt-caked stone steps up to the rear of Elaine's house.

'That's a convenient short cut to the pub,' Linda pointed out, as they carefully ascended the final two extra steep steps that brought them up onto the level patio, outside the entrance to the kitchen.

'Actually, it was intended as a short cut to the church,' Elaine motioned to the adjacent church steeple, faintly silhouetted against the darkening evening sky. 'This house was the original rectory, where the tithes were paid, back in the eighteenth century.'

'How old is the building?'

'There is a stone in the side wall with 1789 carved into it, but the church across the road, is much older. The Church of England sold the rectory to a private owner after the Second World War, and it's been a guesthouse since about 1960. Mother and Aunt Iona bought it as a going concern in 1970 – obviously Iona didn't get to see it until 1972, when she got out of prison. Old Joe can remember when it was still a rectory, he told me that when he was seventeen, he clambered up the drainpipe and squeezed through an open window into one of these bedrooms, then he seduced the vicar's daughter! Only he didn't say, "seduced".'

Elaine's hand gripped the metallic, aged doorknob and twisted, causing the interior spindle to rotate with a soft clicking sound, she then gave a gentle push and the back door into her kitchen swung silently open.

'Elaine! Didn't you lock the door when we went out?' Linda exclaimed, astounded by her friend's *laissez-faire* attitude to home security.

'Oh I don't usually bother – until the trees drop their leaves, nobody passing in the road can see that the house is here, besides, most of the time I have total strangers living here anyway, so if someone wanted to rob me, they could easily do so.'

'Are you ever worried about the people who stay here?'

'Not really, it's almost always inoffensive middle-aged couples – anyway this section of the house is separated from the rest.' Elaine explained, while unsuccessfully trying to stoke some life into the grey and white embers of the fire. 'My bedroom and bathroom are upstairs, you get to them via a staircase behind that door over there.' She pointed across to the opposite corner of the room.

'So you are sort of self-contained out here then?'

'Yes, I had a new bathroom fitted a few years ago – it's my one luxury! A relaxing soak with a good book, a glass of wine and half a dozen scented candles flickering away, is my idea of heaven,' Elaine smiled at the thought, while she piled kindling wood on top of some screwed-up newspaper, in the fireplace, before striking a match.

'Oh, I've just remembered, I brought a bottle of champagne with me, to celebrate our reunion, I'll just get it from the car.' Linda declared with a sudden rush of verve.

'Just follow the path around the side of the building, it will be quicker than going through the house, because the front door is

261

doubled locked, and I can never remember where I put the damn key,' Elaine instructed.

Linda reappeared into the kitchen a few minutes later, clutching the expensive looking green and gold bottle and was surprised to see the fire was now roaring away, fuelled by several additional logs.

'Great, Champers! I'll plonk it in the freezer, that should bring down the temperature,' Elaine advised, taking the heavy bottle from Linda. 'In the meantime, shall we sample some of Joe's homemade fruit wines?'

The two women sat down on the sofa, in front of the fire and sipped the ruby-red, syrupy liquor that Elaine had poured from an already uncorked bottle.

'God! This is really delicious, well worth getting your bum pinched for!' Linda laughed.

'Does that officially make me a prostitute, in the eyes of the law?' Elaine asked, trying to keep a straight face.

'What do you mean?'

'Trading sexual favours for material gain!' Elaine put her glass down on the coffee table, clapped her hands like a demented seal and burst out in a gush of manic giggles. Linda immediately joined in, making it a duet of alcohol-embellished laughter.

'Who bought Grenchwood from your aunts?' Linda asked, when she had sufficiently recovered from her fit of the giggles.

'A publishing millionaire got it for a song, which is why, when all the debts and Aunt Iona's legal fees were paid off, they could only afford to buy this place. He then spent the following twenty-five years trying to restore Grenchwood to its past glories. Quite an expensive task, especially as the poor building had been abused by generations of schoolgirls, for almost fifty years. I suppose you know it's been a posh hotel for last five or so years?'

'Yes – but I only found out last week – after I did a search on the internet. So, have you still got anything from the old school?'

262

'They auctioned the contents before the new owners moved in, so what didn't get sold, is crammed upstairs in the attic room. Mother told me that she saved some personal items, in an old chest, but I've never gone through it. Oh, she did keep "*the chair*" – she said it was quite valuable.'

'What *the* chair . . . the one in her office, the one that was used for executions!'

'Yes, this is it,' Elaine tapped her left hand down on the sheet-covered seat positioned next to the sofa. Linda jumped to her feet and pulled back the loose throws, which entirely covered and distorted the shape of the fine antique, wing backed chair.

'God, so it is!' she squealed, as the characteristic gold and cream leaf pattern of the Queen Anne chair, once again became visible to her after so many years. 'Wow! I didn't think I would ever see that again!'

'At least it's in more harmonious circumstances this time!' Elaine chortled, topping up their glasses with the remainder of the blackberry wine.

'You said you had some more things upstairs in the attic?'

'Mother said there were some books and ledgers up there in a trunk, but I doubt whether there would be anything of real interest.'

'You haven't been tempted to look inside the trunk?'

'No – the only times I ever go up to the attic room, is to get the Christmas decorations and then return them a couple of weeks later.'

'Let's go up and take a look, you never know what gems of nostalgia we might uncover,' Linda effused, her voice bubbling with excitement.

There was a negative pause from Elaine, before she answered, 'Oh, it is a terrible mess up there, and the light bulb barely gives out enough light to see what you are doing.'

Linda began to snigger.

'What are you laughing at?' Elaine complained to her simpering companion.

'You're frighten that there might be spiders up there, aren't you?'

'Well yes, the thought doesn't attract me to the suggestion.'

'Don't worry I'll go up on my own and bring the trunk down.'

'I'm not sure you will be able to, it's bound to be quite heavy.'

'Let's give it go and see,' Linda pleaded, sensing that Elaine was warming to the idea.

'All right, I'll get the key,' Elaine smiled, rose from the sofa and manoeuvred her way around the kitchen room, to the old pine Welsh dresser. Opening the middle drawer, she fished out a bunch of keys, which she held aloft and jingled for Linda to see. Plunging her hand into the drawer again, she came up with a torch. 'You had better take a torch up with you as well. There are some small gabled dormer windows in the roof, but at this time of night the light that they afford is extremely limited.'

The two women eagerly trotted up the wide staircase of the main house and along the landing until they came to an inset of a half a dozen steps, which disappeared from sight around the side of the wall. Linda poked her head into the space and followed the line of the stairs up another dozen shallow treads until they stopped at the foot of a gloomy brown coloured door, made from sturdy wooden planks.

'You know what this reminds me of, don't you?' Linda whispered.

'Yes, of course I do! At least we don't have to worry about being caught "out-of-bounds" by some beastly prefect,' Elaine laughed, handing the torch and keys to Linda. 'The light switch is to your right when you open the door, and the trunk is over by the large chimney breast, good luck!'

264

Linda advanced up the stairs to the locked door with a mounting sense of excitement and curiosity. Using the key that Elaine had isolated for her, she placed it into the lock and turned. Silently the door opened and pivoted towards her, dropping herself down a couple of steps Linda pulled the door fully open and fastened it to the hook on the wall. Using her free right hand to search in the dark shadows before her, she located the cold brass light switch and flicked it with her index finger. A faint coat of insipid light illuminated the continuation of the stairway up into the heart of the attic. Venturing on, Linda saw for herself that the source of the weak luminosity was a single, ancient, bare light bulb, which must have been fixed in place, when electricity was first installed into the house, seventy years previously. She switched the torch on and made a sweep of the room with the beam. For one terrifying second, through the clutter in the corner of the attic, she thought that she saw someone staring back at her. She managed to stifle the scream she felt rising in her throat and turn it into an embarrassed choking cough, when she realised that the face, was in fact, the portrait of Elaine's great-grandmother, Victoria Fullman, which used to hang in the headmistress's study. Linda moved closer to the oil painting and marvelled to herself, how the unsparing expression on the old woman's features could still make her feel like a panicky little girl, caught in the act of doing something naughty. The hard, compassionless eyes, looking back at her from the picture, gripped her senses with a strange and deathly feeling of foreboding. Shivering away the sudden anxiety, she cast the torchlight onto the old trunk and noticed within the bright circle where the beam landed, that it had inset carrying handles on the ends. The old wooden, military travelling chest, had its edges and corners braced with narrow strips of riveted iron, adding to the impression that there would be little prospect of being able to move it. Linda pulled at the handle and to her surprise the wooden box slipped along the floor relatively easy. She hastily created a pathway around the strew of cobwebbed covered, usurped junk, that years before, had been consigned to the attic and forgotten about. Linda shoved the trunk to the edge of the stairs and called down to Elaine, 'Can you come up and push against the box while I slide it down the stairs?'

Elaine got into position to counter balance the trunk, while Linda slowly allowed it to roll down the stairs. Carefully they made their descent, Elaine stepping backwards and Linda holding the weight until they finally got it down to the landing. Then they each took a handle and carried the trunk downstairs to the kitchen without too much effort.

'Hope the damn thing is unlocked or we will have to go through this lot,' Elaine jangled the bunch of keys towards Linda and then attempted to lift the lid. 'Oh, good it's opening.'

The initial excitement of opening the ambiguous box, neutralised to a flat feeling of disappointment, at the sight of a sea of boring, antiquated ledger accounting books. Linda picked one up and thumbed through it.

'It's just pages of the day-to-day accounts, keeping track of the outgoings on things, like paraffin or toilet paper,' she moaned.

'Aunt Iona was always very thorough when it came to money – remember getting our allowance when we visited the village at the weekend, it was all carefully recorded down in the book, to the last penny,' Elaine remarked, pulling out some more of the red covered books and placing them on the kitchen table. 'Hang on this is different!'

Using both hands and some considerable effort, Elaine wrestled a larger, brown leather embossed book from below the strata of accounting volumes. Laying it down across the back of the sofa, she hauled the heavy cover open and was confronted by an impressive, sepia suffused, whole-plate print of Grenchwood Hall. Each turned page was greeted with sighs of appreciation, as intimate scenes depicting everyday life at the Hall, captured the faces of long dead gardeners, house maids, butlers and members of the Sumners family.

'The clarity of these old photos is amazing – it's almost as though the people are looking directly into your soul,' Linda raved.

266

'Wonder why the Sumners family didn't take this with them, when they sold up to my great-grandfather?' Elaine mumbled, in a puzzled whisper.

'Perhaps, they thought the photographs belonged at the Hall?' Linda conjectured.

'They certainly don't belong stuffed away in an attic of a B&B,' Elaine lamented, at the ignominious fate of the book.

Linda returned to the trunk, lifted out several more of the annoying accounting books and excitedly announced, 'There's another one!'

Taking the second large photo album over to Elaine, she rested it on the back of the sofa as they had done previously and opened it.

'Oh my God! It's full of the school photos!' Linda screamed with childlike surprise and delight.

'Hang on, I'll get my magnifying glass,' Elaine shouted, hurrying over to the middle drawer of the dresser, where she seemed to keep everything useful.

'1923! God the teachers look a bit mean!' Linda laughed.

Elaine looked through the glass and pointed a finger to the centre of the group.

'That's my great-grandmother, Victoria – the first headmistress,' she said, handing the magnifying glass to Linda.

'Yes, I recognise her from the portrait, she must have been about twenty years younger here though, still, um . . . very intimidating looking, isn't she?'

'She does look like a right old bag! The girls look happy, it's a shame to think that most of these fresh-faced young things will be dead now.'

'If they, were still alive . . .' Linda stopped for a few seconds, to mentally work out the present possible age of the schoolgirls in the photo, 'they would be in their nineties. Let's take a look at the back of the book, we should recognise some of the teachers.'

Linda closed the book, turned it over and pulled open the back cover, 'Shit! It's us, it's the photo we had taken on . . . that day.'

'Gosh, how amazing! I've never seen it – I expect this is the only one that got printed. There we are! Don't we look so young and . . . happy?' Elaine's voice trailed off.

Long forgotten images, of their fellow schoolmates, flooded back into view, causing a myriad of jumbled memories to overload Linda's brain.

'I can't believe I'm seeing all these girls again – and the teachers! Miss Neame was very attractive wasn't she? Wonder what happened to her, in fact, I wonder what happened to all the teachers when the school closed down?' she gushed.

'I suppose most of them got jobs at other schools and Miss Ryan probably retired.'

'Miss Ryan!' Linda exclaimed, quickly searching out her image in the photograph. 'She was very strict, even by the standards of day back then.'

'It was probably because she started teaching at Grenchwood in 1930!' Elaine informed Linda.

'Wow! She spent almost her entire adult life at the school. Do you know what she did during the holidays?'

'I remember my Aunt Iona telling me, that she visited her sister in Scarborough.'

'Oh, I sort of feel sad now, it must have been particularly traumatic for her when the school closed down.'

'Yes, from the moment I dropped this down the crack in the floorboards,' Elaine held her silver e up to her chin. 'Over a hundred people's lives completely changed direction.'

268

Linda decided not to comment, but instead continued to scrutinise the photo and cry out the names of the girls whom she remembered, this roll-call was accompanied with a brief anecdote about them.

'There's bloody Louise,' she slurred, and moved the magnifier closer to study the girl's mouth area. 'I see from the picture that her lip had healed up by then. Which was a shame!' both women instantly rocked with the joy of guilty laughter, after which, Linda wiped the small tears from the corner of her eyes and continued, 'Shall we open the champagne and raise a toast to all the girls who passed through Grenchwood Hall, in its forty-eight years of glorious existence?'

'That sounds like a brilliant idea!' Elaine concurred with the proposal, and rushed off to find some fluted glasses, while Linda brought the bottle from the freezer.

'Gosh! I haven't had real champagne for an age,' Elaine eagerly declared.

Linda picked at the gold foil on the unopened bottle.

'I hate this bit,' she said, apprehensively untwisting the wire caging that secured the bulbous cork. Gripping the neck of the bottle with her left hand and slowly twisting back and forth on the cork with her right, she felt the pressure behind the plug building, forcing it inexorably upwards and with a loud "blop", it rapidly shot out of the bottle. The disengaged mushroom-shaped cork, flew out in a blur and bounced off the ceiling, landing with a dull thud on the arm of the sofa, before rolling under the coffee table. Linda felt the cold fizzy liquid glug out of the bottle and spill down over her fingers. A wisp of white vapour coiled out from the top of the bottle, adding to the visual notion that it had just fired a bullet.

'That was a bit like giving Steve a hand job!' Linda giggled, gently pouring the expensive beverage into the two glasses that Elaine held out in front of her.

'I wouldn't know! About hand jobs, I mean . . . not on how expert you are at giving them!' Elaine joked, slightly embarrassed.

269

'I wish they were over that quick, makes your arm ache after five minutes of . . .' Linda smiled and jiggled her open fist up and down. 'All I get out of it, is a work-out for my right arm and sticky fingers from the lube.'

'Ah! I do know all about sticky fingers!' Elaine grinned, and held up her glass to Linda for them to tinkle together. 'God bless Grenchwood School!'

'And all the girls who sailed in her!' Linda added, with a whoop of laughter.

'Let's see what other historic memorabilia is hiding in the box,' Elaine said, returning to the trunk. 'Oh look at this army jacket, it must have been Donald's, and there's a cap that goes with it.'

Elaine handed the two items over to Linda.

'This looks like my grandmother's academic gown,' she announced, turning around to show off her latest find. 'Wow Linda! You look really . . . sexy in that.'

Adorned in the oversized military jacket, which she had topped off by wearing the peaked cap at a deliberate devilish angle, Linda did look strangely alluring in the masculine attire. Checking herself out, in the wall mirror, she was suitably pleased by her reflection and the fact that Elaine thought she looked sexy.

'Must be something about uniforms I supposed?' Linda giggled to herself, and turned back towards Elaine, who was now standing in the old headmistress's iconic gown and wearing a mortarboard on her head.

'Well, do I look sexy as well?' Elaine asked in amused curiosity.

'You do actually, albeit in a strangely disturbing way. Just a minute,' Linda picked up Elaine's spare reading glasses from the table and placed them tenderly on the bridge of her nose. 'Bloody hell Elaine! You are the spit of Miss Rutherford . . . I mean your mother!'

270

'What do you expect? My gene pool, is more like a gene puddle really! It's a shame that the pub fancy dress party is next Saturday and not tonight, or we could have gone along in these outfits – oh, you need these for yours,' Elaine held up a pair of black binoculars, which, hanging at the end of a tan coloured strap, slowly pirouetted in mid-air. Linda slipped the strap over her head and put them up to her eyes, to watch Elaine in close-up, as she continued to rummage about in the trunk.

'You'll definitely need this,' Elaine gave a little chuckle and then produced a leather side arm holster.

'What is it?' Linda asked, taking it from her.

'It's a gun.'

'A GUN!' Linda shouted, alarmed by the thought that she was actually holding a real firearm. Cautiously, using just her finger and thumb, she opened the top flap of the holster, by pulling on the tiny button strap. A pleasant smell of old leather permeated the air and infiltrated her nasal passages. On the inside of the flap, she noticed a faded blue stamp mark, that read - Tanner & Co London 1940. The brown wooden, grip handle was intriguingly exposed to the touch of her fingers, but Linda couldn't bring herself to take the gun out of the holster and instead she forcibly passed it back to Elaine.

'Don't worry, it won't be loaded,' Elaine said, taking the weapon out of the holster, to study the imprint on the side, near the chamber. 'It's an Enfield Number Two, Mark one revolver – I'm pretty sure that it fires thirty-eights.'

'You seem to know a lot about it?'

'Years ago, when I had my job at the council, I used to go along to a local pistol shooting club, it was a social thing really, but I got quite good and even won a couple of cups.'

'Guns frighten me – are you sure that it's not loaded?' Linda asked warily.

Elaine broke open the chamber and to her disbelief six brass coloured bullets recoiled back out of their snug compartments.

271

'Shit, it is loaded! This must have been the gun that mother kept handy, in case of intruders – it would have been Donald's personal side arm during the war.'

'Oh Elaine, put it somewhere safe!' Linda wailed, wringing her hands in an agitated disposition.

'I'll put it over here, and next week I'll drop it in at the police station, so they can dispose of it.'

Elaine replaced the gun into its holster and took it over to the corner of the room, where she stowed the relic from World War Two, in a wooden fruit bowl.

'Shouldn't you take the bullets out?'

'Yes, I will later, but I think I'd better do that when you are not around – you looked so terrified when I was handling the gun,' Elaine looked amused at Linda's consternation.

'It's not funny Elaine – guns kill people. We've had terrible incidents of people getting shot in the streets of Fulham.'

'Lots of people who live and work in the countryside have guns, old Joe's got a veritable arsenal down in his cottage – guns are only dangerous when they are in the wrong hands,' Elaine spouted dogmatically, and then returned to the trunk, to see what remaining treasure there was still buried within. 'Gosh! There's only another weapon in here. In the wrong hands, this one could be devastating.'

'Oh no!' Linda moaned, half expecting Elaine to brandish a machine gun, but her dread, diverted into an involuntary scream of astonishment, at the sight of what she was actually holding up. 'I don't believe it! The bloody hairbrush!'

'Remember this?' Elaine rather needlessly asked.

'I'm hardly likely to forget it, am I?' Linda broke into a fit of hysterics, her eyes shining bright at the thrill of the memory. 'It seems smaller now and less threatening, or perhaps my backside is just that much bigger now!'

'Well, I doubt whether the brush has shrunk in its thirty years of retirement, so you might be right,' Elaine joked, and passed the implement of punishment from a bygone era, over to Linda, who handled it with the respect and reverence, usually reserved for precious antiques.

'It's quite a sensual thing to hold, the lovely cool polished wood and the way the handle seems to fit so perfectly into your hand.'

'I bet you weren't so appreciative of its design qualities the last time you saw it,' Elaine mocked Linda's assessment and bent over to retrieve the next item from the treasure chest of memories.

'Ha, bloody ha – very funny,' replied Linda, flashing a swipe of the hairbrush across Elaine's jean clad, left buttock.

'*Ouch!*' Elaine lurched upright, 'It certainly hasn't lost any of its sting!'

Both women broke into yet another fit of laughter, but for Linda, mixed with this bout of levity, was the impulsive dark tingle of delight that suddenly coursed through her body.

'What have you got there?' Linda asked, after the laughter and the thrill had subsided.

'It's the . . . punishment record book,' in a split second, Elaine's light-hearted expression had changed to that of a frowned seriousness.

'God Elaine! From the look on your face, anyone would have thought you had just discovered the Dead Sea scrolls!' Linda cackled, trying to keep the atmosphere jocular. 'Do you think . . . my name will be in there?'

'I would have thought so,' Elaine gave a nervous cough and randomly opened the dark blue canvas-covered tome. They both beheld page after page, of neat columns of names and offences, written in an impeccable copperplate hand that assertively recorded the punishments, of erstwhile miscreant schoolgirls.

273

'God, there are so many,' Linda commented, as Elaine continued to leaf through the book.

'Gosh, I'm about seventy pages in and the date is only 1932. Look how trivial the offences are – talking – not paying attention – improper uniform – insolence – out-of-bounds – bad manners in class – the list just goes on and on. It certainly gives you a graphic insight, on how draconian life was, back then – and we thought we had it bad. This writing must be my great-grandmother Victoria's, I'll say one thing for her – she certainly had a very elegant style.'

Elaine continued to pick through the book, until she got to a page where the handwriting changed to a more modern script.

'Ah, 1950, the year when my grandmother Emily became the headmistress, I suppose?' she asked herself in a low murmur, then flicking through another dozen pages, she gave Linda a teasing, supercilious grin.

'Oh there I am!' Linda cried out, on seeing her name inscribed at the end of a short list, written in a third style of pen script. 'The last name in the book!'

'Mother obviously didn't like to use corporal punishment, as much as her predecessors – you are one, of only seven pupils in five years – the first being the famous Charlotte Drummond.'

'Not sure whether I should feel proud or ashamed – I see my offence was recorded as "unladylike behaviour",' Linda chuckled. 'Fighting like an alley cat, would have been a more accurate description.'

Elaine took the bottle of champagne and refilled the flutes. Thousands of tiny embryo bubbles spiralled to the surface where they burst, causing a delicate spray that tickled Linda's lips, when she raised the glass close to her mouth. After pausing for a moment to reflect on the unexpected contents that they had found in the wooden time capsule, she inhaled the luscious honey aroma into her nostrils and took a generous sip.

274

Elaine emerged from another visit to the trunk, struggling to open an old corroding Huntley and Palmers, oblong biscuit tin.

'Here, let's have a go,' Linda said, taking the garishly litho printed box from Elaine and then immediately managed to prise the lid off. 'There, it's off!' she proclaimed, with a satisfied smile of achievement playing around her lips. Inside, lying loose, they found six medals, along with a small, claret coloured, round-ended case that had a gold crown embossed upon it. Elaine clicked the tiny brass button and opened the leather case, to find another cross-shaped, silver medal, adorned with a white and purple ribbon.

'These must be Donald's medals that he won in the Second World War. The one in the little case must be quite important.'

'I think it might be something called a Military Cross,' Linda speculated.

'Do you know about medals then?'

'Steve is interested in military paraphernalia, so a couple of years ago we went to an auction, where he bid for a Military Cross medal and I'm sure it looked just like this one.'

'Did he get it?'

'No, the bidding went way too high for us, we were pretty broke at the time – I think a museum bought it for about eight hundred quid.'

Elaine hesitated and then smiling at Linda, she said, 'He can have these for his collection. I'd rather that someone who would appreciate them, have them – I'll just throw them back in the trunk and never look at them again.'

'You can't just give them to him, he's rolling in money now, I'll get him to give you the market value for them – he'll give you a fair price, Steve is a very honest person.'

'All right, I won't argue with you, I can see you have that determined look in your eye.'

275

The women clinked their empty glasses together to seal the deal, and then Elaine edged her way around the piles of the indiscriminately strewn bric-à-brac, en route to the fridge.

'You've missed this,' standing by the open trunk, Linda called over to Elaine, who was starting her return journey from the fridge, encumbered by two bottles – the nearly finished champagne and an unopened Chardonnay.

'What is it?'

'It's another photo album, perhaps belonging to the Sumners' family?'

Elaine tipped out the remaining champagne into the glasses and joined Linda, who was sitting on the sofa studying the monochrome pictures, which had been haphazardly stuck on the chocolate brown pages, with ivory coloured, ornate corner tabs.

'Oh, my gosh! This is our family photo album!' Elaine imparted with a shrill start. 'That must be Donald, my grandfather, or . . . father.' she pointed to a handsome looking man, with an easy smile and a gentle expression in his eyes. He was dressed in full military regalia, having been carefully posed in a photographer's studio, with an incongruous painted backdrop of a medieval landscape behind him. 'I've never seen this book before.'

Linda looked at the pin sharp image of the dashing young man's face, a picture which just oozed vitality and she couldn't help but consider, that the decomposed arm, which she pulled out from under the floorboards, belonged to this human being. The thought sent an unpleasant cold shiver down her spine.

'I've never seen a picture of him before – it's been strange all these years, not knowing what the man, who fathered me, looked like,' Elaine revealed, gazing at the photographs with transfixed eyes.

'He looks . . . well, rather nice, not how I had pictured him, at all,' Linda said softly, unsure of how Elaine was going to react.

'Yes he does, doesn't he? Look, here they all are on Redcar beach in 1936, making sandcastles. And here, walking along

276

the front at Whitby Bay, dad proudly holding hands with his two little daughters.'

Each of the many snaps on the first twenty pages, showed scenes of happy family holidays and celebrations, the very quintessence of the perfect nineteen-thirties middle-class family. Elaine gaped in wonderment at the pictures, which featured her mother and aunt as very contented little girls. With each page that she turned, Amelia and Iona became a little older and taller, and their father's presence became more occasional. The last photo in the book was of the two girls, now in their early twenties, sitting either side of their father on a low wall, to the front of Grenchwood Hall.

Linda screwed her eyes up to better focus on the tiny facial features. Amelia was smiling, happy and carefree, whereas Iona's expression did little to hide the uneasiness that she must have been feeling, while holding her father's hand. Sitting ramrod upright in the middle, Donald Rutherford stared impassively at the camera lens, despite being in his early fifties, the greying hair on his temples gave him a distinguished, debonair look of an aging Hollywood matinee idol. Linda concentrated her focus on his face and noticed, what was either a blemish on the original negative, or he had a deep scar disappearing from his forehead up into his hairline.

'What do you think that mark is on his head?' Linda asked.

Elaine took a closer squint at the photograph and confirmed, 'It must be the scar from his operation.'

'What operation?'

'Mother told me the whole sad story before she died,' Elaine sighed. 'As you can see from the early photographs, grandfather wasn't always . . . how should I put it . . . a sex fiend. She said, that when she was a child, he was the most wonderful father and the perfect husband to grandmother.'

'Something happened during the war?' Linda surmised out loud, in a high-pitched expectant tone of voice.

277

'No, he came through the war unscathed – in fact, according to mother he was a bit of hero – hence the silver cross thingy. After the war, he wasn't demobbed, instead they gave him a jeep and he travelled around Europe collecting men that had truanted during the battles.'

'Truanted? Oh you mean those who went AWOL.' Linda couldn't help but snigger at Elaine's inappropriate usage of the scholastic concept.

'What does AWOL mean?'

'It's an acronym for "absent without leave" – in other words desertion.'

Elaine pondered the phrase for a few seconds before she declared, 'When you think about it – really it's the same kind of thing as playing truant.'

'I suppose so,' Linda quickly agreed, hoping that Elaine would get back to the more interesting story about her grandfather's mysterious scar.

'Anyway, it was early in 1947 and his stint was almost over – he was driving to an American airbase in Southern Bavaria called Landsberg, to catch a plane home. Then he was going to retire from the army for good, to become a music teacher at Grenchwood. His car skidded on some black ice – it left the road and hit a telegraph pole. Fortunately, an American patrol was following and managed to get him to their field hospital at the airport, where they patched him up and flew him straight to London, for an emergency operation on his head injuries. The surgeon didn't give my grandmother much hope for his survival, but after being in a coma for forty-eight days, he suddenly woke up. He remained in hospital for the next fourteen months, slowly recovering and learning to walk again. After another three-month stretch at a recuperation hospital, he finally came home in 1949, outwardly, apart from the scar on his forehead, looking as good as new.'

'Outwardly? So there was still something not quite right about him, then?' Linda asked.

'Yes, I can only describe it in the layman's terms that mother used, but he was suffering from a form of hypersexuality, which gave him "Jekell and Hyde" mood changes.'

'What the hell is hypersexuality?'

'In the accident, the frontal lobes of his brain were damaged and this affected his libido, and more dangerously, he lost his sense of sexual restraint – basically he would be fine most of the time, but then get sudden and uncontrollable sexual urges, which he found too irresistible to refrain from.'

'Oh my God! How on earth did your grandmother manage?'

'At first, Emily thought his sexual demands were just a physical response, to the fact that he had been away for so long. When she couldn't cope with his attentions anymore, she started to slip her own prescribed tranquilizers into his tea, but her supply of drugs couldn't keep up with his periods of rampant sexual desire.'

'Did she seek medical advice about him?' Linda asked.

'No, she was too embarrassed to talk about it to her doctor, this was back in the fifties, it wasn't seemly to discuss sexual matters – not like now, when it's all that everybody talks about!'

'So what happened?'

'On Friday and Saturday nights, he started to go down to the village and play the piano, in any of the three pubs that were there then. He soon got involved with various women, most of whom were either war widows, or bored wives wanting a fling. After a while, he caused a lot of jealous resentment between the women that he was seeing, and the men weren't too happy to have him around either. So one by one, he got barred from all the pubs and that's when the real problems started up at the school. Grandmother had managed to keep him away from the girls, by not letting him teach music, but instead, getting him to do the maintenance and upkeep of the building, which had been badly neglected during the war years. So there was this man, suffering from a pathological desire to have sex, surrounded twenty-four

279

hours a day, by over a hundred and fifty females. It didn't take too long before grandmother found out that he had been knobbing two of the younger teachers.'

'Not Miss Ryan!' Linda exclaimed.

'No! But I'm sure grandfather would have – given half a chance!'

'Did he try it on with any of the girls – the pupils I mean?'

'Yes, and the strange thing is, none of them complained, in fact, they apparently vied for his attention,' Elaine accompanied this statement with an uneasy laugh. 'The problem intensified during the summer holidays – suddenly the school emptied out and left just the immediate family. It was then his desires grew darker, and he started to have sex with poor Iona, who kind of allowed him to, on the condition he didn't interfere with her younger sister.'

'God! How terrible for Iona, she must have been at her wits' end.'

'Yes, and all the time Amelia had no idea of what was going on, because during the term times, she had been away at university for the previous four years.'

'What a burden for your poor grandmother and aunt – Iona must have dreaded Amelia coming back for the summer holidays.'

'He had been on his best behaviour, that summer of 1955 and Iona thought they were going to get through it, without Amelia finding anything out or being molested by him, and then, just two days before the end of the holiday – it happened,' Elaine gulped back a sob of retrospective distress, and Linda instinctively held her hand in a supportive gesture.

'Iona and Mother were re-decorating the top floor bedrooms, while grandfather had the floorboards up, running in some electric cable. Everything was fine and they had all been joking around, then Iona went downstairs to get some more paint. When she came back into the room five minutes later, grandfather was on top of mother. Iona snapped, picked up the long bladed scissors and stabbed him in the back with them.'

280

'Why didn't they go to the police straight away?' Linda enquired.

'Well, Amelia and Iona were in a state of shock and totally out of it, so Grandmother Emily took charge. She knew that the resulting scandal would force the closure of the school – as it in fact did, when his body was eventually found.

'Why did they stash the body under the floorboards?'

'Not the most original place was it!' Elaine sniffed, her moist eyes smiling again. 'But my grandmother didn't have many options – the floorboards were already up from where he had been working, so she just scooped out the tiny shell insulation, and lined the bottom with sand from the long jump pit. Then she managed to slide his body into the void between the floors and swept the shells back in, on top of him – banging the floorboards down the best she could. With her husband's body safely entombed, she locked the segregation door in the corridor, swore her daughter's to complete secrecy, and hoped that nobody would ever set foot in that part of the building again. You realise that his body was directly above your bed in the dorm – that stain which kept reappearing on the ceiling was some type of chemical residue that had seeped into the ceiling plaster.'

'God, I'd forgotten about that! I used to like looking at it, last thing at night, thinking it was my guardian angel and saying goodnight to it before I went to sleep, to give me luck for the next day,' Linda said, stopping for an instant to wistfully recall her childish superstition, before pursuing the original thread of their conversation. 'How did your grandmother explain his absence, when the new term began?'

'She just told the returning teachers and people down in the village, that he had gone off with another woman, and as luck would have it, a barmaid, whom he had previously been seeing, packed up and moved on, at about the same time – so the gossips in the village, had them doing a moon night flit together.'

'There must have been a smell . . . you know when he was decomposing,' Linda threw her hands up in disgust.

281

'Yes, I suppose there was, but most of it must have floated upwards and into the empty room – besides if you remember, there were quite a few nasty smells drifting around the building when we were there,' Elaine snuffled some air into her nose with amusement.

'You're right – I well remember that horrid smell of greens and cauliflower wafting around the corridors – yuck! And fish on Fridays, that ponged up a bit, not to mention the laundry, what on earth did they boil up our clothes in, back then?'

'In the winter, the dorms smelt of a mixture of paraffin and sweaty socks,' Elaine added to the list of dubious odours. 'I guess one more stench was hardly noticeable.'

'Did they really think that his body would never get discovered?'

'I would imagine that both Amelia and Iona knew that one day it would be, but they also thought that day, would be way off in the future, when they would be too old to care – you see, they didn't envisage the school ever closing. Grandmother put the stark "out-of-bounds" warning up on the door, and in those days that was enough to deter the most inquisitive of girls, against trying to gain access to that part of the top floor. Besides, not many pupils attending Grenchwood had the skills to pick a lock, so if you didn't have a key, then entry was just about impossible. The other entrance, the one that Charlotte found, connected straight down to the kitchen and had been bricked up since the thirties, so essentially, there was only one way in. When you think, if my chain hadn't slipped down that particular crack in the floorboards, in that part of the room, he could still be hidden there, and it's possible that Grenchwood Hall would still be a girls' school today.'

'Yes . . . it's almost as if, fate took a hand,' Linda considered the possibility for a few seconds. 'And of course, if the school was still going, you would be the headmistress now!'

'I doubt whether I'm headmistress material, I'm too soft, the place would be a constant riot of underage sex and drug parties, if I was in charge.'

282

'Not if you had someone like Miss Ryan there as your deputy,' Linda joked, 'A teacher to put the fear of God into the pupils.'

'I don't think you are allowed to do that these days. Do you think Miss Ryan is still alive – if she started in 1930 and was, say twenty then . . . she would be ninety-three now!'

'She could be alive – my grandma was older than that when she passed away. Probably in an old people's home in Scarborough, ordering the staff about and muttering on about how things were different in her day,' Linda smiled at the image that she had just conjured up in her head and then her thoughts returned to Elaine's story. 'So what happened when Amelia discovered that she was pregnant?'

'Well an abortion was out of the question, even if they could have found somebody to do it. Grandmother took her away to Scotland to see great-aunt Davina, who was Donald's sister, and explained what had happened, leaving out the part that her brother was dead and instead, telling her that he had cleared off after the rape. She agreed that Amelia could stay with her until the baby was born and then they would try to have it . . . I mean me, adopted. But when I arrived, Mother refused to let me be adopted . . .' Elaine's voice faltered and she glanced at Linda with tears beginning to drench her eyes. 'Which means she did love me, didn't she? Even though she left me after a year and returned to Grenchwood.'

'She had to do that, she could hardly have had you back at the school – having the unmarried daughter of the headmistress, parading her baby around a girls' boarding school in the fifties, would have been just unthinkable. Remember, once you were old enough, you stayed at Grenchwood every holiday, it would have been the same scenario, if Amelia had married and had a child, they would have still gone off to boarding school at the age of six or seven. Imagine how awful it must have been for her, seeing you every day at school and never being able to tell you the truth, the frustration must have been immeasurable.'

'Yes, and I was a constant reminder of that appalling day. Before she died, Mother told me that she had planned to tell me that

283

she was my real mother, when I reached the age of twenty-one. But not who my father was, or anything else about the circumstances of my conception. Whether she would have done, I don't know, still that's all water under the bridge now.'

#   #   #

The day had flown by, in a warm whirl of laughter, memories and a few tears. Linda and Elaine's reunion had been an emotional roll-a-coaster ride, the breathtaking journey had dipped, twisted and soared, but now had finally drawn to a stop. Fourteen hours had passed since the two friends had met up again for the first time in thirty-three years, but the intensity and excitement of the day had taken its toll. Grudgingly they decided to retire to their beds, both happy with the prospect that tomorrow would be just as exhilarating.

CHAPTER TWENTY-FOUR
19th October 2003

9.30am

Linda crept along the darkened corridor and gently pushed open the kitchen door, to see if Elaine was up and about yet. Peering into the room, she saw her sitting at the book-cluttered table, wrapped in a pink dressing gown and totally engrossed in the large photo album that contained the pictures of Grenchwood Hall, taken at the beginning of the twentieth century.

'Oh morning,' she looked up with a brilliant smile, 'you needn't have got up so early – I'll get you some coffee.'

'Thanks. What time is it? I just got up and didn't bothered to check for a change.'

'Nine-thirty,' Elaine informed her.

'Nine-thirty! I've just had about the best night's sleep, since I don't know when! It's so utterly peaceful here – I was out for the count, as soon as my head hit the pillow. I've only just woken up, a few minutes ago – over eight solid hours of uninterrupted sleep – bliss!' Linda stretched her arms above her head and arched her back, listening for the faint pops that her lower vertebrae made, as her spine straightened out.

'Is it noisy in Fulham then?'

'Yes, there's always someone coming home from a night out, shouting and swearing, or the sound of a police siren wailing, or the traffic constantly revving up at the junction. The people who work in the city, that live nearby, seem to set off for the office at about 5am, so you get their car doors banging away as well. I think I only ever get about an hour's sleep before I'm disturbed again – then I can't get back to sleep, and just when I do, the bloody alarm goes off!'

Elaine handed a mug of piping hot coffee over to Linda, and said, 'I'll make us a fry-up in a few minutes.'

'I had a thought . . . about this photo album,' Linda suddenly remarked, pointing to the open book lying on the table. 'I was thinking about what you said about it.'

'What was that?'

'That it doesn't belong here, shut up in the attic.'

'Yes, it is a shame.'

'Why don't we return it to Grenchwood – right now . . . today I mean, and at the same time, see the old school in its new guise as a hotel. We could even stay the night – my treat!'

'I'm not sure, do you think they would want it?' Elaine's natural reluctance to revisit the old school was clearly imprinted on her face.

'Of course they will want it – it's marketing gold dust. They might even offer you some money. Go on Elaine, the last memories I have of you at Grenchwood, are simply awful, let's go back and lay to rest the ghost of that time forever. We can go down to Grench village and see how that has changed.'

Elaine looked into Linda impassioned eyes and felt her doubts start to wilt under her intense gaze.

'Oh all right then, what harm can it do? And, it would be good to see the old place again, after all these years,' she agreed, with a warm, appeasing smile.

286

'Great! After breakfast we'll clear up last night's mess and then take a spin over to Yorkshire, we should be there by mid-afternoon – I hope they'll still have some rooms available.'

'Sod clearing up, I'll do that when you have gone home, let's just get ready and go after breakfast – make a day of it,' Elaine suddenly enthused.

#   #   #

As Linda turned into the drive of Grenchwood Hall Hotel, the voice on the car radio, announced that there were just a couple of minutes to go, until the one o'clock news. Slowing the car down to a stop, Linda switched off the radio so that they could both sit in silence and imbibe the sight of the old school building, which neither of them had seen for so long.

Linda finally broke the edgy stillness, by saying what they both were thinking, 'It just looks exactly the same.'

'I suppose it's looked exactly the same for over three hundred years, but the grounds look different, neater – oh, I see why, there's a golf course now,' Elaine said, pointing across to an electric golf buggy, trundling along a fairway to their right. Linda crawled the car along the driveway and into the newly black tarmaced car park, which stretched the entire width of the historic building's frontage.

'The old limestone chippings have gone then,' Linda observed, while parking the Land Rover into a space at the far end of the marked bays.

'So have the raised beds, with all those lovely rose bushes in them, in fact, I think we are parked where they used to be,' Elaine made this estimation, from the image she had of the old estate, indelibly stamped in her mind's eye.

Linda twisted around in her seat and reached into the back of the car to retrieve the old leather-bound photograph album.

'Well this is it! Let's go through those old front doors again,' she said trying to remain upbeat, but looking at Elaine's pale, blood drained face, it was obvious that upsetting thoughts had been fermenting in her brain during the journey. Without saying anything and wearing a forced smile on her lips, Elaine looked back and nodded her agreement. In silence the two women began their march across the car park, over to the main entrance. While walking, both had a desperate urge to look up towards the window of the secret room, but neither dared to do so. After pausing to exchange a glance and take a deep breath, they ascended the well-worn stone steps and entered into what was now the hotel's entrance hall.

'Oh my God! I knew that it would have changed, but it's totally unrecognisable!' Linda burst out with shock and astonishment, at the vision before her. The original, dark oak panelled corridor had been sympathetically re-modelled to create a light, spacious and atmospheric reception area. Casting her eye around the rest of the visible interior, Linda almost gasped out aloud, at the opulent seating and bar areas. Turning to Elaine, who looked equally shocked by the sumptuous surroundings, she whispered, 'I don't believe this is the same place, do you?'

'No, It looks incredible!'

Linda slowly advanced in the direction of the young, bright-blonde haired girl, sitting behind a large, elegantly carved, antiqued reception counter, which looked like it could have come straight out of a grand eighteenth-century coaching inn.

'Good afternoon,' said the smiling receptionist, who wore a black badge with gold lettering, which advised the reader that her first name was Lauren.

'Hi, um . . . could I speak to the manager please?' Linda replied, unsure how to approach the subject of the photo album.

'Is there something wrong?' Lauren's expression changed to a concerned frown at Linda's question.

'Oh no, it's just that we have brought something with us, which the hotel owners might wish to see.'

The girl's features now fluctuated into a look of total confusion. Linda carefully placed the bulky, venerable-looking tome down on the desk top, for her to see.

'It's a set of very old photographs that were taken here, at Grenchwood Hall, about a hundred years ago,' she explained.

Lauren looked at the first plate.

'Oh yes, I can see that it's this building, but everything else looks so different – all those flower beds and a horse-drawn carriage,' she said, picking up the phone and pressing a green button. 'Hello Mr. Parry, I have two ladies in reception who have something that you might be interested in . . . it's a book full of old pics of Grenchwood . . . yes, about a hundred years old apparently.' The young receptionist replaced the phone and smiling at Linda, politely asked, 'Would you like to follow me and I'll show you to Mr Parry's office?'

Stepping out from behind the counter Lauren strode purposely towards the back of the building, with Linda and Elaine pursuing her a few feet behind. Passing close to the grand staircase, they were both most impressed to see how the dark wooden varnished balustrades now gleamed against the backdrop of the plush red carpet that covered the stairs. Making their way further into the corridor, the surroundings became far more familiar to them, with the austere dark oak panelling and lofty coved ceiling, being the prevailing architectural features. The door that just over thirty years previously, had served as the entrance to Miss Rutherford's study, came into view. It looked exactly the same, except that now, the imposing brass plate bearing the appellation "Headmistress" had been replaced with an oblong of shiny white acrylic, with the words "General Manager" etched in black, vinyl san-serif lettering. Linda felt her heartbeat accelerate as she crossed the threshold of the manager's office, only to find a room that was the embodiment of minimalist modern office design and not furnished in the style of a Victorian drawing room, the way that she had remembered it.

'Good afternoon, I'm very pleased to meet you. My name is Daniel Parry, I'm co-owner and General Manager of

289

Grenchwood Hall Hotel – Lauren tells me that you might have something very interesting for me to see?' said a smart-looking, grey haired man, who courteously shook their hands, as he welcomed them into his office.

'I'm Linda Watson and this is my friend Elaine Rutherford,' Linda continued to act as spokesperson for the pair. 'Elaine's mother and aunt used to own this building, when it was a girls' boarding school, and yesterday when we were sorting through some old things, we found this.' Linda passed the album over to Daniel.

He immediately picked up his reading glasses, from the top of the solid maple-wood table that dominated the room. Stooping over the table, he opened the album and peered down at the photographs, with a look of thoughtful fascination on his face. Taking his time to carefully examine each sepia print individually, finally he stood back upright, stroked his chin in contemplation and declared, 'This is just an amazing chronicle, of life at Grenchwood Hall in a more genteel age – is it by chance for sale?'

Linda looked at Elaine, indicating that it was her decision. Elaine nervously searched for the right words, before saying, 'Well I thought . . . I mean, we thought, that these photos should be reunited with the hall – they should be kept here always.'

'How much would you want for them?' Daniel Parry asked, not picking up on the fact that Elaine was offering the historical artefact gratuitously.

'Nothing – we just want to return the book and while we are here, perhaps stay for the night for old time's sake.'

'That is very generous of you Ms. Rutherford, and of course you must both stay as my guests, it's the very least I can do,' Daniel acknowledged Elaine's benevolence and immediately picked up his phone, to check with the receptionist about the availability of rooms. Linda smiled warmly at Elaine, pleased with the outcome of their meeting; she then wandered casually over to the bay window. The view was exactly how she had remembered it, except this time, there was no friendly blackbird foraging for worms in the grass, as there was, the last time she stared out across the lawn covered expanse.

'Linda . . . Linda . . .' Elaine called over, but her voice failed to penetrate the cocoon of deep wistful thoughts that her friend had woven herself into, while gazing out of the window. 'Linda!' Elaine raised her voice a few decibels, which shook Linda, back into the present time.

'Oh sorry! I was lost in thought,' Linda apologised.

'They only have one suite available – it's a double on the top floor. Did you want to share a room?'

'The top floor?' Linda repeated, in a woolly tone that did little to convey that she had grasped what Elaine had asked her.

'Is there a problem about the top floor,' Daniel cut in, looking concerned by Linda's perplexed expression.

'No, of course not, it's just that . . . when we were here at school, that floor was out-of-bounds to us!' Linda regained her composure and managed to extricate herself from her hazy demeanour with a joke. She then addressed Elaine's question, 'Yes I'm fine about sharing, if you are?'

'Please don't feel that anywhere at Grenchwood is out-of-bounds now,' Daniel laughed. 'I would also hope that you will dine with us tonight in the restaurant, again as my guests.'

'Thank you.' Both women answered together.

'Please let me show you to your suite – it's called The Cullingworth, and is situated to the front of the building, with panoramic views over towards the village of Upper Grench. The original central part of the building dates back to the early eighteenth century,' Daniel lapsed into his instinctive sales patter concerning the rooms and building, as he led the way out of his office and down the corridor back to the reception. He stopped and turned around with a half-smile of contrition on his face. 'Of course, you already know all of that, sorry, it's a habit of mine to rattle off boring spiel about the hotel.' After briefly pausing at the

291

front desk for Lauren to hand him the keycard, he gently ushered Linda and Elaine over to the lift.

'Gosh! Imagine what fun we would have had with this, if it had been installed when we were here,' Elaine whispered, smiling at Linda, as the lift doors separated to allow them admittance into its steely-grey, metallic interior. During the short journey upwards, the etiquette of an awkward silence was meticulously observed, broken only by the "ding" that signalled that the doors were about to slide effortlessly apart. Stepping out into the airy, well-lit and generously carpeted corridor, both Linda and Elaine exchanged disbelieving glances at each other.

'It's just so different – much wider and so luxuriously decorated! This passageway used to be so dingy, with a bare wooden floor, and a door on the left and right, every ten feet or so,' Elaine spouted out.

'I thought this was out-of-bounds for you two,' Daniel jokingly queried.

'It was, but we did sneak up here a few times,' Elaine smiled an impish grin back at him.

The further they marched down the corridor, the faster Elaine and Linda's hearts began to beat. Just as they were approaching the end, Daniel mercifully announced they had reached their suite and stopped. He inserted the keycard into the slot and pushed open the door allowing them both to enter.

'Oh my God! This is so beautiful,' Linda exclaimed with sheer delight, at the vision of luxury before her.

'I hope you will both be very comfortable in here, and as I said before, feel free to use any of the hotel's facilities, including the mini-bar,' Daniel said, giving them a friendly wink. 'It's all on the house, or should I say the hotel. Thank you again for bringing the photos back to Grenchwood, they are a unique link to the past, which we will use to great effect around the building.'

Daniel Parry returned to his office and the two excited women were left to marvel about the splendour of their

292

surroundings, and how utterly different everything was from their days at the school.

'I thought for one awful moment that we were going to be . . . in the . . . actual room,' Linda stammered nervously.

'Actually, despite everything changing so much, I don't think I could have gone into that room – my legs were turning to jelly as we walked down the passageway,' Elaine expressed her feeling of uneasiness about being so close to their former hideout. 'Where exactly are we now?'

'The bedroom part of the suite, would have been Charlotte's old room, the far end where the bathroom is, would have been the room next to Charlotte's and this living room, where we are standing, would have been part of the first room in the locked off section,' Linda explained, using the former room layout as her reference.

'So behind this wall,' just above the reproduction Georgian fireplace, Elaine gently smoothed her hand across the cool magnolia painted plaster, 'is the actual secret room, where we used to hang out?'

'Yes, it must be, because the corridor came to an end, about thirty-five feet after the door to our rooms.'

'Well, this is as close as I'm getting to that damn room – remind me to always turn right, when we come out of our door,' Elaine joked, smiling again.

'Let's go down to the village – while it's still nice outside. The weather forecast said there is a storm coming in from the west, we might as well make the most of the sunny weather while we still have it.'

Elaine readily approved Linda's suggestion, so after a few minutes, they vacated their newly acquired apartment and wandered back down the corridor, still agog at how everything seemed so completely different.

'It's weird being able to take a lift downstairs,' Linda said, pressing the button to call the cage to the top floor.

293

'It's all very weird, the place has had one hell of a makeover, since we were here – it's totally unrecognisable inside.' Elaine sighed, with a tinge of disappointment.

'Well you didn't expect it to still have dormitories did you?' Linda playfully jibed at Elaine's comment.

'No of course not, but apart from the headmistress's study, all the room sizes have changed. I can't work out where our old classroom is . . . or rather was.'

'I'm pretty sure that it forms part of the restaurant. Just think, when we have our meal tonight, we will probably be sitting very close to where we sat, for all those boring lessons about algebra and logarithms – whatever they used to be!'

The blurry mirrored doors cascaded opened and they stepped inside, only to hear a plaintive cry of, 'Can you hold the lift!' ringing up the passageway. Linda was immediately sent into a sense of panic, as she searched for the correct button to keep the doors open.

'Oh thank you!' gasped, an out of breath, red-faced lady in her seventies, who on reaching the lift opening, steadied herself, by leaning against its open door. 'It's my husband, he's very bad on his feet.'

The noise of two walking sticks, periodically prodding down onto the thick carpet with a muffled thud, heralded the slow arrival of the said husband.

'Thank you for waiting ladies, hope I'm not delaying you too much,' the man cheerily said, as he came into view.

'Of course not,' Linda reassured him.

'It's me knees, they're buggered.'

'I'm sorry to hear that,' Elaine said, taking his arm and helping him inside the lift.

'You'd never guess, looking at the state of me now, that forty-five years ago, I was a professional footballer!'

294

'Is that what caused the damage to your knees?' Elaine asked.

'No, when I retired from the game, I spent the next thirty years laying bloody carpets – that's what did for me knees,' the man gave a little ironic chuckle.

'Did you play for someone famous?' Linda inquired keenly, not wanting to allow their conversation to fizzle out, and spend the duration of the descent in an uncomfortable silence.

'No, I did the rounds of the southern, third and fourth division clubs – Southend, Leyton Orient, Gillingham and Aldershot.' The man proudly listed the teams that he had played for, none of which meant a thing to either Linda or Elaine.

'We were forever moving house, I dreaded the end of the seasons when he was out of contract – never knew where I'd be next,' laughed the man's wife. The lift doors opened into the reception area and the old couple shuffled slowly out towards the bar.

'They were a nice old couple,' Elaine mumbled under her breath, and then, in a more distinct voice she added, 'I wonder how much of Upper Grench village we will recognise?'

CHAPTER TWENTY-FIVE
19th October 2003

1.05pm

Melissa had strategically seated herself in the elegantly furnished lounge bar, just off of the main reception area, and waited for Steve to meet her there on the completion of his morning round of golf. Sipping a coffee while pretending to read the Sunday papers, she indulged herself in her favourite hobby of people-watching. Unfortunately, the barroom was almost empty, save for two couples who were together on a weekend break and an elderly looking man, with a smart military bearing, sitting up at the bar, knocking back a double malt whisky every five minutes or so.

The raw material that she had to work with was a bit limiting; the two couples had almost hidden themselves away in the corner of the room and were talking in revered hush tones, so it was hard to eavesdrop on their conversation, which she had all ready decided, would be mind-bogglingly dull anyway. The elderly gentleman sitting at the bar, whom she had mentally given the nickname of the "Major", looked more interesting. Perhaps he was waiting to rendezvous with a high-class prostitute and the chain-drinking of the double whiskies, was to afford him the Dutch courage that he needed. Melissa decided, that at his age, he would be better off taking a shot of liquid Viagra, and then it dawned on her, that the man was probably only three or four years older than her own husband. This realisation deflated her amusement and motivated a panoramic sweep of the almost empty lounge, across to the entrance. The giant grandfather clock next to the door, gave the time as ten minutes past one, a cursory check with her wristwatch confirmed this. Through the open doorway, she could see the pretty young receptionist studying the contents of some kind of old leather-bound book, which would not have looked out of place on the *Antiques Road Show*. The young girl made a phone call and then, along with two other women, who she could only see the backs of, disappeared down the rear corridor and out of sight.

Melissa exhaled a sigh of boredom and thought that if Steve didn't get to the bar soon, she would ask the Major up to her room and see if he still had the ability to stand to attention. Just then, her lover loped through the doorway, smiling to himself and seemingly completely unconcerned that he was over an hour late, on the agreed meet-up time.

'Steve! Where have you been?' Melissa hissed.

Steve frowned innocently and sat down on the seat next to her.

'Am I late then?'

'You said you would be finished, at the latest, by mid-day. It's too late to go out for some lunch now, so we'll have to get something sent up to our room.'

'Sorry! It was just that, two guys up here from Birmingham invited me to join them, so we made up a threesome.'

Melissa sniggered, 'I didn't know you liked threesomes – perhaps we should have invited Linda along?'

Steve made faint wheezing laugh, like the sibilant noise a radiator makes when being bled.

'It's hard enough to get Linda to have sex when it's just the two of us, I can't see her being too enthusiastic about taking part in an orgy.'

'A threesome is hardly an orgy – anyway, I think she might be all the more interested, if she knew that I was the third person.'

'What do you mean?' Steve asked, genuinely taken aback by Melissa's comment.

'I've caught her checking me out.'

'Get out of here! You're making it up.'

'I have! I caught her eyes perving down at my tits – just for a second, when she opened the door to me, and once, when I bent over to pick something up, I'm sure she was ogling my bum.'

'Rubbish! She was probably checking to see, what ridiculous label you had on your clothes – you're all obsessed with designer labels.'

'Who knows what she got up to, when she went to school here. She probably had a torrid lesbian affair with her best friend, the one that she is visiting this weekend. That's why, she never mentioned being here at school to you – she was too ashamed!'

'I don't think thirteen year old schoolgirls have affairs, torrid or any other kind.'

'Oh, I think you'd be surprised to find out what thirteen year old girls get up to,' Melissa giggled, unable to keep a serious face for any longer.

'You're pulling my plonker aren't you?'

'Not yet, but I'm sure it's on my list of "things to do to you", when we get up to our room. Now, can you get us a couple of glasses of wine before we go up.'

Steve smiled, and with his usual good grace, accepted that Melissa had once again managed to wind him up, for her own personal enjoyment. He meandered his way around the other tables and over to the bar, where Melissa could see he was exchanging some pleasantries with her Major.

'What were you and the old guy at the bar talking about?' Melissa asked, as soon as he returned to her, carrying two glass goblets of white wine.

'He said, I was a reckless man, to keep such a beautiful woman waiting,' Steve answered, with a smirk curling on his lips.

'Did he?' Melissa laughed, but was pleasantly flattered in the way that she always was, when she received a compliment from a man. She looked over to the bar and the old man raised his crystal-cut whisky tumbler to her, in an admiring salute. She lifted her wine glass back at him and giggled like an embarrassed schoolgirl.

'Perhaps you would like a threesome with him?' Steve quipped.

'I might,' she flashed a riposte, 'I may have to bring him on as a substitute, if you start to tire in extra time.'

After finishing their drinks, Melissa and Steve strolled through the reception area to the lift, where Melissa impatiently stabbed the call button several times.

'Oh! The bloody thing seems to have got stuck on the top floor – it's been there for over a minute now, let's take the stairs.'

Before he had a chance to disagree, she had grabbed Steve's hand and led him across to the foot of the sweeping staircase.

'If you were at all romantic, you would carry me up these stairs,' Melissa said, with the serrated edge of a challenge cutting through her words.

'You're right,' Steve agreed too readily for Melissa's liking, and before she could stop him, he had hoisted her over his shoulder and was advancing up the stairway.

'Not a fireman's lift you fool,' she screamed, pounding on his backside in a half-hearted attempt to get him to put her down. All pleas were steadfastly ignored, with Steve manfully continuing up the second set of stairs to the top floor. Having passed a very surprised couple coming the other way down the corridor, he waggled their suite card key into the slot and then pushed the door open with the sole of his shoe. Once ensconced in their bedroom, Steve carefully lowered Melissa down onto the large double bed.

'There you are, safely delivered to the boudoir, hopefully that was romantic enough for madam!'

'It wasn't romantic, it was embarrassing!' Melissa laughed, trying to rearrange her tousled hair.

'I can see that, from the flushed colour in your face,' Steve observed, enjoying his fleeting moment of ascendency.

'What do you expect, with all the blood rushing to my head!'

'All my blood is rushing to another part of my anatomy,' Steve smirked.

'Right then, if that's the case, it's time for your surprise – I'll just be ten minutes,' Melissa declared, daintily stepping over to her case and unzipping it.

'Not another ten minutes!' Steve groaned. 'We've been here over twenty-four hours now and we haven't even had a shag yet!'

'Just ten more minutes, I promise you, it will be worth the wait,' Melissa expertly teased him, and then pulled out a large black plastic bag from her case.

'What's in there?' Steve asked, intrigued by the emergence of the mystifying bag.

'You'll find out in ten minutes.'

Before Steve could make an attempt to snatch the bag away from her, Melissa rushed across to the safety of the bathroom, where she locked herself in. Steve was baffled by her behaviour, but mixed with this feeling, was a sense of submissive stimulation, at being continually orchestrated by his mistress. To quell the suspense that was rising, mostly from his loins, he passed the time looking out of the window, at the several games of golf, taking

300

place below him. In his head, he pretended that he was commentating at the British Open, making sage comments on the various shots and having a genial conversation with the great golfing guru, Peter Alliss.

The bathroom door opened with a slight creak, the image he detected in his peripheral vision, caused his golfing fantasy to instantly vanish and be replaced by a much more sordid flight of fancy. Melissa was standing dressed head to toe in an authentic, contemporary schoolgirl uniform, with her hands placed on her hips she struck up a sultry pose.

'Hello Sir, are you going to teach me a lesson?' Melissa lisped, and then slowly lifting a bright red lollipop to her matching coloured lips, she acquainted the sticky ball with her darting tongue. 'As you can see from my badge, I'm the "Head Girl" and you are about to find out why I'm called that.' Strutting into the middle of the room with a sexy swagger, she took hold of Steve's hand and escorted him over to the bed, where she firmly pushed him down, so that he was sitting meekly on the end. Stepping back, she threw the saliva-coated confectionary across the room, lifted the side hems of her very short skirt and twirled around to reveal a pair of navy blue schoolgirl knickers. The result of this display was immediate and very noticeable upon Steve.

'The woman in the shop said these blue knicks would have that effect on you!' Melissa giggled, while she concentrated on undoing Steve's belt and trouser buttons.

'What woman, in what shop?' Steve managed to breath out his question.

'The woman in the school outfitters.'

'The woman in the school outfitters said that!' Steve spat out his words of disbelief at Melissa, while she pulled his unfastened trousers down to his knees.

'Yes, I explained to them what I was planning to do,' Melissa let out another raspy guffaw.

'You did what!' Steve growled.

301

'Don't worry, I didn't mention you by name, you silly sod, I just told them I wanted to spice up my sex life.'

'Weren't they shocked?'

'Well, no. Not at all. Apparently it's a very common fantasy, which they're all in favour of, as it helps to keep their cash register ringing away through the quiet months, after the schools have gone back in September.' Melissa casually informed him, while she took off her gold and blue striped tie and started to unbutton her white blouse. Flinging open her top, she smugly revealed her rounded bare breasts to Steve's appreciative scrutiny.

'Hold your hands out,' Melissa ordered, standing up close to Steve, in just her school knickers and white ankle socks.

'Why?' Steve replied, confused by where the interaction was going.

'Just do it Steve,' Melissa said in a quiet but assertive voice. Steve held out both his arms in front of him and quickly Melissa looped the school tie around his wrist and tightened the knot.

'What . . . are you doing?' Steve half protested, but Melissa just pushed him down so that he was lying flat on the bed. She then clambered onto the duvet, turned around and adopted a kneeling posture, her bronzed naked thighs straddling his chest. Encased in the drum tight, blue knickers, her buttocks were gently swaying just a few inches in front of his face, while he could feel her hands gently liberating his erect penis from the snare of his underpants.

'Now, what was that little chore that Linda hates to perform?'

Steve stared intently at Melissa's bottom as it rocked with a tantalising attraction back and forth, in time with the ticking wall clock. With each lean forward, he felt the head of his penis being expertly caressed by her moist lips and swirling tongue, while her two hands soothingly rubbed his groin and scrotum.

302

After a few minutes, Melissa interrupted her exertions and twisted around to take a look at the abandoned, ecstatic expression on Steve's face.

'Was this worth the wait then Steve?'

Steve moaned out a garbled sound of admiration for her labours. The weight of her body suddenly lifted off of his chest, causing him to open his eyes, to capture the erotic sight of Melissa bending over, in readiness to divest the last item of her school uniform. She deliberately thrilled him, by very slowly, rolling the blue cotton pants down her flawless pear-shaped behind, inch-by-inch the sinuous dark crease that separated the swells of her two shadowed buttocks became exposed to his eager view. Once the band of material, had reached the top of her slender thighs, it was loose enough to drop down her legs to the floor. Melissa then returned to her former dominating position of sitting astride Steve's torso, tilting forwards she firmly commanded, 'Time for you to show your appreciation Steve!'

303

CHAPTER TWENTY-SIX
19th October 2003

6.25pm

Returning back to the hotel, from their Sunday afternoon nostalgia trip down at the local village, Linda and Elaine were delighted that the general appearance of Upper Grench had changed little, from the memories that they held in their heads; it was just the walk there and back that seemed to have become longer.

'I was so pleased to see that the Copper Kettle was still there!' Elaine proclaimed as soon as Linda had closed the door to their rooms. 'Do you think that the same people own it?'

'The shop may have been sold several times in the intervening years, but they probably wouldn't have wanted to change the name, for goodwill reasons,' Linda theorised.

Elaine looked slightly disappointed.

'Only, I thought that the lady taking the money near the door, looked a bit like the waitress who served us, when we went there on your first weekend. Obviously she is a lot older now – about her mid fifties, it would be about right, age wise – wouldn't it?'

'Elaine! You can't possibly remember what that girl looked like!' Linda mocked her friend's fanciful assumption. 'I can tell you what has changed though.'

'What?'

'The price! Nearly twenty pounds for the same order that we had back then, for ten bob.'

'And the other thing that has changed – we won't get hauled into the headmistress's study tomorrow!' Elaine's comment caused them both to burst into laughter at the embarrassing recollection.

After a few seconds, the outburst of hilarity subsided into reflective smiles and a strange silence presided over the room; this was intruded on by the curious beat of a muffled pounding noise, coming from the next suite. The two women looked at each other with expressions of unease.

'You don't think the old secret room is haunted do you,' Linda said, in a serious tone.

Elaine stood closer to the dividing wall.

'It could be, given what went on in there, but if I'm not mistaken, those sounds are being made by two people, who are very much alive,' she responded to the question by making an uneasy joke.

Linda concentrated on the different acoustic squeals and groans emanating from the adjacent rooms.

'Wow! Somebody's having a good time, judging from the shrieks of delight coming through the wall.'

'Yes, "coming" is the optimum word there I think!' Elaine sniggered. 'I think I'll have a shower and freshen up before we go down for our meal.'

'I'll have one after you,' Linda said, still craning her ear to catch the essence of what was going on next door.

'We could shower together, like we did at school, after games,' Elaine flashed a cheeky smile at Linda.

'If I remember correctly, that hardly ever happened, we used to fool Miss Neame, by splashing water around the floor, near

305

to where we were changing, and then dampen our towels to make it look as though we had showered.'

'That's right – we weren't very hygienic back then, were we?'

'To be fair, neither was the shower, just four small heads dribbling out lukewarm water, with most of the wall tiles cracked, and covered in some sort of horrible sooty mould.'

'I hope the showers have improved now.' Elaine said, unbuttoning her blouse, while walking through to the bathroom. Linda concentrated her hearing on the compelling sound of the sexual shenanigans radiating from through the wall. After indulging herself for a few minutes, she felt guilty about her snooping and so switched on the television to obscure the steamy vibrations.

#   #   #

Just over two hours later the two women were finally ready to go down for their evening meal.

'I'm not sure that this is really suitable to wear to a posh restaurant,' Elaine cast a nervous doubt about her appearance, as she glanced at herself in the large wall mirror.

'Nonsense, you look . . . you look wonderful,' Linda's compliment was un-mistakenly sincere and reassuring. 'Anyway, everyone goes to restaurants casual nowadays – dressing up is so eighties.'

'Thanks! I think it was in the eighties that I last went to a proper restaurant. Are the lovers next door having a bit of a break – I can't hear any sounds of action?'

'Yes, the pounding of distant guns stopped about twenty minutes ago,' Linda laughed.

'Gosh! Wouldn't it be embarrassing if we walked straight into them, as we left the room.'

'Yes – it would be difficult to look them in the eye, after listening to their "goings-on" for the last couple of hours.'

306

'Imagine if we had to share the lift down with them!' Elaine's bright brown eyes were wide with excitement, as she carefully opened the door just enough to poke her head out. Taking a quick look down the corridor, she whispered, 'It's all clear, come on,' and beckoned Linda to follow her.

'Jesus Elaine, this is just like being back at school, only now we are sneaking out of the top floor, rather than sneaking into it,' Linda panted as they scampered down the passageway towards the lift.

#   #   #

Having wined, dined and forensically reviewed the previous thirty years of their separation, at just after midnight, they found themselves making the reverse journey, somewhat unsteadily, along the top corridor back to their room.

'That was marvellous, and how kind of Mr Parry to insist that we have a bottle of champagne. That's two bottles in two days, after not having any for over ten years – you must visit me more often!'

'I'd like that,' Linda said, thinking to herself how lucky she was, to have found Elaine again. 'And you must come down and stay with us – we can spoil ourselves with some retail therapy in the West End shops.'

'Ssshhh! They're still at it!' Elaine hissed, cupping her ear to the wall.

'Elaine! Come away,' Linda playfully rebuked Elaine for her eavesdropping, taking her firmly by the arm she led her into the adjoining bedroom, where they both toppled over and landed across the super king size bed, descending into yet another fit of giggles.

'Who made you head prefect?' Elaine slurred. 'Do you think they have taken a break from all that shagging, anytime this evening?'

'I should think so – they probably came down for a meal, to refuel.'

307

'Who do you think they are then? The young couple, who were sitting over in the corner, holding hands and whispering to each other all evening.'

'No, the girl struck me as being a bit too refined, to come out with some of the rather coarse things I heard being said earlier,' Linda snorted.

'What about the old couple who we met earlier today, who asked us to hold the lift?'

'What the crippled, carpet laying, ex-footballer?' Linda asked incredulously. 'I hardly think the poor man was up to some of the high jinks we heard going on next door – do you?'

'I suppose not – unless his wife was doing all the work,' Elaine spluttered out an inebriated chuckle and attempted to rise from her prone position. 'Oh, I'm just too pissed to care now.'

For the first time since they had slept in the school dormitory together, Linda watched her friend get undressed. Back then, disrobing in front of each other was a nightly ritual, and nudity was an accepted part of school life, devoid of any noticeable sexual undercurrent. Elaine, who was totally unaware of Linda's interest, wobbled slightly whilst trying to release her feet, from the tangle of her trousers, which she had allowed to fall down her legs and were now rolled around her ankles. Linda jumped up off the bed and held Elaine's left arm to help steady her, while she finally managed to kick off the offending garment.

'Thanks,' Elaine smiled and puffed out her cheeks. 'I've heard of bondage trousers, but I didn't realise I was wearing a bloody pair.'

Her institutionalised upbringing had left Elaine with few inhibitions about same-sex nudity. Standing face to face with Linda, she casually reached behind her back and unclasped the hooks on her bra strap, allowing it to fall down her arms and join the trousers on the floor, forming an untidy pile. Linda's eyes were inadvertently gripped by the way Elaine's nipples instantly reacted to the cool air and became slightly erect.

308

'Opps! That happens to me, at the local supermarket.'

'What?' Linda asked sheepishly, and followed her brusque question with a hard empty swallow, but was still unable to disengage her eyes, from focusing on Elaine's very full breasts.

'It happens, when I go down the chilly, frozen produce aisle – you know, I'm sure that some men loiter around that section, hoping to see women with organ stops protruding through their sweaters,' Elaine gave a sniffy chortle and collapsed back down on the bed. Feeling slightly intimidated by Elaine's brazen striptease, Linda decided to withdraw to the bathroom and change into her pyjamas. When she re-emerged into the main room a few minutes later, she found Elaine fast asleep, and the only noise other than her friend's deep breathing, was the continuing stifled sound of the marathon sexual encounter, going on in the next suite. Linda pulled the sheets over Elaine and then snuggled down on her side of the large bed, feeling very contented and relaxed, knowing that the start of a rare restful good night's sleep was just seconds away.

CHAPTER TWENTY-SEVEN
20th October 2003

8.35am

'That was a very nice breakfast, but not as good as yours Elaine,' Linda praised her friend's gastronomic expertise, while they waited patiently in the hotel reception area, for the lift to descend to the ground floor.

'Thanks – I do get a lot of compliments on my full English, especially the size of my portions,' Elaine cheekily replied with a definite twinkle in her eye.

The lift doors opened like mechanical stage curtains, and behind them were the elderly couple that they had met the previous day.

'Good morning ladies,' the man chirpily greeted them. 'You're both early birds this morning, I hope you have left us something to eat.'

Linda took his arm and helped him totter over the narrow metal furrow where the lift casement and the reception floor joined.

'We're early this morning, because I've got to drive back to London and go to work I'm afraid.'

'Oh what a shame, still I hope you've had a good weekend.'

'Yes thank you, it's been a great weekend,' Linda said, giving Elaine a covert smile. After bidding farewell, the old couple doddered off toward the restaurant, while at the same time, Linda and Elaine travelled at speed in the lift, to the top floor.

'What a nice man, shame about his knees – must be awful not to have full use of your legs,' Elaine deliberated quietly, while they tramped down the corridor to their room.

'We'll just get the cases and then be on our way,' Linda sighed a deep breath of resignation, at the prospect of the unpleasant task she would have to undertake later that day, breaking the news to her staff, that she was going to sell the business. They gathered their luggage from the room and Linda pulled their suite door shut.

'That's that then, Grenchwood Hall revisited – mission accomplished,' she forced out a cheerless laugh.

'Yes, except for one last thing,' Elaine said, suddenly running down towards the end of the corridor. 'Before we go, I have to conquer my silly, irrational fear of being close to the secret room,' she called back to Linda, who slowly followed her up the passageway.

Inside the room, Melissa heard the running footsteps and through the strip of clear light at the bottom of the door, she could see the shadow of two feet, standing directly outside.

'I think breakfast has arrived, I'll let them in,' she called to Steve and then opened the door, only to see a shocked looking woman, holding a small suitcase, staring back at her.

'Oh, I'm dreadfully sorry to have disturbed you . . .' Elaine began her apology, but couldn't think of a legitimate reason, why she would be positioned immediately outside the woman's door.

'Did you get the wrong room?' Melissa grinned. 'Don't worry – they all look just the same, don't they? What's your suite called?'

'Um . . . Cullingworth.'

311

'Oh, this is Blackshaw – I think Cullingworth is the next one along,' Melissa poked her head out of the doorway, to point out which room she meant, and to her total amazement, her eyes collided with Linda's, who was still following Elaine down the corridor. Their jaws dropped open, in a simultaneous shocked reaction at seeing one another.

'Melissa? . . . What . . . are you doing . . . here?' Linda managed to utter a confused, disjointed sentence, as she approached ever closer. Melissa was comprehensively dumbstruck, but the look of horror in her eyes conveyed the fact that she was not best pleased to see Linda.

'What seems to be the problem,' a very recognisable male voice, called out from within the room. Every drop of blood in Linda's body froze, as Steve's face appeared from out of the open doorway. Standing totally rigid like a shop window mannequin, she just stared straight through her immediate surroundings. The case and shoulder bag that she was carrying, fell to the floor, landing with a soft thud on the thick carpet. Steve's expression of jarred shock, mirrored her own, with neither of them being able to articulate a single syllable, until he eventually moaned out, a long and heartfelt, 'Fucking hell.'

The expletive re-animated Linda, who then angrily pushed passed Melissa into the room.

'What the hell have you done?' she shouted, in a trill, high-pitched yowl, that was so high, it was almost inaudible.

'How . . . did you find us?' Steve's response was suitably feeble, but it was all that he could muster.

'Find you? I wasn't looking for you, we were just staying here – in the next bloody room, listening to you two, fuck each other's brains out, all of yesterday!' Linda screamed, while she frantically beat her arms against her sides, like a frustrated young bird, trying to get airborne for the first time. 'It's fucking over Steve – I never want to see you again.'

312

Turning to Melissa, Linda delivered a withering warning, 'And I expect, Rod will feel the same about you – you fucking little whore!'

'Please don't tell Rod! We can work something out – he'll divorce me and I'll lose Taylor – I'm begging you!' Melissa dramatically dropped to her knees and pulled on Linda's short jacket.

'Get off me!' Linda struggled to free herself from her tight double-handed grip. 'I said get off me, you bitch!' Still Melissa held on, continuing to plead for forgiveness. Linda's right palm slapped down hard across Melissa's left temple, causing her to release her hold. Pivoting around in a semi-circle on her knees, she collapsed onto the floor and continued to sob hysterically. Linda had an alarming flash back, to the time when she saw Iona in precisely the same position, wearing the same anguished expression on her face. The disturbing image burned into her retinas, causing the room to time-shift, back to how it appeared when she first saw it, with bare floorboards and half painted walls. This startling, vivid echo from the past, set off a surging panic attack, which in turn, activated an overwhelming urgent need within her, to get as far away from the malevolent room, as she could. Stumbling over her discarded suitcase, Linda retrieved her shoulder bag and then ran off down the corridor. Steve tried to follow her, but with a towel tightly wrapped around the lower half of his body, his restricted leg movement meant that he resembled a half-naked robot, clumping ungainly down the passageway, making no appreciable headway.

Steve looked ludicrous as he bunny-hopped back towards Elaine, who was standing paralysed by the bewilderment that the previous sixty seconds had caused.

'Please can you go after her – don't let her drive, she might kill herself.' He begged.

'Yes of course!' Elaine's brain switched back on, and she rushed after Linda, who was by now, seventy yards ahead of her and careering down the first flight of stairs. By taking the waiting lift, she made up some valuable time on her absconding friend. Limiting herself to a conspicuous, hurried walk in the peopled

313

reception area, she immediately resumed her haste once through the main doors. Running down the old stone steps that led out of the building, Elaine then zigzagged between the standing cars, quickly threading her way diagonally across the car park, where she knew the Land Rover was parked. Looking through the car's side window, she was relieved to see the distraught Linda, still sitting hunched in the driver's seat and not preparing to drive off in an uncontrollable frenzy. Tapping gently on the glass, she provoked the sobbing woman to lift her bowed head from her tear-moistened palms, and utter in a crushed voice, 'Oh Elaine, what am I going to do?'

'Move over, I'm going to drive you back to my place – give you some time to think,' Elaine ordered assertively.

'What about our luggage?'

'Sod the luggage, we can come back for it later.'

Elaine started the car up, released the hand break, pushed the gear selector into drive, and they were away. Keeping to the one-way car park directional system, they were filtered into a lane that passed back close to the main entrance. Linda looked across to see Steve, now with his shirt and trousers on, but his feet still bare, recklessly bounding down the front steps and running towards them, his face haunted with a desperation that she had never seen before. Elaine accelerated away from his pleas to stop, turned left and sped up the drive.

The solemn atmosphere in the car made it feel like they were in a funeral cortege, on the restrained, onerous journey to the cemetery. Not knowing, what to say, neither woman wanting to be the first to break the sensitive silence. Linda's mind was rapidly playing through a myriad of different outcome scenarios to her personal crisis, each one ended in the same final result of divorce.

With just a few miles to go, until they would be back at Elaine's house, Linda piped up with a snuffled question, 'Would it be okay, if I stayed with you for a few days?'

'Yes of course you can,' Elaine smiled sympathetically. 'You can stay as long as you like, but it's really incumbent on Steve to move out, after all, he's the one in the wrong.'

'Yes I know, but I can't stand the thought of staying in the house and being just a few doors up the road from that little bitch.'

'Sorry, I didn't realise she was your neighbour – yes, I can see that would be very awkward,' Elaine agreed.

'I don't really want to stay at my mum and dad's – they would be horrified about what has happened and overreact to everything. Sadly, they would probably drive me completely mad in a few hours.'

'It's no problem, I haven't any bookings for next week, so the house will be empty.'

'If you are sure?'

'Yes, like I said, you are welcome to stay for as long as you need to.'

Elaine pulled off Basington's main road and up the compacted earthen track, which led to her house. When they arrived back in the kitchen, the first thing on Elaine's agenda, was to go straight to her stock of assorted alcoholic beverages, which were haphazardously crammed together on a Victorian occasional table that jutted out from an alcove. After pausing for a moment to make a decision, she picked up a bottle of brandy and poured out two generous measures. Carrying the two, highball glasses, she carefully picked her way around the discarded ledger books that were still lying untidily on the floor, after being deposited there on Saturday night. Linda cut a sorrowful figure, sitting passively dejected on the sofa, in a post-trauma induced daze. Elaine offered a glass to her and she gratefully accepted it.

'Get that down you – it's good for shock and it will warm you up until the fire gets going,' Elaine said.

Turning around, she set about building a pile of quartered logs in the fire grate. Linda's rapt thoughts were disturbed by the sudden rasping sound of a match head striking against the abrasive

315

side of the matchbox. Soon the roaring of the flames stretching up into the chimney and the cracking of the burning wood, dominated the otherwise still mood of the room. Elaine refilled their glasses with another brandy and slumped down next to Linda. Sighing, she whispered, 'Have you considered what you are going to do?'

'I've mulled a lot of things over, trying to see a way that we can continue living together, but I just can't see beyond his betrayal. And of course, all I can hear going around and around in my head, is the sound of their ecstatic love making. I just can't believe it – only a week ago, Melissa and her husband were guests in my home, and all the time, she was shagging Steve – right under my nose!' Linda let her pent-up anger bubble up to the surface with her irate outburst.

'Do you think they have been "at it" for a while then?'

'They must have been, you don't travel two hundred miles up a motorway for a knee-trembler, she must have had this planned – which is why . . . they were so keen, for me to visit you this weekend,' Linda's voice softened, as in her mind, she started to analyse the events from the previous week and realised how she had been totally manipulated. 'The bitch even had to fuck him at my old school, in some sort of spiteful gesture of her dominance over me. Well, I hold all the aces now, and I'm going take immense pleasure mentally torturing her, by not telling her husband about her affair, straight away – I'm going to torment her for week or so, like a cat playing with a mouse. She'll be in hell, never knowing when I'm going to turn up, to spill the beans on her dirty weekend away with my Steve.'

'What do you think he will do, when he finds out?' Elaine asked, finishing off her brandy in one gulp.

'I don't know. Steve told me that his nickname in the business world, is "Ruthless Rod", so if he takes that ethos into his private life, I would think he will want rid of her. They both dote over their daughter, so I expect there will be an almighty battle in court, over who gets custody of her.'

316

'It's a shame that an innocent little girl's world, will come crashing down, through no fault of her own, and then she becomes the rope in a bitter tug-of-war between her parents,' Elaine's comment caused a lull in the conversation, while they both considered the unintentional damage that the exploding bombshell of the illicit liaison would cause.

'I'll get us another drink,' Elaine said, bursting the bubble of quiescence that had enveloped the room. Linda reached for her jacket, which was draped over the back of the nearby chair; searching in the pocket she pulled out her mobile phone and switched it on.

'Six missed calls, all from Steve,' she announced, not bothering to look up, as she scrolled her list of text messages. The first three were from her office, and the last, was again from Steve. She clicked it open and read the wording out aloud to Elaine, 'I'm so sorry, please call me at home so we can sort this mess out.' Linda gave a dismissive laugh, and then muttered to herself, 'I think it's going to take a lot more than a phone call, to sort this out, Steve.'

'The signal is not great here for mobiles, so if you want to phone him, better use my landline, I'll make myself scarce,' Elaine advised.

'I don't want to call him, but if it serves to tighten the screw of suffering for them both, I feel I should,' Linda almost smiled at the vengeful thought. She looked at her wristwatch and calculated that at nearly one o'clock, they should have arrived back in London by now. Elaine made a tactical withdrawal to the top of her garden, to give Linda some privacy to make the call.

With her heart pounding, Linda's finger trembled slightly, as she pressed out her own landline number, all the time in her head she kept repeating to herself to be strong and not to cry. The phone was answered after just one ring, and she heard Steve breathlessly whisper, 'Hello?'

'It's me, I'm ringing to tell you that I'm staying with Elaine, and I won't be coming back until Saturday, when we can get

317

things started on the . . . divorce,' Linda's voice faltered on saying the word divorce.

'No wait! This was just a silly, stupid fling – Melissa means nothing to me – I love you,' Steve entreated.

'It sounded like she meant a great deal to you – judging from the passionate commotion coming through the wall from your room, that I was forced to listen to, for most of Sunday,' Linda's resolve not to cry weakened, and she felt the first tear slowly slip down the curve of her cheek.

'That was just sex – it didn't have anything to do with love . . . only, we haven't had sex for so long, I just . . .'

'Couldn't resist it,' Linda finished Steve's stalled sentence, and felt a surge of anger, at his suggestion that she was somehow culpable in the whole sordid affair. 'How dare you try and blame me for your adultery!'

'I wasn't . . . it's just, well we haven't, have we?'

There followed a period of strained silence, while each waited for the other to continue.

'Look, we've got too much to lose, to let one stupid mistake destroy everything that we have together,' Steve took the initiative.

'You mean, you have too much to lose, no more lucrative contacts from Rod. And Melissa might lose Taylor – all I'm losing, is an unfaithful husband and a treacherous neighbour.'

'If we split up, we would have to start again, what type of property would we each be able to afford on a single income – nothing in London that's for certain?'

'So you're basing our relationship on property prices!' Linda exploded down the phone with indignation.

'I'm certainly not basing it on physical contact in the bedroom!' Steve couldn't resist the temptation to bite back, with his own indictment.

The accusation struck home, putting Linda on the back foot. Determined to retake the moral high ground, she turned the conversation back to the salient fact of his two-timing.

'So, how long has this "fling" been going on then?'

'It was just this once,' Steve lied.

'I suppose there have been other women over the years.'

'No! I promise you,' he lied again.

'I don't believe you Steve. I'm going to divorce you and sod the ramifications of the fucking housing market!'

'No please, you're upset, I can understand that, after a few days you'll see things differently,' Steve appealed, but midway through his sentence the line went dead. He threw the phone down onto the sofa in annoyance and walked stiffly over to the front room window, trying to gather his thoughts. Staring mindlessly down the road, he noticed Melissa purposely striding towards his house, immediately he went to open the front door, where they converged on one another.

'Have you spoken to her yet?' Melissa asked, as she passed by him and entered the front room.

'Yes, I've just got off the phone with her.'

'How did it go?'

'Not that well, we sort of got into an argument over the extenuating circumstances surrounding my weekend with you.'

'You mean her "no sex please, we're British" attitude.'

'Yes, and then she said that she wanted a divorce.'

'She is bound to hurt at the moment, and wants to lash out at you,' Melissa calmly analysed the situation. 'Hopefully we can't talk her out of leaving you, and stop her from bringing me into it. We both have far too much to lose if Rod gets wind of this.'

'Yes, that's what she said.'

319

'I've been on the net and found the address of the friend that she was staying with over the weekend – I presume she is still there?' Melissa asked, and Steve nodded. 'Good, we'll go up and see her tomorrow and I'll plead with her, face to face, woman to woman, not to break my family up. I'll use all my persuasive powers on her.'

'They might not work on the female of the species, and I don't think she's in a very conciliatory mood at the moment,' Steve moaned.

'Well, she'll have calmed down a bit by tomorrow and with any luck she will be in a more practical mood about her immediate future,' Melissa said, with an introspective expression on her face.

'What have you got in mind then?'

'If all the begging and pleading to her doesn't work, you can offer her the house to keep quiet.'

'Now just hang on a minute!'

Think about it Steve, her business has just gone belly up. The chances of future, high paid employment, will be uncertain to say the least. I doubt whether she would want to move back in with mum and dad – so you would be giving her a chance of financial independence.'

'But what about me!'

'You would still have your thriving consultancy business, which brings you in a very tidy sum – for the time being, you can rent a bachelor pad and we can carry on – "carrying on", if you see what I mean. The alternative is – Linda tells Rod; you both separate and split the equity that is in the house. Of course then, the only work you can expect finding in the financial sector, will be cleaning out the bank's offices. Rod is not nicknamed "Ruthless" without reason, he will make sure your name is "Mudd", nobody will touch you with a barge pole, for fear of offending him.'

Melissa could see Steve checking over her strategy in his mind, as he looked blankly past her at the far wall of the room, he

320

then suddenly returned his gaze to her eyes and announced, 'You're right, we might just get away with it – it's worth a shot. When do you want to go up and see her?'

'Tomorrow morning?'

'I have a meeting at lunchtime that I can't put off.'

'Steve! This is our very future we are talking about here – put them off,' Melissa urged, annoyed by his bizarre prioritizing.

'No I can't, Rod arranged it. If I don't show, he's going to wonder why.'

'Okay, when will you be able to get back here?'

'I would think about four o'clock. How are we going to travel up there, I haven't got a car?'

'We can use my Mini – I'll think of an excuse to tell Rod, why I'll be home late tomorrow and arrange for someone to babysit Taylor, until he gets in at about seven-thirty.'

'Will he believe you?'

'Yes, he believes everything I tell him!' Melissa laughed, 'I'll see you at four tomorrow then. Don't call her and say that we are coming up – it will be better to catch her cold, give her less time to think about things.'

'I don't think she'll be taking any of my calls,' Steve said dejectedly to himself, and wondered just how he had managed to mess things up so completely.

CHAPTER TWENTY-EIGHT
20th October 2003

1.28pm

The phone conversation with Steve, had left Linda highly agitated, causing her to pace up and down the narrow space between the kitchen table and the open trunk. Over and over in her head, the acrid words that they had just exchanged were running on a never-ending loop, pricking at every cell in her brain and making her want to scream with frustration, or lash out at something. It hadn't gone the way she thought it was going to, and some of the unexpected things that he had said, disturbed her. The back door swung open, assisted by a gust of cold wind and Elaine clattered back into the kitchen, clutching an armful of onions that she had just pulled up.

'How did it go?' she asked, with an uneasy look on her face.

'Not very well – he said it was partly my fault, because we don't have enough sex,' Linda blurted out, fighting back the tears of despair she felt overflowing from her eyes.

'Cheeky bugger! You've been together for a long time – it wouldn't be natural if you were still going at it like rabbits every night. How often, do you do it?'

Linda looked away for a moment; wiped her eyes with the cuff of her sleeve and then turned back looking sheepish.

'Not very often,' she whispered.

'Once a week – once a month – once a year?'

'It's been a very long time. I've been so busy and away a lot, and he has been working all hours. We just never seem to get the chance. Or rather, I never seem to get the chance, he has obviously managed it several times, but not with me.'

'Let's go out for a short walk, before the rain gets here,' Elaine said, looking out of her kitchen window, at the black and grey clouds sweeping in from the horizon. 'Clear your mind for a while and release some of that built-up adrenalin.'

She took down one of her several wax jackets, that were hanging on the coat stand and handed it to Linda, who dutifully put it on with the grace of a sullen schoolgirl, after which, they stepped out of the back door, into the bracing cold air. Due to the inclement weather, it took a greater physical effort to re-trace the same route that they had blissfully tramped a couple of days previously. The strong westerly wind bent the tall trees that surrounded the house and scattered their red, orange and yellow leaves, to all parts of the garden, like oversized flakes of confetti swirling in a churchyard. Elaine tried to speak, but the howling noise of the wind blowing through the leaves and branches, drowned out her words. Doggedly they marched on, battling against the elements in silence, but it wasn't long before the blackened sky let loose its threatening cargo. The resulting rain fell like thick steel needles, bouncing up like particles of exploding glass marbles, as it impacted with the hard, dry earth. They decided that it was time to return back to the warmth of the house, and so, for another fifteen minutes continued to trudge on, until they muddled their way into the welcoming shelter of Elaine's kitchen.

'It's amazing how the weather can change so quickly at this time of year. On Saturday, it seemed like we were still in the height of summer, and now, just forty-eight hours later, it feels like winter is here,' Elaine said, sitting on the very front edge of the old winged back armchair, robustly drying her hair with a towel.

323

'Yes, on Saturday, everything in my garden seemed rosy,' Linda sighed mournfully, 'and now, I'm in the middle of the most gigantic storm.'

'Sorry, I keep putting my foot in it, don't I?' Elaine apologised, for inadvertently drawing a parallel to Linda's domestic strife.

'No, I'm sorry – it's not your fault – it's mine. Steve had a point – we were living together like brother and sister. Men have needs don't they?'

Elaine poured out the remainder of the brandy, which produced two quadruple measures and handed Linda a tumbler.

'Women have needs too – didn't you miss the sex?' she asked, bluntly.

'No not really, I've never been that fussed about it.'

'Haven't you!' Elaine spluttered out her surprise. 'What about when you were first married?'

'I faked enthusiasm for his sake, but I just didn't get what all the palaver was about. I remember the girls at work, going on in raptures about this and that, and how they couldn't get enough of their boyfriend's cocks. Even the shy, less extrovert women joked about sucking willies, like it was the most natural thing in the world. I played along with them, but couldn't believe what they were saying. Even allowing for some exaggeration, it seemed that I was the odd one out, in thinking that men's cocks look ridiculous and repulsive. Whether they have sprung to attention or are dangling there between their legs, they just look silly. I'm not remotely aroused by the sight of one, and the thought of putting it in my mouth makes me,' Linda made a violent gagging gesture.

'They're certainly not aesthetic to look at,' Elaine giggled, pleased that a thin smile had flickered across Linda's lips for the first time that day. 'I think our genitalia is a much better design. I was flashed at few years ago, by some middle-aged man who, for all the world, looked like he could have been a bank manager.

Strangely my natural reaction was not to scream, but just to laugh out aloud.'

Linda's faint smile turned into a lazy grin, as she imagined the scene. 'Weren't you frightened?'

'No, he just ran off, probably very disappointed by my somewhat contemptuous response.'

'About twenty years ago, I got an obscene phone call when I was alone at home. At first, I thought it was funny. He asked me what colour knickers I had on, and for some silly reason I played along with him, thinking it was someone I knew, who was playing a joke on me. Then he kept calling back, always when I was alone in the house, and each time he was more threatening.'

'Now that is frightening – it was obviously somebody who could see your house and knew when Steve was out.'

'Yes exactly. I called up British Telecom, who were sympathetic, but didn't seem to have a solution on how to stop him, other than, changing my number. I didn't want to do that because of the hassle it would have caused, but I was also scared that one day, he would try and break into the house, and attack me.'

'Yes, you hear of these horror stories, about being attacked in your own home, mercifully, like they say on *Crimewatch*, such incidents are extremely rare – apparently you've got far more chance of winning the lottery jackpot. So what did you do?'

'We got an answering machine and screened our calls through it. He obviously didn't find it as much of a kick, describing the nasty things he wanted to do, to a tape recorder!'

'So who do you think it was?'

'Almost certainly a neighbour, who could see our comings and goings.'

'How spooky. You must have suspected all the men in your street.'

'Yes, it did make me feel nervous about who I was taking too. It just goes to show that beneath the outward veneer of respectability, people hide all sorts of secrets and perversions.'

'Is that true of you also?' Elaine responded, with a look of intrigue.

Linda averted her eyes from Elaine's stare.

'I suppose we all flatter to deceive in life. In my case, I've deceived myself mostly,' she conceded.

'How?'

'By trying to be someone I'm not.' Linda inhaled with resignation.

'Who are you then?'

'Well, I'm not a happily married, successful business woman, that's for sure,' Linda threw her head back and laughed with spurious contempt, as she circumvented the question and then batted it back with a top-spin of irritation. 'And what about you?'

'You already know the answer to that – let's face it – I'm really no better than Steve, am I? I've had meaningless affairs with women, who were in long-term partnerships. I never gave a second thought to the emotional carnage that would have occurred, if we had been found out. I wanted to stop doing it, but the raw excitement was like a drug. I would have periods where I abstained, but the need would build up to a point where it was the only thing I could think about, and then I would have to make a phone call.'

'Was it because you and Yvonne were no longer having sex?'

'Yes partly. Although I would have still done it, even if we were sexually active – it was the buzz it gave me,' Elaine self-consciously confided.

'Do you think that's why Steve and Melissa started having it off with each other – the thrill of breaking the rules?'

'Probably, forbidden fruit is always sweeter, or more tempting.'

'Melissa is very attractive, I would think most red-blooded men would find it hard to say "no" to her,' Linda pouted.

'She's not as attractive as you,' Elaine thoughtfully flattered her friend.

'Elaine, you say the nicest things, even if they are un-true – my ego needed a big boost!' Linda smiled.

The initial bout of drinking large neat brandies had sparked energy into their *tête-à-tête*, and a temporary lifting of their moods. They had both deliberately set out to drown their sorrows, but as the evening wore on, and as more wine and spirits were imbibed, the slurred conversation became more and more surreal.

Elaine tilted her head right back and turned her glass upside down, allowing the last few drops of wine to drain out and drip into her open mouth. She then declared dolefully, 'Oh Linda, this is all my fault, I'm so utterly worthless!'

'Elaine, for God's sake what do you mean, it's all your fault – you had nothing at all to do with it,' Linda contradicted Elaine's rash statement.

'I told you I'm a jinx – if I hadn't stupidly gone back down the corridor, to confront my irrational fear of that bloody room, none of this would have happened.'

'You mean I'd have been none the wiser,' Linda interposed, and then expanding on her intervention, she continued, 'I would have found out sooner or later, Steve is a terrible liar – he would have slipped up sometime. Anyway, it was my idea to go back to the old school, you didn't want to go – I had to persuade you. If anything is to blame, it's the bloody secret room, drawing me back again, to unleash another trauma into my life. I mean, what are the odds that the two most intense moments of my life, would have taken place in the same fucking room, of a building, that is located over two hundred miles away, from where I normally live!'

327

'If I hadn't dropped my silver necklace down between the bloody floorboards in the first place – everything would have been different,' Elaine whined, in an unremitting pursuit of self-martyrdom.

'Yes, it would have been, but then you could say that about virtually everything we ever do. If I hadn't bought you the silver e that Christmas, somebody else would have discovered your grandfather's body – a builder most likely, or possibly it would still be there. Or, if my granny hadn't died . . . when she did,' Linda stopped in mid-flow to swallow hard, 'we would have never even met.'

'I don't care what you say, I know I'm the catalyst for all of this – I really wish I had never been born,' Elaine sobbed and wallowed in an alcohol induced attack of self-loathing. Nothing that Linda could say or do was going to convince her otherwise. For the next hour the conversation descended into ever decreasing circles of crushing self-guilt and blame. Cutting through the superficial outpourings, the ominous beginnings of an uncontrollable pit of despair were welling up deep inside Elaine. Eventually, emotionally exhausted from the day's events, Linda decided it was time to drag herself off to her room. She whispered a soft 'Goodnight' and tiptoed out of the kitchen, leaving the semi-conscious Elaine, curled up on the sofa, still mumbling incoherently in her shallow sleep, about her culpability in the whole catastrophic day. Stumbling unsteadily around her room, Linda undressed down to her underwear, but then remembered that she had left her night-things, along with her other clothes, back at the hotel. Unable to fight the urge to sleep, she collapsed face down onto the soft duvet and fell into a deep slumber.

#   #   #

After a few hours of dreamless sleep, the alcohol levels in Linda's blood system dropped to the point, where her brain sent an automated wake up call to her body. Her eyes opened with a shock, without moving her head she blinked a few times to focus on the adjacent illuminated clock face, which showed a time of thirty-eight minutes past one. The high winds had stopped blowing and a

328

silence had settled in with the darkness of the room. Linda concentrated on the complete stillness of her unfamiliar surroundings and then she heard it – a faint tap, followed by another one, and then another. The pattern was a slow rhythmic beat, like the regularity, of the barely audible tock sound that a Grandfather clock makes in an adjoining room. The strange noise aroused her confused curiosity, and without hesitating to consider it any longer, she erratically shuffled her way out of the bedroom and into the dark passageway. Wandering stealthily down the unlit corridor, the measured rapping sound became more distinct and was definitely coming from the kitchen. As she got closer to the entrance of the kitchen, the more the irritating disturbance sounded like a slow handclap. She quietly stalked through the open door and peered into the moonlit room. Just at that moment, from over in the corner, another clear slap sound reverberated out. Inching forward into the core of the room, Linda detected some movement in the cave-like darkness, followed by the report of another fleshly smack. Her eyes quickly adjusted to the dimness of the surroundings, and to her utter disbelief, there before her, was Elaine. She was kneeling on the armchair, with the old school hairbrush in her right hand, about to deliver another smack down onto her own prominent naked bottom that plumped-out at a slight angle, behind her.

'Elaine! What the hell are you doing?' Linda shouted her unnecessary question.

The fall of the suspended hairbrush was momentary delayed by the verbal intrusion, while Elaine twisted her head around to face Linda.

'I'm punishing myself for being so . . . wicked,' she bemoaned, in a morose monotone. The brush plummeted down in a swooping arc, causing a loud splat of naked flesh, as its hard, polished wooden back, landed firmly across her right buttock.

'Stop it!' Linda cried out, and reached out to switch the wall lights on, thinking that the shame of the stark exposure would bring Elaine to her senses. Instead of the expected recoil of humiliation, Elaine remained passively calm and without changing her indecent posture, calmly offered the hairbrush to Linda.

329

'You do it to me,' she ordered resolutely.

'Don't be so ridiculous!' Linda protested, averting her focus down from Elaine's fixed stare, to the two red oval marks, on each of the beaten cheeks of the bare posterior offered up to her.

'Please, you must do it for me,' Elaine appealed.

'No . . . I couldn't . . . I couldn't hurt you.'

'You would be helping me – don't you see, I need to feel punishing pain, to release me from this unbearable anguish – if you don't, I'll start cutting myself again,' Elaine continued to press, using the unsubtle intimation of blackmail.

'No . . . I'll . . .' Linda swallowed nervously, her wide eyes still riveted on Elaine's naked rump, she was comprehensively lost for words.

'Please!' Elaine turned around and thrust the hairbrush into Linda's hand; she then resumed her submissive position and waited, tightly gripping the worn fabric on the top edge of the chair. Linda took the hairbrush and stepped closer, without uttering a word she patted it down across the centre of Elaine's well-presented bottom.

'Harder! Much harder, make me feel it,' Elaine instructed firmly.

Linda doubled her effort, and the second blow made a slightly louder slap.

'Harder!' Elaine twisted around to confront Linda. 'Imagine I'm the bitch who stole your husband!'

Elaine's harsh words provoked an instantaneous loss of temper within Linda. This time the heavy wooden brush landed with resounding crack across the naked twin globes, pancaking them flat, and causing Elaine's face to jerk forwards into the upholstered high back of the chair. Without stopping to think about what she was doing, Linda launched a second heavy blow, rapidly followed by a third and a fourth. Elaine's hips swayed and writhed under the burning impact of the stinging spanks, again and again the wooden oval rained relentless smacks down onto her now flaming

330

rear end. Linda suddenly dropped the hairbrush to the floor and watched with astonishment, how Elaine's back arched violently, while she repeatedly pummelled her upper body against the cushioned back of the chair. Breathing loudly, and clearly gripped by an overwhelming emotional release, she twisted her rocking head around and looked directly at Linda. As her whole body shuddered with unmistakable elation, Elaine transfixed Linda with a perplexing, mixed expression that compounded gratitude and bewilderment. Physically spent, she then dramatically draped herself backwards over the arm of the chair, so that her body bowed upside down, and she was looking up towards the ceiling. Holding this crab-like position for a few seconds, she then slowly toppled over the side and landed sprawled out, at Linda's feet.

Linda looked down at Elaine with a demeanour of addled shock on her face, comparable to someone who had just been brought out of a deep hypnotic trance.

'Oh my God! What have I done?' she bent down and helped Elaine up onto her feet. 'I'm so sorry, I don't know what came over me.' Linda flung her arms around Elaine, hugging her close to her, their cheeks and torsos pressed tightly together. For a few moments all either of them could hear, were the pants of their excited breaths, exhaling into each other's ears. Linda allowed her hands to slide down to Elaine's waist. Drawing back her head, she stared at her friend's large, glistening brown eyes and was completely unable to resist the sudden and overpowering urge that blitzed her thoughts. Without any warning, she leaned in and passionately kissed her, on her full, pouting mouth. There were a couple of seconds while Elaine absorbed the potency of what Linda's kiss was proposing, and then she responded with an equal fervour. Their lips lingered, pressed earnestly together, and locked in a classical lover's sweet embrace for over a minute, before Elaine peeled back from the hold, to take a searching stare at Linda. Without having to ask, she could distinguish the answer that she was hoping for, shining out from Linda's two adoring, blue eyes. In an instance, the look dispelled any remaining qualms and sanctioned the resumption of their tender clinch. Linda let out a faint gasp of pleasure as she felt a tongue probing at her lips; she

331

instinctively let her hands drift further downwards, until she could gently stroke Elaine's seared bare buttocks. The more passionate and intense the kissing became, the harder Linda kneaded the soft, rounded nates. Eventually, Elaine pulled back from the sultry smooch, this time she didn't look at Linda, but grabbed her hand and pulled her across to the stairway that led up to her bedroom. Un-shackled from her self-imposed perpetuity of sexual constraint, Linda followed willingly, feeling a quivering, nervous thrill in the pit of her stomach. The last time that she could remember the same exhilarating feeling of being out of control, was years before, at the amusement park, when she was strapped into the seat of a roller coaster, that was rolling slowly towards the first death-defying descent. Elaine advanced up the narrow stairway with Linda gliding up behind her, watching with unfettered desire, the alluring reddened bottom that she had both viciously beaten and lovingly caressed within the past ten minutes. They both made straight for the bed, Elaine pulled her sweatshirt over her head as she walked. Now standing completely naked, she turned to Linda and patted the top of the bed, indicating that she wanted her to sit down. Linda was completely subservient to Elaine's dictate, and without any delay, she sat down exactly on top of the hand mark depression in the bed linen. Linda felt Elaine reach around her shoulders to release her bra strap, once it was off, she then pushed her down so she was lying across the bed. Kneeling over her, Elaine set about the task of smothering Linda's breasts with lustful hungry kisses. The kissing stopped, and Linda felt a finger and thumb pluck at the two cotton strips, which stretched around each side of her knickers. Elaine began to cautiously tug the underwear down, assisted by Linda who lifted her bottom up off the top surface of the duvet. In one dramatic unveiling movement, the silken material slid all the way down her legs and off. Totally nude and acquiescently recumbent, like a fictional expectant virgin in a tawdry romantic paperback, she was primed for a life-changing experience. Elaine clambered up beside her and began tenderly stroking the soft curve of Linda's stomach, just above the pubic hairline, whilst at the same time, kissing her neck and shoulders. Linda lay passively beneath Elaine's stroking hand, allowing her hips to wriggle slowly in time with the small concentric movements, which had now journeyed to the top of her

332

inner thigh. She opened her legs fractionally wider, and Elaine's feather light fingers reached their ultimate destination. Linda let out an instant groan of delight and her body gave an involuntarily tremor, at the waves of pleasure generated from the exquisite stimulation of her firmed clitoris. Elaine was thrilled with the affirmative response, and after a few more minutes teasing and rubbing the engorged labia, she smoothly eased just her middle finger into Linda's warm, well-lubricated vaginal opening.

'Oh God!' Linda called out, as a tingling quiver of charged energy, joyously ran through her nervous system. Her breathing became heavy, and between every other gasp, she moaned out a rapturous, 'Yes!' and squirmed down against the searching finger inside her. Elaine changed her position and knelt at Linda's side, so that she could bury another digit into her soft, viscous vagina. Linda's gyrations and thrusts became more intense as her thighs clamped closely together, in a spontaneous reaction to her pelvic contractions. Elaine had to fight hard to free her hand, which was now trapped between Linda's squeezing thigh muscles and in danger of being badly crushed by the pressure. She managed to wrench it from the vice-like grip, and was rewarded for her efforts by Linda, who wailed out a long guttural moan, as her whole body stiffened at the peaking point of orgasm. With an inner glow of satisfaction, Elaine observed Linda, slowly coming down from her point of climax, still with her eyes tightly shut, but breathing more evenly. Leaning over, she bent down and kissed Linda on the tummy and then repeated the kiss again and again until she had worked her way up to her lips, which sported a mellow, satisfied smile. Linda opened her eye's and whispered, 'Thank-you.'

'Are you sure you're finished? If you're not, I can always go down on you,' Elaine softly proposed, poking her tongue out and seductively licking her lips.

'What, munch my rug?' Linda drawled, in a dream-like voice.

'Munch my rug,' Elaine repeated, and then burst into laughter. 'Where did you get that from?'

'Oh, a so called friend told me about it, sometime ago,' Linda replied, remembering the conversation in her kitchen that she had with Melissa, just eight days earlier. Twisting her body into Elaine's so that they spooned, she then grabbed Elaine's arm and pulled it around her. 'Hug me Elaine.'

Elaine was more than happy to comply with her request and cuddled her tightly into her breasts. As she drifted off to sleep, the cadence of their breathing and heartbeats syncopated, making it feel as though their bodies had merged into single entity.

CHAPTER TWENTY-NINE
21st October 2003

7.45am

In the grey moments just before waking, the significant highlights from the previous day's far-reaching events, projected silently across Linda's closed eyelids, like a disjointed home movie from the sixties, flickering away on the living room wall. Her eyes slowly opened, and for the briefest of moments, she thought it had all been an extravagant dream. One surreptitious glance to her left, where Elaine was lying naked and sleeping peacefully, indisputably clarified her exact circumstances. Suddenly, a set of pin sharp recollections, from the previous day's exploits, tumbled into her brain, inciting a furious clash of conflicting emotions. With this whirl of thoughts continuing to confuse and disorientate her, she eased herself out of the bed and gently walked across to the window. Leaning over a mahogany, bow-fronted chest of drawers, she contemplated the beautiful sight of a diffused pale sun, rising over a mist-covered hillside. Thirty feet down the side of the banking that attached to Elaine's property, the low-lying mist had blanketed all but the roof of old Joe's cottage, so that it appeared to be floating in a pool of cloudy, peace and calm.

'Nice bum!' Elaine's voice abruptly broke the moment of rare tranquillity, causing Linda to snap her head around. A blush quickly seeped into her cheeks, on confronting her friend for the first time since their impromptu sexual intimacy. Her first thought was to cover her own nakedness, but that consideration dispersed when Elaine stretched out a welcoming hand towards her, and she automatically reacted by advancing the three steps to be at her side.

'I expect you hate me this morning' Elaine continued, with a worried frown creasing her brow.

Linda sat down on the bed beside her, before answering, 'No, of course I don't.'

'You should, I took advantage of your vulnerable state last night.'

'I thought it was the other way around,' Linda sniffed out an ironic laugh.

'Well, I promise I won't ever mention it again,' Elaine said apologetically, and then jumped up off the bed and grabbed her dressing gown. 'I'll run you a bath.'

Linda watched Elaine slowly walk through to the en-suite bathroom and then heard the sound of water gushing into an empty bathtub. She felt peculiarly discontented by what Elaine had just said; she wanted to talk about what had happened, in fact, she wanted to shout from the rooftops about it. Elaine re-entered the bedroom with a benevolent smile on her face.

'You get into the bath and I'll bring you up some breakfast,' she instructed.

'Nothing to eat for me thank-you, but I would like a black coffee,' Linda replied.

Elaine gave her another knowing smile.

'All right, I'll be back up in a few minutes.'

Linda wandered over to the bathroom doorway and was very pleasantly surprised by the quality of the black and white themed, contemporary suite that greeted her. In the centre of the room stood a brilliant white, large double ended roll top bath, with centrally mounted Georgian style chrome taps, both of which were now disgorging torrents of water into a thick layer of bubble bath froth. To test the temperature of the water, Linda bent over and

336

dipped her hand through the foam, unusually for her, it felt just right. Pulling her arm out again, she blew away a part of the clinging white glove of suds, adhered to her skin, and created a short-lived blizzard, of tiny white foam particles that criss-crossed in front of her eyes, like agitated bees. With the taps still running, she stepped over the high-sided bath and gradually lowered herself into the half filled tub that now resembled a vat of soft vanilla yogurt. Linda relaxed back, resting her head against the cool porcelain curve of the bath; this allowed her chin to drop down into the sweet-smelling bubbles, so that just the top half of her face and head were visible. Wrapped completely in a cocoon of warm water, she couldn't help but ruminate, on how, over the course of just one extraordinary day, her life had changed forever. The strangest thing was, she felt almost relieved that fate had finally interceded after all these years and forced this to happen. The door opened and Elaine walked in carrying a small tray, which she carefully placed down on top of a stool, before pushing the whole ensemble over to the side of the bath.

'I've done some toast, to go with your black coffee – you should really get something inside you,' she said, conscientiously looking after her guest.

Linda's face crinkled into a smirking grin, as Elaine's words revived glowing images from their passionate encounter to spark in her mind.

'I thought you weren't going to mention last night, ever again,' she giggled, and held her wet hand to her mouth, like an embarrassed schoolgirl.

Slowly realising what Linda's suggestive remark had meant, Elaine's eyebrows lifted and a small smile bowed on her lips. She turned around and rubbed the condensation off the mirror to check her face, at the same time, she let her dressing gown slip down on to the tiled floor.

'God Elaine! Look at your bottom – it's covered in bruises!' Linda shrieked out, immediately springing up in surprise, her naked upper body was bejewelled in a mix of shiny, sliding foam suds and dripping shimmering water droplets. Elaine tried to twist around to take a look for herself, but it was impossible to see anything, so she tilted the angle of the pivoted wall mirror and studied her damaged posterior in that.

'Gosh, it is a bit marked – isn't it?' she said, with more than a hint of pride in her voice.

'Oh Elaine, I'm so sorry, how could I have done that,' Linda moaned a heartfelt apology, her face crimsoned by a combination of the hot steam and a sudden feeling of guilt.

'Nonsense! It would have ended up like this anyway, you just speeded things up a little,' Elaine exonerated Linda from any blame with a dismissive wave of her hand. 'Actually, great-grandmother Victoria would have been very pleased with your technique and . . . um . . . enthusiasm.'

'I did get a bit carried away – do you think it was her spirit that was guiding me?' Linda laughed, reoccupying her previous horizontal position.

'Considering that I single-handedly managed to close down her precious school, I wouldn't be at all surprised. I should show my bruised bum to old Joe and tell him that he did it, with his pinching,' Elaine giggled.

'I think the poor old guy might suffer a major heart attack, if you did!' Linda warned.

'He might, but if he did survive the shock, it should be worth at least twelve bottles of his homemade hooch! Budge up a bit I'm going to join you.'

Linda sat up and drew back her legs, so that her thighs were up against her breasts. After stepping into the vacated half of the bath, Elaine lowered herself down, causing the water level to rise up, almost to the overflow aperture.

'You can put your legs down over mine if you like,' Elaine suggested, and after some careful manoeuvrings, they both reclined comfortably into the warm and fragrant water. Linda took a sly, approving look at Elaine, whose half-submerged, well-rounded breasts, looked like two pink atolls in an Arctic seascape.

338

Dissolving knots of white froth that resembled tiny floating icebergs enhanced the composition of the bizarre tableau still further.

'Do you remember bath night at school?' Linda said, breaking the silence with an appropriate subject matter.

'Yes! Our turn was Monday night, if I remember correctly. Imagine, just one bath a week!'

'It wasn't really a bath – you were only allowed three inches of water and ten minutes,' Linda laughed, feeling settled again, and enjoying the silky sensation of her legs smoothly rubbing against Elaine's. 'It was more like sitting in a lukewarm puddle.'

'Yes, there were only six baths, so just half the dorm went in at a time. Then you also had to wash your hair with a bar of that awful green carbolic soap, which stunk to high heaven.'

'That's right, and Miss Ryan would threaten to use it, to wash out the mouth, of any girl she caught swearing,' Linda said, screwing her face up in disgust.

The laughing stopped, and once again they were unsure of how to continue their conversation, this resulted in another period of uneasy stillness, while the two women watched each other attentively.

'You want to tell me something, don't you?' Elaine whispered, pulling nervously at her silver e that was hanging just above the cobalt coloured water.

'Yes . . . I do,' Linda began, after swallowing a nervous lump in her throat that felt like it was the size of a golf ball. 'Do you remember when I said, I was trying to be someone, that I wasn't?'

'I do seem to remember you saying something cryptic, about not being a successful business woman,' Elaine frowned, racking her brain to recall Linda's exact phase.

'That's right, but what I really meant was . . . I've been playing the part of a heterosexual woman for all these years, even though, I've always found women much more attractive than men.'

339

Elaine stared at Linda with an expression of stunned incredulity.

'Now just hang on, you're not basing this in any way, on last night's drunken heavy petting session, are you?'

'No! I've always known that I was sexually attracted to women. Last night was the first time that I've allowed myself to do anything about it.'

'How old were you, when you first realised this?' Elaine asked, still unable to fully comprehend the implications of what Linda was revealing to her.

'I'm not sure, but when I was about seven years old, I remember my parents buying me a plastic, battery operated, Chad Valley projector. You used it to beam strips of coloured slides onto the wall of your bedroom, like an old magic lantern show. Each strip was a story, like Dick Turpin's ride to York, or Aladdin's Lamp, that sort of thing.'

'Yes, but what bearing could they have had on your sexuality?'

'Well, one of the strips was the story of Joan of Arc, and in the last frame, she was tied to the stake, about to be burnt.'

'So?'

'Seeing her tied up and vulnerable, made me feel really good inside – a sort of pleasurable buzz of electricity flashed around my body that I hadn't ever experienced before. Even now, I only have to see the words "Joan of Arc" and I feel strangely aroused!' Linda confessed, and straight away felt rather foolish.

'Wow! How kinky, and you were only seven! I hope you are not planning to tie me up against the apple tree and set fire to me, while you dance around the garden pleasuring yourself!' Elaine screamed, and they both burst out with laugher at the silliness of this idea. 'So what about when you were older, what were the signs then?'

'I suppose my obsession with stories set in girls' public schools.'

'Lots of teenage girls used to read those type of books, it didn't mean that you were an apprentice dyke.'

'I know, but I was so obsessed with them, I even . . .' Linda arrested her speech mid-sentence.

'You even did what?' Elaine asked quietly, but there was no reply. Instead, Linda stared down into the bath water, with an expression of repugnance, stamped on her flushed and glistening face.

'Linda, what did you do?' Elaine pursued her line of questioning with mounting uneasiness.

Linda looked up with eyes full of shame.

'What did you do that was so bad?' Elaine asked firmly, unable to contain her curiosity any longer.

'I heard Mum and Dad talking about how they would inherit a large amount of money one day, because my dad was an only child, and my granny owned her own house. I . . . I . . . prayed to God, that she would die, and leave her money to Dad, so that I could go off to boarding school. And within two weeks, it had bloody happened! While she was getting a scuttle full of coal from the bunker in the cellar, she fell down the sodding steps and broke her neck. I was the one who found her – it was just terrible!'

'Jesus, I thought you were going to say that you murdered her!' Elaine said, feeling relieved that her friend's guilty secret was nothing more horrible, than a young girl's selfish wish.

'I felt like I *had* murdered her! I still feel terrible about it now.'

'It was just an unlucky coincidence.'

'I know, but how awful must I have been, to wish my own grandmother dead, I've been haunted by it ever since.'

341

'You were just a child at the time and having a rough time at school. I remember praying for things to happen, when I was little girl, of course they never did, in my case.'

'That was just it, I prayed for something and it happened, I got what I wanted most – I then became convinced that I had some sort of special power, to strike people down, just by asking God to fix it for me!'

Elaine couldn't help but smile at Linda's admission.

'Like you were part of some celestial Mafia, who went around liquidating anyone who got in your way!'

Linda started to see the funny side of her declaration of guilt.

'It didn't take long for me to discover that my special powers were somewhat limited,' she giggled. 'I prayed to have that girl at school, Louise Bennington, terminated, but sadly, she *didn't* meet with an unfortunate accident. But you can see how ruthless I was back then – I was prepared to kill *again*!'

Elaine stretched over the side of the bath to pick up the colourful tin tray, with the coffees and toast on it, which she politely offered to Linda. Taking a couple of seconds to weigh things up, she gratefully accepted her cup, but still refused anything to eat. Elaine devoured a piece of butter-soaked toast, then after this brief interlude of quiet, she swigged her cooling coffee and continued in a sarcastic vein, 'Okay, so we have established that as a child, you liked to watch women being tied up and set on fire, and you had magical powers, which enabled you to make your dreams come true.'

'Sarky bitch!' Linda chuckled at Elaine's flippant appraisal of her intimate confessions.

'What about when you were at school, did you fancy other girls?'

'Yes of course I did!'

'Even at Grenchwood?'

342

'Yes!' Linda answered abruptly, annoyed with Elaine's sustained refusal to believe her.

'Who then? Oh, I know – Charlotte of course. I should think most of the school fancied Charlotte!'

'Yes, I did like Charlotte – she was both very beautiful and unobtainable, in a movie star sort of way. You *must* know that it was you who I was madly in love with, but I could never bring myself to say it, for fear of rejection or ridicule.'

Elaine stared deeply at Linda, taking in what she had said, and then replied, 'I felt the exactly the same way – if indeed, a thirteen year old can be in love. And of course, I was also too scared to say anything, in case you thought that I was some kind of freak.'

'I kissed you once, when we were at school' Linda softly confided.

'No you never, I would have remembered. I longed for you to kiss me.'

'You were asleep at the time – we were up in the sick room, and I just couldn't resist it.'

'And I didn't wake up?'

'I don't know what I'd have done if you had,' Linda laughed. 'I hadn't thought it through that far.'

Elaine broke out into a fit of excited giggles, 'Gosh, I wish I had!'

She then turned on the hot tap to reheat the cooling water. Wafting her hand back and forth, like a flipper, to disperse the fresh steaming water to both ends of the bath, she realised that her fingers was unintentionally stroking the inside of Linda's thigh.

With a teasing smile, she asked, 'Is that better for you?'

Linda shut her eyes gave out a satisfied moan of pleasure, 'Yes, it's lovely, thank you.'

343

Elaine carried on for a few minutes, until the water felt hot again and a new layer of bubbly foam had formed on the surface.

'So, if you knew that you were gay, after leaving school, why on earth did you go and marry Steve?'

'I was too scared to admit it to myself, and I certainly never, for a moment, considered telling anyone, *especially my parents*. I just couldn't come to terms with the implications of not being regarded as normal. We both know how totally different things were in the seventies – I wasn't brave like you. I buried my inclinations, because I'd been programmed by society to believe, such feelings were wrong and deviant.

'The prescribed route in life, was to go out with boys, marry one and then have children. It would have broken my poor father's heart, if I'd told him that I preferred girls to boys. My mum and dad grew up in a generation that definitely didn't regard homosexuality as normal, and I wasn't strong enough to confront their certain indignation, hostility and disappointment.

'All my life, I've been over-concerned about pleasing my parents and living up to their high expectations of me. So I did the same thing that thousands and thousands of other secretly gay people have done throughout history and got married, as soon as I could. Keeping my secret thoughts safely locked away in my head.'

'Why did you choose Steve?' Elaine asked, placing her empty coffee cup back on the tray.

'Steve had very long hair back then, plus he has quite effeminate facial features, so to be quite truthful, he looked quite girly, and unlike most of the blokes at college, he was quite sensitive and gentle.'

'So apart from his dangly parts, he was the perfect substitute woman?'

'You could say that,' Linda muttered thoughtfully. 'I did a very selfish thing back then, didn't I?'

'Did you love him?'

344

'Yes I did – I mean I do, but more in a brother-sister sort of way.'

'And Steve has never suspected anything?' Elaine continued her questioning.

'I've never given him any reason to suspect anything, other than not being overly keen on shagging, which I've always put down to the fact that I have a lower sex drive than him. My secret fantasies have been, just that, very secret. He doesn't know why I like to watch the women's tennis on TV, even though I hate sport, or why I always queue up at the same cashier's till at the bank, just to see her smile at me, or why I buy trashy women's magazines, crammed with pictures, of female celebrities in their swim suits.'

'So what are you going to tell him on Saturday?'

'I'll tell him that I want a divorce, but I won't land Melissa in it with Rod – you were right, I can't bring myself to ruin little Taylor's life, just to get revenge on her mother – as much as I would like to punish the conniving little cow,' Linda answered with an angry, but controlled edge to her voice.

'I felt that last night!' Elaine joked, embellishing a pained expression on her face.

'Sorry about that,' Linda apologised with insincere regret, and a mischievous grin forming on her lips. 'But I have to say, I *really* enjoyed it, and from what I saw, so did you!'

Elaine flicked some water at Linda, who retaliated with a splash aimed straight back at her head. In no time at all, the two women had regressed to carefree teenagers, their girlish laugher, together with the splatter of water hitting the floor tiles, echoed around the bathroom.

Eventually the juvenile cavorting wound down and Elaine asked, 'What shall we do today?'

'I'll need some more clothes and underwear for the rest of the week. Can we go shopping?' Linda proffered, with a childlike squeal of excitement.

345

'Yes, we can drive over to Ashbourne, they have some lovely shops over there.'

'Great! That'll give me the chance to do some more spanking,' Linda announced to a startled Elaine.

'Pardon?'

'My credit card! I'm going to spank the plastic until it can't sit down!' Linda shuddered with laughter, at the look on Elaine's face.

CHAPTER THIRTY
21st October 2003

11.15am

During the twenty-five minute journey, the atmosphere in the car differed greatly, from the trip back from the hotel the preceding day, with the two women chatting enthusiastically about their respective shopping agendas. Taking directions from Elaine, Linda pulled off the main road and into the large, open-air car park, close to the town centre of Ashbourne. She ploughed the car across a series of large puddles, caused by the previous night's rainfall and parked up in between the grey-white, tyre worn lines of a bay, close to the exit for the shops. After switching the engine off, for some reason Linda trotted out the little maxim that her father used to say, 'All a shore that's going ashore.'

'I'll get the ticket,' Elaine offered, and without waiting for an argument, she skipped off towards the machine.

Linda waited by the car and watched Elaine, as she slalomed her way around the larger pools of surface water that dimpled the tarmac and impeded her most direct route. On reaching the ticket dispenser, she put her money into the slot and pressed the green button, but the coinage immediately reappeared in the returned change pouch, causing a metallic jangle to ring out across the shimmering asphalt.

'It's not working, I'll have to go over there,' Elaine shouted back to Linda, while pointing to another ticket machine on the far side of the car park.

Linda gazed around the periphery of the parking area and spotted a portable farm shop, selling food. Feeling hungry, she paced over for a closer look at the blackboard that was fixed up on the side of the serving opening. The list was almost entirely connected to meat produce, but close to the bottom her eye was attracted to the word "cake". As she got nearer, she could make out the words "Oatcakes - six for a pound". Unzipping the small side pocket on her handbag, she reached in and took out some coins that she kept there as an emergency parking meter fund.

'Could I have six oatcakes please?' Linda asked, offering up two shiny silver fifty-pence pieces, to the woman behind the high counter.

'Hey-up me duck, course you can,' the woman replied, and then quickly wrapped the cakes in a plain white paper bag, before handing them down to her. Linda started back over to the car, where she knew Elaine would be sticking the ticket on the windscreen. On the way, she couldn't resist opening the paper parcel and sampling one of the oatcakes. She was surprised to find that the cake had a slippery moist texture, undaunted she took a bite. The slimy unpalatable consistency of the cake, made it feel like she was eating, cold sticky, oat-flavoured blancmange. With some difficulty she finally managed to swallow her mouthful of the gluey, batter-like concoction.

'I've got us some cakes, but they taste a bit funny,' she imparted the duel strands of information, while offering the top oatcake to Elaine.

'I'm not surprised, these need to be cooked!' Elaine's hand flew to her mouth as she tried to suppress a bout of giggles, at the comic absurdity of her friend's gastronomic blunder. 'You stick them on a griddle and have them with your breakfast!'

'I wondered why they were so gooey,' Linda laughed, joining in with Elaine's amusement, but feeling embarrassed about

348

her lack of knowledge, concerning northern cuisine. 'To be fair, we don't have these down south.'

'That's because you are all too busy, eating cockles and whelks!'

'Yuck! I'd much rather eat a raw oatcake, than put one of those in my mouth!' Linda exclaimed, and then deposited the bag of oatcakes into the glove compartment of her car. 'We can have them with breakfast tomorrow.'

As they strolled over to the corner exit of the car park, Elaine interlocked her arm tightly around Linda's, eliciting a notion to form in Linda's mind on whether this was a "more than just friends" gesture. She then reasoned to herself, that she had often seen two women walk arm-in-arm, and never speculated about their sexual identity. Elaine's arm then suddenly slid down, and before Linda could think or react, she had grabbed hold of her hand and given it an affectionate squeeze, answering any residual doubts Linda may have about Elaine's intentions. They continued side-by-side into the shopping area, their arms swinging together like a couple of teenagers, subliminally announcing to the world that they were lovers. At first, Linda felt a touch uncomfortable about this daring, public display of their sexual union, to the milling shoppers of Ashbourne, but after a few minutes, she began to revel in the strangely liberating sensation it gave her. Elaine appeared completely at ease with their physical statement, pointing out things in shop windows, and casually chatting away about the minutiae of consumerism. Although Linda was responding to Elaine's comments, she had half an eye on how the other shoppers were acknowledging, what was, in her mind, an audacious declaration. She was cognisant of the fact that they were getting many more attentive stares, from the outnumbered men, who were begrudgingly shopping with their female partners. At last, Elaine guided her into the lingerie department of a fashionable town centre store, and much to Linda's relief, a place where the male of the species was rarely sighted.

'They have some lovely stuff in here, I think I'll treat myself as well,' Elaine breathed into Linda's ear.

For the first time in twenty minutes she released her hand and stepped away from her side, to prowl off around the display cabinets, like a predatory feline, waiting to pounce on its stalked prey.

'What do you think of these?' she asked, waving over to Linda, who was looking at boxed sets of the more reasonably priced underwear. The type designed, not for the titillation of passion, but to be used primarily on a day-to-day basis. Linda smiled her approval back at Elaine, and then continued to concentrate on her own purchases. Several minutes later, they both reunited near the lingerie department doorway, each holding the first, of the plethora of designer carrier bags that would hang from their arms by lunchtime.

#   #   #

'Shall we have something to eat in a pub?' Elaine proposed, looking at her wristwatch. 'It's nearly one-thirty – two and half hours have just whizzed by – it's amazing how time flies when you are having fun.'

Rain was starting to fall again, and the chill in the air was augmented by a strong, gusty wind, which was spiralling a mixture of leaves, tumbling styrofoam cups and general litter, into little tornados, which whipped across the road at knee height. Feeling cold, Linda readily agreed to Elaine's suggestion, so together, they quick-marched towards the market square, in search of a suitable place to have lunch. As they approached the bustling town centre, the heavens suddenly opened, which caused the crowd of meandering shoppers to abruptly scurry for cover. They disappeared into the shops, cafes, restaurants and pubs that fringed the square, like a group of frightened squirrels, seeking the refuge of the nearest clump of tree.

Spotting a large, former coaching inn, Elaine and Linda scampered across the road and sheltered for a few seconds in the recessed doorway, to recover from their unexpected sprint. Once composed, they stepped inside the warm, smoky bar, with its low black-beams and welcoming open fire that crackled away in the corner. There were about a dozen or so other patrons sprinkled

350

around the room, mostly men sitting in twos and threes, all of whom seemed to be absorbed in conversations about football, or racing. Selecting a table that distanced them from the other drinkers, the two women carefully deposited their bags down around it, like they were attentively positioning presents under a Christmas tree. After an exhausting morning of frenzied shopping, Linda delegated herself to go up to the bar for some much-needed, thirst quenching drinks, and at the same time, order the meals.

Returning to the table, she fastidiously placed down two half-pint glasses of lager, on top of the stained beer mats and asked, 'Are you pleased with what you bought this morning?'

'Gosh yes! It's been a while since I've had a really good spend up! What about you? Have you got everything you will need for the rest of the week?'

'Nearly, I've just got to get some more toiletries and I'll be fine.'

'On the way back to the car, we can pop into Boots the chemist for them. The weather out there looks terrible, I suppose we should try and get home fairly soon, in case this gets any worse,' advocated Elaine, her attention being assailed by the driving rain, rattling violently against the windowpanes.

'When I was getting the drinks, I overheard the young barmaid say, that the storm is set to be quite bad. She's been listening to the radio, and there have been reports of trees being uprooted, over in Staffordshire – apparently it's heading our way.'

'Oh, that doesn't sound good – still we are only twenty-five minutes away from Basington, so hopefully we'll be back before it gets too bad.'

'Elaine,' Linda said softly, signalling to Elaine that she wanted to say something confidential, by leaning in closer towards her, 'did you the see people looking at us, because we were holding hands?'

351

'Yes,' Elaine giggled, 'that does freak some people out, especially men. They don't quite know what to read into it – do they?'

'I think that some of the men who were staring at us, knew exactly what to read into it! I had this strange feeling that they could tell what we had been up to last night,' Linda retorted, scanning the room with an embarrassed, furtive expression in her eyes.

'Trust me, they were making up their own stories – I think the old guy in that second antique shop that we went to, was about to come in his trousers, by the time we left!' Elaine snorted a gleeful suppressed laugh.

'Shhuuusssh' Linda admonished her, with a long hiss: worried that somebody might be eavesdropping on their intimate conversation.

'I did it on purpose,' Elaine gathered herself and spoke in a serious tone, to a puzzled looking Linda.

'What do you mean?'

'I held your hand like that, to see how you would react – to being outed.'

'Outed? I don't understand.'

'Outing means – that you reveal your true sexuality to the world, well, in this case, just the town of Ashbourne,' Elaine explained, with a twinkle of mischief in her eyes.

'I see,' Linda's breath thickened, and then she continued in a hesitant voice, 'Did . . . I pass your little test then?'

'With flying colours! You never baulked once.'

'That's because – I was rather enjoying it – after I got over the initial shock, that is! Holding someone's hand is such an intimate, trusting gesture, I'd forgotten that feeling, it was nice to experience it again,' Linda said, looking longingly into Elaine's eyes.

352

'So, for being such a good little girl, I'm going to buy you a present,' Elaine announced with a slight leer on her face, forewarning Linda that she was about to say something with a sexual slant to it.

'Will I like it?' Linda drawled seductively, playing along by stroking the top of Elaine's thigh under the table.

'Yes you will, it's going to be a lovely . . . book.'

'A book!' Linda spluttered loudly, with genuine disappointment.

'Yes, a ladybird book – do you remember them?'

'I do, they cost half-a-crown when I was growing up – I had quite a few. Which one are you getting me?'

'The Joan of Arc story!' Elaine burst out laughing. 'I saw it in one of the bric-a-brac shops that we looked around. I didn't say anything at the time, in case you wet your knickers, thinking about Joan all tied up and helpless!'

Linda slapped Elaine's leg, in a pique of feigned anger, and issued her retort, before stopping to think where she was, 'Right! And because you have been such a *bad* little girl, I'm going take that bloody hairbrush and give you another sound smacking on your bare bot . . .' feeling the presence of a body looming over her, the sentence came to an emergency stop, slightly too late. Linda nervously cast her eyes upwards, to see the young barmaid standing next to their table, looking slightly bemused and holding two plates of sausage, egg and chips. Without speaking, the girl gently placed the meals down onto the old wooden table top, and then, sporting an undisguised sly smile on her face, took a pace back and asked, 'Would you like some sauce to go with that?'

'Um . . . yes, sorry . . . I, mean no . . . I mean, no thank you,' Linda managed a confused, cringing response, to the query, while her face lit up cherry red with abject mortification. She waited until the young girl had returned to her position behind the bar and then hissed, 'Oh my God! How very, very embarrassing!'

'Amazing!' Elaine started to snigger. 'That was a really spectacular way to "come out". I suppose the hand holding was a bit too subtle for you – was it?'

Both women shook with shared laughter at Linda's gaffe. When they had managed to sufficiently control their spray of schoolgirl giggles, Linda continued, 'I suppose this is what my life will be like now?'

'How do you mean?' Elaine asked, her fork with two speared chips on it, hovered a couple of inches away from her mouth.

'Well, I hope that we will be seeing a lot of each other from now on – if you want to, that is?'

Elaine continued to delay the eating of her hot chips.

'What are you trying to say?'

'I've decided to approach Jim about buying the Poacher's Pocket.'

'What!' Elaine returned the fork laden with chips, back to her plate, realising that she would be unable to eat, while the startling conversation was in progress.

'I might as well! What else am I going to do? I'll have the money from selling my business, and I'll have half of whatever profit there is, after we sell the house. The rest, I hope I can get from the bank. It's an ideal opportunity for a fresh start.'

'So, we will be neighbours then?'

'More than neighbours I hope!' Linda gave Elaine's leg a tender squeeze. 'I thought – if you are agreeable, we would be business partners and run the pub together?'

'Business partners?' Elaine repeated, with a guarded intonation to her two-word question.

Linda managed to swallow the tight knot lodged in her throat.

354

'No, I mean partners in every sense – if you will have me. I know this is all very sudden, but the events over the past few days have changed my life completely – I know it sounds crass, but I just want to be with you forever. I never stopped loving you Elaine, from that day I waved goodbye, when you were looking down from the sick room window. Even though we have been separated for all those years, you were always in my head – I never stopped wondering about how you were, hoping that you were happy and being loved by somebody special.

'I've spent my whole life being frightened by my real desires and inclinations, but now I feel free, it's like I'm breathing for the first time, and I don't want to waste another single second. So what do you say? Do you want us to live together?'

Elaine looked totally stunned by this unexpected outburst, she sat, staring blankly back at Linda, making no attempt to answer her earnest proposal. Linda looked expectantly into Elaine's emotionless eyes, and as the excruciating seconds of silence ticked past; she felt that her dream of a new utopian lifestyle was beginning to fade away. Elaine's deep brown eyes suddenly started to liquefy. There was a loud clatter, as the knife that she was holding dropped onto her plate, which aroused the curiosity of the other drinkers in the bar. Throwing her arms around Linda's neck, she held on with a vice-like tightness.

'Of course I'll be your partner!' she whispered, half laughing and half crying. For a few precious moments nothing or nobody else in the world mattered, and they were lost in each other's embrace. When they disengaged themselves, the young barmaid, was once again standing next to their table, quickly returning them back to worldly reality.

'Is everything all right with your meals?' she asked innocently.

'Yes thank you!' Elaine replied, 'Everything is just fantastic!'

CHAPTER THIRTY-ONE
21st October 2003

3.45pm

With his head lowered in deep thought, Steve walked with a stiff-legged, almost military gait as he emerged from the tube station. A few minutes later he rounded the last corner of his short journey, where he looked up and caught sight of the distinctive, olive-green coloured front door of his house, about fifty yards further up the road. Flicking back the end of his coat sleeve, he held the material above his watch and checked the time. Breaking his stride, to stand still for a second, he made sure that he was seeing the position of hands correctly, and said to himself, 'Three forty-nine.'

Nervously he checked again to make sure. Satisfied that it was the correct time, he felt momentarily mollified by the fact that he had made it back before four o'clock. Quickly glancing up the road again, he could see that Melissa's bright yellow, limited edition Mini Cooper, was parked outside her house, ready for their journey. The second he put the front door key into the lock, his mobile phone began to ring out its relentless and impatient summons. Steve chucked his briefcase down in the hallway and rooted around in the deep pocket of his raincoat, he pulled out the phone along with a screwed up tissue, which he tossed at the waste paper basket, but missed. Before he had a chance to speak, he heard Melissa's voice.

'I'll drive down the road and wait for you around the corner, you leave from your back garden, go down the alleyway, and I'll pick you up where it comes out, near the old pub,' she ordered.

Steve was about to reply, but the line went dead. Without waiting, he did exactly what he been instructed to do. Letting himself out of the patio doors in the back extension, he took the six strides it required to get to the back garden gate, which still retained the sharp smell of a recent coat of creosote. Opening the gate, he turned right, only to stop dead, when the glint of a silver thread from a spider's web flashed, like a laser beam right in front of his eyes. Carefully he detached the long anchoring strand from the fence and the web collapsed in on itself and hung limply on the opposite wall. Steve felt guilty about destroying the intricate masterpiece of arachnid engineering, but continued to forage his way down the narrow overgrown passageway that divided the two sets of adjacent rear gardens. Stepping over various types of domestic rubbish, which had been dumped out of sight and out of mind, into the alley by inconsiderate neighbours, he finally finished the seventy-yard trek by squeezing past an abducted supermarket trolley. Venturing out into the main street, it wasn't difficult to locate Melissa's car, which shone out like a beacon of Day-Glo yellow, against the myriad of dull grey shades that surrounded it. Steve walked towards the car, trying to casually brush off the withered remnants of the dried vegetation that irritatingly, had adhered to his suit trousers during his brief urban safari. He opened the door of the Mini and attempted to engage Melissa with a smile, but she continued to look stolidly ahead, tapping the rim of the steering wheel with an agitated tempo. As soon as he had sat down into the front passenger seat, Melissa cut out into the moving traffic, causing a black taxicab to break hard, in order to avoid a collision. The aggrieved driver, who was looking for a fare, pulled up beside them at the next junction and made his expected derisory remarks, about the prowess of women drivers. Unperturbed by the haranguing, Melissa simply turned to her right and blew him a kiss, at which, his annoyance dissolved into a loud chuckle, and he pulled away in the opposite direction.

'Bloody taxi drivers, they think they own the road,' Melissa muttered under her breath.

'You did cut him up a bit,' Steve reluctantly informed her.

'He should have been anticipating other road users. That's what it says in the *Highway Code*,' Melissa informed Steve with the misplaced authoritative zeal, of somebody who had just passed their driving test. 'What do you think of the car?'

'It's nice – very bright colour though,' Steve mumbled.

'Yes, I can't believe that bloody taxi driver didn't see me! Rod bought it for me – for my birthday this year. It's a special edition, hence the unusual colour. I hardly ever use it, so it stays locked up in the garage for most of the time. Rod refuses to let me drive his car and rarely ever lets me drive him, in this one. He says I'm a typical "school-run mum" driver – bloody cheek, I passed first time.'

'Did you?' Steve's surprise was clearly evident in his voice, as he stamped his foot down onto a non-existent brake pedal. 'How many lessons did you have?'

'Sixty-eight.'

'Sixty-eight! Your instructor must have been a very patient . . . and rich man,' Steve sniggered.

'Oh shut up!' Melissa shouted, annoyed by the sarcasm being cast on her driving ability. She decided that it was time they changed the subject away from her driving, back to the business in hand. 'Are you clear about what we are going to say to Linda?'

'Yes, hopefully she has calmed down now and will be in a more forgiving mood,' Steve answered optimistically.

'I wouldn't bank on her forgiving you Steve – she was staying in the next room to us. It's one thing to find out that your old man is having an affair, it's quite another thing, to hear him actually having it off, with the other woman,' Melissa tempered Steve's expectations. 'Just be prepared to offer her the entire proceeds from the sale of your house.'

'I'm not sure that Linda is that money orientated,' Steve conjectured.

'Everyone has their price, believe me – I know what I'm talking about. Dangle an extra hundred thousand pounds in front of her and she'll be far more cooperative about keeping stum, about our little roll in the hay.'

'So, do you have a price?'

'Yes, of course I do. And I've already cashed in. The moment I got pregnant with Taylor, I hit the jackpot. A child was the one thing that Rod didn't – and *couldn't have*, with his wife, Philippa. I wasn't expecting him to leave her, but I was sure that I would be comfortably off for quite a few years. He wasn't going to let his precious only daughter, grow up on a no-hope council estate, was he?

'So *why did* he leave Philippa?'

'I'd like to say that he was madly in love with me, or that he just wanted to trade in his old wife, for a younger prettier version, like men do with their cars. The truth is, he is obsessed with Taylor and couldn't bear the thought of only having visiting rights every other weekend, so he dumped Philippa and asked me to live with him. I certainly didn't need asking twice, but I made sure that it was on the understanding that he would marry me, once his divorce came through. Which, to be fair to him, he did.'

'So you both got what you wanted then – a luxurious lifestyle for you, and Rod got the child that he never thought he would have?'

'Yes, it does seemed to have worked out that way, well for Rod and me – Philippa was the loser, I suppose.'

'Didn't you feel a bit guilty about that?'

'I did at first. I had met Philippa several times and she seemed very nice. But like they say – all's fair in love and war.' Melissa glanced at Steve, and detected a curl of disapproval on his lips. 'For fuck's sake Steve, it was okay for you, growing up in your cosy middle-class cocoon – I grew up on a rundown council estate in Essex. I quickly realised that my main assets, were my looks and body. So I learnt at an early age, how to use them, to get what I wanted in life. As a girl, I had to share a cramp bedroom with my younger sister – I was forever dreaming that one day, somehow I would live in a fantastic house, with all mod-cons and luxury furnishings, and fly off around the world, on fabulous holidays.

'When I was about sixteen, I opened the newspaper and saw a picture of this shrivelled up old man, with his absurdly glamorous, much younger wife hanging onto his arm. Bingo! In an instance I had clocked the answer to my search for a better life. So after leaving school and armed with good secretarial qualifications, I temped at a lot of top offices in London, with the sole aim of bagging myself a very rich man. It took a few years, but eventually everything fell into place when I started work for Rod.'

'Well, you certainly executed your plan to perfection,' Steve conceded, with a rueful smile. 'I'm sorry, who am I to cast stones. I'm hardly a totem for moral decency, am I? Do you regret anything about your decision to marry for money, not love?'

'No not really, love doesn't seem to last that long in most marriages. Of course, there are the downsides – although I got the big expensive house that I craved, it's become a bit of a gilded cage. I get lonely at nights, at least twice during the week, Rod stays over at the company flat, when he has to have conference calls with the Far East, in the middle of the night. Then there are his business trips away, and let's face it, Rod is pretty old – how would you like to have sex, with a woman older than your mother?'

Steve grimaced, 'I wouldn't!' and for a fleeting moment, he almost felt sorry for Melissa.

'So, you can see now, why I wanted our weekend away, to be like a proper romantic break, the sort that a happily married couple would take together – as strange as that might seem, that's my fantasy. It will never happen with Rod, because he is only interested in doing things that include Taylor.'

'If he's so besotted by having Taylor with him, why does he want her to go away to boarding school then?'

'He wants the very best for her in everything. She wouldn't stay at the school over the weekends, he would send a driver to pick her up on Friday evening and take her back Monday morning. He would still get his *darling girl* all to himself, Saturday and Sunday, to indulge in those father-daughter things that he is so fixated with. He knows how the system works in this country. You get your offspring into a good school, where they make friends with the *right* people. They then get the best university places and of course the best jobs, where they start in a managerial position. After that, they just take all the credit for the team of foot solders working below them, or resolutely blame them, when things go wrong. Well, that's what happens – doesn't it?'

Steve gave a nod of endorsement to Melissa's cynical evaluation of the enduring British class system, before asking, 'So you don't want Taylor to benefit from that advantage?'

'I'm just being selfish actually, if she goes away to school during the week, I'll never bloody see her, unless I'm prepared to stand in all weathers at the side of a football pitch on Sunday mornings. Anyway she won't need a good job, Rod has stacks of money and he can set her up in something.'

'Like what?'

'I dunno, something that just needs overseeing, like an art gallery or a posh frock shop.'

'So tell me, how many times have you played "happy families" with other men, while you have been married to Rod?'

'A few times, not that often.'

'And Rod has never suspected anything?'

'No, he is usually too wrapped up in his work to notice anything, or he is out and about taking Taylor to football practise, or dance class, or riding lessons; she's always doing something – of course I'm incredibly careful, you never know who is watching. After all my planning, I can't believe that the most atrocious piece of bad luck caught us out. So now, we have to put things as right as we can, before Rod finds out and the shit hits the fan.'

361

Two hundred miles away, Linda and Elaine were journeying home after their successful shopping expedition. With the storm getting stronger, the gale force wind was snapping an assortment of branches from roadside trees, creating an obstacle course on some of the country roads. After taking over twice as long, as the drive usually took to complete, they pulled into the concealed track, which led up to Elaine's house.

'Oh shit, the old beach tree has come down!' Elaine shouted in mid-jolt, as Linda made an emergency stop, causing the Land Rover to skid to a halt, just a few feet away from the outstretched branches of the stricken tree. 'You'd better park the car over in the pub car park, it will be safer there, another tree might come down on it, if you leave it here.'

Linda edged the Land Rover back out onto the main village road, and then they continued along to the Poacher's Pocket car park. Jim Guthrie stuck his head out of one of the first floor windows and shouted something across to them, but his words were lost in the furious whistling of the wind that blew relentlessly across the open space of the pub forecourt. They both trotted over to the side of the entrance porch, to use the wind-breaking effect it offered and looked up at Jim, who was struggling to hold the window open. He signalled that he would come down, and a few seconds later they heard the bolts of the main door clack open.

'Come in,' Jim beckoned them inside, 'Elaine, the electricity is out and the telephone lines are down as well.'

'The beech tree near the entrance to my driveway has come crashing down, blocking the way up to the house, it's probably brought the overhead power line down with it. That's why we've put the Land Rover in your car park, is that all right with you?' Elaine explained.

'Yes of course it's okay, I was calling over to tell you to be careful where you walk – there might be a live power line lying on the ground, if you step on it – it could be goodnight Vienna!' Jim advised, in his usual jocular manner. 'We can't seem to get a signal

362

on the mobile, so Finola has driven over to her friend's house, in the next village, where she can call up and report the power cut. I have to open up in twenty-five minutes, and I'll only be able to use the gravity pumps for the beer, anyone wanting a lager is going to be disappointed. On top of that, all our ovens are electric, so I don't know what we'll do about the meals this evening?'

'It sounds like a bad news day Jim . . . but Linda does have a piece of good news for you,' Elaine said, teeing Linda up, to divulge her intentions.

'Have you Linda?' Jim's thick black eyebrows compressed together displaying his genuine puzzlement, at what kind of possible good news, Linda could impart to him.

'I'm seriously considering making you an offer for the pub – if I can get a financial package worked out,' Linda gleefully blurted out.

'Really?' Jim took a moment for her proposition to sink in. 'But you haven't looked around the place or scrutinized the books or . . .'

'I'll do all that, when I know I can definitely afford to make you an offer, probably in a week or two,' Linda interrupted. 'I'm selling my events company, so if that goes through okay, and if I get enough money from the sale of my house . . .'

'So you and your husband are going to run the pub.' It was Jim's turn to interrupt.

'No!' Linda suddenly paused for a few breaths, while she looked at the gold band on her left hand. Using the forefinger and thumb on her other hand, she abruptly twisted the ring off and stuffed it into her handbag. 'No, my marriage is over – I'm going to run the pub with Elaine.'

Jim Guthrie's eyebrows were having a most intensive workout, now they had bounced up his forehead and disappeared under the awning of his uneven fringe; their brief, but lightening quick trip, fuelled by pure astonishment.

'I'll be the other side of the bar from now on, Jim,' Elaine informed him with a board grin.

Although he was suffering from a near terminal case of information overload, Jim managed to collect his thoughts and offered a response, 'At least you will be safe from old Joe's bottom pinching.'

'Yes, and I can threaten to ban him,' Elaine gushed with enthusiasm.

The two buoyant women exited the pub, leaving Jim in a state of stunned contemplation, as he watched them link arms and run together to the car. They gathered their shopping and then, with the various bags blowing like wind socks from their arms, they rushed across the road to the foot of the steps that climbed up to the back of Elaine's house. Having scaled the steep flight of steps, taking extra care not to stand on anything resembling a cable, they opened the back door into the kitchen, which seemed strangely hushed and dark.

'Oh bugger, I forgot that the power cut has gone and shut down all of my freezers and fridges,' Elaine shouted, but still automatically flicked down the temporarily redundant triple light switch, out of habit.

'Does that mean that the food is ruined?' Linda asked.

'As long as I remember, not to open any of the doors, it should be all right for about twelve hours. Do you still want to take over the pub? Imagine the headache that this kind of thing causes Jim and Finola.'

'I'm not worried, in my job, things went wrong all the time, I just had to fix them the best I could. Do you have many power cuts then?'

'This is only the third since I've been here, but I must give them credit, they usually get the electricity back on in a few hours. In the meantime, we can get the fire going, and I have hundreds of tea light candles that I use up in the bathroom, when I'm *indulging* myself,' Elaine answered, shooting Linda a cheeky smile.

In no time at all, tiny twinkling candles had been placed about the room and the combined light that they produced, projected overlapping, flickering shadows, which danced about in the nooks and crannies of the walls.

'I've just got to pop upstairs for a few minutes,' Elaine said, slowly stepping around the indistinct barricade of assorted furniture and piles of ledgers.

Linda kicked off her shoes and bounced up onto the sofa, perching with her legs folded back up beneath her, awaiting Elaine's return. Gradually, the soporific effect of staring into the flames of the fire, caused her to fall into a state of comfortable drowsiness. Just at the point when her nodding head began to descend onto her chest, she was awoken with a start, by the hollow cadence, of stiletto-heeled shoes clip-clopping down the wooden staircase. She looked up and there stood Elaine, with a long golden silk lounging robe wrapped tightly about her.

'Ta-dah!' Elaine exclaimed, dramatically peeling the robe away, to reveal that she was wearing the new satiny black lingerie that she had purchased earlier in the day.

'Imagine, just how hot, Joan of Arc would have looked, if she had been wearing this, when they tied her to the stake!' Elaine giggled, and placed her hand over her mouth in mock regret. 'Opps! "Hot" might have been an insensitive thing to have said!'

'Blimey Elaine, you look . . . you look, really fantastic!' Linda squealed in delight.

'Do you truly think so?' Elaine asked, while doing a slow twirl in the hope of garnering further words of approval from Linda. 'You don't think I'm too old for sexy undies, stockings and suspenders?'

'Don't be silly, you have a fabulous figure,' Linda continued to compliment.

'It's been a while since I've dressed up, and I certainly haven't worn really high heels for an age – I was really wobbling, as I came down the stairs.'

365

Linda leapt up from the sofa and stood close up to Elaine.

'It's like being back at school!' she said.

'What do you mean?' Elaine asked, looking confused, as she searched her memory for anything that would connect her appearance, with their time at school together.

'Our heights!' Linda laughed, at seeing the look of concerned bewilderment on Elaine's face. 'At school, you were about three inches taller than me and you are again on those stilts.'

'Oh I see! Yes, come to think of it, you do look a lot shorter than me from up here.'

In the soft candlelight, Elaine's laughing eyes were like two illuminated dark brown orbs. Linda couldn't resist slipping her arms around her, enfolding her in a comforting embrace.

'We're going to be great together Elaine – I just know it.'

Linda expected Elaine to return her poignant hug of solidarity, but instead, she felt her wrists being gripped.

'Undo my bra,' Elaine assertively ordered, in a hushed low voice, as she tenderly guided Linda's hands up to her brassiere clasp.

While her fingers fumbled with the unseen, fiddly bra hooks, Linda raised her mouth up, teasing the tip of her tongue along the line of Elaine's full lips, forcing them to part slightly wider.

'Sorry, I feel like an inexperienced teenage boy,' she whispered her apology for the infuriating delay.

'Well make your mind up,' Elaine sniggered quietly.

'Where would I get one in this little village,' Linda saw her joke and raised her.

'If you can't find one, I'm sure old Joe would step in.'

The bra strap snapped open, curtailing any further volleys of nervous witticisms. Elaine allowed the black lacy demi-cupped material to slip down between their two bodies, where it landed silently on the carpet. Linda could hardly believe what she was doing; it was like she was bursting open a secret compartment in her head that had been securely locked all her life. Straight away, her hands went to Elaine's soft breasts, capturing the two nipples between her fingers, gently rolling and tweaking them until they hardened. Stooping slightly, Linda lowered her head close to the left pillowy summit and with her lips pursed in readiness, she expelled a light huff of warm air over the areola. Resembling a vampire preparing to take her first exquisite draw of blood from a sleeping victim, she slowly opened her mouth wider. Firmly pressing it over the erect nipple, she dynamically flicked her tongue back and forth across the protruding cerise nub, before sucking hard at the soft, plump flesh. Elaine rewarded and encouraged her efforts by making vociferous panting sounds of gratification. Lifting her eyes to glance at Elaine's face, Linda suspended her velvety oscillations for a moment, to ensure that the delicious spectacle of the breathless murmurs of delight, being expressed, would be forever burnt into her memory. The sight of Elaine's blissful expression, stoked her own escalating passion and after another brief pause to draw breath, she eagerly returned to her deft tongue gymnastics. This time her attentions were centred on Elaine's right breast, and the soft, responsive vocal payoffs it produced, once again floated around the room. After enjoying the matchless sensation for a few minutes, Elaine gently walked Linda backwards over to the sofa, and when she felt the backs of her legs touch the edge of the cushioned seat, she obediently sat down. Dropping into a kneeling position, Elaine's hands quickly reached for the button and zip of Linda's jeans to undo them. Eagerly she pulled the scrunched up denim material down her outstretched legs, struggling for a second or two with the tightness, but eventually the tug of war was won. Falling back with the effort, she held the faded blue jeans above her head in a victory salute. By the time she had managed to look up again, the freshly debagged Linda, had pushed her knickers down and kicked them off into the corner of the room. Elaine contorted around and pulled off her shoes, then smiling seductively, she inched her way back, crawling on all fours, until she knelt between Linda legs. Without breaking eye contact, she placed her

367

hands on the inside of Linda's warm thighs and after steadily spreading them wider, hoisted them up, onto her own shoulders. Emitting a long, deep and satisfied sigh, Linda eased forward, lifting up her buttocks slightly, so that the outer lips of her vagina, seamlessly docked with Elaine's soft, moist rotating tongue, which vigorously twisted and stabbed, like an opportunistic cat, stealing the cream.

CHAPTER THIRTY-TWO
21st October 2003

6.55pm

'Take the next right and we should almost be there,' Steve instructed, using a small map torch, to track their route around the maze of country lanes that surrounded the village of Basington.

'Is it always this dark in the countryside? I can't see a bloody thing, but it looks like there's a pub up on the left – shall we go in and see if they know the whereabouts Linda's friend's B&B?' Melissa asked.

'Yeah, good idea, they're bound to know where it is and give us the final directions. If the place is open, that is – it looks closed,' Steve answered, while surveying the unexpected darkened windows of the public house. 'Oh, that's our car over there, perhaps they're inside – what shall we do?'

'There are some flickering lights coming from the bar, let's go in – if Linda is in there, she'll hardly be likely to create a major scene in public,' Melissa said, opening the car door. They braced themselves against the multiple gusts of swirling wind and ran over to the pub entrance. Steve gave the door a shove with his shoulder and it jarred wide open, along with Jim Guthrie's mouth, as he watched a man abruptly tumble into his candle-lit snug bar.

'Sorry about that, I wasn't expecting it to open quite so easily,' Steve offered his apologies for the slapstick entrance, while

369

Melissa fought hard to push the door shut, against the invisible resistance caused by the gale blowing in.

'I'm afraid we've had a power cut, so I can only offer you spirits, bottled drinks, or ale drawn up on the hand pumps,' Jim explained the reason for the subdued lighting and the restricted stock of drinks.

'I'm actually looking for my wife – her car is parked out in the front,' Steve said, pointing through the window at the dark shape across the car park. 'The Land Rover Discovery.'

'Linda's car?' Jim questioned, sporting his now habitual raised eyebrow look, of doubt and surprise.

'Yes, I'm Linda's husband,' Steve confirmed.

'Her husband,' Jim repeated in a vacant tone, giving his brain a chance to compute a viable reason, as to why Linda's partner – who she said she was leaving – would have turned up from London, accompanied by a very attractive younger woman. 'Sorry, she's not in here – the car is parked outside because the driveway, up to Elaine's house, has been blocked by a fallen tree. If you walk straight over the car park, to where the pub sign is, directly across the road you'll see a set of stone steps leading up past a small cottage – at the top of the steps you'll come out at Elaine's kitchen. Almost certainly they'll be in there – just tap on the window to get their attention.

'Thanks very much, is it okay to leave our car in your car park?' Steve asked.

'Yes sure, we're not going to get inundated with customers on a night like this.'

Jim agreed to a second parking request that evening. He then watched through the window, as the couple headed across to the road, following the directions that he had advised.

Finola appeared from the back room.

'Did I hear you blathering to a customer?' she asked.

370

'Not exactly, it was Linda's husband, with a woman friend.'

'What, Linda who is thinking about buying the pub?' Finola questioned, with an uncharacteristic hint of worry in her voice.

'Yes,' Jim turned to his wife with a pensive frown on his face, 'He didn't say anything about the pub. You would've thought he would have mentioned it, if he was aware of her intentions to buy this place.'

'I wonder what yer man wants? I hope to God he isn't going to block the deal from going through.'

'I'll just give Elaine a quick call, to warn them that they are about to get some visitors,' Jim announced, and then lifting the phone to his ear, he heard a flat silence and exclaimed, 'Shit! I forgot the bloody telephone line is down.'

#   #   #

Steve and Melissa waited at the side of the road for a fast approaching car, their eyes dazzled for a second by the reflection of the headlights, which bounced up off of the wet tarmac surface. Instead of passing them by, it suddenly turned off into the pub car park, leaving it safe for them to cross the road. Steve led the way up the steps, taking them two at a time. He was nervous about meeting his wife again in such abnormal circumstances, but wanted the situation sorted out, one way or another. At the top he stopped and waited for Melissa to catch him up.

'Well this is it,' he murmured to himself, while striding across a thick carpet of spongy wet leafs that had fallen and congregated on the kitchen patio. At first glance, the inside of the building looked dark and deserted, but with his head craned to the side and his nose almost pressed against the windowpane, he could make out the faint glow of shimmering candlelight, coming from the far corner of the large room. Steve tapped on the glass and peered in, trying to detect any movement from the interior of the room. He tapped again, this time a bit harder, still there was no reaction from within.

371

'Try the door,' Melissa suggested.

'We can't just let ourselves in,' Steve protested.

'Well I haven't come all this way to stand outside in the bloody wind and rain,' Melissa countered, taking hold of the brass doorknob, she twisted it and the door swung silently inwards. Cautiously, the two uninvited guests entered the building and nervously wound their way around the darkened room. As they moved further in, they could see that the limited light source was coming from the fireplace and the tiny tea lights, dotted about on the eclectic furnishings.

'Jesus Christ!' Melissa screamed, suddenly happening upon Linda and Elaine engaging in a fervid bout of oral sex. Linda's eyes sprang open in horror on hearing the profanity; she turned her head to the left and was thunderstruck to see the face of her nemesis, looming out of the shadows at her. Frantically wriggling, she tried to disengage herself from the hold that Elaine had on her upper legs. Alerted to the fact that something was wrong, Elaine released her grip and bobbed up to see Linda's look of complete panic. Following the direction of Linda's horrified stare, she screwed her head around to see two dark figures, standing no more than ten feet away from her.

'What the fucking hell are you doing in my kitchen!' Elaine screamed out in fright, on seeing the two interlopers, gaping at her from the darkness.

"I'm sorry . . . we knocked a few times . . . you obviously didn't hear us,' Steve attempted to apologise, but was hypnotised by his wife's involvement in the surreal sexual exhibition that he had voyeuristically witnessed.

'It's hardly likely that she would hear anything, while wearing Linda's thighs like earmuffs,' Melissa chipped in gleefully.

Realising how exposed she was, Elaine grabbed for her robe, while behind her, Linda hopped on one leg, hurrying to pull her jeans up the naked lower half of her body.

372

'See I told you Steve! I said that Linda had been checking me out,' Melissa couldn't resist the chance to crow in celebration, after literally stumbling upon the proof that she needed, to substantiate her earlier discounted allegation. 'You *must* believe me now!'

'Shut up Melissa!' Steve shouted, snapping out of the spell that the Sapphic scene had cast over him, he turned a building anger towards his wife. 'What the hell were you up to Linda? You catch me out having a meaningless affair, and within two days it's turned you into a raging lesbian. Is this your idea of getting even with me?'

'No of course not!' Linda fired back her own broadside. 'I haven't been a lesbian for just the last two days – I've been one *all my life*. I fell in love with Elaine when we were at school together, and I'm still in love with her!'

'Don't be so fucking stupid – you were both just children at school. You haven't even seen her for over thirty years for Christ's sake – how on earth, can you be in love with a woman, who you have only really known for four days?'

'I don't care what you think Steve, I've decided that my future is with Elaine now – we are going to start a new life with each other and take over the pub in the village.'

'What! You don't know the first thing about running a pub,' Steve spat out a dismissive rebuke.

'Well, that's what we are going to do. It won't be so different from my old job, I'll still be dealing with people and organising things, while Elaine looks after the catering side of things.'

'How are you going to finance this grand project then Linda?' Melissa asked, remembering the reason why they had made the trip up to see her.

'Not that's got anything to do with you, but I'll have the money from the sale of my business and whatever I get from my share of the house – I'll get a loan for the rest.'

'Steve has agreed to let you have the entire equity from the house sale,' Melissa dramatically jumped in with the planned inducement.

'Why? Why would you let me have everything Steve?' Linda asked, confused by the offer.

'To buy your silence, about our little fling, of course,' Melissa continued to elucidate. 'If Rod finds out about it, he'll make sure that Steve never sets foot in the city again, and I'll spend my foreseeable future, going to court in an expensive custody battle over Taylor.'

'I should tell him, the man has the right to know what a total slut his wife is,' Linda couldn't resist the temptation to hurl an insult at Melissa.

'Okay, I deserved that, but let's face it, you haven't been totally honest with Steve have you? Marrying him, when you knew all a long that you could never really give him your true love and passion in the bedroom. You've used him Linda.'

Melissa's words cut Linda to the quick, but she still attempted to retaliate, 'That's not fair, I do love Steve but . . .'

'Not in the same way, as you love Elaine?' Melissa contemptuously finished off Linda's arrested sentence. 'Look, why don't you do everyone a favour, including yourself, by keeping your mouth shut and taking what's on offer. That way, we all get what we want and nobody gets hurt.'

'NOT TRUE! You're all going to get hurt!' a deep voice from the back of the room, boomed out from the pitch darkness.

'Oh please tell me, you're here to fix the electricity,' Elaine wailed.

'I'm sorry my dear, I'm here to even up the score,' the sinister figure answered and then moved forward just enough, so that his features were irradiated by the dim orange glow of the candlelight.

'*Rod!*' Melissa breathed out in shocked disbelief. 'How did you . . .'

'I simply followed you – all the way up from London, I lost you for a few minutes in the maze of country roads around here, but then I saw your Mini in the pub car park, shining out like a little flare, and as I pulled in – there you both were, crossing the road,' Rod gave a mocking laugh and shone his powerful torch-light straight at Melissa, the intense beam rendered him indistinguishable again. 'You never use your rear view mirror, except to check your make-up, and besides, I was in a pool car from work that I'd fitted with false plates, so you wouldn't have recognised the motor anyway. Why was he in a car with false plates? – I hear you all asking yourselves – let me tell you. I've known since Saturday that you and Steve have been "having it off" behind my back. On Thursday night, when you were picking Taylor up from her friend's birthday party, I came home to find the answer phone light flashing. It was a message from your sister, thanking us for the baby clothes that you sent over to her, and saying she was looking forward to seeing you at Christmas. She didn't mention anything about your trip that was supposed to be happening just two days later. Naturally, it aroused my suspicions, things didn't quite add up, so I employed a firm of professional private detectives to trail you. When I dropped you off at the station on Saturday, a waiting woman investigator, watched you purchase a ticket to Ravenscourt Park Station, she promptly phoned her partner to meet her there in the car, and then they carefully pursued you up to the hotel in Yorkshire.'

'The couple that sat at our table, outside the pub – I knew I'd seen the woman before – she was waiting for a lift, at the tube station in the morning,' Steve blurted out, angry with himself for not realising at the time.

'Correct Steve, and the photos that the man took of the pub, happened to include you and Melissa, having a cosy little drink together. He emailed the pictures to me that afternoon – you can imagine my surprise, to see the guy that for over a year, I have been helping to make a small fortune in commission, gazing lovingly into the eyes of my wife.'

375

'Rod we can work this out, it was just a stupid spontaneous thing that we both regret,' Melissa appealed, shaking her head slowly from side to side, trying to emphasise her deepest remorse.

'I'm sure that you do regret it now, but only because you have been caught with your pants down. And from what I heard, while I was waiting to surprise you, Linda caught you at it as well – what a double whammy! So now it's retribution time. When I was Head of House at school, before I thrashed miscreants, I would give the boys a long lecture, so I could watch them squirm like a maggots on a hook – consider this your lecture,' Rod repositioned his torch so it spotlighted the fact that he was pulling out a Beretta 9mm pistol from inside his camouflaged combat jacket. 'This is how I'll be administering your punishment.'

With the demeanour of a professional hit man, he calmly delved into another pocket and produced a silencer, and then using his left hand in a quick twisting action, he adeptly attached it to the end of the short barrel.

The sight of the gun, gave rise to a unified intake of breath, the involuntary noise of disbelief, softly punctured the deathly quietness that had fallen over the room.

'Now hold on Rod, you're completely over-reacting, put the gun down and lets talk this through,' Melissa tried to pacify her husband, but he ignored her suggestion and carried on.

'You see, I've had since Saturday to plan a suitable revenge – just out of interest, I'll tell you what *was* going to happen, before I rashly decided to see where you were both sloping off to.

'This afternoon, I was about call for Steve and tell him about a business colleague I knew, who wanted to meet him. Knowing that he can't resist the prospect of making easy money, I was going to offer to drive him over for an initial meet-up. Of course, we would have really headed off to a private estate that a friend of mine owns in Surrey. Once off the beaten track and into the wooded area – BANG! BANG!' Rod pointed the pistol at Steve's head, as he made the childlike gun shot noises. 'Two bullets in the back of the head and then I'd have buried him in the thick

376

undergrowth, returned the car to work, changed the plates back and arrived home at the normal time. A week later, using Steve's mobile, I'd have send an intriguing text to my darling wife, giving her instructions to urgently meet him down in the Surrey woods. Imagine how surprised you would have been Melissa, when instead of meeting lover boy, it was your husband waiting for you. After a few pleasantries, it would have been BANG! BANG!' Rod aimed the gun barrel at Melissa, who flinched and tried to back away, but the old trunk blocked her retreat.

'Stop pointing that thing at me, you know you won't really use it!' Melissa decided to call her husband's bluff. 'You wouldn't want to leave Taylor without her mother.'

'Don't worry about Taylor, I'm sure that Philippa will make the perfect step-mother.'

'Phillppa!' Melissa squealed with incredulity. 'You must be joking!'

'For the last ten years, I've been leading a double life, even though I stupidly divorced Philippa, I never stopped loving her. You can guess where I have really been, when you thought I was working late at the office and staying overnight in the company flat.'

'So you were cheating on me first, you bloody bastard,' Melissa squawked, as her mind reeled at the implications of Rod's revelation. A burning anger inside her began to consume and replace the feeling of fear in the pit of her stomach, as they stood motionless, staring their contempt at each other.

'I don't see it as cheating, because I've never considered you as my real wife,' Rod dismissively answered.

'Anyway, I can't see Philippa agreeing to look after *my* child.'

'She already has,' smiling defiantly, Rod parried Melissa's attack, before making a wounding verbal thrust of his own, by adding, 'and I think she'll make a great success of it. Let's face it – Taylor's always been just a meal ticket to you, hasn't she?

'That's not fair, you know I love Taylor, more than anything!'

'Rod, *please* for God's sake put the gun down, you are frightening everyone,' Linda called out from the far end of the room, hoping that he had sated his appetite for retaliation, by just scaring them all half to death.

'Sorry Linda, I'm going to need it – now that my curiosity has fucked up the meticulous Plan A, I will have to change to a hastily conceived Plan B. Which is, to kill you all, get Taylor from my parents and then, before the police discover your bodies, fly to Cyprus on a private jet, that I've already chartered.'

'Rod you can't possibly think that you will get away with this, the police will soon work out what has happened and come after you,' Linda again tried to be the voice of reason.

'I will get away this, because I've been planning my escape from this country for some time now. You see, I've been stealing from my own company for a number of years and the Serious Fraud Squad are closing in on me. Early next year, I'm expecting to be charged with theft and false accounting, following that, there'll be a long, drawn-out, expensive show trial. At the end of which, there's the real possibility that I'll be banged up for five or six years. Alternatively, I can go and live a luxurious lifestyle with Philippa, in my villa just outside Kyrenia, safe in the knowledge that Northern Cyprus doesn't have an extradition treaty with the UK.'

'So why don't you just do that, why do you have to kill us,' Melissa implored.

'Because, you took me for a bloody fool Melissa. Me! The person who has provided you with everything you could have ever dreamed of. So one way or another, you have to go. I'm not prepared to take any chances over Taylor. She is my whole life – this way, you'll be out of the picture for good, no messy divorce, no fucking visiting rights. I'll know that she'll always be with me in Cyprus. Besides, I really want to kill you, I've fantasised about

378

doing away with you for some years, you scheming little gold-digger.'

'Rod, I promise you, I won't contest the custody of Taylor, just put the gun away and walk out of the house,' Melissa begged, seeing the ice cold, morbid intent in her husband's eyes, which seemed twice their normal size, magnified by the thick lenses of his glasses. She half glanced over at Steve and could tell from his tense stance that he was setting himself, for a desperate spring across the cluttered room. Unfortunately, the slight nod to her left, was enough to redirect Rod's attention.

'Don't even think about it Steve, you'd be a dead man before you got halfway across to me,' Rod growled, and then tailgated his stark warning, with a contemptuous flick of the pistol in Steve's direction. Confident that he had rebuffed any planned offensive action from his only physical threat in the room, he continued to address his wife, 'Anyway Melissa, why should I believe a lying little trollop like you? I'm sure that if I did let you go, you'd quickly revert to type, try to keep Taylor with you, and poison her against me.'

'Rod, please just calm down and think for a minute, I know that you have a axe to grind with Melissa and me, but Linda and her friend have nothing to do with this – at least let them go,' Steve appealed, trying to evoke the remnants of any public school chivalry that Rod might have retained from his youth. While his would-be executioner considered the plea, Steve still tried to edge, closer to him.

'Sorry Steve, if I'm going to make a clean getaway, to a new life in Cyprus, I can't afford the risk of leaving any witnesses. You've heard the term "collateral damage" in the news reports – well, that's what Linda and her friend are. They just happened to be in the wrong place, at the wrong time.'

Without any warning, Melissa began to walk towards Rod, with her arms bizarrely outstretched, in a last futile gesture of appeasement. Linda heard a sound, like a tree branch snapping twice in lightning-quick succession, followed almost instantly, by a spray of atomised blood droplets and brain tissue landing on her face. Melissa's lifeless body crumpled downward, landing with a sickening thud onto the top edge of the open trunk, she then twisted slowly sideways and dropped out of sight. Rod swivelled around to point the gun and torch at Steve, there was a loud click and every light in the room came on simultaneously. Thinking that somebody had entered the kitchen behind him, Rod panicked and swung his body around in a half circle, to confront the intruder. In the blink of an eye that it took Rod to realise the reason for the sudden illumination, was the reconnection of the electricity supply, Steve had already propelled himself across the expanse of flooring that separated them. He crashed into Rod's chest and they both staggered back into the Welsh dresser. In a lemming-like mass suicide leap from a cliff, finely crafted ceramic figurines, tumbled from the shelves. Each exquisite piece plummeted to the tiled floor, and within a second of the slamming impact, most of Elaine's lifetime collection of Staffordshire pottery had been destroyed. The two battling men, resembled a couple of ballroom dancers, spinning around with their opposing arms extended out to the side, as Steve tried to prevent Rod from turning the gun towards him. Another crack reverberated around the room, motivating Linda and Elaine to instinctively duck down for cover. The men continued to grapple with each other, enmeshed in a ferocious death struggle that saw them collapse over the top of the pine table, knocking an assortment of books and plant pots flying. Linda watched, but was frozen to the spot, more by disbelief than fear, as, almost in slow motion, the two combatants rolled the length of the table and then crashed to the kitchen floor, in front of the Aga cooker. There was another sharp cracking sound, the aftermath of this discharged bullet, was a brief snowstorm of plaster dust, drifting down from the ceiling. A few seconds later, a strange, more muffled pop sound filled the room, followed by complete silence. Like a drunk who had fallen over in the street, Steve staggered falteringly up to his feet. Overflowing with sudden relief, Linda impulsively started towards him, but on seeing the same look of haunted anguish on Steve's face that she had witnessed at the hotel on Monday morning, she stopped dead in her tracks. The front of his bright white shirt was stained red with blood, and his arms were twitching with spasmodic, jerking movements, as he tried to pull them up to the wound. Steve's head

380

suddenly snapped backwards, recoiling in synchronisation with the penetrating blowouts of two more bullets that hit him under the chin. He fell against the already decimated Welsh dresser, rebounded forwards, and landed facedown on the debris, of what was once Elaine's cherished earthenware collection. Rod's head popped up above the end of the table top, minus his glasses, making it appear for a second that somehow a third person had joined the fray. Using his left hand to gain purchase from the heavy wooden table, he levered himself up. Once standing upright, he slowly raised his right arm and angled the gun directly at Linda's head. An eardrum-shattering explosion pulsated around the room as a .38 calibre cartridge, serrated the top of Rod's left shoulder, throwing him off-balance and causing him to discharge his gun harmlessly into the skirting board.

'Run for the front door Linda!' Elaine screamed, setting herself for a second shot. Tightly gripping the old service sidearm that they had discovered in the trunk a few days before, she pulled the trigger and the sound of a second jarring blast bounced off the walls of the kitchen. The lead shell, missed Rod's head by a few inches and punched a neat, round hole in the fridge door, incrementally adding some more CFC gases into the atmosphere. Linda pulled open the door that led into the darkened passageway, allowing them to both escape from the kitchen. The sound of two 9mm rounds studding into the closing old oak door, issued their starting orders for the race through the house.

Rod searched frantically on the floor for his missing glasses, without them, his vision was severely impaired, but every instinct screamed to him that if he let the women flee the confines of the building, his chances of making it to Cyprus that night, were practically zero. Elaine reached the front door first and anxiously twisted the small brass knob, but to her mounting horror, she realised it was not going to open.

'Oh shit, oh fucking shit, I double locked the front door this morning and the key is back in bloody kitchen,' she cried, her hand shaking with panic.

'How are we going to get out,' Linda hissed in a frightened wheeze.

Two more bullets buzzed up the hallway, one breaking a panel of coloured glass in the side window, the other imbedding itself into the top of the door frame.

'Quick get up to the attic, we can barricade ourselves in,' Elaine ordered, and then she fired off two shots into the dark void that she knew their assailant would have to venture down, to take another pot shot at them. Rod heard the sound of two pairs of feet slapping up the staircase, so he felt safe to rush down into the front hallway. Reaching the foot of the stairs he looked up, but without his glasses, all he could see was a blurred movement near to the top. He raised his gun and fired twice, hoping to at least bring one of the two women down, but his reactions were a split second too slow, and instead, the rounds thudded into the painted plaster wall. By the time he had bustled up the stairs, Linda and Elaine had reached the first tiny flight of steps that connected up to the attic room. Keeping low and twisting the top half of his body around the newel post, Rod strained his eyes to see if the women were still in his sights. What he couldn't make out, from the fuzzy imagery, was at the other end of the long landing, Elaine had taken a kneeling position, anticipating his arrival. She fired off a shot that clipped the acorn finial just above his head, sending prickly splinters of wood, arrowing into his face and left eye. The needle pricking pain in his eye temporarily blinded him, but it also incited an angry reply from his trigger finger, the aimless shell implanted into floor, just a few feet in front of him. Elaine sprang up the concealed narrow staircase, to where Linda was struggling in the semi-darkness, to release the hooked catch, which had held the attic door open, since the previous Saturday evening. A loud metallic clink, announced to the two terror-struck women that the door was free, whereupon Linda used the doorjamb to haul herself through the architrave frame and up into the attic. She desperately began searching for something large and heavy, with which she could wedge between the steps and the door, to help strengthen its resistance to being kicked in. Immediately that Elaine jumped above the level of the open doorway, it was painfully apparent to her, that there was

382

nothing to grab hold of, to pull the heavy wooden door shut, and even if she could, there were no sliding bolts to hold it closed. Only when exiting from the roof space, was it possible to push the door shut and lock it with the key.

'Elaine look out!' Linda screeched, spotting the dark green material of Rod's combat jacket, slowly emerging in the caliginous depths of the enclosed staircase. Elaine held her revolver in her two hands and leaned back, so that her body was horizontal and parallel with the wooden risers. There was another movement at the foot of the stairs, which stimulated an instantaneous reflex squeeze, in the tip of Elaine's right hand forefinger. A booming report rang out, but instead of the expected sound of a thirteen stone man collapsing onto the floor, there was just the limp thud of a heavy material coat landing in a heap, on the tiny quarter landing. Having used his jacket as a decoy to entice Elaine into firing her last bullet, Rod knew that he could now pursue his prey, without the danger of being shot himself. In a flash, he had stepped into the base of the stairway and fired up into the blackness of the attic, thinking that he would be certain to hit his adversary. Fortunately for Elaine, she was still lying in her reclined position and felt the bullet whine over her head, before slamming into one of the thick wooden rafters, which spanned the underside of the roof. Confused as to why he had managed to miss a sitting target, Rod started to slowly advance, step-by-step up the staircase, to investigate the reason. At the same, Linda had hoisted above her head, a large jardinière that she had previously selected to help with the fortifying of the door. Using all of her strength, she desperately hurled it over Elaine, and down the flight of steps. Appearing suddenly from out of the gloom, the heavy vessel landed on Rod's outstretched right arm, which was primed to fire the kill shot into Elaine's prone body. Unbalance by the startling collision with the weighty pot, he staggered back down the stairs, slipped and then tumbled backwards, eventually landing face down at the bottom, amid large chunks of highly glazed green pottery. Elaine could see that during the fall, Rod had dropped the gun and was now frantically groping around with his hands, desperately searching the darkened steps behind him, to regain the vital weapon. Realising that this offered her a brief window of opportunity, to get out of the line of fire, she flipped herself up into

383

the body of the attic. Bouncing up to her feet in one fluid movement, she felt the old light bulb brush the top of her head – sensing that now, their only ally would be the obscurity of their surroundings, she reached up and yanked it out of its porcelain fitting. Ushering Linda into the jumbled hinterland of the attic, Elaine guided them both around the amassment of discarded furniture, garden paraphernalia and packing cases that clustered together to form a maze-like construction, which filled the entire room. Mindful that heavy objects could assail him from above, Rod cautiously began his second climb up the stairs. He pressed his left hand against the wall to steady himself, and touched the sticky wetness of the bloodstain that his flailing arm had deposited there, when he had stumbled backwards seconds earlier. Keeping his body crouched well down, and holding the gun above his head, he crept back through the doorframe ready to react to any movement that his restricted eyesight discerned. Close to his right side, mounted on the wall, he could make out a brass plate light switch; carefully he nudged the tiny metal knob downwards with the heel of his hand, but nothing happened. He cursed God for his bad luck, but then, noticing the dark green coloured torch discarded by Linda on Saturday evening, he immediately rescinded the profanity. Gladly picking it up, Rod tested its worth by switching it on – at once, a translucent yellow beam of light, illuminated the archaic collar-and-tie style roof joists. Stepping into the attic room, he was confronted by a bewildering labyrinth, made up of the piles of tangled chattels, which years before had graced the teachers' rooms at Grenchwood Hall. Quickly he flashed the torch around the darkened room, trying to determine a hiding place, where the two women might have concealed themselves.

'Come out, come out, wherever you are?' Rod hissed, in a timbre reminiscent of a deranged character actor, hamming it up in a horror movie. 'As much as I like a game of hide-and-seek, I have to catch a plane tonight.'

Linda pinched her nose, in an attempt to thwart the build up of tiny specks of disturbed dust, from continuing to invade her nostrils. She hunched down, her forehead covered in beads of cold clammy sweat, while her body was petrified by the numbing, intense nervous tension that prevented her from exhaling.

'Sorry ladies, I can count to six – I know that you've run out of bullets, while I still have . . .' Rod paused, as two questions invaded his thoughts – how many shells did the magazine hold, and how many rounds had he already fired off? 'More . . . than enough . . . to despatch the two of you.' He finished the second part of his threatening sentence with far less assurance than he had begun it. Maddened by the sudden uncertainty of the situation, he lunged into the confusion of the dishevelled passageways, angrily pushing down boxes of junk and sweeping his torch around the obscure recesses, hoping to catch sight of his quarry. Rod had never contemplated the far-fetched possibility that he was going to be involved in a running gun battle, and so had never bothered to check the ammunition capacity of his newly acquired weapon. Every few seconds, shafts of torchlight punctured through the narrow gaps contained within the heavily loaded, freestanding set of shelves that separated the two cowering women, from the rampaging madman. The ever-nearing proximity of their would be killer, paralyzed Elaine and Linda with a resigned hopelessness, as any second, they expected the shelving unit to be toppled over upon them. Rod suddenly desisted from his frenzy of demolition and turned towards the far corner of the roof space, where he thought he had detected a noise. Squinting through a small triangular void, afforded to her, by a hard backed novel, leaning at an obtuse angle against an ebonised elephant bookend, Elaine could just make out that Rod's attention had been drawn to the opposite corner of the room. Spotting the chance to add to the diversion and give them the possibility to attempt a break for the stairs, she threw the light bulb that she had earlier ripped from the overhead fitting, down the channel of space, between the wall and the shelves. It landed with the thin sound of a delicate glass ornament breaking, but the indistinct noise was enough to convince Rod that he would definitely find the two women hunkering down behind the jumble of cardboard boxes. Furiously, he pushed and kicked his way through the remaining upright objects that impeded his way, all the time aiming his torch and gun between the butting rafters. Having got to within eight feet of the sloping corner area, peeping out from

385

just above the thick cross beam, he could make out the hazy features of a face looking back at him. Without stopping to deliberate the situation, an impetuous double tap of the trigger sent two bullets blasting into the head from almost point blank range – there was an immediate loud clatter of wood scraping against the rough floorboards, followed by a resounding bang that sounded like a sash window being slammed shut. Peering over the substantial crosspiece timber, Rod passed a circle of torchlight across the floor, where he discovered that his poor eyesight had played a trick on him, fooling him into shooting a two-dimensional portrait of an old headmistress. While he contemplated his mistake, the noise of scampering feet from the other side of the room, alerted him to the fact that his intended victims were making an attempt to escape from the attic. Whirling around, he could distinguish two shapes moving in the gloom, raising the gun and torch clamped together in his two hands, he took careful aim. The beam of light bounced a reflective glint off of Elaine's contact lenses, giving her eyes the eerie animal-like glow that poachers use as a target, when "lamping" their prey in the darkness. Rod squeezed the trigger, but instead of the now recognisable crack of a shell exploding out from the suppressed barrel, there was just the hollow sound, of the firing pin clicking. He pulled the trigger again, but it was the same discouraging noise – frustrated, he heaved the spent Beretta at the women, but it sailed wide of its mark, smashing against the brick wall behind them. Realising that he had to cut them off before they made their getaway down the stairs, he charged forward through the fallen wreckage of the old paint pots and boxes of Christmas decorations that littered his path. They were all about to converge near the head of the stairs, but Rod fell to his knees after tripping over an unseen threadbare footstool. In a desperate attempt to prevent their descent down the stairs, he stretched out a hand and grabbed hold of Elaine's ankle – his vice-like grip pulled her off-balance, toppling her over onto the floor with an echoing clump.

'Run Linda!' Elaine shouted.

'No, I won't leave you!' Linda screamed, tugging at her arm, in a hope that the extra weight, might help prise Elaine away from Rod's clutching hand. Elaine managed to shove Linda away, and quickly repositioning her grasp on the wartime revolver, she brought the metal stock down across Rod's skull with all of her strength. The steel lanyard ring, embedded into the bone, provoking a white-hot, excruciating flash of pain to sear his nerve endings. Both of Rod's hands flew to the radiating point of suffering, allowing Elaine to scramble away. Grabbing her friend by the hand, Linda helped her stand upright, and then together, they bounded down the narrow flight of stairs. By the time that they had both sprung off the bottom tread, out onto the first floor landing, Rod had wiped the streaming blood from his head wound out of his eyes and re-gathered himself. Staggering to his feet and summoning all the speed that he could muster, he launched his bid to stop the women from leaving the building, frantically pursuing them, by almost throwing himself down the attic stairway. Elaine and Linda raced along the landing, stopping for a fraction of a second at the top of the stairs, to glance back at the sickening sight of Rod, starting to sprint after them. Supporting each other for stability, they hurtled down the main staircase as fast as they dared, knowing that a misstep would mean certain capture. With each elongated stride down the flight of stairs Rod was gaining on them. Running for all they were worth up the hallway, they burst into the brightly lit kitchen, to find old Joe cradling a double barrel shotgun into his right shoulder and pointing it directly at them.

'Joe he trying to kill us!' Elaine screamed.

'Get out of the way!' Joe shouted back. His abrupt demanding words made the two women automatically dive for the floor, while Joe braced himself with his index and middle fingers pressed across the two triggers. A split second later Rod appeared in the doorway, his facial expression had just the time to adjust from anger to consternation, before Joe snapped both triggers back. The resulting lethal cacophonous chorus, sparking from both barrels, signalled the end of Rodney Baxter's life. The increased recoil from discharging both cartridges at the same time, caused Joe to fall backwards, landing into the open trunk, where he lay with the smoking barrels pointing up at the ceiling. Elaine and Linda rushed over to help him back to his feet.

'Don't worry about me, just get out of here!' Joe commanded, as they hauled him upright. Elaine hurriedly led the way to the back door with Linda right behind her, when suddenly Linda stopped. Looking across the kitchen and seeing the nightmarish image of her husband's lifeless body, lying in a pool of blood and broken pottery, she felt drawn to go to him. A hand grabbed hold of her wrist.

'You can't do anything for him my love – he's dead, now get over to the pub,' Joe firmly instructed, and Linda was reluctantly forced out through the kitchen door and across the leaf-covered patio. They stuttered their way down the overgrown, slippery limestone steps, and then, holding hands Linda and Elaine dashed across the road together, with Joe trailing behind them, trying to keep up. Struggling against the wind and rain, which still teemed down, it was only when they got to the pub car park that Linda realised that she had nothing on her feet.

'No need to leave our boots outside tonight,' she murmured mournfully. Elaine gave her hand a comforting squeeze, and then pushed the heavy black door to the snug bar wide open. Jim Guthrie was in the process of pouring a pint for one of his die-hard regulars, who had braved the inclement conditions, to partake in his nightly quota of ale. He glanced up at the trio of incoming customers, smiled and then continued to concentrate on his quest to deliver the perfect pint. Something in his subconscious made him take another look up – there standing before him, were three dripping wet, bedraggled figures, Elaine with just a wet, transparent silk robe wrapped around her, Linda with completely bare, mud splattered feet, and Joe holding up a shotgun. The savage trauma and violent deaths that they had just witnessed, induced a strangely sedating effect upon the two women. Jim studied the dazed look on each of the three chalk-white faces.

'What the hell has happened?' he exclaimed, allowing the beer that he was pouring, to overflow the top of the glass and run all over his hand.

388

There were a few seconds of silence before Elaine spoke, in a soft calm voice, 'Something terrible has happen up at my house – can you call the police?'

Rendered speechless by the myriad of questions that were flashing through his brain, Jim continued to stare back at them, while he placed the over full pint glass on the bar.

'Can you call the police Jim, there are dead people up there,' Elaine repeated her request in a deadpan tone.

'Finola!' Jim yelled at the top of his voice.

'What's all the shouting about Jim?' Finola asked, as she appeared almost immediately from behind the curtained entrance to their private accommodation.

'It's Elaine, there's been a terrible accident up at her house.'

'Jaysus Christ! What on earth has happened?' Finola squealed, seeing the inappropriate and unkempt attire that the women were wearing.

'There was a madman trying to kill them. I thought I heard gun shots and went up there, armed with my shotgun – I found two dead bodies in the kitchen, and then Elaine and her friend came running in, being chased by the bastard,' Joe said, explaining the events to the shocked onlookers, by using the most economical amount of words possible.

'What happened then?' Jim snapped.

'I blew his bloody head off!'

'Joe saved us – he was trying to kill us, I just don't know what would have happened if Joe hadn't shot him,' Elaine interjected.

Linda started to shake violently with shock, and tears began to stream from her eyes.

'I just can't believe that Steve is dead,' she whimpered.

Elaine, who had also started to cry, put a comforting arm around her shoulder and then guiding her backwards towards the nearest chair, pressed her to sit down.

'Jim get some brandy, no I'll get the brandy. Yer go and see if yer can get through to the police,' Finola ordered, taking charge of the situation, she then rushed around the other side of the bar and bolted the front door. 'Brian, can yer run upstairs, there's a cupboard at the top, on the right – in it, you'll find some blankets.' The startled middle-aged customer jumped off his stool and scurried up the stairs.

'The line's been reconnected, the police are on their way!' Jim announced, bounding back into the snug. Finola hugged the two crying women and whispered, 'Don't worry nobody can hurt yer now!

CHAPTER THIRTY-THREE
24th December 2003

12.15pm

Fresh from its recent trip through a nearby garage car-wash, a brief burst of midday sun, highlighted the gleaming clean bodywork of the Land Rover, as it manoeuvred gently up to a stop, behind a white Ford Focus, parked neatly at the top end of the gravelled driveway.

'I've been dreading this moment,' Linda said slowly, taking a deep draw of breath, hoping it would subdue her misgivings.

'It's going to be great,' Elaine reassured her. 'I can't wait to meet your parents again after all these years.'

'Yes but, we are here as a couple, with all that involves – I'm not sure how they will react. They are bound to say something crass and embarrass me.'

'Calm down, you have done the hard part – you have told them about us – it's not like you're going to announce it, while your dad carves the turkey on Christmas Day.'

'It was peculiar explaining things over the phone, I couldn't see their faces, I couldn't tell what they were really thinking. Since then, I expect they have been arguing about where they went wrong, bringing me up. It's stupid, I know, but I always carry this feeling that I have somehow let them down.'

'Enough soul searching, you have not let them down, that's a ridiculous thing to say – now let's go in before it starts raining, or even snowing. After all, it is Christmas Eve, it should be snowing – it always snows in the films on Christmas Eve,' Elaine giggled.

They got out of the car, collected their cases from the boot and strolled over towards the front door of the smart detached bungalow.

'Look at all the lovely lights!' Elaine squealed, with a nip of distilled childlike enthusiasm.

'God yes, Mum said that Dad had gone mad this year,' Linda laughed, while giving the doorbell a quick stab with her gloved index finger. They stood back and listened to the melodic chimes from within, which were accompanied by the less harmonious sound of a small dog yapping. After a short wait that seemed like an age to Linda, the door opened and there stood Jack Middlewick, holding in his arms a gorgeous black and white Shih Tzu dog.

'Linda! And Elaine!' he announced excitedly.

Liz Middlewick pushed past her husband.

'Who did you think it was going to be – Father Christmas? You daft old sod,' she laughed, and hugged her daughter. Then she did the same to Elaine. 'Come in, come in – we're letting all the cold in.'

Elaine immediately recognised Liz, who apart from her grey hair, looked much the same, as she did all those years previously. Jack had changed, he seemed smaller than she had remembered and now was bald, wore gold-framed glasses and sported a white goatee beard.

'Oh, Mr Middlewick you have a beard now!' Elaine blurted out.

'He looks ridiculous doesn't he?' Liz laughed. 'I don't know who he thinks he looks like, but he won't shave it off, no matter how much I go on at him about it.'

'I think it's very distinguished – you look a bit like . . . Sean Connery,' Elaine dealt out a measured compliment.

'In his dreams!' Liz cackled. 'Come to think about it, in my dreams as well!' Her laughter was contagious, relaxing Linda as she joined in with her mother's high spirits.

'Did you see all of those Christmas lights that he's put up?' Liz continued.

'Yes, they look really lovely, I can't wait for later, when it's dark, they should look breathtaking,' Elaine continued with her cordiality offensive.

'They do look fantastic, but God knows what our electricity bill will be next month!'

'There's a fabulous smell coming from the kitchen, Mrs Middlewick. Have you been doing some of your wonderful baking this morning?' Elaine switched her flattery over to Liz.

'Stop all this Mr and Mrs nonsense Elaine, call us Liz and Jack,' Liz gave Elaine another quick supportive hug. 'No, I don't bother with baking anymore. I just buy stuff from the supermarket, bung it in the oven and heat it up!'

Jack led the small group into the lounge.

'Look what I found in the loft, when I was up there getting the decorations down,' he said, flourishing a hand towards the Ker-Plunk game set up on the low coffee table.

'Dad! We are in our forties, not teenagers,' Linda protested, although she was inwardly pleased to see her old Christmas present again.

'See! You silly old sod, I said nobody would be interested in playing games,' Liz chided her husband.

393

'Actually I'd love a game Jack,' Elaine came to Jack's defence.

'Great, but first I'll get everyone a Christmas sherry,' Jack said, pretending to dance with an imaginary partner across the room to the drink's cabinet.

'I swear he's going bonkers,' Liz smiled at her husband. 'I'll get some mince pies to go with the sherry.'

'I'll help you,' Linda murmured, giving Elaine a surreptitious wave good-bye, as she followed her mother out of the room.

'I've made the double bed up in Grandma's old room, for you and Elaine,' Liz said, in matter-of-fact tone.

'Mum, are you and Dad okay with this?' Linda asked, catching hold of her mother's right arm as they walked down the hallway.

'Okay with what?' Liz replied, with a mystified look on her face.

'With me and Elaine . . . being . . . partners,' Linda hesitantly chose her words.

'Yes of course! Why wouldn't we be,' Liz answered, with a confused, negative shake of her head.

'I just thought.'

'You just thought what? That your father and me would be disgusted or ashamed of you? I can't lie, we were a bit shocked when you first told us. We might be a bit ancient, and your father seems to be going through a second childhood, but we understand the ways of the world. If you are happy, and you clearly are, then we are happy – very happy!' Liz pulled Linda close to her and wrapped her arms tightly around her.

There was the sudden cracking sound of a heap of marbles crashing into a plastic dish, accompanied by hysterical laughter flowing out from the lounge.

'Thanks Mum – I think this is going to be the best Christmas since . . . 1969!'

THE END

Printed in Great Britain
by Amazon

41014109R00236